Cécile Lainé

MW00830959

El planeta gris

Claudia Rodríguez Mandujano

For additional resources, visit:

www.towardproficiency.com

ISBN: 978-1-7341686-8-6

Agradecimientos

Mi talentoso ilustrador, Alkinz

Mis padres increíbles, mi esposo y mis dos hijas

Y también:

Mi traductora, Claudia Rodríguez Mandujano

Mi editora, Anny Ewing

Mis estudiantes

Para Olivia y Sophia

Personajes

Tea

Issa
la hermana mayor de Tea

Nen
la madre de Issa y de Tea

Eru

Sorya
la jefa del pueblo

Les Racas

Ptero
el robot de Tea

poder = power

peligroso = dangerous

4

Vamos a hablar con Sorya.

Sorya es la jefa del pueblo...

...y Tea va a regresar al campamento de les Racas.

No Tea. Estoy de acuerdo con Issa. Es muy peligroso...

¡Tea!

6

Voy a regresar al campamento de les Racas.

Voy a buscar información sobre nuestra madre.

BRRUUM

PLAF

ZIS ZAS

¿Mamá?

¿Tea? ¿Eres tú?

TRRRIIIS

Tea, mi pequeña Tea...

Llegamos.

Mamá, ¿tus ojos?

Les Racas me torturaron. Estoy ciega*.

Pero Tea, desde que* estoy ciega, mi poder es aún más* fuerte.

ciega = blind
desde que = since
aún más = even more

quedarse = stay

Eru...
Hace mucho tiempo que no nos vemos.

Sé por qué estás aquí, Nen: tu poder es aún más fuerte.

¿Tal vez* puedo ayudarlas a combinar sus poderes...?

Ahora, siento el agua en todo nuestro planeta.

tal vez = maybe

¿¿QUÉ PASA??

No tenemos chance, pero...

18

FIN

En tu opinión

1. ¿Por qué no hay agua en el planeta de Tea?

2. Issa puede sentir el agua, pero Tea no puede sentirla. ¿Tiene que tener un poder especial para ser una heroína?

3. Nen, la mamá de Tea, es ciega. ¿Nen necesita ver para ser una heroína?

4. ¿Quién creó a Ptero el robot?

5. ¿Quién es Eru?

6. ¿Ptero está "muerto"?

7. Ahora hay agua en el planeta de Tea. ¿Qué va a pasar después?

8. Una alianza entre dos generaciones salvó el planeta de Tea. ¿Nuestro planeta necesita de una alianza similar?

Cécile Lainé

Cécile es profesora de francés en los Estados Unidos.

Le encanta contar historias.

Alkinz

Alkinz es ilustrador en Indonesia.

Le encanta crear ilustraciones estilo manga y animé.

Claudia Rodríguez Mandujano

Claudia es de la Ciudad de México.

Le encanta viajar y saber de otras culturas.

Glosario

A

a to, at
acuerdo agreement
  estoy de acuerdo
  I agree
agua water
ahora now
al to the
alianza alliance

allí here
años years
aquí here
atacan are attacking
aún still
ayudar to help
ayudarlas help you
azul blue

B

bravo well done

buscar to look for

C

campamento camp
casa home
chance chance
ciega blind
cinco five
combinar combine

compañía company
con with
contigo with you
crea create
creó created

D

de of
del of the
desde since
después after

diez ten
distracción distraction
donde where
dos two

E

el the
él he
ella she
en in
entender understand
entre between
era was
eres are

es is
especial special
esta this
  esta noche tonight
está is
estás are
estoy am
ey hey

F

fin end
fueron were

fuerte strong

G

generaciones
generations

gris gray

H

hablar to talk
hace it does
  hace cinco años
  five years ago
  hace mucho tiempo
  it has been a while

hay there is
hermana sister
heroína heroine
hora hour
hostil hostile
hoy today

I

importante important
información information

ir to go

J

jefa leader

L

la the
les the

lindo beautiful
llegar to arrive

M

madre mother
mamá mom
más more
me me

mi my
minutos minutes
mira look
moto motorcycle

mucha a lot of
mucho a lot of

muy very

N

necesitan they need
no not
noche night
norte north

necesitan they need
no not
noche night
norte north

O

ojos eyes

opinión opinion

P

para for, in order to
pasa is happening
pasar to happen
peligro danger
peligroso dangerous
pequeña small
pequeño small
pero but

piensas think
planeta planet
poder power
por qué why
puede she can
pueden you can
puedo I can

Q

que that
  tenemos que
  we have to
qué what

  por qué why
quedarse stay
quién who
quiero I want

R

rápido quick
regresar to come back

robot robot

S

salvó saved
sé I know
sentir to sense
sentirla sense it
ser to be

siento I sense
similar similar
sobre about
sus your

T

tal vez maybe
tenemos we have
  tenemos que
  we have to
tener to have
tiempo time
tiene has
  tiene que has to

todo all
tomaron they took
torturaron they
  tortured
tu your
tú you
tus your

U

un a, an

una a, an

V

va is going

vamos let's go

van are going

ver to see

verde green

vez time

  tal vez maybe

voy I am going

Y

y and

De la misma autora

Alice (also available in Spanish)
When Alice finds out she and her family are moving in a month, she is far from happy. Her friend suggests she make a list of the most important things she wants to accomplish before she leaves. Alice writes four items on her list and sets off on a quest to discover what truly matters to her.
French: Marseille, France
Spanish: Liberia, Costa Rica

Khadra
Khadra is trying to deal with her recent falling out with her best friend, Alice. As she reflects on Alice's betrayal, she makes an unlikely new friend and finds unexpected purpose in helping him survive a dangerous situation. Set in Marseille, France, this second installment of the Alice series takes the reader on a journey of compassion and perseverance. Khadra can be read either separately from Alice or as a sequel.

Camille
When Camille finds out her beloved dance teacher, choreographer, and studio owner is leaving, she is worried about her future. She fears that Studio Pineapple, where she has been dancing for five years, is going to close or be sold to someone she won't get along with. But she soon finds out that while changes are hard, they often bring an opportunity to grow and blossom. This third installment of the Alice series can be read as a sequel or independently of the first two stories.

Cécile Lainé

Cécile Lainé

Cécile Lainé

Cécile Lainé

34154294R00024

The ART *of* ALLUSION

The ART *of* ALLUSION

Illuminators and the Making of English Literature,
1403–1476

Sonja Drimmer

PENN

University of Pennsylvania Press

Philadelphia

Publication of this book has been aided by
a grant from the Millard Meiss Publication Fund of the College Art Association;
the International Center of Medieval Art and the Samuel H. Kress Foundation; and
a Publications Grant from the Paul Mellon Centre for Studies in British Art.

 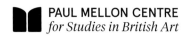

Published by
University of Pennsylvania Press
Philadelphia, Pennsylvania 19104-4112
www.upenn.edu/pennpress

Printed in the United States of America on acid-free paper

1 3 5 7 9 10 8 6 4 2

Library of Congress Cataloging-in-Publication Data
Names: Drimmer, Sonja, author.
Title: The art of allusion : illuminators and the making of English literature,
        1403–1476 / Sonja Drimmer.
Other titles: Material texts.
Description: 1st edition. | Philadelphia : University of Pennsylvania Press, [2018] |
        Series: Material texts | Includes bibliographical references and index.
Identifiers: LCCN 2018004665 | ISBN 978-0-8122-5049-7 (hardcover : alk. paper)
Subjects: LCSH: Illumination of books and manuscripts, Medieval—England.
        | Illumination of books and manuscripts, English—15th century. | English
        literature—Middle English, 1100–1500—History and criticism.
Classification: LCC ND2940 .D74 2018 | DDC 745.6/709420902—dc23
LC record available at https://lccn.loc.gov/2018004665

For my mom and dad

The fifteenth century, it may well be said, was one of the most curious and confused periods in recorded history. . . . Not the least curious and confusing of its aspects is the story of the book production in that century.

—CURT F. BÜHLER, *The Fifteenth-Century Book*

CONTENTS

INTRODUCTION

A miniature produced in the middle of the fifteenth century offers an illuminator's vision of textual production (Figure 1, Plate 1).[1] In the center of the composition a man sits in a canopied chair with a slanted tablet resting on its arms. He consults a codex, open on a set of shelves nearby, while seeming to write on the roll that slinks over the edge of his tilted desk. Warmed by the fire at his feet and joined by a watchful cat whose gaze echoes his own, the man enjoys the ease of his cozy environs. The circular walls that embrace him rhyme with the set of round, tiered shelves at his side, a visual simile that compares composition to domestication, a relocation of preexisting texts by writing them anew.

This miniature precedes the following lines from *The Fall of Princes*, in which the author, John Lydgate (circa 1371–circa 1449), pauses to reflect on the value of old texts:

> Frute of writyng set in cronycles old,
> Most delitable of fresshnesse in tastyng
> And most goodly and glorious to behold
> In cold & hete lengyst abydyng
> Chaunge of sesons may do yt no hyndryng
> And wherso be that men dyne or fast,
> The more men taste, the lenger yt wil last.[2]

In the image, the illuminator has visualized the harvesting analogies, cued by but not in direct correlation with Lydgate's metaphor that compares literature to an everlasting fruit. Just outside the window of the study, a man can be seen sowing in a plowed field.[3] Writing, this visual juxtaposition proclaims, is a creative act of reuse.

Expressing a commonplace, Lydgate praises the backward glance at these old texts as a sustaining activity. Similarly, among the most lapidary—and oft-quoted—verses in the oeuvre of Geoffrey Chaucer (d. 1400) is the nearly proverbial

> For out of olde feldes, as men seyth,
> Cometh al this newe corn fro yer to yere,

FIGURE 1. *Man writing*. John Lydgate, *Fall of Princes*, Bury St. Edmunds (?), c. 1450. San Marino, Huntington Library HM 268, fol. 79v.

And out of olde bokes, in good feyth,
Cometh al this newe science that men lere.[4]

Likewise, John Gower (d. 1408) opens his *Confessio Amantis* declaring,

Of hem that writen ous tofore
The bokes duelle, and we therfore
Ben tawht of that was write tho:
Forthi good is that we also
In oure tyme among ous hiere
Do wryte of newe som matiere,
Essampled of these olde wyse.[5]

These three poets composed some of the first monumental works of Middle English verse that were disseminated in multiple manuscript copies during the fifteenth century.[6] And all three of them imagine the English author's act of composition as a continuative one, an enterprise of renewal rather than pure invention. This poetic imagery has long been recognized as a hallmark of vernacular creativity in late medieval England: influenced by scholastic modes of composition that flourished in universities from the thirteenth century onward and shaped by the growing popularity and demand for translations of Latin and French literature, the first major works of the English literary canon were forged with the tools of intertextuality.

The cornerstone of what came to be England's canon was laid between the end of the fourteenth and the first half of the fifteenth century, against the background of two defining conflicts with lasting impact: the Hundred Years' War (1337–1453) and the Wars of the Roses (1455–1485).[7] Between these years, Geoffrey Chaucer, John Gower, and John Lydgate translated into English and radically revised stories with a long literary pedigree, stitching them together in vast, compilative works. And from the turn of the fifteenth century, royals and gentry alike commissioned "authoritative-looking manuscripts of [these works] that match those in Latin and French in handsomeness and regularity, and were dignified with the kind of apparatus of presentation that had hitherto been reserved for Latin and French texts."[8] Significantly, many of these manuscripts contain images that were integral to the rising prestige of English as a literary language. Yet despite the significance of the contribution of manuscript illuminators to English literary culture, they are seldom discussed in the major narratives of its development.[9]

This book offers the first study devoted to the emergence of England's literary canon as a visual and a linguistic event. While the year 1400 is invoked commonly as a "watershed" that witnessed a vast increase of vernacular literary production,[10] Kathleen Scott has pointed to the "less realized fact that from the beginning of this period, indeed not long after secular limners themselves had become officially established [in 1403], Middle English texts came very quickly and professionally to be produced with illustrations."[11] This bumper crop grew by and large in the flourishing commercial environment of London, "where sufficient numbers of authors and copyists were located to facilitate the development of commercial and labour systems necessary to support a definable book trade."[12] In addition to the authors and copyists who turned out these texts, illuminators disposed them in manuscripts with illustrative and ornamental programs that announced—or tried to announce, at any rate—that the English language had arrived.[13]

The newly enlarged scale of vernacular manuscript production generated a problem: namely, a demand for new images. Not only did these images need to accompany narratives that had no tradition of illustration, but they also had to express novel concepts, including ones so foundational as the identity and fitting representation of an English poet. Illuminators had, in Brigitte Buettner's useful formulation, to create "objects of cognition rather than mere recognition."[14] From where might these images derive? The question is imperative because a manuscript culture is inherently a culture of the copy. Yet liturgical manuscripts could not be relied on to provide adequate source material for the subject matter of these poems nor could illuminated books containing legal or scientific texts. Furthermore, while scholars have discussed the presence and influence in late medieval England of both Continental illuminators and manuscripts, the manuscripts of Middle English verse under examination in this study seldom adopt wholesale Continental models and at times exhibit little receptiveness to them at all.[15] For example, regarding a form of imagery that became increasingly common over the course of the fifteenth century, Joyce Coleman has remarked that "while the English came to presentation iconography much later than the French, they did interesting things once they got there."[16] These "interesting things," as I will argue throughout this book, derive in large measure from the mixed redeployment of pictorial conventions from diverse genres of illuminated manuscripts.[17]

A central premise of this book is that the work of illumination both responds and contributes to the entry and circulation of new ideas about English literary authorship, political history, and book production itself in the fifteenth century. My aim is not to devise a theory of literary illustration drawn from English texts; rather, I reverse this operation by examining how images think about English literature. In this introduction I provide a foundation on which to lay claims regarding illuminators' generation of these thoughts through allusion, what William Irwin has defined as an indirect reference that "calls for associations that go beyond mere substitution of a referent."[18] What we encounter in the manuscripts of Chaucer, Gower, and Lydgate is a technique for image production that recalls the strategies of literary production that these authors assume. Just as these poets embrace intertextuality as a means of invention, so did illuminators devise new images through referential techniques—assembling, adapting, and combining image types from a range of sources in order to answer the need for a new body of pictorial matter that these poets' works demanded. Allusion, in other words, emerges as the dominant mode of pictorial invention in Middle English literary culture.

Taking my opening image as emblematic of a form of authorial portraiture that emerged in this period, which shows a writer composing while consulting other books, I do not observe how it reflects authors' projections of their own identities or activities. As I discuss in greater detail in Chapter 2, the poets whose works are at the center of this study—Chaucer, Gower, and Lydgate—were seldom portrayed in the act of writing (just once, in fact). Rather, I follow here Jeffrey Hamburger's dictum that "art's work . . . is to provide an implicit theory of the image where medieval texts provide none. The work of art itself shapes, structures, and defines our experience in essential ways."[19] Such images as the one with which I opened and will examine in greater detail are illuminators' idealizations of the process of literary production. As such they betray the extent to which the idea of a book's multiplicity—that is, its derivation from the judicious selection and reconfiguration of preexisting material—had penetrated the culture of book production at this time.

The Late Medieval Writer at Work

It is around the mid-fourteenth century that the poetic imaginary of authorship exemplified by Lydgate's and Chaucer's agricultural analogies and Gower's more sober praise of ancient volumes was pronounced in a new visual imaginary of learned authorship.[20] This visual conception typically shows a man seated between an exemplar or reference book and a book in which he is writing, a configuration that appears to have been developed by artists almost simultaneously across central and northern Europe.[21] To appreciate the magnitude of this change, we only have to look at the tenacious tradition that preceded it. Until the mid-fourteenth century, representations of venerable authors at work had abided by the same conventions for almost a millennium.[22] During this long period, author images had conformed to the "remarkably homogenous"[23] prototype provided by the Evangelists in the earliest illustrated Gospels. The standard depiction appears in two variations. In the first, the Evangelist poses frontally, standing with a scroll or book in hand. In the

FIGURE 2. *St. Matthew. Lindisfarne Gospels*, Lindisfarne, late seventh–early eighth
century. London, British Library Cotton MS Nero D iv, fol. 25v.
© British Library Board.

second variation, exemplified in the image of Matthew from the *Lindisfarne Gospels*
(Figure 2), the Evangelist is seated with a bound book balanced on his lap, pen in
one hand, and with his zoomorph hovering above his halo, blowing the trumpet of
divine inspiration.[24] One of the most significant features of this portrait's conception of authorship is the writer's focus on one book and the absence of the *armar-
ium* rich with tomes, which is visible in a related manuscript.[25] Priority here is placed
on the single Book, and its origins in the Word of God rather than the words of
other men. Moreover, although the author is shown in the act of writing, the page
with which he makes contact is blank: as an emblem of wisdom and truth, its power
is "unmitigated by reference to [its] actual function."[26] According to this formula,
authors are shown as scribal subordinates to a transcendent dictation.[27]

INTRODUCTION

FIGURE 3. *Bede writing*. Bede, *Life of St. Cuthbert*, Durham, c. 1175–1200.
London, British Library Yates Thompson MS 26, fol. 2r.
© British Library Board.

The same formula, minus the Holy Spirit or zoomorph, was retained in non-scriptural imagery as well. A typical example is the image of Bede preparing his *Life of St. Cuthbert* (Figure 3).[28] Enclosed within a private space that recalls contemporary church architecture, Bede sits before a slanted, anthropomorphic lectern with legs, feet, and even a draped torso. The torso's contours mimic arms extending a blank book outward, much like the angel often seen supporting Saint Matthew's scroll. There is a suggested naturalism in the evening sky flanking the author, but the author himself is placed against a hieratic gold background that is aligned with the church-like structure above. The gold leaf appears to cascade from above and pour into the author himself, implying in both its composition and color that although Bede's writing is not officially prompted by the Holy Spirit, his inspiration nevertheless issues from the Church. Moreover, the location of Bede's hand proclaims his intermediary role: poised at the seam between the gold and blue backgrounds, or the other world and this world, the author's text is what sutures the two. While Bede's *Life of St. Cuthbert* is not a scriptural text, the visual notion of his authorial work is modeled on a paradigm of sacred authorship: one man, one writing surface, one book. His authorship, as the Evangelists', is a conducive act, and he is the vessel through which the Word of the true *auctor*, God, flows.

These two images dovetail with ideas about authorship that had presided in written culture before the emergence and growth of universities in the twelfth century. Agency in these images is accorded first to God and second to the ancient *auctores* whose words were embodiments of divine wisdom.[29] Benjamin Tilghman has furthermore suggested that these conceptualizations extended to manuscript producers themselves who "may thus have seen a divine agency guiding their own hands: the work of angels through the labor of agents."[30] Changes in readership beginning in the twelfth century—from meditative, monastic reading to interactive, academic reading encouraged by the universities—necessitated an alteration to the format of books in order to facilitate study. This change drew attention to the ways in which the individual himself creates knowledge, not through inspired innovation *ex nihilo* but rather through intellectual and physical engagement with preexisting material made by other individuals.[31] This theory of authorship was codified in a now widely cited passage by Bonaventure:

> The method of making a book is fourfold. For someone writes the materials of others, adding or changing nothing, then this person is said to be purely the scribe. Someone else writes the materials of others, adding, but nothing of his own, and this person is said to be the compiler. Someone else writes both the materials of other men, and his own, but the materials of others as the principal materials, and his own annexed for the purpose of clarifying them, and this person is said to be the commentator, not the author. Someone else writes both his own materials and those of others, but his own as the principal materials, and the materials of others annexed for the purpose of confirming his own, and such must be called the author.[32]

In short, one can copy the contents of one book to create another book (*scriptor*); compile a new book from copying the material of many books (*compilator*); copy the material from one or many books and add commentary (*commentator*); and create one's own words and copy into the book the words from others for support (*auctor*). Bonaventure's categorization of the four ways is, however, not hierarchical;[33] rather, what his distinctions articulate is an inclusive formulation of writership encompassing a range of activities that "combine[d] into a single continuum two functions which seem fundamentally different to us: composition and the making of copies."[34] "To make a book" was not simply a metaphor for the intellectual labor of producing literature but also a literal description of giving form to that literature: no matter where individuals sat on Bonaventure's continuum, they would at some point turn their heads and take into their hands written material that once existed in another place.[35] Over the next two centuries, this notion of writership extended beyond scholastic discourse to influence vernacular poets' conceptions and representations of their own work.[36] Recent scholarship on the critical engagement of scribes, as well as the scribal labor of authors themselves, has gone far to illustrate the porous boundary between these occupations.[37]

Immersed within this changing landscape of book production and attentive to an altered discourse that embraced craft, illuminators supplied a new visual model to express this modified vision of authorship.[38] This visual model, which began to appear in the fourteenth century, is typified by my opening image (Plate 1). What is remarkable about this image in particular is its elaboration of the extended analogy it precedes. While Lydgate's verses first invoke the comparison of *reading* to the consumption of succulent fruit, the illuminator has added a further activity to the miniature: in addition to reading the open codex at his side, the man portrayed works on an unbound or unfurled sheet before him, presumably writing on it. Although his hands are not in view, the inkhorn that penetrates the right-hand side of the desk implies his occupation. And this occupation exists in an interstice that puts his identity in doubt: is he an author, a commentator, a compiler, a translator, or a scribe?[39] Any distinction we could hope to make is obscured by the open codex that has attracted the man's attention. It is clear enough from both the academic formulation of authorship expressed in Bonaventure's outline and vernacular poets' praise for the consultative act that such a distinction did not truly obtain in the later Middle Ages. What this image and others like it demonstrate is how this occupational continuum was understood and visualized by illuminators.

The illuminator's representation of the scene in these visual terms hypostatizes intertextuality, elevates the consultative act, and centralizes the patchwork nature of the book as the product of assembled and adapted models.[40] A prominent feature of the image is the tiered set of shelves to the writer's right, supplementing the cantilevered surface extended over his chair. Given its location within the composition, the furnishing is as important as the presence of the reference work in establishing movement between books as *the* mode of intellectual creativity. The increasing prominence of structurally impressive and accessorized work spaces in miniatures of writers at work, which crop up during this period—especially their presence when not necessitated by the adjoining text—gestures toward limners' own conception of what constitutes textual production. In other words, the illuminators who painted such images enfolded into them their own idealized notion of the making of a book. In doing so, they codified intertextuality as a physical act, similar to the kind performed by the scribe copying from an exemplar and the artist drawing from a model book.[41]

Literary scholars have developed a sophisticated language for discussing intertextuality as a product of transmission in a manuscript culture, whether through theories of translation, variance, or *mouvance*.[42] I propose here that this attentiveness to the multiplicity of a text's origins and signifying gestures is likewise suited to an examination of the illumination in manuscripts containing Middle English verse. What my opening image—an emblem of a broader phenomenon—suggests is that illuminators were as integrated in the culture of adoption and adaptation as their scribal and authorial counterparts. When charged with producing a new corpus of imagery to accompany this new corpus of text, illuminators resorted to the techniques of invention that were essential to the development of this literature.

Agents of Allusion, Beyond Word and Image

In opening with these ideas my purpose is to channel conversations about English literary illustration away from the topic of textual and visual interchange that has dominated them. Scholarship on the illumination of Middle English literature—an "opportunity rich but neglected field"—is sparse.[43] Two significant publications have, however, drawn greater attention to the visual properties of these manuscripts: Kathleen Scott's *Later Gothic Manuscripts*, which gathers together and provides information about 140 English (albeit not exclusively literary) manuscripts of the fifteenth century; and the important introductory volume *Opening Up Middle English Manuscripts*.[44] Outside of these guides, literary scholars have taken the lead in approaching the illumination of Middle English literature, examining it chiefly as a response to the text it accompanies. Regarding this scholarship, Derek Pearsall observed that "the comparative neglect of vernacular text illustration by art historians is to some extent compensated for by the attention they get from literary scholars. But literary scholars have their own preoccupations, and a distorted impression of the production circumstances of vernacular text manuscripts and the function of illustration in them may arise from the concentration of these scholars on the relation of the image to the text, as if the significance of the image began and ended in its fidelity to the text."[45] In accordance with a primary interest in literature, these analyses have prioritized text in a number of ways, viewing images as accurate visualizations of the text or inaccurate visualizations, as simplifications of the text, in the service of its structure, as finding aids, and as evidence of reader response.[46] While these works have helped move images into English manuscript studies' field of vision, they nevertheless perceive the image subsequent to the word, and by extension as subordinate to it.[47]

Since the majority of illuminations in Middle English manuscripts fail to hold up to the standards of aesthetic excellence that traditionally have compelled art historical research—a topic I explore in greater depth in Chapter 1—they have been overlooked by art historians.[48] But other obstacles, beyond the aesthetic, have repelled art historical attention. Because this body of illumination is neither attached to religious texts nor designed to serve the needs of monastic individuals and communities, it cannot be assessed for its visionary potency, as, for example, in the studies of Jeffrey Hamburger and Jessica Brantley.[49] Nor can it be appreciated for its centrality to spiritual programs of salvation or reform directed at the laity, as elucidated by Lucy Freeman Sandler, Kathryn A. Smith, Aden Kumler, Alexa Sand, and Michael Camille, in their studies of devotional manuscripts produced in England.[50] Nevertheless, at the same time that these publications have produced important analyses arising from visual and verbal interchange, their readings extend far beyond the call and response of text and image, opening on to interpretive vistas that encompass identity formation, religious mediation, political expression, social regulation, and the cultural construction of vision itself. Lucy Freeman Sandler and Kathryn A. Smith in particular have produced a significant body of scholarship on English manuscript illumination of the fourteenth century, which has had a formative impact on my understanding of literary manuscripts produced in the following period. Both scholars take an intrepid view of illumination as a communicatively powerful apparatus that is flexible enough to pictorialize both word and narrative, and at the same time to give form to preoccupations indicative of a broader cultural landscape that reaches out far beyond the borders of the book. Moreover, while invested in the agency of patrons, both Sandler and Smith attend to the decisive role of illuminators in the production of meaning as well as the "constitutive role played by images" in late medieval lay culture.[51] It is from these capacious approaches to the illuminated manuscript that I take my cue.

Likewise instrumental in devising an approach to the objects under examination here is art historical scholarship treating the illumination of literary manuscripts from France, in particular the work of Brigitte Buettner, Anne D. Hedeman, Sandra Hindman, Erik Inglis, and Claire Richter Sherman.[52] Together, their works have provided a model for conceptualizing visual historiography, an issue of central importance in the final part of this study. Yet because there are some fundamental differences between French and English literary production, I have had to bear these differences in mind while deploying the methods applied by the scholars who attend to the Continental material. Much of the research on French historical and mythographic illumination draws rich rewards from the evidence of collaboration between authors, translators, patrons, and the illuminators of their texts. No evidence for such collaboration survives for English literary manuscripts. Furthermore, this scholarship at times posits strong relationships between the ideological agendas of the men who commissioned literary works and the programs of illumination in the manuscripts that contain them, which they owned. *The Canterbury Tales* had no such patron, and illuminated copies of it postdate Chaucer's death. No manuscript of the *Confessio Amantis* can be linked securely to either of its two dedicatees, Richard II and Henry Bolingbroke; and the same holds for manuscripts containing the long historical poems of John Lydgate. Instead, what survives exclusively are illuminated manuscripts produced for individuals who had little or nothing to do with either the circumstances in which or the people for whom these poems were originally composed.[53]

One way in which scholars have recuperated the verve of literary illumination is through theories of visual translation.[54] Richard Emmerson has been the most productive proponent of these ideas with respect to English literary manuscripts, and while ultimately he and I differ in our approaches, Emmerson has made important advances in elucidating a body of material that has been underresearched. In an essay that criticizes "the notion that images dumb-down the word [which] characterizes much literary historical scholarship,"[55] Emmerson proposes visual translation as the lens through which to view illuminations. He advocates that "to appreciate the complexity of a manuscript image, therefore, we need to avoid privileging the unachievable, and undesirable, model of accurate content and instead focus as much on *how* the image represents as on *what* textual features it represents. This crucial desideratum in approaching a visual translation recognizes the heuristic principle that an interpretation of an image should not separate form from content."[56] Emmerson's endeavor to follow the lead of Mieke Bal (and other semioticians) and examine words and images as cotexts on equal footing has produced invigorating studies, yet the concept of translation nevertheless requires a hierarchical or at least sequential relationship that accords primacy to the word. The standard operating procedure of manuscript producers was to copy the text first and then supply images and ornamentation; but these images and ornamentation were not circumscribed by the text and were sometimes irrelevant to it. To inquire into illuminators' translations of texts into images is tantamount to inquiring into poets' translations of Latin and French texts into English: it is only one part of the story.

What I propose is attentiveness to the allusive act as a means to understanding how illuminators gave visual form to ideas and preoccupations arising from vernacular literary culture at large rather than from exclusively the text at hand. Chaucer's, Gower's, and Lydgate's poems are explicitly intertextual and are self-conscious realizations of what Julia Kristeva considers the essence of poetic language as "an intersection of textual surfaces."[57] More than a mosaic of translated sources, they are a convergence of discourses from the scholastic and homiletic and documentary to the hortatory and the legal and the ludic and so on. In referring to the illuminator's practice as "allusive," I mean to suggest an affiliation between the illuminator's artistic methodology and the Middle English poet's own; at the same time, I am deliberately avoiding the term *intertextuality* in order to allow for the possibility that the illuminator's tactics transcend the word on the page.[58] To modify Gérard Genette's formulation, then, the illuminator's allusive act involves "an enunciation whose full meaning presupposes the perception of a relationship between it and another *image*, to which it necessarily refers to some inflections that would otherwise remain unintelligible."[59] Appropriating idioms from the visual discourses of religion, courtship, legal procedure, narrative history, and even propaganda, illuminators leveraged allusion itself as the chief tactic for visual inquiry about a literature too young to have its own conventions as material texts.

Process and production are essential here. Earlier, I cited William Irwin's definition of allusion.[60] But, while Irwin stresses the necessity of authorial intention, I construe allusion here as necessarily a condition of process and facture—that is, arising from the operations of the illuminator's craft. The idea—now enshrined in the term "intervisuality"—that images produce meaning by reference to other images is not a new one in the history of art. However, intervisuality tends, at least in its original sense, to prioritize reception over production, asking how images "are perceived by their audiences to work across and within different and even competing value-systems."[61] I take allusion instead to prioritize production, considering it as an act that leaves traces of artistic thought, deliberate or subconscious. Paul Binski has summarized a common late medieval image of invention as threads "woven together by mind and hand, a process that entailed that material was first 'drawn in' before something new could in turn be 'drawn out.' . . . An inventory of material having been formed, it was drawn upon, summoned in a process of recollection, which moved the mind to invention."[62] Moreover, the etymology of allusion in *alludere* (to play with) suggests its aptness to my purpose.[63] Binski cautions that while "the notion of the ludic was an important one in medieval thinking," we ought not "to underestimate the seriousness of intent of the playful, its capacity to draw on orthodox sources in the service of unorthodox outcomes, and its fully rational ability to ambiguate accepted aesthetic solutions."[64] Allusion not only circumvents the false binary between exemplar and copy and between tradition and innovation; it renders convention a necessary prerequisite to the inventive act.[65] In this case, it is the invention of a pictorial corpus for a new corpus of literature, each as indebted to preexisting material as the other.

This study is founded on the premise that illuminators were integral participants in the production of literary culture, whose images were not just responsive but constitutive. They worked in tandem with—but, significantly, at a chronological remove from—the authors whose works they coproduced in processing the broader cultural stakes that a new vernacular literature claimed. In illuminating it, they offered audiences a visual matrix within which to situate such authors as Chaucer, Gower, and Lydgate in a cultural market that had yet to accommodate major works of English literature for consumption by elite and powerful audiences. Through their depictions, illuminators asked what exactly is an English author? What is his value in a literary economy? From whom does he derive his authority? What are the social arrangements that validate literary work in English? How does the book object itself locate verse in a specific, contemporary moment? How can decades-old English verse have agency in a political environment very different from the one in which it originally emerged? It was by harnessing visual allusion that illuminators articulated these central questions and provided difficult, at times evasive, answers regarding both literary and cultural authority. Turning our attention to these as the sorts of issues that illuminators contemplated opens an exit ramp off the loop that word-and-image studies can threaten to circumscribe.

Conceptually, the path of this book is divided into three parts that move from the makers of manuscripts (illuminators and scribes), to representations of the makers of the texts they contain (authors), to the illuminated narratives they depict (two chapters devoted to separate case studies of manuscripts with prolific illustrations of historical narratives). Its temporal focus—between the years 1403 and 1476—signals my investment in the importance of "makers" in the process of English literary production: in 1403, scribes and illuminators merged to found what came to be called the Stationers' Company, and in 1476 Caxton set up the first printing press in England. It was between these two years the verse that later became the archetypal English literary canon was—literally—made.[66]

Critical to this study is an understanding of the circumstances in which and mechanics of how these manuscripts were made. I tackle this subject in Chapter 1, which offers an account of the professional conditions of manuscript illumination in late medieval London. Recent scholarship, which I address in this chapter, has elevated the scribe to a central position in the dissemination of English literature and has spotlighted the ways in which these professionals edited and organized poetry for consumption by a range of audiences. Here, I unite archival research into London's book trade with recent developments in the study of scribes to provide a picture of the activities of manuscript illuminators. Their professional practices created a set of conditions that had an impact on how illuminators went about their labor and in turn had consequences for the images they produced. These conditions include illuminators' anonymity and indifference to individuation, their professional versatility, and the collaborative and decentralized nature of their work. In characterizing illuminators' practices and habits, I provide a foundation in the realities of the book trade for the larger claims made throughout the book.

Chapter 2 initiates a suite of chapters devoted to illuminators' confrontations with one of the most significant developments in the history of English literature: the invention of the vernacular author. The chapter opens by posing a deceptively simple question: who is Geoffrey Chaucer? This is precisely the question that illuminators faced when embarking on the illustrative programs for the manuscripts that contain his works. In this and the following two chapters, I consider how illuminators responded to the challenges presented by the emerging concept of a contemporary writer of English poetry at a time when, in the words of J. A. Burrow, "There [was] no sign in England of the specialized, professional, vernacular writer."[67] After introducing these core issues, the chapter examines the five, very different images of Chaucer in manuscripts of *The Canterbury Tales* as documents of illuminators' indecision about the status of the English author. In contrast to previous scholarship, which ascribes to these images a celebratory attitude to Chaucer's excellence, I argue that the status of the "father of English poetry" and the image commensurate with this status was by no means a settled matter.

The third chapter turns to the pictorial identity of John Gower, a figure who was twinned with Chaucer in the earliest rosters of the English literary pantheon. Gower's *Confessio Amantis* was one of the most widely disseminated works of nondevotional English poetry in the fifteenth century, second only to *The Canterbury Tales*. Its appeal sprang from its profile as a compilation of over 140 tales, each related in Middle English and Latin of Gower's own creation. A visual feast of multivocality, the poem disposes Latin and English in a complex arrangement on the page. What is more, the poem is thrust into action by Gower's metamorphosis before the reader's eyes: deciding that the authenticity of his poem hangs on its emergence from a young lover, he takes on this persona for its duration. The poem's complexities—its multilinguality, generic hybridity, and divergent narrational personae—challenged illuminators with questions about the author's identity. In this chapter, I investigate images that depict the moment when the eponymous Lover kneels down to begin his confession. Illuminators strained to locate an appropriate guise for the confessing author: some portrayed him as a blushing youth, others as a graying old man, and others endowed the character with biographical references to the historical Gower himself. Other illuminators neutralized these vexations by endowing the confessing lover with a gesture that was immediately recognizable to the late medieval viewing audience: that of the arms crossed over the chest. Delving into the semiotics of this gesture, I expand on its synonymity with humility, a humility that expressed submission to another's will. In making this gesture of subordination the Lover's—and by proxy, Gower's—denotative attribute, illuminators sanctioned the author's dismissal as a controlling agent over his own work. This argument has implications for our understanding of the political interventions made in the *Confessio*, a topic of ongoing debate that I take up in detail in Chapter 6.

The final chapter in this section extends the inquiries of the previous chapters to representations of John Lydgate, often referred to as England's first (if unofficial) poet laureate. The authorial ambiguities stoked by Chaucer and Gower are eschewed by Lydgate, who markets himself consistently throughout his vast poetic corpus as a dutiful servant to his royal patrons. There is a similar consistency in visual representations of Lydgate, which typically portray the poet kneeling and in a monk's habit. Scholars have referred to these representations as conventional scenes of book presentation, yet such a categorization does not encapsulate what these images express. This chapter brings together all prefatory images to Lydgate's works, not one of which proclaims Lydgate's identity as an author. Furthermore, multiple prefatory images to his poems dispense with the figure of Lydgate altogether, illustrating his patrons or sponsors instead. This and other nuances of Lydgatean representation have gone largely unremarked, and as I will argue, its classification as authorial portraiture maps a category backward onto images that would neither have been conceived as such in production nor perceived as such in reception. Instead the images give a visual form to the central paradox that motivated them: the paradox of Lydgate's successful self-promotion through acts of self-negation. The paradox found visual expression in devotional images—*ex voto* portraits—which configure Lydgate as a devotee. In the position of a devotee, the author vouches that the purpose of his poetry is to elevate the target of his vows, and this is a promise that illuminators took up with brio.

The chapters that make up the final part of the book move beyond illuminators' considerations of authorship to reckon with the consequences of the authorial indeterminacy that their images articulate. Acknowledging the precarity of Chaucer's, Gower's, and Lydgate's canonical status *as* authors liberates us to seek out the ways in which their works were made to have value for audiences who did not accept on faith the author's name and historicity as a single point of perspective around which the meanings of a work were organized, as a guarantor of cultural significance, or as a promise that an expensive copy of his work was a worthy investment. Audiences appear instead to have valued English verse for its elasticity, its openness to manipulation and instrumentalization. Both literary and art historical scholarship, no matter how theoretically committed, are often originalist in that they tend to bend in a philologically motivated arc toward the moment of a text's inception or an object's facture. Or, if a text or object is held under inspection in later moments of its life, the resulting inquiry is classified as reception study that presupposes a break between creator and consumer. But, in line with manuscript studies that confound this break, the final part of this book examines the illuminator's agency in dislocating literature from its natal moment and interpolating it into the later moments of its recurrent production.

Through two case studies of manuscripts made for royal patrons during the politically tempestuous Wars of the Roses, I discuss how the copresence of images and text defied both canonicity and absolute authority in the very moment of canon formation. Like Gower, who was "obsessively concerned with the relationship between past and present,"[68] and Lydgate, who was similarly inclined, illuminators deployed visual allusions to effect contact between past and present, a project in sympathy with partisan participants in the political conflicts that bedeviled England during the second half of the fifteenth century. These chapters hone in on issues of temporality of critical concern to both literary and art historical studies.

Chapter 5 focuses on a magnificent manuscript of John Lydgate's *Troy Book* (London, British Library Royal MS 18 D ii), which bears the traces of its conflicted production throughout its pages. The manuscript was commissioned by Sir William Herbert (d. 1469) and Anne Devereux (d. circa 1486) as a gift for the king—either Henry VI or Edward IV. But work on the manuscript was interrupted, and the unfinished book was kept in the possession of the Herbert family. Over the ensuing seventy years, the descendants of Sir William and Anne contracted illuminators and a scribe to complete the illustrative program and complement the manuscript with additional texts, including texts that replicate verses painted on the walls and ceilings of two of their residences. This chapter delves into the stratigraphy of the manuscript, cross-referencing its original images of royal praise with illuminations in other copies of Lydgate's *Troy Book* and with the illustrations and texts that were added later. Both comparisons divulge the larger aims of the original program to promote the legitimacy of self-interested cooptations of the past.

If the British Library's copy of Lydgate's *Troy Book* exposes the aggravations in producing history in English for the king, a sumptuous manuscript of Gower's *Confessio Amantis* offered the monarch a far shrewder political tool. Commissioned after Edward IV's deposition and subsequent return to power in 1471, a copy of the *Confessio Amantis* (New York, Morgan Library and Museum MS M.126) emerged from a volatile period in English political history. To restore the public's faith in the vigor and validity of their reinstated king, Edward's faction unleashed an avalanche of persuasive material, including new chronicles, positive "eyewitness" accounts of his victorious return to London, and newsletters of his success, in addition to staging spectacles in celebration of his venerable lineage. At the same time, Edward embarked on a campaign to reshape his own image through the patronage of manuscripts and tapestries with an almost exclusive focus on historical content. Chapter 6 addresses how this milieu furnishes a context for understanding the illuminations in the Morgan *Confessio*. Cued by the techniques of historical revisionism that defined persuasive material disseminated by supporters of Edward IV, the producers of this manuscript effectively revised Gower's poem not to act as one of royal counsel but rather to function as a catalog of royal models the king could claim for himself at any given time. Collected within this manuscript is an exhibition of historical images to which the patron might—and did—allude in fashioning his public identity.

The allusive images described in these chapters exhibit the integrality of the illuminator to the rising prestige of English literature. Moreover, they present an alternative narrative of literary canonization, in which the value of the first major works of English poetry was not guaranteed by the poets responsible for them. Rather, when manuscripts containing such poems were commissioned by elite clients, they were valued for their amenability to the opportunistic manipulation that illuminations fostered.

But, if this is the case, then why are there no narrative illustrations in any manuscripts of *The Canterbury Tales*? It seems illogical that such a rich collection of stories deflected full cycles of narrative illumination. By way of conclusion, I examine briefly Caxton's first two printed editions of Chaucer's *Canterbury Tales* from circa 1476 and circa 1482, capping off the chronological span of this study. While the first edition lacked illustrations, the second edition contained—like some of its manuscript counterparts—images of the pilgrims as tale tellers. Caxton, the savvy entrepreneur who printed these books for a broad market, exploited the *Tales'* appeal to an English populace that could envision itself in any one of its pilgrim authors, an operation that resembles kings' alacrity to see themselves in the heroes of history. Caxton realized quickly his audience's expectation that English literature worth reading was English literature worth looking at as well. This is a history that, until now, has never been told.

PART I

ILLUMINATORS

CHAPTER 1

The Illuminators of London

Because medieval illuminators are so often anonymous, they were,
in a sense, already "dead" before Roland Barthes pronounced the death
of the author in 1968.

—ALEXANDER, "Art History, Literary History," 55

Over the course of two weeks in 1456, the wardens of St. Nicholas Shambles in London issued a number of payments for the refurbishment of the missal designated for the high altar of their church.

Item payde for a large bukkes skyn the xx day of Janyuer for the massboke of the hye awter xxii d.

Item payde the same day for ii reede skynnys for wynges and lymnyng to same boke viii d.

Item payde for new wryting and amending of a defawte in the same booke ii d.

Item payde the xxvii day of Janyuer for a peyr of clospis of syluyr and gylte for the masboke that longeth to the hye awtyr xxii d.

Item payde the xxx day of Januar for tyssewis for the same claspis viii d.

Item payde the iii° day of ffebruar for garnysshyng of the howse of the saide masseboke iii s.

Item payde the iii° day of ffebruar for bynddyng of the saide masboke of the hye awtyr vi s. iii d.[1]

These scant lines are typical of the accounts of book production that survive from fifteenth-century London, and they are remarkable both for what they disclose and for the amount of information they withhold. One of the first things that a reader of this account might notice is the variety of materials and activities required for the book to be restored: there are the skins, the gilt silver clasps, the fabric for the clasps to be fastened to the binding, the garnishing of the "house" (perhaps a display case of wood) for the book, the writing, the illumination, and the binding. Among this passage's other disclosures is the information that the churchwardens paid to have their missal not simply amended but also supplied with a new binding and complemented with new writing and illumination. It also registers the costs of certain materials and kinds of labor, and it records that a sequence of payments was made between January 20 and February 3. Among the many questions it does not answer is whether the materials were procured and the activities commissioned were completed over this two-week period, or whether this was simply the amount of time over which payments were made. It names not a single individual, and it is unknown how many contributed to this campaign nor whether—if multiple individuals were indeed involved—their work was coordinated by a central contractor. Nor does it specify whether those who labored on this book were full-time professionals in the book trade with membership in the Stationers' Company or whether they were simply freelancers. The nature and content of both the writing and the illumination are unspecified as are particulars about the ornamentation of the book's "house." A number of entries combine payment for materials and activities that may or may not be related or have been provided by the same person, and perhaps in these cases the wardens visited multiple workers but only tallied the amount of money spent on a given day. Finally, and most typically, the book that these entries describe no longer survives (or, at the very least, its whereabouts are unknown), foreclosing the possibility of pairing archive and object and extrapolating further information from the conjunction. The renowned *Lytlington Missal* (1383–84) and the more granular details of its commission are prized for the information that, together, they divulge about book production; but for every *Lytlington* there are dozens of unnamed and lost missals like the St. Nicholas Shambles one, the production histories of which are riddled with uncertainty.[2]

Such uncertainty aggravates inquiry into late medieval London's book trade. The questions multiply for the nonliturgical manuscripts under consideration in this study because no such records survive for their production.[3] However, mitigating this uncertainty is an important surge in scholarship over the past twenty-five years on the professional conditions of copying manuscripts of Middle English verse in late medieval London, prompted in part by the discovery that a small number of scribes were "integral participants in those acts that founded a national, London-centered literary tradition repeatedly engaged in producing copies of Chaucer and Gower's poetry."[4] Yet illuminators, or limners as they are called in Middle English, have not been the subject of so significant a discovery, in part because the greatest information we have about their activities comes from illuminated manuscripts themselves. And manuscripts can be cagey informants. As D. F.

McKenzie showed in his study of Cambridge University Press in the eighteenth century, the codex itself is not always—or at least not always in isolation—the most reliable evidence of its own production history; recourse to the archive can act as a check against its sometimes dissembling transparency.[5] Documentation of London's late medieval book trade is neither as loquacious nor as number rich as the information at McKenzie's disposal. Nevertheless, in this chapter, I take a cue from his insights and muster evidence from archival sources such as inventories and account books in order to supplement what can be drawn from manuscripts themselves with information about limners' professional activities.

This chapter contributes to an ongoing conversation about the nature of London's book trade from 1403 to the end of the fifteenth century by concentrating chiefly on the role of manuscript illuminators within it. My focus here is on London and the surrounding areas, including Westminster, because the greater metropolis was the hub for the production of manuscripts containing verse by Chaucer, Gower, and, to a lesser extent, Lydgate, and because the majority of manuscripts under discussion in the pages to follow originated in London or its environs. While it would be difficult to establish a causal connection between the rise of vernacular literary production, its illumination, and the formalization of the commercial book trade, it is nevertheless true that "not long after secular limners themselves had become officially established [in 1403], Middle English texts came very quickly and professionally to be produced with illustrations."[6] Jonathan Alexander modified his remarks, quoted in the epigraph, about the illuminator's death on arrival by commenting on the necessity of inquiring into the broader structures that come together in the creation of a book as well as the training, practice, and cultural exposure enjoyed by these anonymous artists.[7] Following these provisos, my purpose in this chapter is not to identify the names and hands of individual limners responsible for illustrating the manuscripts under consideration in this study. Rather, I identify the peculiarities of their profession that bore on how these manuscripts emerged, developed, and ultimately produced meaning.

In the Introduction, I articulated that a central argument of this study is that the work of illustration both responds and contributes to the entry and circulation of new ideas about English vernacular literary authorship, political history, and book production itself in the fifteenth century. The purpose of the present chapter is to locate the wellspring for these new ideas in the dynamics of a profession in which "writing, decorating, and binding books were skills for hire."[8] These "activities, or at least ways of thinking about [these] activities, were rather fluid."[9] A reading of well-known sources and provision of new evidence from London's parish records, documents of civic administration, and Livery Company accounts and inventories bolsters this view and draws out its significance for the illuminations under examination in this study. Three key conditions emerge from these observations, and these conditions underpin the arguments of the chapters to follow. First, illuminators were avowedly anonymous and indifferent to individuation. I see anonymity, therefore, not as an impediment to be overcome by the historian but rather as a norm that, as such, is a meaningful situation. Second, illuminators were versatile. Consequently, enfolded into the miniatures they produced is knowledge not only derived from the pictorial models at their disposal or the adjacent text at hand but also from the texts they may have copied, the bindings they may have provided, and the books they may have sold. Third—and this is a point that has already been acknowledged with respect to late medieval London—manuscript production was not only a collaborative but also a decentralized affair. As a result of this final condition, a book was not perceived of as the product of a single or singular source but was rather, in its physical facture, a "multiauthored" object. It was in these conditions of anonymity, versatility, collaboration, and decentralization that manuscripts of works by Chaucer, Gower, and Lydgate were illuminated.

Who Were the Limners?

The inaugural year of this study—that is, 1403—is somewhat artificial, but it is a useful marker not only because of the outburst of vernacular manuscript production that occurred after 1400 but also because of an administrative document that attests to the growth of London's book trade.[10] It was in 1403 that the Court of Aldermen of London consented to a petition from the text writers, limners, and "other good people" who also bind and sell books to combine into a single company.[11] Until this point, limners and text writers had operated as separate craft misteries, subject to independent self-governance.[12] The petition of 1403 was the only official statement regarding the company's organization until 1557, when the Company of Stationers, as it then came to be called, was incorporated.[13] First among the requests in the 1403 petition was permission to "elect each year from among them two worthy men, the one a Limner and the other a Textwriter, to be wardens of the said crafts."[14] The following requests largely concern the regulation of their trade, and two things about this petition are worth commenting on: the first is that, at this early date, each of the two wardens is classified as holding a different profession—the one a limner and the other a text writer; but by mid-century, both wardens are labeled as stationers, representing all of the crafts that fell within the company's purview.[15] Second, the "other good people" are those who *also* bind and sell books, "impl[ying] that both binding and bookselling were trades commonly practised by textwriters and limners."[16] And so it was that in 1403, limners, text writers, binders, and vendors "joined forces to promote, protect, and regulate" the trade in which they were allied by a common investment—that is, the production and sale of books.[17]

The later choice for the title of the company is suggestive of its members' protean capacities. Although the reason for the term's application to the book trade remains uncertain, Blayney concluded that in definition, *stationer* meant simply *bookseller*, but that in practice it "seems to have been an all-purpose synonym applicable to any maker, binder, or seller of books."[18] It is not known how or why members decided to call themselves stationers, but they certainly made the decision official by the middle of the century: in 1441, the wardens elected to the company are not distinguished by craft and are simply referred to as "Stacioners."[19] In addition, after 1461, there is not a single known record of an individual called a limner working in London.[20] Of course, limners did not go extinct; rather, they appear to have opted for a different job title, and those who were formerly "limners" show up in later records with the description "stationer" after their names. The term *stationer* certainly could refer to a manager, middleman, or contractor, but this is not necessarily the case; when I refer to a stationer here, it is not in the sense of a contractor but rather as one who could be responsible for copying text, illuminating, binding, selling books, or any combination of the four.[21] It is important to remark at this early juncture that not all individuals who illuminated books within the City boundaries were necessarily members of this company, as anyone who had gained his or her freedom of the City could practice any trade he or she desired; likewise, not all limners in the larger area of London worked within the jurisdictional boundaries of the City.[22] Nevertheless, the formation of the company and the nature of its membership I have just sketched offer a useful starting point for characterizing the profile of illuminators—whether members of the Stationers' Company or not.

Records that document limners' places of work put them in proximity to one another and other members of the book trade, but within independent, discrete premises that preclude centralized cooperation in the style of a commercial scriptorium.[23] One of C. Paul Christianson's most significant contributions to our knowledge of the book trade in medieval London is the evidence he assembled for a concentration of book producers and vendors occupying small tenements in the area around St. Paul's Cathedral, particularly on Paternoster Row.[24] On this development, Christianson remarks,

> Such attestation of sixteen, and perhaps eighteen, book-trade artisans in these small Paternoster Row shops thus supports an hypothesis that the mode of manufacture for manuscript books in fifteenth-century London was quite different from that practised in monastic scriptoria. Instead of labouring in large workspaces, many artisans may have worked independently in small

quarters, not in concert in a single shop, and a book was therefore presumably created on many different sites, none of them, however, any great distance apart, perhaps many of them separated by only a few yards or a flight of stairs.[25]

None of these premises would have accommodated the kind of workshop where head artists and scribes trained teams of apprentices to work in a similar style or on their behalf. What existed in London was, rather, a small, amorphous, and loosely affiliated community of individuals who earned their livelihoods from the production of books—by Christianson's count, 260 of them. The business of books in late medieval London "was not conducted in uniform ways, but included both organized commissions and contracts involving patrons, stationers and artisans, as well as much more ad hoc activities. It was not simply 'commercial' in ways that we now understand the term."[26] It was a system that relied on collaboration but was predicated on independence.

Questions about the degree to which book production was supervised remain open in part because of an absence of documentation that attests to such coordination.[27] Perhaps this is because no documents were required when the same person who copied text also illuminated it, when the working relationship between the two was so intimate as to obviate the need for written contracts, or when the situation of manuscript production was simply ad hoc.[28] Similarly, the paucity and "brevity of the language"[29] of instructions to illuminators is a remarkable feature of English manuscripts from the fifteenth century, one that differentiates them from their Continental counterparts. Although in France, Italy, and the Low Countries instructions to the illuminator are commonly found in the margins of and on the incompletely trimmed edges of pages, and authors frequently directed the illustrative programs of manuscripts containing their works, no instructions of this scope or nature survive for manuscripts of Middle English literature.[30] Guide letters for decorated initials survive aplenty, to be sure, but beyond them only isolated examples of laconic instructions survive in English manuscripts, three of which I describe in Chapter 3. The vast majority of these instructions—such as "hic imago" placed in a blank space in a manuscript of the *Confessio Amantis* filled with signs of scribal incompleteness and emendation—appear more like *aides mémoires*, common devices among artists who spent multiple days on projects.[31] In the far more prolific instructions they have excavated and in the specialized tasks allocated to different artisans they have encountered in commissions, Mary Rouse and Richard Rouse find evidence for a "division of labour," "serial production," and highly particularized "distribution of work" in the Parisian book trade.[32] These conclusions are not ones that we can extrapolate to the London scene. The production of a manuscript in London was a "collaborative yet essentially divided" enterprise, and it was not a uniformly systematic one.[33]

Books Without Masters

The difficulty of grasping the conditions of manuscript illumination in late medieval London can find no better illustration than in this fact: for the entirety of the fifteenth century, there are only three illuminators whose names can be attached to surviving works of art (Herman Scheere, John Siferwas, and William Abell). The "painful fact," as Kathleen Scott put it, is that "English book illustrators of this period simply did not sign their work."[34] Until relatively recently, the idea of attempting to establish an area of artistic study lacking artists' names (or the names of canonical monuments and objects) would have been unthinkable, and it is for this reason that the study of late medieval English manuscripts has remained peripheral to the field of medieval art history.[35] It was long considered necessary to invent what Jonathan Alexander referred to sardonically as "the Master of this and the Master of that."[36] But rather than lamenting this anonymity as an obstacle, I want to linger on the significance of this professional attitude as an important precondition that impinged on the development of the illustrated manuscript of Middle English poetry. Such books, and the images within them, were themselves loci for changing cultural attitudes toward authorship and authority—a subject I tackle in the following three chapters.

Counterintuitively, maybe even paradoxically, the significance of anonymity in the professional practice of London limners can be drawn out by reference to one of those three limners who can be paired with a surviving work, William Abell. As we will see, while Abell has been represented as the master of a school of illumination—and therefore as evidence that such masters and schools existed—the details of his career and revisions to his oeuvre cast doubt on this characterization. Abell has been known to art historians since 1947, when an exhibition at Eton College featured the college's Consolidation Charter (Figure 4) for which a record of payment to its illuminator survives.[37] Significant about this receipt is the accident of both it and its accompanying charter's survival: Abell neither signed the charter nor took any other measures to ensure that future viewers would recognize the work as his. Since the Eton College exhibition in 1947, scholars have uncovered a fairly substantial dossier of records relating to Abell's life and work, a dossier I can expand.[38] Yet none of these documents records Abell's direct participation in the production of a surviving work, and the ascriptions of manuscripts to Abell's hand have rested on visual observations alone. In 1971, Jonathan Alexander published the first list of works attributed to Abell, a list that amounted to twenty-one items.

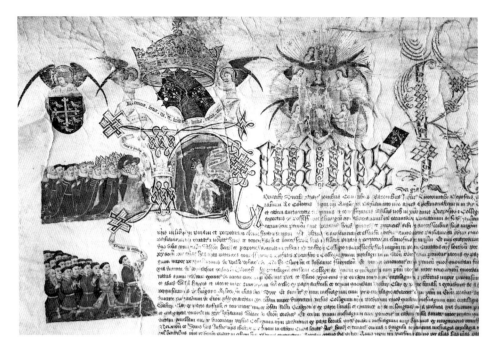

FIGURE 4. Eton College Consolidation Charter, Westminster/London, 1446. Eton, ECR 39/57. Reproduced by permission of the Provost and Fellows of Eton College.

FIGURE 5. Eton College Consolidation Charter, Westminster/London, 1446. Eton, ECR 39/57 (detail). Reproduced by permission of the Provost and Fellows of Eton College.

FIGURE 6. King's College Cambridge Charter, Westminster/London, 1446.
Cambridge, King's College Archives KC/18. Reproduced by kind
permission of King's College.

Although Abell's single attested work is the Consolidation Charter from 1446, Alexander highlighted as his baseline a manuscript from fifteen years later with no verifiable relationship to Abell.[39] As a result, a large number of manuscripts with resemblance to this later work were ascribed to him. It was only with the 1996 publication of Kathleen Scott's catalog of illuminated manuscripts that this list of Abell attributions was pared down to nine.[40] In her reassessment of Abell's oeuvre, Scott provides a meticulous description of the illuminator's style, with which I concur; it is only through extended observation and high-resolution photography that I have decided to shave Scott's list down by two items. The works I ascribe to Abell include Eton, ECR 39/57, the Eton College Consolidation Charter of 1446 (Figures 4 and 5, Plate 2); King's College Archives KC/18, a charter for King's College, also made in 1446 (Figure 6); the Worshipful Company of Haberdashers Grant of Arms of 1446 (Figure 7); San Marino, Huntington Library HM 932, the Statutes of the Archdeaconry of London of 1447 (Figure 8); London, Society of Antiquaries MS 501, a genealogical roll from circa 1447–55 (Figure 9); one miniature in Cambridge, St. John's College MS H.5, Stephen Scrope's *Epistle Othea*, circa 1450–55 (Figure 10); and Cambridge, King's College MS 40, a Bible concordance of the mid-fifteenth century (Figure 11). Despite Scott's important amendment, Alexander's original article is still often cited, and because of this, Abell is still treated as an artist who presided over a school of illuminators. Additionally, he is often cited as the collaborator of a scribe with whom he only appears to have worked once, possibly twice.[41] Because Abell illuminated far fewer surviving works than is commonly thought, his status as an artistic master who oversaw a school of illuminators and influenced their style—the closest thing we had to a solid case for such a master in late medieval London—is less secure.

FIGURE 7. Worshipful Company of Haberdashers Grant of Arms, London, 1446. Reproduced by kind permission of the Worshipful Company of Haberdashers.

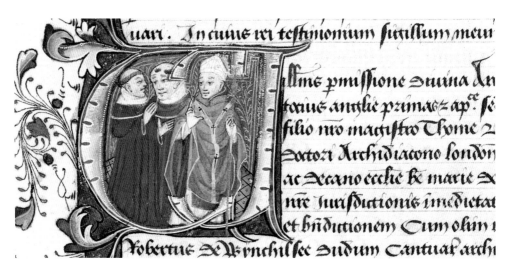

FIGURE 8. *Archbishop William Courtenay accompanied by two clerics.* Statutes of London. London, 1447. San Marino, Huntington Library HM 932, fol. 10v (detail).

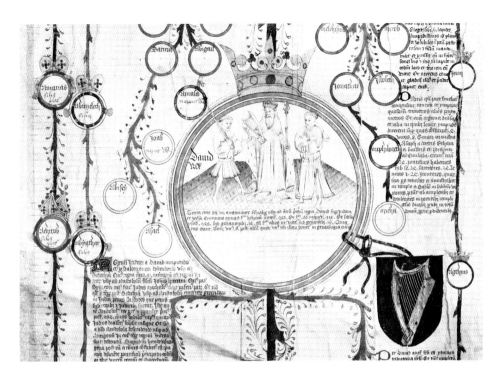

FIGURE 9. *David and attendants.* Genealogical Roll, London, c. 1447–1455. London, Society of Antiquaries MS 501 (detail). By kind permission of the Society of Antiquaries of London.

FIGURE 10. *Presentation of the book.* Stephen Scrope, *Epistle of Othea*, London, c. 1450–1459. Cambridge, St. John's College MS H.5, fol. 1r. By permission of the Master and Fellows of St. John's College, Cambridge.

FIGURE 11. *Hiram before Solomon*. Bible concordance. London, c. 1450. Cambridge, King's College MS 40, fol. 32v (detail).

The details of Abell's career between 1446, when he first shows up in the archive, and his death in 1474, likewise offer little evidence to suggest that he presided over an artistic school. The Eton College record from 1447 for one pound, six shillings, and eight pence is the earliest known documentary attestation to Abell, along with an unrelated rental record from the same year for a garden property in the parish of St. Egidius beyond Cripplegate in London.[42] What these two documents reveal is straightforward: in 1446–47, William Abell was living in the city when he received the commission from Eton College to illuminate its Consolidation Charter. At around the same time, he illuminated the Confirmation Charter for King's College, Cambridge (1446), providing for them a design nearly identical to Eton College's.[43] Three years later, William Abell, limner, was named supervisor of the will of Thomas Ffysh, onetime warden of the Company of Stationers: in this will, Abell was also given the remaining term of Ffysh's two apprentices. So, by 1450, Abell was sufficiently advanced in his career to take on the responsibility of managing apprentices. According to the will, Abell's responsibility was to "tech Enforme and fynd" the apprentices, but the manner and degree to which Abell incorporated their labor into manuscripts on which he himself worked is unknown.[44] Regarding the clearest case of collaboration by multiple illuminators in a manuscript worked on by Abell (Cambridge, St. John's College MS H.5), Scott writes of the second illuminator, "He appears, from the confidence and quality of his style, to have been a fully trained collaborator rather than a learner or an assistant to Abell in his shop."[45]

After this date, only a slender dossier attests to Abell's professional activities. In 1452, he served the first of his numerous stints as joint churchwarden for the parish church of St. Nicholas Shambles. In the wardens' accounts and related inventories, he is referred to variously as a limner and a stationer.[46] As warden, Abell was responsible for covering whatever arrearages the church incurred during his tenure, and a series of items from an account of 1471 shows the church making up these debts to Abell, who paid for candle wax and reparative work on books and possibly executed some of this work himself. For example,

> Item payed by William Abell sumtyme on of the churche wardeynce for reparacions of diuerse books and linkes for daily light in party of contentacion of his olde arreragez atte his laste accompte ffirst for mendyng of a masse booke that was all to toryn rent and brokyn for newe renewyng and glewyng of the same . . . ii s.
>
> Item by the same William in party of payment of the saide arreragez for newe mendyng of an olde portos [breviary] that was alle to rent and amendyd in writyng in diuerse places and was newe glewed ageyn and newe bownde with an newe coueryng of deres leder lined with newe rede leder with a peyre of newe plate claspes price in all . . . xiii s. iiii d.[47]

As with the accounts cited at the beginning of this chapter, these items raise the question of which—if any—of the services listed were carried out by Abell himself. It is possible, but by no means certain, that he played a supervisory role by delegating this work to others. Similarly, it is possible that the three contiguous shops Abell rented on Paternoster Row for five years starting in 1469 (and which his wife continued to pay for two years after his death in 1474) were used for the book trade, but nothing in the records indicates as much, and these shops could have hosted any number of businesses.[48]

William Abell is an important figure because he is the illuminator for whom the most abundant documentation survives and because one of these documents offers details about a work that is extant; what is remarkable about this documentation is how little of it relates explicitly to his work in the book trade. If it seems as if Abell was the core, originator, or master of a group style, it is only by accident of the surviving Eton College receipt and charter and by the misperception that he was the illuminator responsible for a greater number of surviving works than he was.[49] Kathleen Scott's keen ability to localize and date manuscripts has been essential to advancing our knowledge about fifteenth-century English manuscript production. But just as she has located plausible links between the hands responsible for some manuscripts, she has also advocated a measured approach that is worth underlining. Among the important caveats Scott has issued is a reference to the work of one illuminator, which "will probably always be difficult to distinguish from other English borders of the period. This, of course, is true of the work of the many anonymous and (as yet) undifferentiated English illuminators of the fifteenth century."[50] In line with this observation, I would argue that there are so many other manuscripts with illumination that resembles to greater and lesser degrees the style in works attributable to Abell as to suggest that a variety of illuminators were learning the trade from one another, being exposed to each other's work, but nevertheless functioning independently. Long ago, A. I. Doyle and M. B. Parkes stated that the physical proximity of practitioners in the book trade "would enable them to draw on each other's skills and imitate each other's products," and it appears from the surviving work attributable to and erroneously identified with Abell that this was indeed the case.[51] Refining of the body of illumination that can be identified with the hand responsible for the Eton College charter (that is, Abell's) implies that the act of identification is itself possible (if a manuscript can be rejected from this corpus, it necessarily follows that a manuscript can be admitted to it). What is important to acknowledge is that this operation is the exception, rather than the rule, for late medieval London. The case, then, of William Abell points to the challenges—often insurmountable—in seeking out the hands of individual illuminators when the institution in which they worked did not encourage them to individualize their own hands.[52] In the chapters that follow, I will not name illuminators or attempt to track their careers across books.[53]

Although Abell's résumé discourages us from attempting to identify limners' hands, it does place us in a better position to understand something of limners' professional mentalities. Further evidence from a variety of civic, commercial, and parish records exhibits anonymity and flexibility as common traits among limners. Professional titles and receipts are particularly evocative of the limner's protean capacities. Aside from taking on the general title of "stationer" by the mid-fifteenth century, like the "stacioner" who was paid by the Carpenters' Company in 1485 "for gildyng of letters on our tabill & for the parchement,"[54] limners up to that point do not always appear in records exclusively under that rubric. Christianson's *Directory* includes forty-two limners, eighteen of whom (or 43 percent) are also known by other professional titles.[55] In 1464, when the wardens of London Bridge were preparing for the entry and coronation of their new queen, Elizabeth Woodville, they paid John Genycote three shillings "for writing and limning six ballads, delivered to the Queen at her approach."[56] The small scale of the commission makes it likely that Genycote was responsible for both the writing and the limning, although other commissions are not so straightforward. In 1499, the churchwardens of St. Margaret's Westminster paid "Thom Herte xx s. in parte of payment of xl s. for the makyng writtyng notyng lumynyng byndyng and for the stuffe of iij newe fastis that is to sey, the visitacion of our ladi, de nomine Jhu and transfiguracion of our lorde, that is to witte in v antiphoners and a legende, iiij graelles, iiij masse bokes and iiij procession-ares."[57] It is probable that this Thom Herte is the same Thomas Harte who is re-ferred to as a stationer in Chancery records from 1463 to 1467.[58] Perhaps Herte was paid to cover some services he would not carry out himself but would rather facili-tate. But maybe not. William Abell is a good reminder that one referred to as a sta-tioner could also be a practitioner of any of the crafts required to make a book.

The dynamism of a limner's professional activities is borne out elsewhere. In a case argued before the Commons, the limner Thomas Elbrigge alleged that he was retained in 1419 by the stationer William White to serve him as an illuminator of books for two years and was promised, in addition to his food and drink, a hun-dred shillings per year, which White never paid.[59] This suit would *seem* to support the idea of specialization, but just three years later, Elbrigge was in court (his pro-fessional title is not given) suing the limner John Bradley, for forty shillings as well as for a book valued at forty shillings. The Plea Rolls do not specify why Elbrigge sought compensation from Bradley or why the latter had "unjustly detained" a book, but perhaps Elbrigge had risen to a managerial position and was demanding compensation for services not rendered. Alternatively, he and Bradley could have been limner-collaborators or simply friends vying for ownership of a book.[60] The one signed work by an illuminator aside from Scheere and Siferwas is not illumina-tion but rather the binding of London, Lambeth Palace Library MS 560, impressed into which is the declaration "Iacob illuminator me fecit."[61] Evident from this brief review of several figures are both the challenges in determining just what roles were played by people named in documents as limners or scribes who were paid for illu-mination and the probability that this is the case precisely *because* so many limners did not function in that capacity exclusively.

Inventories and account books frustrate even further any chance of discerning a division of labor. Bookkeeping practices in the fifteenth century are not especially different from today's, and invoicing often itemizes according to the cost per unit or activity without indicating the individual responsible for procuring or executing ei-ther.[62] In addition to the example with which I opened this chapter, the wardens of St. Nicholas Shambles also recorded the following for 1454: "Item payde the ix day of September for stuffe and writing of a kalender for the masboke of the hye awtyr xxi d. Item payde for lymnyng for the same kalendyr vi d."[63] Was the material for the book purchased in one location but brought to another one nearby for limning and writ-ing? Were both purchased on the same premises and provided by the same individual but merely itemized for the sake of transparency in accounting? Similarly, the wardens of the same church in the 1480s paid John Rowland "staycionar" for quires of vellum written and noted with the service of the visitation of our lady—that is, embellished with musical notation—and for binding, covering, and clasping other volumes.[64] Did Rowland already have the unbound objects in his shop? And if so, was he the person who copied and noted them? What complicates this picture even further is that he was paid wages as parish clerk for the year. So did the parish keep a stationer on retainer to record their inventories and accounts? Rowland's case is mirrored in that of Thomas Fferour, "clarke of Seynte Andrews," who was paid in 1487–88 by the wardens of St. Mary at Hill "for mendyng of an olde antyphoner, to peace it, to wryte it and to note yt and also to newe bynde yt, 6s 8d."[65] The imprecision of records is similarly on view in the case of John Barber, the stationer who was paid by the wardens of St. Dunstan-in-the-East "for amendyng of the bokes of the cherche swyche as were fawty."[66] In sum, none of the surviving documents suggests that book producers held particularized or compartmentalized positions.[67]

A premise that undergirds current scholarship on English manuscript illumination of the fifteenth century is that limners had partitioned their profession to such a degree that some specialized as "border artists" while others specialized in figural illustration.[68] It is significant that before Kathleen Scott, the foremost authority on English manuscript illumination of the later Middle Ages was Margaret Rickert, whose scholarship followed the predominant methodological trends of her day in, first, defining individual styles and establishing the oeuvres of single master artists and, second, assembling evidence for artistic schools and classifying their participants as illustrators, decorators, and so on.[69] Both of these habits are apparent, for example, in her christening of Herman Scheere as the master illuminator responsible for bringing a fashionable Continental style to London[70] and in her magisterial reconstruction of the *Carmelite Missal*, which ascribes its decorative program to anywhere between three and over a dozen illuminators.[71] Rickert is something of an unsung pioneer in the study of English illumination, although her techniques have been adopted widely, influencing the study of such canonical manuscripts as the *Sherborne* and *Lytlington Missals* and of the *Great Bible*.[72] Yet, as the opening vignette to this chapter illustrates, the production of such celebrity manuscripts is not representative of how all books were made. The study of English manuscript illumination owes much to these methodologies as applied to blockbuster manuscripts, but these methodologies are not always commensurate with evidence about English manuscript production in the later medieval period. There is no indication in surviving documents that the basic vocabulary of the professional artistic organization common on the Continent and particularly in Italy and France—school, atelier, workshop, master, assistant, historiator, maker of vignettes—was in use in the book trade of fifteenth-century London.

Anonymity and the absence of specialization are, as the preceding discussion has shown, important characteristics of London limning. Limners were not working in a master-centric system that placed a premium on asserting singular, "authorial" identities, nor were they required to mark their products as their own work, a requirement among illuminators in cities like Bruges.[73] Additionally, limners had visual models, patterns, and even pounced designs at their disposal so that images they produced were, as often as not, reliant on an appropriation and selective redeployment of preexisting work. And, as other scholars have argued, a book got made because a variety of people working in kaleidoscopic coalitions and occupying various métiers made it. These conditions are not applicable to illuminators alone, and, as I will now go on to discuss, they echo the practices of other professional book producers in London.

The Copyists of Middle English Poetry: An Aspect Shift

Recent research into the scribes responsible for copying out works of Middle English verse has contributed to a richer, more varied picture of how these manuscripts came about. This research has shown that as with limners, scribes who produced these Middle English manuscripts often did so in informal ways, both within the City and outside of its civic borders. Some of these scribes may have been professional text writers, and others may have worked in adjacent professions that entailed paralegal and administrative work but that allowed them to copy verse as a sideline. In what follows, I address this important research, partly because knowledge about scribes is essential to a holistic conception of the illuminated manuscript. In addition, my purpose is to consider this recent work in light of my contention that the anonymity and versatility of manuscript producers had a formative impact on the illuminated manuscripts of Middle English verse that they made. The conditions I previously ascribed to illuminators could, as I discuss here, be applied more broadly to all producers of Middle English verse manuscripts made within greater London.

Scholarship conducted since the 1990s on the scribes responsible for copying vernacular poetry during the fifteenth century has strengthened the long-mounting suspicion that many of them were members of the civic secretariat and clerks whose day jobs were devoted not to copying out manuscripts of verse or scripture but rather to the many documents that greased the wheels of London's commerce and bureaucracy.[74] The nomenclature of these individuals can be somewhat confusing—and it was slippery in the fifteenth century itself—but, for the sake of convenience, when I refer here to scriveners and clerks, I mean specifically individuals who were paid to copy administrative and legal documents, some but not all of whom were members of the Scriveners' Company (although it is important to note that *scrivener* was not so narrowly defined or consistently used in the later Middle Ages); when I use the term *scribe,* it is in the most neutral sense, to mean simply anyone who copied out text, regardless of its content or of the individual's professional affiliation.[75] One group of manuscripts offers an example of why it is important to contextualize the work of illuminators alongside our increasing knowledge about scribes. Eight copies of John Gower's *Confessio Amantis* are believed to contain the work of one scribe, the famous "Scribe D" first identified and named as such by Doyle and Parkes.[76] All but one of these manuscripts contain figural illumination.[77] Linne Mooney and Estelle Stubbs recently identified this scribe as John Marchaunt, chamber clerk and common clerk of the Guildhall between 1380 and 1417.[78] While this theory has not gained universal acceptance, it is possible that this scribe—whether John Marchaunt or "Scribe D" or even a group of professionally related individuals—was also responsible for the sort of work associated with scriveners. If a scrivener was a major participant in the production of these early manuscripts of the *Confessio Amantis*, then their pictorial elaboration is all the more noteworthy. They demanded that a person accustomed to copying legal and business documents produce manuscripts of verse and furnish their production with space for images and decorative illumination, and required a liaison between scribes and illuminators who may have come together commonly for the elaboration of official documents and collections, such as charters, grants, and custumals, but not necessarily for books with narrative or poetic content.[79]

The genesis of recent work on the scribes of Middle English verse is Doyle and Parkes's landmark study from 1978, which had three significant consequences. First, it demonstrated that three of the scribes who were responsible for a single manuscript of Gower's *Confessio Amantis* also worked on other manuscripts of Middle English poetry; second, it argued that one of these scribes was Thomas Hoccleve, clerk of the Privy Seal and poet in his own right; and, third, it put paid to the idea that Middle English poetry was produced in large, organized scriptoria overseen by the poets themselves. According to Doyle and Parkes, and the others who have followed, the manuscripts themselves show signs of simultaneous copying by multiple scribes, independent copyists whose work sometimes was and often was not coordinated by a separate contractor or middleman.[80] Their views have been widely accepted, but it was only in the first decade of the twenty-first century that scholars attempted in earnest to identify these independent craftsmen. A number of scholars, including Mooney, Stubbs, and Simon Horobin have assembled evidence that many of the scribes responsible for works by Gower, Chaucer, and other English poets were members of the Scriveners' Company as well as those who worked as clerks for the Guildhall or for the companies of London.[81] The project to identify these scriveners received momentum from Mooney's 2006 article, which argues that the Scrivener (i.e., scrivener and member of the Scriveners' Company) Adam Pinkhurst was the scribe responsible for a number of *Canterbury Tales* manuscripts, including the celebrated, illuminated Ellesmere copy.[82]

Recent scribal identifications rely chiefly on paleographical evidence, and there remains disagreement over whether there are sufficient grounds for ascribing manuscripts of Middle English poetry to named individuals.[83] There are, of course, important exceptions, specifically in cases where scribes have signed their work and where such identity between the hand of a signed work and another sample of writing exists as to almost obviate the need for justification (Hoccleve is the highest-profile example; Ricardus Franciscus, discussed in Chapter 6, is another). But rather than intervening in the debate over the accuracy of these identifications, I want to propose here that insights from the history of art may have something to contribute to the epistemological questions that motivate this debate. Lawrence Warner has recently urged the "need for a serious conversation concerning the methodologies of scribal attribution, and the desires and imperatives that lead to those methodologies' employment even where no obvious need or reason presents itself."[84] After taking up Warner's invitation, I will propose ways in which this discussion intersects with concerns about the illumination of the manuscripts that these scribes copied. Part of the impetus for my contribution here is that the naming of "Chaucer's own scriveyn" as Adam Pinkhurst has exerted the same gravitational force as that of the Old Master, pulling ever more works into its orbit and ultimately reframing an entire body of manuscripts, by both adherents and detractors of this identification.[85] In addition, the discourse of scribal attribution is similar to that of late nineteenth-century connoisseurship. That this is the case suggests that recent theoretical conversations about connoisseurship may lend a useful framework that would circumvent the conundrum of individual attribution while still allowing us to appreciate the value of this current scholarship.

While connoisseurship has, unfortunately, acquired a negative connotation and suffered a diminished reputation, it is one of the oldest methods of art historical scholarship and one that is in complete sympathy with paleography. Richard Neer has usefully referred to paleography as "a connoisseurship of words,"[86] and, indeed, connoisseurship itself is one branch of *Sachphilologie*, or the philology of objects.[87] In definition, it is "the attribution of artifacts to particular hands, or times, or places."[88] All of this is to say that when I invoke connoisseurship, it is not in a derogatory sense nor in relation to judgments about quality; and, more important, when I do so, it is because, as a cornerstone of art historical scholarship, it has received the kind of extended interrogation that Warner proposes might benefit recent paleographical analysis.

It was in the nineteenth century that the erstwhile doctor and politician Giovanni Morelli (d. 1891) gave connoisseurship the kind of analytical backbone that characterizes contemporary paleography. Morelli's method was simple: to focus on features of a painting (*Grundformen*) that are most likely to manifest the painter's unconscious, idiosyncratic, and thus most diagnostically useful habits.[89] In this respect, the ductus, minims, and graphs of paleography play an analogous role to *Grundformen*, wherein the stem, limb, and shoulder of, say, an *h* could be seen to parallel the forensic utility of an earlobe or a tear duct in Morelli's schema. Morelli had his champions and detractors, and his detractors expressed their hesitation in terms similar to those that have been leveled at efforts to identify scribal hands. First, "ears or fingers could take many different forms even in the same painting by one master,"[90] just as letters could take a variety of forms in the same document by one scribe.[91] Second, individual components—so the skeptics suggest—are tenuous reference points for individual hands since not only do they vary widely, but also in isolation they are easily replicated; it is, rather, the manner in which components are contextualized and brought together that is more diagnostically significant.[92] Likewise, paleographers have argued that an overall appearance "on the basis of an examination from a distance of about 20 to 30 inches" is a more reliable diagnostic than individual letter forms.[93] These echoes suggest to me that the ways in which later art historians have grappled with and responded to Morellian connoisseurship may prove useful to the current debate in paleography.

Two ways in which scholars have recuperated connoisseurship are to admit and embrace its inherently subjective foundations and to adopt a more capacious form of attribution that does not attempt to identify individual hands, thereby eschewing "a modern . . . notion of a corporally defined . . . self within which resides artistic genesis (and genius)."[94] Attending to the former helps answer the problems of the latter. Regarding the matter of objectivist criteria, we might say that scholars have not identified incontrovertible proof that the same individual is responsible for X and Y manuscripts; rather these scholars have identified visual features that have forced an aspect shift. Taken from Wittgenstein's example of the duck-rabbit illusion, an aspect shift (*Aspektwechsel*) is that process by which the same entity transforms into another without undergoing any change in form; the change, rather, originates in the fuzzier act of perception, grounded not in rational inference but in intuition.[95] The term *aspect* is a fortuitous one because it also has a currency in paleography, taken to mean the "general impression on the page made by a specimen of handwriting at first sight."[96] (Any art historian who has experienced flutters in the presence of a work by an artist whose hand he recognizes can relate.) According to Richard Neer, "stylistic criteria are whatever criteria must be met for the requisite aspect-shift to occur."[97] For Neer, verifiability is not always important; it is the aspect shift that counts. Marian Feldman explains the significance of Neer's assertion: "Because attributions based solely on stylistic analysis [for which, read, connoisseurial criteria] are unverifiable, we may be using stylistic analysis to answer the wrong sorts of questions (that is, who made it) when we might instead pose different questions with respect to artistic and communal identities."[98] In the case of the copyists of Middle English poetry, scholars have identified stylistic criteria that justify looking in the direction of certain clusters of scribes, some who were probably clerks working in and around London and Westminster. And in this respect, they have identified visual criteria that constitute, if not an *individual* style, then certainly a *communal* one, which has demanded a recontextualization of the manuscripts containing the first multicopy, major works of Middle English poetry.[99] Daniel Mosser and Linne Mooney's recent research into the "hooked-*g* scribes" illustrates the fruitfulness of a group-oriented approach. While it would be difficult to corroborate with absolute certainty the parsing of hands that they assert, their focus on a number of interconnected individuals who collaborated with and were influenced by one another is profitable.[100] Because traits or motifs in an anonymous profession did not belong to one individual but were rather common property, by focusing on the motif, or in their terms, "graph" of the hooked *g*, Mosser and Mooney identify evidence for what is in Feldman's terms "a network of skilled practitioners who interacted closely with one another in their training and crafting yet did not necessarily work always and only in one particular spatial location or with one group of crafters."[101]

Communal style is a useful concept because it reorients questions away from the thorny matter of individuals and instead toward the direction of conditions. It focuses on diagnostics not to arrive at the identities of who is behind a work of art but rather to group this work of art into a milieu and then inquire into the impact of their decision to associate, collaborate, or even operate in a given, corporate style. For example, if we speak of the variations of a script as a style or a calligraphic idiom, we could focus not on how a particular hand in one document appears in another but rather that a script and scribal motifs characteristic of documents are chosen for luxury manuscripts of Middle English poetry. This affiliation is exemplified in the pen-worked initial that heads Richard Pumfrey's 1447 entry in the Scriveners' Company Common Paper (Figure 12) and the ornamental initials that adorn *The Canterbury Tales* in Oxford, Bodleian Library MS Rawlinson Poet. 223 (Figure 13), the latter of which Mooney and Mosser ally with the "hooked-*g*" group.[102] Likewise, Bodleian Library MS Rawlinson C 48—a manuscript of John Lydgate's *Siege of Thebes* and some of his shorter poems—is preceded by strapwork, flourishing, and a pen-drawn crown labeled "magister" (Figure 14), which is reminiscent of the ornamental first membranes of the Common Plea Rolls copied by clerks working in Westminster (Figure 15).[103] Scribes were trained to work in a range of hands, so the use of cursiva or a documentary script in this example is not proof positive that the person who copied the Lydgate manuscript was a clerk of Westminster. However, it does help to

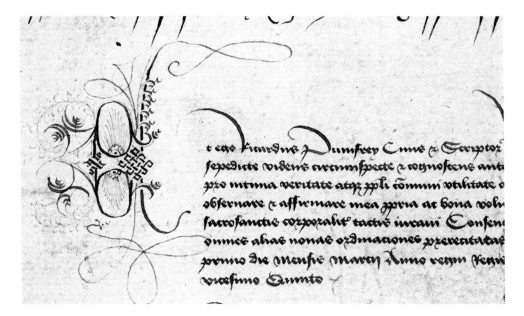

FIGURE 12. Subscription to the oath by Richard Pumfrey. Scriveners' Company
Common Paper, London, March 1, 1447. London, Guildhall Library MS 5370, p. 72
(detail). Reproduced by kind permission of the Worshipful Company of Scriveners.

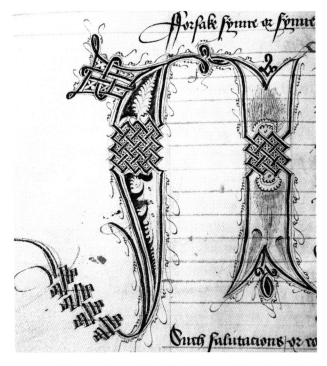

FIGURE 13. Strapwork initial. Geoffrey Chaucer, *Canterbury Tales*, London,
c. 1450–1475. Oxford, Bodleian Library MS Rawlinson Poet. 223, fol. 208v (detail).
By kind permission of the Bodleian Libraries.

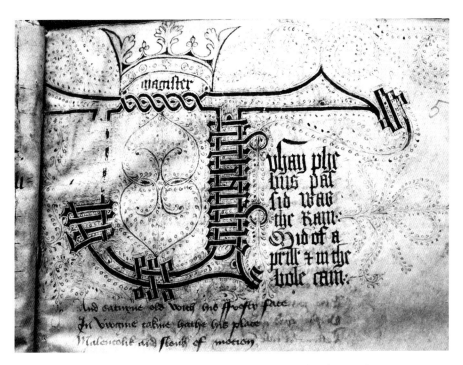

FIGURE 14. Strapwork initial. John Lydgate, *Siege of Thebes*, London or Westminster(?), c. 1475–1500. Oxford, Bodleian Library MS Rawlinson C 48, fol. 5r (detail). By kind permission of the Bodleian Libraries.

FIGURE 15. Strapwork initial. Common Plea Roll, Westminster, Easter Term, 1466. Kew, National Archives CP 40/819 (detail).

date and place the manuscript, as well as to suggest that the person who made it perceived a documentary script and embellishment as appropriate for verse by Lydgate. For some, this aspect shift opens the manuscripts to questions regarding the motivations and politics of the men who took on this extracurricular labor, unrelated to their day jobs if they were indeed scriveners. For others, this aspect shift gives a material foundation to larger issues already pursued along literary lines: namely, the intermingling of legalistic and bureaucratic discourses in the earliest canonical works of Middle English poetry.[104] These are matters beyond the purview of this study, but they do bring me to issues that are germane to my interests here.

The existence of style communities among scribes likens the dynamics of copying to the dynamics of illumination I outlined earlier. As with illumination, the copying of Middle English verse was not driven by singular dynamos or masters but was instead distributed across a variety of groups, often loosely affiliated individuals who imitated each other and who worked both within company structures and outside of them as freelancers. Seeking to identify their names and build up oeuvres and schools around these names might be at odds with this anonymous and collaborative practice.

Furthermore, like their illuminator counterparts, scribes responsible for legal documents appear, increasingly over the fifteenth century, to have been versatile. In 1442−43, Winchester College paid five shillings and fourpence to a "clerico Kirkeby" both "for writing various documents and for illuminating the letters patent of 9 February 1443."[105] Likewise, Richard Frampton, a figure known well to paleographers as a member of London's civic bureaucracy and a clerk for the House of Lancaster, received a number of commissions for both writing and illuminating.[106] It is possible he delegated the illumination to colleagues, but the contracts themselves only specify payment to Frampton "pour p'chemyn et pour lymenere d'un nri portos" [for parchment and for illuminating one of our breviaries] and "pour p'chemyn limnature et scriptura" [for parchment, illumination, and writing].[107] The possibility that Frampton carried out illumination seems more like a probability in light of Estelle Stubbs's comment that "Frampton was paid for doing his own flourishing for one of the Great Couchers and was a skilled and artistic craftsman in his own right."[108] And a rare, draft copy of a grant of arms to Louis de Bruges (1472) indicates that clerks at the very least had access to and the ability to apply pigments for limning: the draft contains a quick version of the arms to be granted to Louis, and it seems reasonable that—for this informal document—the clerk simply executed the illumination himself (Plate 3).[109] Naturally, the fair copy also contains an illuminated version of these arms, and the adroit penwork executed by the clerk who produced the fair copy suggests the possibility that it was the clerk who provided the arms here as well (Figure 16).[110] Another grant, this one for the Armourers' Company in 1453, contains a deftly drawn figure of St. George (Figure 17).[111] Anne Sutton

FIGURE 16. Grant of Arms to Louis de Bruges, Westminster(?), 1472. London, British Library Egerton MS 2830 (seal not pictured). © British Library Board.

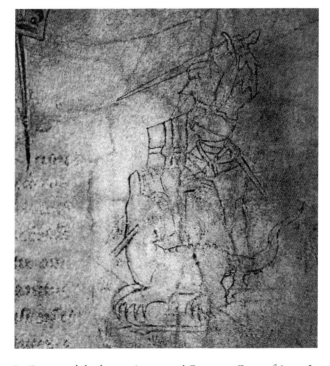

FIGURE 17. *St. George and the dragon.* Armourers' Company Grant of Arms, London, 1453. London, Guildhall MS 12112 (detail). By kind permission of the Worshipful Company of Armourers and Brasiers.

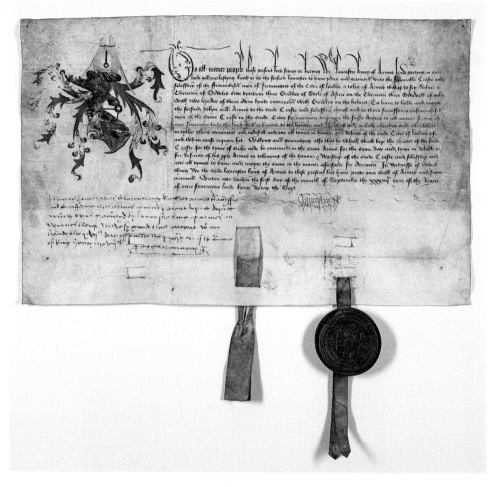

FIGURE 18. Ironmongers' Grant of Arms, London, 1455. London, Worshipful
Company of Ironmongers. By kind permission of the Worshipful Company
of Ironmongers.

has drawn attention to the "artistry and sophistication" of the fifteenth-century
clerk's penwork, artistry that extended beyond flourishing and strapwork to encompass figural drawing of exceptional draftsmanship.[112]

As with the manuscripts cited earlier, invoices for documents such as charters
are vague and suggest clerks' versatility. In 1455, a scrivener named Thomas Fermory was paid by the Ironmongers to create their company grant of arms. According to the company's accounts, Thomas was paid "for makyng [i.e., composing]
and writyng of the [grant],"[113] yet nothing else in the account mentions the grant's
illumination. The question this item raises is whether Fermory was responsible for
simply writing up the text of the grant in his capacity as scrivener, or did he also
produce the illumination of the company's newly granted coat of arms? The grant

ILLUMINATORS

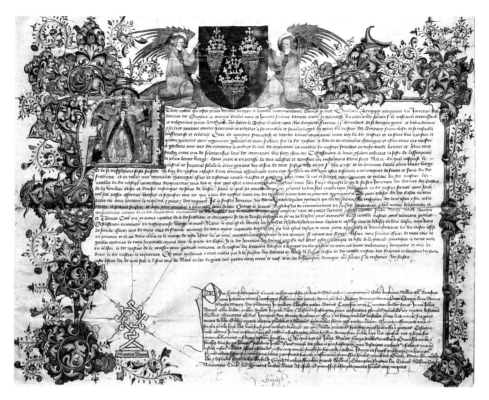

FIGURE 19. Drapers' Company Grant of Arms, London, 1439. London, Worshipful Company of Drapers. By kind permission of the Worshipful Company of Drapers.

itself survives, and if the quality of its illumination is indicative, then perhaps Fermory was responsible (Figure 18, Plate 4). The arms are not the work of a virtuosic artist, and the rate of three shillings and fourpence (which also included a supplication to the king) is closer to the sum awarded Kirkby for his work on the Winchester College letters patent than the one pound, six shillings, and eightpence that Abell earned for his work on the Eton Charter (Figures 4 and 5, Plate 2).[114] The account for the Drapers' Company Grant of Arms from 1439 is, while more granular in its itemization, silent on the identity of the individuals they hired.[115] According to the Wardens' Account of 19 Henry VI (1441), Drapers' paid

> for devysyng and for wrytyng of a dede of armys & for a notares signe 6s 7d.
> for lymnynge of þe same dede 5s.
> for gravinge of þe comune seal 23s 4d.[116]

The grant is among the most elaborate to survive, containing not only an ornamental border with profuse gold leaf but also a depiction of the Virgin of Mercy and angels supporting the company's arms, as well as the notarial mark of John Daunt (Figure 19). While I cannot hope to show that Daunt was responsible for the illumination as well as the text, it is tantalizing to propose that John was related to the painter Thomas Daunt, who was paid in 1436 to paint the heraldic images for the Duke of Bedford's funeral procession.[117]

The degree to which clerks' drawings featured as part of the decorative repertoire of documents during the fifteenth century recommends a consideration of their contribution to the visual—pictorial, even—aspects of literary culture. If clerks participated in copying the texts of Middle English poetry that contain illumination, it is possible some of the decisions about this illumination were influenced by the nature of the documentary illumination that they themselves may have provided or at the very least accommodated and anticipated in their more routine labor.[118]

Changing Roles, Changing Styles: A New Proposal

Art historians have never extended much charity to English illumination of the fifteenth century, "the dull stepchild of art historical studies."[119] Jonathan Alexander wrote, "In the later fourteenth and fifteenth centuries it would be hard to argue that English art was of European importance. . . . Later in the fifteenth century, considering what was available in England, it is not surprising that Edward IV bought books from Flanders. . . . A final conclusion would be that, as far as the evidence permits us to see, royal discrimination was not particularly outstanding, but neither for much of the time was native talent."[120] "Coarseness" and "crudeness" are commonly ascribed to late medieval English illumination, and similar epithets have even been applied to the lavishly illuminated prayer books that, as Kathryn A. Smith remarks, long "posed an aesthetic challenge" to art historians whose "scholarly priorities" lay elsewhere.[121] Janet Backhouse coined a delightfully evocative description in its own right when she wrote that "manuscripts identifiably illuminated in England during the final decade of the fifteenth century and the first ten years of the sixteenth await serious study, preferably by someone prepared to enjoy rather than to despise their splendid vulgarity."[122] On the less colorful side, Kathleen Scott, as well as Margaret Rickert before her, observed major changes in habits of manuscript illumination in the fifteenth century.[123] The most significant changes observed are an increasing flatness and schematization and a zeal for pen-drawing as opposed to, or often combined with, illumination of saturated colors. And Paul Crossley has noted that even within exhibition contexts, the display of English manuscripts (along with other media) produced during this period "had become the fragile epiphenomenon of hard social forces," that is, mere evidence of patronal will and historical circumstance.[124]

While the influence of Lollardy and religious reform has been cited as the cause for English illuminators' retreat from naturalism and rejection of the splendorous International Gothic style that had prevailed in the fourteenth century,[125] such an account does not agree with what we know about the prolific and sometimes dazzling devotional image making that continued in the sectors of sculpting, cloth staining, and wall painting throughout the fifteenth century.[126] And, as Kathleen Kennedy has recently shown, Lollard antipathy to images is belied by the profusion of Wycliffite Bibles with decorative illumination.[127] Rather than hypothesize a historical cause for the obvious change in style, I recommend we follow analytical bibliographers in positing that changes in the manner of production precipitated changes in the visual appearance of the book.[128] The growing commercial and paracommercial book trade along with its attendant demands, the increasing versatility of book producers, and the absence of artistic schools led by masters resulted in the less finessed forms that have at once attracted derision and deflected art historical attention.

The questions that remain to be answered are how did the anonymity, versatility, and decentralization of book producers affect the production of manuscripts of Middle English poetry? How were the words of Chaucer, Gower, and Lydgate shaped by the professional conditions of those who complemented them with images? To these questions, I can provide three responses, which will underpin the discussions to follow. First, scholars have remarked on the oddity of the illustrative cycles in the earliest manuscripts of major Middle English poetic texts—the paucity of narrative illustration; the focus on narrators, tale tellers, and authors; the unusual formats and alternative locations of miniatures even in cases when the text remains unchanged. If shifting coalitions of book producers with experience illuminating and copying liturgical books and legal documents were responsible also for the copying and dissemination of Middle English verse, then the unconventionality of these illuminations—in terms of their placement, quantity, and subject matter—could well be attributed to the decisions of those whose experience lay in illuminating a very different sort of material. When it came time for limners to illuminate these new works of English literature, they looked to sources and templates in other corners of artistic and textual culture.

Second, limners, like other members of the book trade and professional sectors that required the copying of documents and records, participated in a variety of capacities in the production of literary culture. If the decisions they made in illuminating poetry seem idiosyncratic, it is because they were not governed by the conventions that develop naturally in highly regulated, insular trades. But, though idiosyncratic, their decisions were by no means uninformed. On the commercial book trade in late medieval Paris, Mary Rouse and Richard Rouse commented,

"Illuminators like the Montbastons, the Mauberge Master, or the *Fauvel* Master manifested neither depth of understanding nor even undue curiosity, with respect to the texts they illustrated. . . . The illuminator's practice included a hasty and no doubt reluctant scanning of the proximate text itself only when unavoidable."[129] While this assessment is itself debatable, as this study will show, such superficiality is by no means on display in the work of London illuminators. Exposure to, immersion in, and perhaps even supervision over the variety of steps required to make a book—from text writing to binding—meant that when limners did produce illuminations, they did so with both a capacious and a fragmentary awareness of the literary culture to which they were contributing. This capacious and fragmentary awareness prompted them not simply to consult the adjacent text for guidance when illuminating it but rather to ask (and sometimes be flummoxed by) such questions as "What exactly is an English author, and how am I supposed to portray him?"; "Who is responsible for this—or even *a*—book?"; "How do I depict a historical episode in the absence of a suitable model?" Their illustrations exhibit an attentiveness not only to the immediate text at hand but also, and more significantly, to the overarching preoccupations of literary culture at the end of the Middle Ages.

Third, the anonymity and the piecemeal production of the books on which they collaborated dispersed the authorial impetus behind the poetry they illuminated. A lack of delineation among those who produced these books meant that at any one time a scribe could be a bookbinder, a limner could be a scribe, and a scrivener could be a dabbler whose doodles show up professional illuminators. In circumstances like these, where no one person could claim definitive responsibility for any one unit of cultural output, it is entirely reasonable that visual recognition of the poet as *auctor* is the exception rather than the rule—a subject I will tackle in the following chapters.

PART II

AUTHORS

CHAPTER 2

Chaucer's Manicule

The author, named or unnamed, *has always been* a way for those who produce texts . . . and those who use, read, censor, or celebrate them to describe the place of those texts in the world. And the text's place in the world has often needed close description.

—ALEXANDRA GILLESPIE, *Print Culture and the Medieval Author*, 15 (emphasis in original)

Conflicting views on the nature of personal identity have confounded the very concept of the portrait as a significant genre of representation because they affect the answer to a basic question presented by art works of this kind: "Who is the who that is being represented?"

—BRILLIANT, *Portraiture*, 13

The Pictorial Invention of the English Author

Who is Geoffrey Chaucer? The body that lies buried in Poets' Corner in Westminster Abbey? The author of *The Canterbury Tales*? The narrator of *The Canterbury Tales*? The pilgrim within *The Canterbury Tales*? The Clerk of the King's Works? The customs official? The character hoisted in the talons of an eagle to the House of Fame? This question prods us to recall the discursive formulation of categories like the author; spurs us to contemplate the quandaries that invoking the author's name stimulates; and challenges us to consider yet again "who is the who that is being represented." But for the manuscript illuminator, or limner, in fifteenth-century London, this question was a matter of professional concern. And limners found the question challenging.

The pictorial program in the celebrated Ellesmere manuscript of *The Canterbury Tales* manifests this anxiety in its indecision about Chaucer's ontological status with respect to the text (Figure 20). In its most renowned image, Chaucer is not presented as an author at all but, like any one of the other twenty-two pilgrims (Figures 21 and 22), is positioned somewhere in the middle of the manuscript. Astride a horse, "Chaucer" appears beside the text column rather than being constrained by a framing device within the text, and he precedes the second tale that his avatar pilgrim relates.[1] This representation makes sense since Chaucer is, of course, a pilgrim on his way to Canterbury.

FIGURE 20. *Chaucer*. Geoffrey Chaucer, *Canterbury Tales*, London, c. 1400–1405. San Marino, Huntington Library MS EL 26 C 9, fol. 153v.

AUTHORS

Yet features of this same image also indicate that the illuminator who portrayed Chaucer was aware of his exceptionality and his status as the creator of the text that contains him. For one, his figure is appreciably larger than the pilgrims portrayed by the manuscript's first illuminator (Figure 21) and appears to have been the only pilgrim depicted by a second illuminator.[2] Even more notably, his is the only figure that points at the text, an engagement with the written word that seems to place

FIGURE 21. *The Friar.* Geoffrey Chaucer, *Canterbury Tales*, London, c. 1400–1405. San Marino, Huntington Library MS EL 26 C 9, fol. 76v.

him outside of its fiction. His location in the world outside of the text is effected also by the penner hanging from a cord around his neck.[3] Additionally, his horse is poised above a patch of grassy earth, whereas the preceding pilgrims are set against the bare folio, without any hint of landscape that might set them apart.

But character and author are not the only available ontological categories. Writing on the conflation of pilgrim and author in Chaucer's poetry, Ann Astell

FIGURE 22. *The Second Nun*. Geoffrey Chaucer, *Canterbury Tales*, London, c. 1400–1405. San Marino, Huntington Library MS EL 26 C 9, fol. 187r.

AUTHORS

submits that "not only does Chaucer fictionalize himself as a writer in . . . Chaucer the pilgrim; he creates in each of the pilgrims a different persona of himself as an artist."[4] The first and second limners formulated Chaucer according to Astell's initial proposal, visualizing him as the poem's meta-author, intrinsic to its expression but extrinsic from its action. A third limner, did not "get it wrong" but instead used the Chaucer image as a baseline, finding in each of the pilgrims an affinity with their author: a response, whether deliberate or not, to Astell's corollary. We see this in the limner's depiction of the five pilgrims that follow Chaucer's figure (Figure 22). All are rendered in comparable dimensions to Chaucer's and likewise are placed atop a verdant mound, with no visible markers of any categorical distinction between Chaucer and his fellow pilgrims.[5] They, too, are authors of a sort. Far from disclosing the author's identity—physiognomic or otherwise—manuscript illuminators of this period only convolute the already tangled thicket of transactions between author and persona inhabiting Middle English verse.

The different actions of the first, second, and third illuminators disclose just how protean the idea of an English author was at the turn of the fifteenth century and how subject his public face was to the inclinations of illuminators working semi-independently. Just as Middle English prologues' "construction of authorship is rhetorical: a way of talking about intention that has not yet begun to locate that intention fully in the person of the author,"[6] so too does the prefatory miniature express a mode of thinking about the author before the conventions of vernacular authorship were established. As a document of illuminators' mediation of a text's origins, the Ellesmere manuscript records their struggles with the invention of the vernacular author and the difficulties in assigning him full responsibility for the text at hand. While some might see in the fifteenth century "a growing interest in portraying literary authors whose status both endorses and is endorsed by the inclusion of their images along with their texts,"[7] the indecision that marks many of these images paints a fragile picture of authorial identity and calls into question the relationship between textual creator and the text itself. Certainly, the differing opinions that the renowned Troilus frontispiece continues to provoke—a body of scholarship to which I will not contribute here—attest that similar problems extend beyond *The Canterbury Tales*.[8] For the audience of the Ellesmere *Canterbury Tales*, its ensemble of narrators enunciates the evasiveness of the poem's author and interferes with the reader's ability to ascribe a centralizing point of hermeneutic coherence to one, specific person.

In this and in the following two chapters, I consider how illuminators responded to the challenges presented by the emerging concept of a contemporary author of English poetry at a time "when there [was] no sign in England of the specialized, professional, vernacular writer."[9] These challenges also formed a central preoccupation of the texts that illuminators illustrated; yet limners' responses to these challenges do not replicate in picture the anxieties that are voiced in the texts they illustrate. Rather, manuscript producers, informed by the dynamics of their profession, parallel in a uniquely visual mode the anxieties then in literary circulation. We can read this anxiety in illuminators' common suppression of the author's identity *as* a writing *auctor*. Throughout the fifteenth century and across Western Europe, the most common subject for prefatory illustration in religious and secular literature alike was a depiction of the author.[10] Yet, when limners of Middle English works portrayed Chaucer, Gower, and Lydgate, their status as authors responsible for the work at hand are almost never made explicit; of the dozens of images that purport to represent them, there is only one that depicts the figure in the act of writing—that is, in the pose affiliated conventionally with the *auctor*.[11] Just one. And this one exception is far from conventional. This fact alone differentiates the visual record of literary canonization in England from its counterpart in France, where, as Deborah McGrady, David Hult, Sylvia Huot, and others have shown, images of the author in the act of writing were essential to the elevation of the vernacular, providing, in Jeanne Krochalis's words, "a logical, visual reinforcement of . . . *auctoritas*."[12] Yet limners refused all but once to render English poets in this pose. This refusal should not be taken casually. In a culture that pressed accessories and attributes into declarative service, and within which physiognomic likeness was often subordinated to type in articulating identity, the refusal to depict English authors with a pen in hand discloses unease with the protean category of the vernacular author.[13]

In many ways, limners obscured English authors' participation in the creation of the book that the reader has in his or her hands. What makes this aspect of the manuscript history of the Middle English literary canon so noteworthy is not only the long-standing tradition of the writing-author portrait (as I addressed in the Introduction) but also the long-standing expectation that educated audiences would evaluate the nature of a work by the nature of the individual responsible for it. In Conrad of Hirsau's twelfth-century *Dialogues*, the pupil fires a series of questions at his tutor centered on the introductory material to a work, demanding, "I also want to find out about the introductory page: what is the difference between a title, a preface, a proem, and a prologue; between a poet, a writer of history, and a writer of discourses?"[14] Uniting in one line of questioning the paratextual apparatus of the book with the agent responsible for the work, the pupil demonstrates a medieval audience's awareness of the scribe and artist's mediation of the authorial voice. "What is interesting about frontispiece illustration in the later fourteenth and fifteenth centuries," write Pearsall and Salter, "is the sophistication with which it begins to work variations on these fairly simple models and the responsiveness shown to the nature of the text and its relation to its audience."[15] More recently, this proliferation of authorial guises has been examined in depth by Ursula Peters, with respect to manuscripts of German and French literature.[16] When it came to the depiction of contemporary English authors, a different set of conditions predicated the illuminator's practice: not "what is the text's relation to its audience?" or even "what is the nature of the text?" but rather "what is the text's relation to the narrator who purports to be responsible for it?" As such, these images provide a rich field in which to explore how the medieval limner, charged with painting prefaces to written prologues, anticipated by several hundred years Foucault's query on the discursive nature of the author.[17]

While, in the Introduction, I addressed how illuminators issued statements about literary production through the formulation of intellectual activity as a physical enterprise—that is, through the corporeal labor of reference and synthesis—this and the following two chapters will concentrate on how illuminators struggled to delineate the identities of the specific authors whose texts they illuminated. To those who authored images, who is the author of a text? How, specifically, does the representation of an author rest on a "semantically significant picture scheme"[18] that disseminates his or her identity across a spectrum of creative agents present in late medieval culture? And how is an authorial identity negotiated via pictorial allusions that substituted for the rejected convention of the writing *auctor*? In responding to these questions, I show that the limners of the earliest major works in Middle English verse produced authors through a concatenation of voices and pictures, a repertoire deriving from pictorial media extending far beyond the parameters of their own texts.

Such an approach is informed by portraiture studies and has two aims: the first is to get out from under the restrictions that word-and-image frameworks can impose on the study of literary illumination;[19] the second is to historicize the vernacular author portrait as a category that did not precede but rather emerged from limners' experiments in representation. Framing images of English authors in a manner similar to how scholars have come to deal with portraiture admits factors exogenous and endogenous to the text and to the historical author into our analyses, if not always smoothly, then certainly productively. Considering an obsolete critical approach to portraiture, Joseph Koerner writes, "Time was when portraiture's power to represent autonomous individuals could be derived, analytically, from the autonomy of the art object, and when both these autonomies were celebrated as representative achievements of the modern age. Such analyses ran roughly thus. Framed off from any context, and internally composed to be beautiful because whole, the independent panel painting already stands opposite its individual viewers as the objective correlative of their individuality."[20] The periodized and materially deterministic view that Koerner describes has been abandoned, and established in its place is a more historically inclusive view of portraiture as the locus of negotiation—a conference among artist, subject, audience, and culturally encoded norms of representation. Scholars have become suspicious of treating the portrait as a reification of the archive, a suspicion that should be extended to treating authorial representation as a hypostatization of the mind behind the text or even the text itself.[21] Late medieval images of English poets have yet to be analyzed with these considerations in mind—considerations that grant much greater agency to their producers.

This and the following two chapters focus on the images that attest to illuminators' confrontations with questions of authorial identity and textual origins. When tasked with pinning a face to a text, illuminators had no choice but to consult their own notions about a text's ontology and the author's ontological status with respect to it. This quandary was particularly pressing when it came to illuminating the metafictional and, following A. C. Spearing's coinage, the autographic works that populated England's literary scene in the later Middle Ages.[22] The arguments that illuminators frequently offered arose not only from the texts in front of them but also from the cache of images that made up the intellectual storehouse of their profession. From these images, I argue that the tradition of authorial portraiture for Middle English poets is an indeterminate one that discloses, more than anything else, the hesitations and reluctance of its makers. The consequence of this argument, to be explored in later chapters, is that whatever authority is allowed the rhetorical "I" of the text is a contingent authority, drawn not from the virtuosity of language, truth of content, or prestige of its author but rather from copy-specific features of the manuscript itself. Without a sense of the "true" origins of a text, literature was, in this period, a flexible cultural production open to opportunistic manipulation and instrumentalization that illustrative programs could—and did—provide.

The Problem of Chaucerian Representation

Sitting astride his own horse and riding into the middle of the Ellesmere manuscript, Chaucer was at the vanguard of an illustrative tradition of indecision (Figure 23). No autograph copy of Chaucer's works survives, and debate continues as to whether he actually had a hand in overseeing the production of *Canterbury Tales* manuscripts.[23] But if Chaucer ever did formulate a plan for an illustrative program to *The Canterbury Tales*, it could not have been one that would accommodate a conventional author portrait, certainly not one based on scriptural models. As any medieval author would have known, *W* (the first letter to the poem) is uniquely

FIGURE 23. *Chaucer*. Geoffrey Chaucer, *Canterbury Tales*, London, c. 1400–1405.
San Marino, Huntington Library MS EL 26 C 9, fol. 153v (detail).

unsuited to framing an image and, lacking a place in the Latin alphabet, had no tradition of historiation in scriptural manuscripts. Later illuminators had to exercise some calligraphic contortions to place a figure in this initial letter, sliding one *V* or *U* over the other, a *W* in only the most generous estimations but workable for historiation. The difficulties posed by the *W* were, of course, only one among numerous complicating factors that illuminators confronted.

Not only was the opening *W* a problematic place for a figure; Chaucer's body itself, a body that no longer existed at the time of these manuscripts' production, presented a further obstacle. The diversity alone of the images—some found before the "General Prologue" and some before one of the two tales ascribed to the Chaucer pilgrim within the *Tales*—testifies both to uncertainties about authorial embodiment and the intellection of illuminators who refused to bow to a convention they did not find appropriate—that is, the image of a man writing. Seven manuscripts of *The Canterbury Tales* contain figural illumination, all of which include depictions of pilgrims or narrators. Among these, five contain images of a potential

Chaucer figure (whether in the initial preceding the "General Prologue" or preceding "The Tale of Melibee," which the Chaucer-pilgrim relates), while the remaining two lack leaves where his image probably appeared originally.[24] A number of these are in related manuscripts (i.e., manuscripts that were either copied from one another or are otherwise affiliated via a common exemplar), and yet the illustrative program is unique to each, whether in terms of composition or iconography or both. Phillipa Hardman has elaborated expertly a point that others have long suggested: specifically, that the distinctions among images that represent "Chaucer" (the quotes are Hardman's) attest to the number of ways in which the Chaucer-narrator or Chaucer-author or Chaucer-pilgrim was constructed by the text.[25]

While we can read variously this multiplicity of Chaucers, I want to coax the conversation in a different direction by focusing on the ways in which the images that introduce *The Canterbury Tales* or Chaucer's "Tale of Melibee" register hesitation on the part of their illuminators. Although attempts to explain these images—to rationalize them—acknowledge tacitly their unconventionality, this unconventionality itself has never featured as an analytic crux. I would like, then, to take this unconventionality in earnest. It is not only notable that Chaucer is multiplied; it is also significant that each version calls itself into question.

This hesitation is observable in the earliest representation of Chaucer, after Ellesmere, which asks a question that it leaves unanswered. Here, in Lansdowne 851, a figure appears in the opening *W* to the poem, standing in an indefinite interior space and extending an open book outward to the right (Figure 24). From the orientation of his head and position of his eyes, it is obvious the man is not reading; nor do his closed lips indicate that he is speaking or prelecting; the gesture of his outstretched arms is one of presentation or demonstration but to whom?[26] It is a strange image. Yet we fundamentally misunderstand it if we attempt to rationalize its "meaning." Rather, what is meaningful about this historiated initial is that it effects a canny deviation from iconographies to which it gestures but does not fully commit. It seems that the illuminator, in thinking through a suitable posture for the figure who introduces the poem, disregarded the need for this figure to match the narrator or to represent someone else entirely. While the opening initial features a presentation, it lacks a credible recipient. So troubled was the Chaucer Society by this ambiguity that their 1868 print edition of this manuscript reproduced on its title page a different image of Chaucer from a copy of another poet's work (discussed later). The point is that the individual or individuals responsible for the frontispiece of this modern edition doubted the suitability of Lansdowne's opening initial.[27]

The same indeterminacy could equally describe the figure's counterpart in Oxford, Bodleian Library MS Bodley 686, a mid-century luxury manuscript that

FIGURE 24. *Chaucer*. Geoffrey Chaucer, *Canterbury Tales*, London, c. 1410–1425.
British Library Lansdowne MS 851, fol. 2r (detail). © British Library Board.

joins *The Canterbury Tales* to a number of works by John Lydgate (Figure 25). The manuscript's scribe executed especially liberal revisions to the text, which include ascribing "The Manciple's Tale" to the historical (i.e., actual, possibly even then living) poet John Lydgate.[28] As with London, British Library MS Lansdowne 851, the limner of Bodley 686 was not governed by any deference to Chaucer's authorship. On its opening folio, a young man points toward the opening verse with one hand and with the other holds a red cap, a gesture of respect, yet again one without any identifiable recipient. Wound round the elegant border on the page is a banderole with the (perhaps patron's) motto, "pences / de mai / pences / de m / Jhc / merci / ladi / help / in god is / al mi truste / in god / as fortune / fauIit / As fort / fauIit" (Figure 26).[29] So while the man inside of the initial indicates the opening verse of the poem, there is nothing to stop us from considering his ownership of

FIGURE 25. *Chaucer*. Geoffrey Chaucer, *Canterbury Tales*, London, c. 1425–1450. Oxford, Bodleian Library MS Bodley 686, fol. 1r (detail). By kind permission of the Bodleian Libraries.

those genteel expressions, particularly since they verbalize the courtesy shown by the action of doffing one's cap.[30] Moreover, because the motto—the letters of which are painted in gold ink rather than written in black—forms part of the illuminated border to the page, it is entirely possible that the illuminator had these in his mind while going about his business of creating the historiated initial. As visual exegetes, we could contort our interpretive capacities endlessly to locate a textual source, appoint symbolism, and pinpoint iconographic analogs for the minutiae of these historiated initials; but ultimately these exercises would miss the point by assuming that the limners responsible for them were themselves iconographers arranging rigid symbols into a coherent statement.[31] Instead, with their odd, noncommittal imagery of a standing man offering a book to or removing his cap for the benefit of no one depicted, the historiated initials fail to issue grand statements about Chaucer—whether as poet, narrator, or pilgrim. And for all this, they are— far more interesting than that—documents of quizzed thought.

The indeterminacy that characterizes these two images is even more explicit in the only other manuscript of *The Canterbury Tales* that depicts a figure in the opening initial.[32] In this, physical traces have left behind evidence of indecision (Plate 5). Within the frame of a distorted *W*, a blond youth with rosy cheeks sits on a turf bench, its verdant green also creating the back to this imaginary chair. The youth

AUTHORS

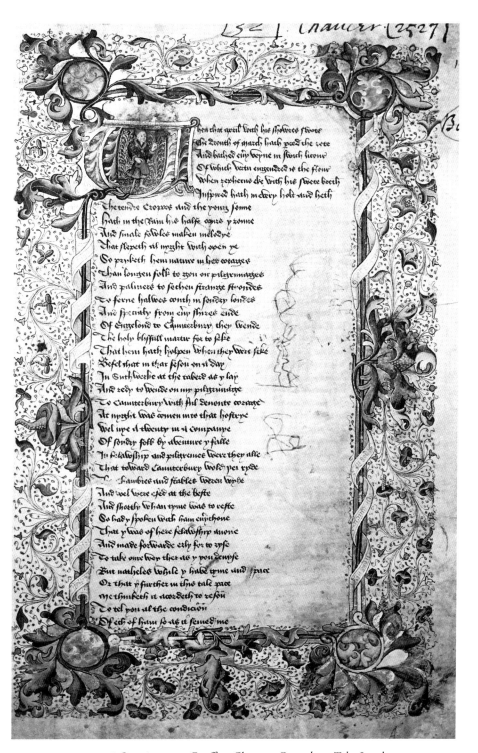

FIGURE 26. Opening page. Geoffrey Chaucer, *Canterbury Tales*, London,
c. 1425–1450. Oxford, Bodleian Library MS Bodley 686, fol. 1r.
By kind permission of the Bodleian Libraries.

crooks his right elbow and supports a cheek on his hand, but his elbow floats freely in the air, unanchored by an armrest or other surface where an elbow might rest. With his left hand, he points downward and to the right, in the same direction as his gaze, but neither his index finger nor his gaze indicates anything in particular. Above, golden rays of sunlight stream down from the right corner, and blue droplets of rain dribble down from the left. In the limited commentary this historiated initial has attracted, scholars have puzzled over its oddities. One has suggested that the image represents Chaucer as he depicts himself in the short poem "Complaint to His Purse."[33] Similarly, casting about for a possible explanation, Derek Pearsall posited the Chaucer figure from *The Legend of Good Women* as its source.[34] These arguments are illustrative of the distances one would need to travel to apply a textually driven logic to a scenario that refutes its application, founded on modernist assumptions of the author's emergence from a coherent corpus. More recently, Maidie Hilmo argued that the scene ennobles the author and captures him in drowsy deflation before divine inspiration strikes.[35] While this and the other meanings assigned to the minutiae in the initial may certainly have occurred to the manuscript's audience, what these attempts to fix a plan to the illumination overlook is the actual process of revision that occurred while the plan was under way.[36]

One can trace this revision in the patterns of overlaid paint, the responsive direction of the brushwork around the central figure, and passages of scraping, all of which enable us to reconstruct the sequence of the limner's activities and pinpoint the moment in that sequence when the plan for the initial's historiation changed. First, the central figure was painted, and it appears that it was designed to appear as it does, with head resting in hand. Whether the left hand was initially meant to be pointing is unclear, but there is no apparent reason to doubt that it was. Next the red backdrop was applied: two small passages to the extreme left and right show green pigment over the red, indicating that the green portion was added after the red backdrop was created. Additionally, roughness in the parchment around the figure's shoulders is evidence of scraping that preceded the application of green pigment. What appears now to be the top of an improbable hillock-chair was almost certainly in conception a continuation of the red backdrop down to the space just below the figure's waist. At that point, a line would have indicated a back wall meeting the floor of an interior space in tipped perspective—the most common method for portraying interiors in illuminations of this time. The limner then filled in the entire space below the (new) register line with green, subsequently overlaying it with the rays of the sun from above. After, he added a perfunctory outline within the green space to sculpt part of it into a bench, which he then dappled with sprigs and flowers. Finally, even after flourishing the backdrop with gold filigree, and perhaps realizing the aptitude of rain to accompany the opening line,

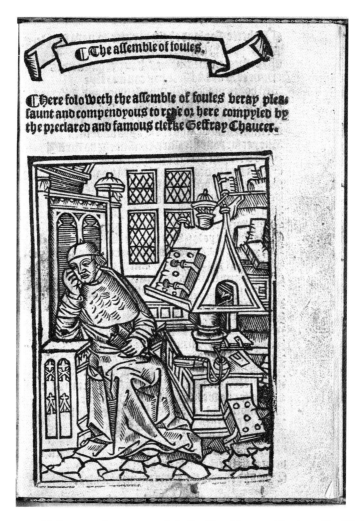

FIGURE 27. *Title page with a man at a desk.* Geoffrey Chaucer, *The Assemble of Foules*, London, 1530. San Marino, Huntington Library RB 31325.

the limner scraped a small patch in the upper left corner and added a blue cloud along with droplets of rain—one of which was placed near the figure's pointing hand. Originally, the figure would probably have been seated on a chair indoors, and it does not seem egregious to suggest that he might have been turning away from a desk, as in the woodcut later used by Wynkyn de Worde to represent Chaucer before *The Assemble of Fouls* (Figure 27). Whatever the original plan, the setting of a seemingly lovelorn youth or melancholic poet in a bucolic environment was not it.

Until this point, I have only addressed images that shy away entirely from the iconography of the writing *auctor*; there is one manuscript, however, that does allude to this convention. Yet even here, in Oxford, Bodleian Library MS Rawlinson

Poet. 223, the conditions in which this convention is acknowledged are unusual. The manuscript is a mid-century luxury production, probably copied by the scribe who was responsible for New Haven, Beinecke Library Takamiya MS 24, or a scribe who trained with him.[37] Among its many elegant decorative letters and borders are two figural illuminations—historiated initials before Chaucer's "Tale of Melibee" and "The Friar's Tale." Within the initial before "Melibee" is an interior scene of a man seated before a lectern, and in accordance with the fine atmosphere of the room, the man wears an elaborate hat of black lined with green, as well as an elegant blue robe held together by a gold chain (Plate 6). Before him, on the lectern, rests an open book with mock letters toward which he directs his gaze. However, his body faces the viewer, and he points with his right hand, either directing our eyes toward the book within the painted image or toward the text of the book we have in our hands. Yet this miniature does not single out the Chaucer-pilgrim who recounts the sententious prose tale of Melibee, because another historiated initial features yet another pilgrim. The initial enframes a depiction of the Friar, standing within a wooden pulpit and against a burnished gold background (Plate 7). His left hand, open and with the palm facing the viewer, is raised in a gesture that might accompany a sermon, although his lips are pressed together here. This volume presents the only instance in the corpus of illuminated *Canterbury Tales* manuscripts in which the tale-tellers are not portrayed as pilgrims or on horseback.[38] Given that the Friar is shown at a pulpit, it seems safe to suggest that the limner was attempting to encapsulate his vocation: a friar is one who preaches (although, interestingly, the limner might have shown him begging or hearing confession or any of the other activities he is said to perform in the "General Prologue"). If that is the case, then it would seem that the vocation of the figure seated before a lectern is that of a reader. The manuscript does not surrender any clues as to why these two figures were the only ones who deserved representation, and the absence of the first folio leaves us ignorant about the appearance of the opening initial to the poem. There is even the question of whether the figure before "Melibee" is even Chaucer or whether it depicts the eponymous protagonist.[39] Just as the line adjacent to the Friar, however coincidentally, labels him ("This worthi limitour this noble frer"),[40] so too does the opening line to "The Tale of Melibee" identify a protagonist of the tale ("a yong man callid Melibe").[41] What is important is that the manuscript does not single out Chaucer nor did the limner endow his figure with an unequivocal claim to literary greatness using the visual terms in which that sentiment is expressed. The Chaucer of Bodleian Library MS Rawlinson Poet. 223 is just one among five disparate attempts to cast the single figure we identify now as "Author," and to do so in a way that circumvents outright comparison to venerable paragons, hard at work at their desks.

At this juncture, it is worth pausing to reflect on author portraits and to estrange them somewhat in order to understand what is so challenging about them as a genre. An author portrait is a special category of portrait because it both produces a corpus and arises from one. Encountered between the covers of a book, it is enframed by the words from which its subject ostensibly arises. And the image seems to tell us that it literally embodies the words that purport to emerge from the exogenous body it represents. The author portrait is, in this respect, a compound icon, the label for which is book length. And because it strives to close a gap between the referent that is both "out there" and "in here," it can beguile the viewer into a forgetfulness of the artist responsible for mediating it. This is historically how author portraits have been analyzed, that is, as attempts made in good faith to capture authors as they represent themselves in their texts. What Chaucer did was confound the equivalence between the words that are his corpus and the actual corpus from which they emerged—this at a time when literary production was still literally in the hands of a host of participants from the poet, to the scribe, to the illuminator, and so on. It is no wonder that illuminators experimented when it came time to represent him. The problem of Chaucerian representation was the instability of its referent and the absence of a suitable precedent for expressing it. This problem was not felt by illuminators alone. In what follows, I explore how this problem was anticipated by one of Chaucer's most devoted followers, who took active measures to forestall it.

Chaucer's Chantry and Hoccleve's Commission

If the Ellesmere representation of Chaucer riding toward the text of "The Tale of Melibee" holds a certain authority—a claim to represent the English author as a wise, venerable figure, guaranteed by its verisimilitude—it is not by dint of features peculiar to the image itself. Rather, it earned its pedigree elsewhere: that is, from a manuscript of Thomas Hoccleve's *Regiment of Princes*, which contains an image of Chaucer with facial features similar to those of his counterpart in the Ellesmere manuscript.[42] It is in this image that we encounter the earliest attempt to anchor Chaucer's authorial identity to a fixed position outside of the fictions of his own narratives. Approximately five to ten years after the Ellesmere manuscript is believed to have been produced, Thomas Hoccleve (d. 1426) composed and commissioned illuminated copies of a poem that gave early momentum to the century-long process of cementing Chaucer's reception as the father of English poetry and the vaunting of the Ellesmere representation of him as the image apposite to that honorific.[43] Like Chaucer, Hoccleve was a government functionary, employed as a clerk by the Privy Seal.[44] He was also responsible for copying at least two leaves of another English poet's work (Gower's *Confessio Amantis*) and is an important figure in the promotion of Middle English verse.[45] In 1410–11 Hoccleve composed *The Regiment of Princes*, a book of royal instruction for Prince Henry of Wales (later Henry V), with the frankly stated aim of raising the prince's awareness of his plight as a government scribe long overdue for his annuity.[46] The book is a disarming hybrid, with a prologue that occupies nearly half its length devoted to a dialogue between Hoccleve and the Old Man he encounters after an insomniac night provoked by money woes. The outcome of this dialogue is the Old Man's advice that Hoccleve write a book to please the king and cultivate his sympathies for the author's financial predicament. The resulting *Regiment of Princes* combines this fictionalized account of the poem's genesis with the poem itself.[47]

Hoccleve's self-promotion as an author has shaped our critical reception of this work, one filled with alluringly autobiographical accounts of personal and professional travails.[48] He complains of the backbreaking labor of writing, bemoans the delayed payments of his salary, and laments the mental collapse he suffered and the attendant anxieties upon his recovery. Although it has become *de rigueur* to acknowledge the disjunctions between the recording and narrating selves within and without his works, the minutiae of a lived life and the mental stresses it carries lends Hoccleve's poetry the reality effect that has tended to authenticate even the "unlived" details he relates.[49] Hoccleve has become, in this respect, the first true witness to Chaucer's apotheosis.

When Hoccleve memorializes Chaucer as the "first fyndere [founder] of our faire langage" and furnishes (in early manuscript copies of the *Regiment*) an adjoining image of the man himself, he encourages his audience to accept this multimedia tribute not as homage but as testimony, authenticated by the autobiographical character of the first half of the poem:

> Allas, my fadir fro the world is go,
> My worthy maistir Chaucer—him I meene;
> Be thow advocat for him, hevenes queene.
>
> As thow wel knowist, o blessid Virgyne,
> With lovyng herte and hy devocioun,
> In thyn honour he wroot ful many a lyne.
> O now thyn help and thy promocioun!
> To God thy sone make a mocioun,
> How he thy servant was, mayden Marie,
> And lat his love floure and fructifie.

Althogh his lyf be qweynt, the resemblance
Of him hath in me so fressh lyflynesse
That to putte othir men in remembrance
Of his persone, I have heere his liknesse
Do make, to this ende, in soothfastnesse,
That they that han of him lost thoght and mynde
By this peynture may ageyn him fynde.

The ymages that in the chirches been
Maken folk thynke on God and on his seintes
Whan the ymages they beholde and seen,
Where ofte unsighte of hem causith restreyntes
Of thoghtes goode. Whan a thyng depeynt is
Or entaillid, if men take of it heede,
Thoght of the liknesse it wole in hem breede.

Yit sum men holde oppinioun and seye
That noon ymages sholde ymakid be.
They erren foule and goon out of the weye;
Of trouthe have they scant sensibilitee.
Passe over that! Now, blessid Trinitee,
Upon my maistres soule mercy have;
For him, Lady, thy mercy eek I crave.[50]

Two manuscripts of *The Regiment* include representations of Chaucer alongside
Hoccleve's third and final homage to "his maister."[51] This final tribute follows a
passage in which Hoccleve advises the prince to seek out good counsel, just as,
Hoccleve claims, Chaucer had advised before him.

Adjacent to these stanzas, in the outer margin of London, British Library Harley MS 4866, is a framed miniature of Chaucer shown from roughly the hips up,
against a deep green background (Figure 28). Dressed in the same black gown and
hood he wears in the Ellesmere manuscript, he likewise suspends a penner from his
neck. And while he grasps the reins of his horse in Ellesmere, in this manuscript he
holds a rosary in his left hand (Figure 29).[52] Here, Chaucer's figure responds to the
words that eulogize him, and he trespasses the bounded space of representation as
his right hand breaks the frame to indicate the word "soothfastnesse." Since the
Ellesmere manuscript is the only (extant) copy of *The Canterbury Tales* with figural
illumination that pre-dates the composition of Hoccleve's *Regiment*, it seems reasonable to infer that the artist Hoccleve contracted to create this portrait did so

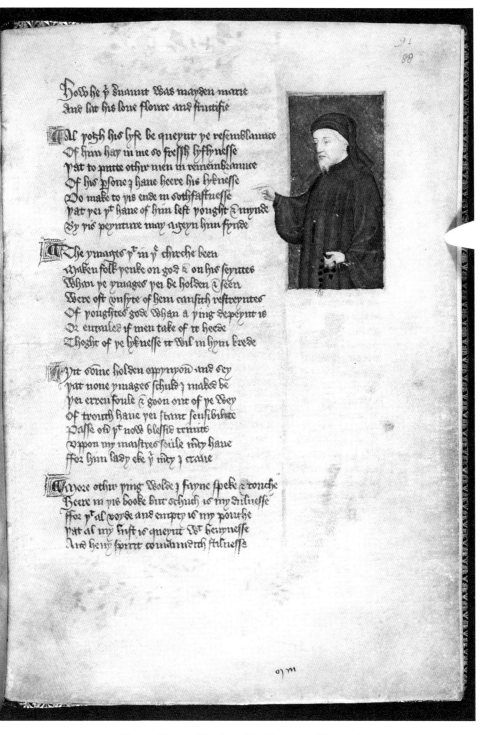

Þothe he þ kunnut was mayden marie
And lat his loue floure and fructifie

Al þogh his lyfe be queynt þe resemblaunce
Of him hath in me so fresh lyflynesse
Þat to putte othir men in remembraunce
Of his psone I haue heere his lyknesse
Do make to þis ende in soothfastnesse
Þat þei þt haue of him lest þought & mynde
By þis peynture may ageyn him fynde

The ymages þt in þe chirche been
Maken folk þenke on god & on his seyntes
Whan þe ymages þei be holden & seen
Were oft vnsyte of hem cansith restreyntes
Of þoughtes goode whan a þing depeynt is
Or entailed if men take of it heede
Thoght of þe lyknesse it wil in hym brede

Yit somme holden oppynyon and sey
Þat none ymages schuld I maked be
Þei erren foule & goon out of þe wey
Of trouth haue þei skant sensibilite
Passe ouer þat now blessid trinite
Vpon my maistres soule mercy haue
Ffor him lady eke þt mercy I craue

More othir þing wolde I fayne speke & touche
Heere in þis booke but soch is my dulnesse
Ffor þt al voyde and empty is my pouche
Þat al my lust is queynt wt heuynesse
And heuy spirit comaundith stilnesse

FIGURE 28. *Chaucer.* Thomas Hoccleve, *The Regiment of Princes,* London or
Westminster, after c. 1411. London, British Library Harley MS 4866, fol. 88r.
© British Library Board.

using either the Ellesmere manuscript itself, a related copy, or a sketch of either as his model. Such affiliations are not so far-fetched: Hoccleve had partnered with the scribe of the Ellesmere manuscript to copy out the text of another Middle English poem.[53]

This image and Hoccleve's verses together offer a critic's bounty, with their invocation of Marian literature, visual and textual eulogy of an English poet, polemic against contemporary religious heresies, and meditation on the value and function of visual representation. In one strain of criticism, the image of Chaucer constitutes a landmark in English art, the mimetic claim of which is authenticated by religious orthodoxy.[54] In a second, related body of scholarship on this passage, the image and text figure in Hoccleve's enterprise both to establish and then insert himself into a literary lineage, fathered by Chaucer.[55] Ever "nobody's man," Hoccleve not only attempts to find a patron in the prince, but he also insinuates his inheritance of the literary legacy that his mentor bequeathed the nation.[56] For Nicholas Perkins, this portrait provides an image of a vernacular author as authoritative adviser, a characterization he supports by comparison to contemporary images of advisory figures.[57] Similarly, Alan Gaylord confers authority on Chaucer's figure here by comparison to images of aged, wise men in other manuscripts.[58] To Andrew Galloway, Chaucer and the accompanying passage present a "state of pensive reflection."[59] Derek Pearsall perhaps goes the furthest in commenting that "it is, expressly, a picture of a wise and pious counselor, one hand raised in grave admonition, the other fingering a rosary. It would have been impossible for Hoccleve to have found an iconographically more powerful way of establishing a 'cult of personality' in which Chaucer, in his very person, embodied the idea of a national literary tradition."[60] Yet there is no necessary equivalence between age and wisdom in late medieval art.[61] I would argue that these comparisons overlook the source of Chaucer's eminence, which is not in how he looks but rather in the conditions of his display.

Hoccleve and his fellow illuminator succeeded where manuscripts of *The Canterbury Tales* failed to provide the poet with a singular body. Part of Hoccleve's goal in this passage is to draft his own membership in the literary lineage that Chaucer founded, but first he has to convince us that Chaucer's *auctoritas* was already in place by this point. To the contrary, Hoccleve's own passage was instrumental in establishing not just Chaucer's greatness, but far more important, his existence, and I mean this literally. Anticipating Caxton's printed epitaph of Chaucer by almost seventy years, Hoccleve's manuscriptual monument was a critical document to Chaucer's historicity and facticity—prerequisites to the condition of an *auctor*.[62] What is important about this monument was the implied necessity of its truth claims. Within a manuscript culture where the author's name could go missing and his face could take on a dozen different hues, Hoccleve and the illuminator he hired rendered proof against the indeterminacies that, as I discussed earlier, beset Chaucer's pictorial reputation regardless.

One way to construe the Chaucer portrait, one that accounts for the socioreligious institutions into which Hoccleve inscribed it, is as a surrogate for a chantry foundation, instituted retroactively to honor the legacy of a great founder. In her analysis of the Chaucer portrait, Jeanne Krochalis argues that Hoccleve's "way of sanctifying poetry—of fixing a halo firmly on Chaucer's head—was to bring a poet into a world hitherto reserved for the holy, the powerful, and the rich: the physical building of the Church."[63] At this, Charles Blyth strikes a note of disappointment in his perception of Hoccleve's inelegance, remarking, "How absurd to think the portrait of a secular poet would have anything to do with icons in churches and their opposition by Lollards. Yet given the importance of the attack on Lollardy in Hoccleve's England and its place in the poem's ideology, the transition must be entirely purposeful."[64] Blyth's dissatisfaction with the comparison to icons would be warranted. But this is not the comparison that Hoccleve is making.

Rather, Hoccleve is comparing the image of his "father" Chaucer to the effigies, often of one's ancestors, that are commissioned in the course of founding a chantry. As defined by Clive Burgess, "The chantry was an arrangement providing for the

daily celebration of masses, either in perpetuity, in which case a property endowment invariably provided the necessary income, or for a number of years, in which
case the service was usually 'found' by a legatee of the individual who was to benefit
from the celebration."[65] The recitation of prayers for the dead had been, of course,
a long-standing practice in medieval Europe. But over the course of the fourteenth
century, the systematic provision for such prayers to be said in perpetuity and the
patronage of chapels and images to facilitate and guarantee their endurance
emerged as a pervasive and characteristically English institution, which "became
increasingly popular in the reign of the Lancastrian kings from 1399," when Henry IV
commissioned a chantry chapel for his father, John of Gaunt.[66] Antje Fehrmann
goes on to argue that "the turning point of royal chantry provision came with the
accession of Henry V to the throne," who fortified his royal claims through mortu-
ary art profuse with imagery and symbolism of dynastic pretensions.[67] Such retrospective actions were not, however, limited to royalty. Recent research on chantry
foundation has shown that "in many cases the task of commissioning a monument
fell to those left behind—widows, widowers, offspring, or designated executors"
and that evidence from tomb contracts "fails to confirm the commonly held assumptions that monuments were ordered soon after death and put in place swiftly."[68]
It is not simply the images of God and the saints that launch the viewer's thoughts
to devout contemplation; it is also the image of the deceased, which reminds the
viewer years after his passing to think of the heavenly host and spare a prayer on the
deceased's behalf. Hoccleve's words here are echoed by the author of *Speculum sac-*
erdotale (circa 1425), who explains that a sepulcher "is also callyd monumentum,
scilicet, movynge the mynde, for be the syȝt [sight] of it shuld the myndes of the
beholders of it be sterid [stirred] for to praye for the dede i-beryed."[69] Similarly,
Hoccleve's declaration that images cause the viewer to think on "God and on his
seintes" allows for the possibility that the images that provoke such thoughts are
the images of the deceased.

Hoccleve's tribute stages itself as an act of foundation in a number of ways. Its
inauguration in a request for the Virgin's intercession sets the stage for this foundation. After Hoccleve laments the passing of his "father," he implores the Virgin,
"hevenes quene," to advocate on Chaucer's behalf, reminding her of an intercessory
debt owed to the poet who wrote verses in her honor. Hoccleve's aims here are, to
be sure, to fortify his own claims to a literary succession of greatness aligned with
ecclesiastical orthodoxy. At the same time, the specifically Marian backbone to this
statement of orthodoxy places it within an elaborate culture of exchange, in which
word and image were not simply commemorative; they were generative, bought
and paid for to stimulate further actions and words that would have a calculative
impact on their beneficiary. The chief purpose of the chantry chapel was to facili-

tate the activities that would redeem its beneficiary's soul, and one of the principal targets of these activities was the Virgin. Only four years after the composition of *The Regiment*, its dedicatee—by then, Henry V—had commissioned his own chantry chapel devoted to the Virgin, a high-profile and high-cost advertisement of the crown's alignment with orthodoxy. This kind of investment in the ecclesiastical economy was anathema to Wycliffe, who polemicized against chantry foundations.[70] Hoccleve's substitute act of foundation may, like Henry V's chantry, have issued an implicit rebuke to Wycliffite heresy, a rebuke made explicit in the stanzas that endorse the production of images.

In addition to his Marian invocations, Hoccleve frames the production of Chaucer's image as the result of patronage, an element of this passage that has not received attention. The verses do not simply direct our attention to an adjacent visual representation; instead, they document Hoccleve's commission, recording, "I have heere his liknesse / Do make, to this ende, in soothfastnesse."[71] Hoccleve's syntax has been described as distinctively writerly, often leading to confusion about his precise meaning.[72] So it is understandable that the final words of these verses, "in soothfastnesse," have been thought to describe both the truthfulness of Chaucer's likeness as well as the "true intention" of its commissioner.[73] The surrounding verses certainly support this reading. But I think there is an equally compelling case to be made for the word's application to Hoccleve's own actions (not just his intentions)—swearing, in truthfulness, that he has caused this image to be made. The point is that Hoccleve is as emphatic about commemorating his own commission as he is about commemorating Chaucer's legacy. What is more, for the readers of the thirty-nine copies of the poem that never had the accompanying image, the passage only memorializes Hoccleve's act, attesting truly that he did, in some *other* book, cause Chaucer's image to be made.[74]

The codicological chantry produced by Hoccleve and the illuminator he commissioned was innovative in its specific application, but it does allude to a tradition of commemorative codices. In Germany, monasteries and churches honored founders in illuminated *Traditionsbücher*, which compiled their images alongside the charters that recorded their foundations.[75] The most renowned example of such a book in England—the St. Albans Abbey Benefactors' Book (circa 1380, with additions throughout the fifteenth century)—is similarly a visual and textual record of those who had donated to the abbey.[76] In the margin, alongside each record of donation is a framed miniature depicting either a full- or bust-length image of the donor concerned, including even an image of the artist who donated the price of the pigments for the images he himself painted in this very book (Plate 8). Each individual points to the object he or she gifted to the abbey or holds up the charter that signifies a grant of land. In the case of the *Regiment* manuscript, Chaucer, the "first fyndere [founder] of our faire langage" points at the English verses by Hoc-cleve that were made possible by the "bookes of his ornat endytyng / that is to al this land enlumynyng."[77] There is arguably no more appropriate commemorative space for Chaucer than in a book of English verse, the output of his endowment in the nation's vernacular.

My reading of this sequence as a codicological chantry localizes the conditions in which the Chaucer portrait should be seen, conditions more specific than the free-floating terms "memorial" or "commemorative image" suggest. For one, these conditions reimburse Chaucer for his good works as a founder of English letters, a not uncommon equation in chantry endowment. Though a church's founder or benefactor may have contributed to its construction or maintenance, she or he may not have provided instructions for the welfare of his or her soul in the explicit terms that a chantry chapel requires. It was left to executors or descendants to carry this out, the role that Hoccleve assumes for himself here. In addition, chantry foundation was itself a good work, for which one could expect spiritual compensa-tion. This sense of fair exchange was never far from Hoccleve's poetic thought, and it is in keeping with his literary modus operandi to honor his mentor with pecuni-ary considerations in mind.[78] In other words, Hoccleve expects payment for his spiritually laudable deed. Beyond its utility for Hoccleve, the framework of the chantry foundation enables us to understand more fully what exactly is going on in the Chaucer portrait and why Hoccleve's truth claims are so important.

Everything rests here on its retrospection, its separation from the—by then—decade-deceased poet whom it "pull[s] . . . out of a merely mythic existence and into historicity."[79] Much has been made of Hoccleve's use of the word *likeness*, al-though the word is not radical in reference to images. Tomb contracts frequently make use of the word and analogs. What *is* so unusual is Hoccleve's choice of the possessive here: "*his* likenesse." In contrast, tomb contracts use the indefinite article when referring to the effigy, requesting "the likeness of *a* chaplain" or "the counter-feit of *an* esquire . . . [and] the counterfeit of *a* lady."[80] Hoccleve is insistent here that his image has an iconic quality and is not merely a symbol of Chaucer's estate or vocation. (And what would that be? Customs official? Diplomat? Clerk of the King's Works? Poet?). Christopher Wood's prescription for the fabrication of like-ness—"to introduce information beyond any warrant," to supply an "excess of in-formation with respect to the apparent function of the image"—correlates well with Chaucer's face here.[81] Sloping shoulders, a snowy forked beard, plump dimen-sions, sleepy eyes, and an animated pose: together, this surplus of pictorial detail, its departure from the conventions of static frontality that characterize the reli-gious icon, all lend Chaucer that "lyflynesse" on which his historicity hangs, re-gardless of its correlation with the empirically observable body of Chaucer.[82]

More than this pictorial surplus, it is the act of replication in which the image originated that confers its credibility. Wood's scholarship on retrospective tombs is even more germane here: he has discussed at length the "evidentiary force" that the tomb of St. Simpertus musters, which derived not only from its abundant physiognomic detail and the rhetoric of likeness it imparts. In addition—and far more important here—the tomb's authenticity grew later out of its service as a model for another sculpture created only fifteen years on. While the tomb sculpture has no verifiable or probable relationship to the physiognomy of the person it represents— that is, Simpertus—the act of replication in creating the copy conferred an authority on both it as an original and its descendant. (The effect is similar to the impact of quoting a text, lending an instant validity to the quote merely by selecting it for re-iteration.) If this scenario sounds familiar, it is because Hoccleve's Chaucer portrait enacts precisely the same procedure on its Ellesmere precedent and inflates its own value in the process.[83] There is, after all, an extant Chaucer portrait alongside the same verses in another Hoccleve manuscript (Figure 30). Yet its failure to replicate Ellesmere and its poverty of detail have relegated it to neglect. For all we know, Chaucer had a snub nose and plump lips. This is, of course, not the point.

It is difficult for us now to conceive of a need to pull Chaucer into historicity. But Hoccleve's poem and pictorial foundation assure us that the need was there. These were early days, when there was a distinct possibility that an English work— no matter how great—could go un- or misattributed. Wills that include bequests of *Canterbury Tales* manuscripts omit unanimously Chaucer's name, even when such wills identify other works along with their authors.[84] The simple fact, as Paul Strohm has shown, was that Chaucer's original intended audience—a small circle of like-minded individuals—not only died shortly after he did but also left behind no intimates or successors to replenish their ranks. The widening of Chaucer's audience (and the concomitant "narrowing" of the Chaucerian tradition) meant that his poetry was read both selectively on the basis of its appeal to fifteenth-century taste and often without regard for the identity of the person who wrote it.[85] Poets like Chaucer and Hoccleve appear not only to have registered this potential but also to have deployed metafictional frames and references to themselves and their works throughout their poetry to preempt it. Chaucer's retraction at the end of *The Canterbury Tales* is arguably the most explicit of such measures, which couches in the humble language of penitence what is after all an impressive curriculum vitae.[86] And, in *The House of Fame*, he acknowledges the necessity of both image and inscription to preserving the memory of what speech is too ephemeral to perpetuate. Hoccleve was aware of this need and commissioned a codicological tomb as a bulwark against his master's oblivion. But unlike a stone monument, this one is immanently capable of replication and distribution. Hoccleve's promise that he

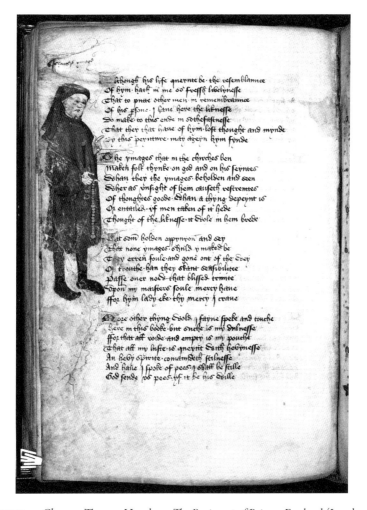

FIGURE 30. *Chaucer*. Thomas Hoccleve, *The Regiment of Princes*, England (London?),
c. 1425–1450. London, British Library Royal MS 17 D vi, fol. 93v.
© British Library Board.

has commissioned a true likeness of his "fadir" acquires even greater historical
credibility in those manuscripts that lack the picture, the thing he promises to have
placed "here."[87] Inducing nostalgia, the passage defers its reader to some originary
moment. But, more than that, its absence from later copies reassures the reader in
its refusal to dilute Hoccleve's claims with a replica. Rather, the unillustrated words
in later copies guarantee that an original, credible, authentic image—the one that
Hoccleve himself commissioned—is out there. Ultimately, Hoccleve succeeded in
contributing to the canonization of Chaucer not because the image he commissioned affirms Chaucer's eminence in any iconographically identifiable way. Rather,
he succeeded because both the image and Hoccleve insist on the former's corre-

spondence to a verifiable historical referent, one worthy of a chantry foundation—even if it only existed in a book. Alastair Minnis's well-known quip (and paraphrase of Walter Map) that "the only good *auctor* was a dead one" was anticipated by Hoccleve, who commissioned a picture that both buried and authenticated the man he hoped would be granted that title.[88]

Chaucer's Manicule

While Hoccleve and an anonymous illuminator worked in tandem to authenticate Chaucer—both as an actual person and as the originator of an English poetic tradition—the illuminators I examined earlier shared this objective but were less audacious in their approach to achieving it. Anxieties about authentication appear to have been the primary preoccupation of those who confronted the problem of Chaucerian representation. Diverse as manuscript representations of him are, one trait is consistent across almost every fifteenth-century depiction of Chaucer: his pointing hand.[89] Whether indicating the first verses of the "General Prologue," gesturing at the opening line to "The Tale of Melibee," guiding the viewer's eye toward a painted book, pointing at a raindrop that replaces what may originally have been a book, or directing his index finger toward Hoccleve's homage, one of Chaucer's hands always exclaims "nota bene." Since the features of all of these images are so different, more than mere coincidence has to account for the near universality of Chaucer's pointing hand. Why did this gesture become Chaucer's virtual attribute? What about it seemed so apt to his condition that illuminators, across roughly a half-century of manuscript production, all chose to render him in this pose?

Pointing with the index finger is the paradigmatic gesture of deixis, the most explicitly social gesture that humans make. It exists solely to effect a convergence of eyes on a single point, focalizing the attention of many on one. Norman Bryson referred to deixis as "utterance in carnal form [that] points back directly . . . to the body of the speaker; self-reflexive, it marks the moment at which rhetoric becomes oratory: were we to visualize deixis, Quintilian would supply us with a vivid, exact picture—the *hands* of the rhetor, the left facing inwards towards the body, the right outstretched with the fingers slightly extended, in the classical posture of *eloquentia*."[90] Quintilian himself, familiar to medievals along with Cicero as the preeminent adviser on all matters of performance in oratory,[91] was specific on this point: "When three fingers are doubled under the thumb, the finger, which Cicero says Crassus used to such effect, is extended. It is used in denunciation and in indication (whence its name of the index finger)."[92] Both Bryson and Quintilian are referring to the pointing finger in actual or envisioned performance as a node between two figures occupying the same time and space. But when placed on a page, the representational pointing hand draws together groups across time: the figure who made the pointing finger and the later figures who, it is expected, will come along and direct their attention to where this finger points.

The pointing hand held an important place in medieval manuscripts, and it was not necessarily indicative of authorship. Rather, the pointing hand often appears in the margin as an artifact of "reading itself, a visual breadcrumb inked into the margin,"[93] or as "marginal notes in figural form."[94] Manicules—those pointing hands scattered by scribes and readers across the folios of manuscripts from at least the thirteenth century in England—"played an important role in the personal process of making a book meaningful."[95] When a scribe or a reader took the effort to draft the outlines of a pointing hand into the margin of a manuscript, she initiated a conversation between herself and an imagined future reader (including her future self), implying that the text indicated is worthy of notice. More than that, the pointing hand enunciates the adequacy of the text on its own terms and that "there is no need to move outside the text at this point. To 'get the point' of a crucial passage, one had only to allow one's gaze to be directed by the pointer, strategically placed beside phrases that needed to be read with care and recalled."[96] Unlike other forms of marginalia, the manicule does not supplement; rather, the pointing hand abrogates the attention it gathers to itself by directing that attention elsewhere. By this process, the manicule proclaims the self-sufficiency of what it indicates.

Chaucer's most characteristic attribute, then, embodies the heuristic thrust of the manicule. It conscripts, with proleptic force, Chaucer's own hand to perform his own validation. It is the coyest of *sphragides*, devices exploited by ancient authors to address directly their audiences and authenticate their own works.[97] Portrayed with his hand outside of the text, marking out his own text, the author becomes the authenticator of the text, at once creating it and assimilating the activity of the approving scribe or reader who finds value in it. If Chaucer's body became inscrutable on the moment of his representation, then the transformation of his hand into a manicule offered a fixed point of reference: the text itself. And if signifying Chaucer was a further problem because no venerable models for versifying in English preceded him—certainly none who were represented visually—then the pointing hand proclaims an English exceptionalism and the English poet's self-sufficiency to vouch for the value of his work.

The self-sufficiency that Chaucer's manicule embodies took on a solipsistic cast in the tradition of printed and painted portraiture that came, from the sixteenth century, to *be* Chaucer. In 1598, John Speed engraved a frontispiece portrait of Chaucer to precede a printed edition of the poet's collected works, *The Works of Our Antient and Lerned English Poet* (Figure 31). Large and central, Chaucer stands

FIGURE 31. John Speed, *The Progenie of Geoffrey Chaucer. The Workes of Our Antient and Lerned English Poet, Geffrey Chaucer, Newly Printed,* edited by Thomas Speght (London: Islip, 1598). Amherst College Archives and Special Collections RBR C393 1598. By permission of Amherst College Archives and Special Collections.

beneath a heading that announces "The Progenie of Geffrey Chaucer" and above a caption that promises "the true portraiture of GEFFREY CHAUCER the famous English poet, as by THOMAS OCCLEVE is described who lived in his time, and was his Scholar." Below rest effigies of Chaucer's son Thomas and the latter's wife, Maud Berghersh. Both portrait and effigial tomb are ensconced in a prodigious array of heraldry and medallions that like Thomas Chaucer's actual tomb, furnishes "an armorial roll-call of the great families of England."[98] The print gathers within itself the dossier of Chaucer's existence, positioning him as "a representative of Elizabethan nationalism."[99] There is debate as to whether the engraving was modeled on the Hoccleve portrait of Chaucer in manuscripts of the *Regiment* or on another sixteenth-century copy. Regardless, what is remarkable about the engraving (and the sixteenth-century illumination on which it was or was not modeled) is not the fidelity to the original Hoccleve portrait but rather its alteration of one key detail: Chaucer's right hand. Here, the author's hand has been turned inward, and it now points to him while grasping the penner that hangs about his neck. Like other portraits of the sixteenth century, this one displaces the "objective attribute that would establish the meaning of a likeness by pointing elsewhere to other meanings or images [with] the gesture toward the body [which] expresses a dream of pure self-reference in and through the sitter's likeness alone."[100] Framed and advertised before a volume of his collected works, genealogically bona fide, and pointing inward toward himself, Chaucer irrupts forth as autonomous, the author of the early modern marketplace of print. But long before that happened, it was the illuminators who made Chaucer's several bodies and who encountered the problems of representation that his many bodies posed. In this, Chaucer was not alone. Fellow English poets John Gower and John Lydgate presented similar challenges to the illuminators of their works, subjects I address in the two chapters that follow.

CHAPTER 3

Gower *in Humilitatio*

Opening a manuscript of John Gower's *Confessio Amantis* can be a disorienting experience. Not only does the first page feature both English and Latin, but the Latin itself is also variable. Baroque and sententious verses introduce the poem, while crisp, straightforward prose summarizes its content. In some manuscripts, the Latin is in red ink; in others, it is in black. In some manuscripts, the Latin is in the margin; in others, it is in the column; and in still others, it appears in both colors and locations.[1] This is a poem of many voices, each with its own textual appearance.

Compounding the polyphony of the page is the illumination that adorns it. The arrangement of words and images that introduces the poem in Princeton University Library MS Taylor 5, for instance, does not pinpoint the author of the many voices on the folio (Figure 32).[2] In the central space of the column miniature, a bicolored figure confronts us from against a star-flecked background. To the right, an inscribed banderole floats vertically beside the miniature's frame, inside of which is the diminutive figure of an aged man within a tabernacle. Further down the folio is a historiated initial *O*, a roundel for a man who gestures toward a cupboard stocked with books. Each of these men "speaks" to us—through the body, in visualized text, and by reference to books—but which of them speaks the words on the page? Is it necessary for us to choose? The ensemble enunciates the evasiveness of the poem's author before we, as readers and viewers, can assign a proper role to each character on the Taylor folio. In this introductory group of images from the manuscript, we find a document of the limner's mediation of a text's origins and the artist's confrontation with the author.

The *Confessio Amantis*, completed in the 1390s, is not only a monument of Middle English poetry; it is also, like *The Canterbury Tales*, an apt work with which to think through issues of authorial indeterminacy. The ambiguity of its author's identity propels the direction and generates the thematic thrust of the entire poem. In brief, the 33,000-line work is a compilation of over 140 narrative exempla, each recounted in Latin and Middle English and offered up as sources of wisdom and entertainment to King Richard II and, in a later version, to Henry Bolingbroke, the

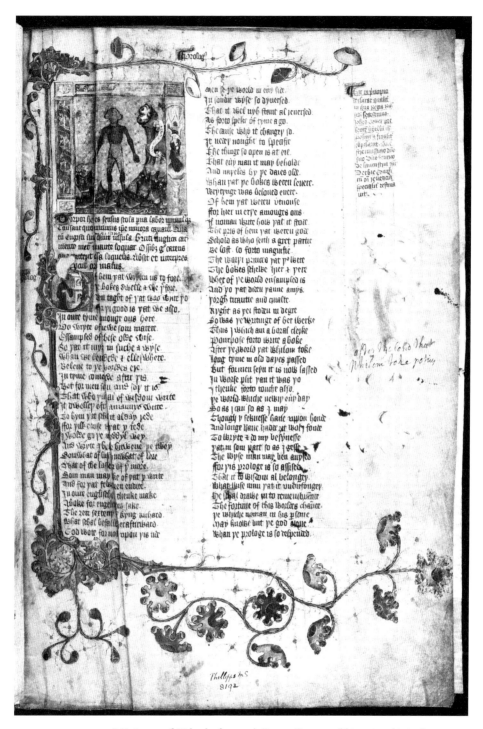

FIGURE 32. Miniature of *Nebuchadnezzar's Dream Statue* and historiated initial of *Gower gesturing to a book cupboard*. John Gower, *Confessio Amantis*, London, c. 1400–1425. Manuscripts Division, Department of Rare Books and Special Collections, Princeton, University Library Taylor MS 5, fol. 1r.

eventual Henry IV.[3] However, before these stories are related, the poem opens with two prologues that set in place its numerous authorial players: the first is an external prologue that describes the circumstances of the poem's production and its intention to restore order to the decadent and divisive world that was prophesied in the Old Testament by Nebuchadnezzar's dream of the metallic statue.[4] The second is an internal prologue that occupies the first 202 lines of Book I. In this second prologue, the narrator downshifts. He concedes that it is not within his power to set the world at harmony, and so he will speak instead of love, a harmonizing force among individuals. From this point forward, he will assume the role of a lover (Amans), making his confession to Genius (Confessor), the priest of Venus. The second prologue sets the agenda for the rest of the work, divided into eight books: seven of these (Books I through VI and Book VIII) are organized according to each of the Deadly Sins, while one book (Book VII) intervenes with a digression on royal education. These books contain numerous stories told by the Confessor to Amans as exempla in order to teach the latter the proper ways of love and, by extension, provide moral counsel to the poem's successive dedicatees. These prologues complicate the identity of the work's author in a number of ways that parallel the complexities of the prefatory miniatures that accompany numerous copies of the poem.[5]

Two aspects of the manuscript history of the *Confessio Amantis* make it an engaging subject for investigating limners' conceptions of authorial identity. First is its provision for a program comprising two prefatory miniatures, neither of which is explicitly a representation of John Gower.[6] Early in the production of these manuscripts, someone—whether Gower or not is unknown—incorporated into the plan for the *Confessio* an illustration of Nebuchadnezzar's dream and a depiction of Amans's confession to Genius.[7] This decision is one of the more curious features of the manuscript history of the *Confessio* (why these two scenes?), although it has been proposed—I think rightly—that they encapsulate the poem's overarching insistence on the reciprocal relationship between the microcosm and macrocosm.[8] However, rather than tracking down the impetus for this decision, I want to develop insights from the actions of limners who were assigned these subjects to depict.

Representations of the lover's confession were a flashpoint for illuminators' discomfort with the identity of the figure they were commissioned to portray. Because of this, I focus for the most part in this chapter on this scene. Essential to the discussion that follows is the condition that when limners of the *Confessio Amantis* painted prefatory miniatures, they were informed not only by the prologues they illustrated but also by the antecedent images that recommended themselves in their contexts.

The chief consistency across miniatures that illustrate Amans's confession to Genius—which appear in fourteen manuscripts of the poem—is the variety of ways in which their artists, together with scribes, construe the command to assign an identity to Amans. In all of these images, a figure kneels before a cleric, the two engaged in the act of confession. While portrayals of Genius are largely similar, variations in the portrayal of Amans treat him as either a youth, an old man, or a figure with potential references to the historical John Gower. These variations in Amans, along with different decisions as to where to place the miniature, disclose illuminators' difficulty with the notion of a contemporary author, a difficulty that is a central preoccupation in the *Confessio Amantis*.[9] Moreover, these inconsistencies, as well as a number of visual allusions in these images, have been overlooked by scholarship that emphasizes the "standardization" of these manuscripts.[10] But repetition of iconography is by no means tantamount to repetition of form. Even in the face of standardization, illuminators of the *Confessio Amantis* found in the images of Amans's confession an opportunity to work through their own queries about authorship. The variation in their responses thwarts easy generalization. However, it is my argument here that such variation affirms the author as a negotiable presence, one which in many instances appears in order to articulate the author's renunciation of his agency as author.

Gower's Many Voices

From the outset, it is difficult to speak of the "author" of the *Confessio Amantis*, since the poem takes shape as a visible chorus of distinct voices, each with a unique appearance on the page.[11] The first voice to speak to the reader is the Latin voice of the text column, often rubricated or underlined in red in manuscripts of the poem. It opens the prologue with a thundering stanza that breaks the silence: "Listlessness, dull discernment, little schooling and least labor are the causes by which, I, least of all, sing things all the lesser. Nonetheless, in the tongue of Hengist in which the island of Brutus sings, with Carmentis' aid I will utter English verses. Let then the boneless one that breaks bones with speeches be absent, and let the interpreter wicked in word stand far away."[12] This is a voice from a distant past. Invoking Carmentis's aid, like the antique poet beckoning the muses, it is an archaic voice. It is also a voice from a long-ago England, populated by the descendants of Trojan heroes. Above all, it is a voice that insists on its orality, as it "sing[s]" (*canam*) and "utter[s]" (*loquar*), and whose only opponent is the tongue (*ossibus ergo carens que conterit ossa loquelis absit*).[13]

In contrast to the archaic speech of the Latin epigraphs is the temporally and geographically particular figure responsible for the Middle English verses that occupy the central columns in every manuscript of the poem. The "I" of these lines (the author-narrator) recounts in one version of the poem that while boating on the Thames one day, he floated past King Richard II.[14] Inviting the author-narrator into his barge, the king charged him "som newe thing [to] booke."[15] And in spite of his infirmity ("Though I seknesse have upon honde, And long have had"),[16] he is gladdened by the opportunity to fulfill his liege's behest. He then recounts a compact history of the world's degradation from a golden age of harmony to the present era of contention and disunity. This account is followed by the tale of Nebuchadnezzar's dream of the statue of precious metals: a dream interpreted by the prophet Daniel to show "hou that this world schal torne and wende / til it befalle to his ende."[17] Because these lines follow on the heels of the author-narrator's own dismal tour of time, it is unavoidable to see a similarity between the two figures. The prologue then concludes with the narrator's wish for the arrival of a new Arion—that is, a poet—whose harping might restore the world to concord.[18]

Although he does not identify himself by name, the writer of these verses is a historically specific figure, coterminous with the implied reader, and familiar as a collection of plausible traits. Beckoned by the king, he attributes to himself a recognizable presence in London's upper social orbit. Commanded to do his "busynesse,"[19] he has a reputation as a writer, confirmed by his frequent use of the vocabulary of books and writing—a feature that distinguishes him from the speaking voice of the Latin verses. And he is ill, and perhaps even old, since he has been so for an extended period. It seems we are on sure footing here, reading words penned by a fully realized "I" whose position we could finger on a map, whose existence we could point to on a timeline, and whose face and demeanor we might even be able to recognize among London's throngs. It seems far from audacious to suggest that *this* is the voice of John Gower.

Yet the very specificity of this person, his nearness to verifiability as Gower, as the author of the work, challenges the certainty with which we could point to him as Gower. By inscribing an avatar for himself into the fiction of the poem's genesis, the author of the work makes it impossible for the reader to ascribe to that avatar full redundancy with the author.[20] "Autobiography," as Paul de Man writes, "veils a defacement of the mind of which it is itself the cause."[21] In identifying himself, Gower confects his own identity from representation.[22] That he recruits two literary figures of potential historical veracity—Daniel and Arion—to index his own poetic ambitions only accentuates his schematism.

What is more, at the precise point when the reader is able to recognize the face behind the words of the prologue, that face evaporates. The opening to Book I—what one scholar has referred to as the "most striking formal incongruence"[23] in the poem—begins with the author-narrator's admission of his own limitations and his concession to pursue a goal less extraordinary than restoring accord to the world:

Forthi the Stile of my writinges
Fro this day forth I thenke change
And speke of thing is noght so strange . . .
And that is love.[24]

While still expressing himself in a voice continuous with that of the prologue's author-narrator, this individual initiates a metamorphosis not just through a change in "style" but also, and more suggestively, through a change of "stylus": he has put aside his star-reaching stile (it cannot be fortuitous that *stile* can mean not only *style* and *stylus* but also *set of steps*) and exchanged it for a stile of lesser aspirations.[25] In turning to these lesser aspirations, the author-narrator sets in motion the textual progress of his own demise and cedes authorial control to become a character of his own tale. He declares that love is something "which wol no reson understonde": "And for to proven it is so, / I am miselven on of tho, / Which to this Scole am underfonge."[26] These verses open with a conspicuous use of anacoluthon, a syntactical bait and switch that obscures the passage from discourse to confession.[27] In Modern English, this might be rendered as "And in order to prove that this is true, I am myself one of those who belongs to this school [of lovers]." This is a difficult phrase to sit with. The narrator offers to provide a proof and instead offers a statement about himself. It may be true that, as J. A. Burrow argues, the "loose syntax" of this sentence "tacitly supports . . . [that] Gower is to *pretend* to be a lover,"[28] but whatever its end, it signals the jagged transition involved in this process.

The final blow is struck by the team of Cupid and Venus, when, after the former shoots a fiery arrow though the dying writer-narrator's heart, Venus demands,

"What art thou, Sone?" and I abreide
Riht as a man doth out of slep,
. . . .
And eft scheo asketh, what was I:
I seide, "A Caitif that lith hiere:
What wolde ye, my Ladi diere?
Schal I ben hol or elles dye?"[29]

The once recognizable figure of the author has crumbled to the ground and died. Resurrected in his place, "riht as a man doth out of sleep," is one who does not know his own identity but whom we recognize as the arrow-struck lover. It is at this point that the eponymous confession of the lover begins.

Contrasting with the syntactically strained progression of the author's death and metamorphosis is the clipped Latin glossular-heading that accompanies its account, either in the margins of the manuscript or rubricated in the columns.[30] In one of the most commented-on passages in the *Confessio Amantis*, the gloss proclaims in Latin, "Here the author, fashioning himself to be the Lover as if in the role of those others whom love binds, proposes to write about their various passions one by one in the various sections of this book."[31] Interrupting the unremarkable language of first-person narration, a commentator punctures the narrative scrim to tell the audience that the author is now one of the characters in the fiction to ensue. Like the anamorphic perspective of a skull superimposed over Holbein's *Ambassadors*, the commentary applies a figure of artifice over the naturalistic structure that governs the central point of the reader's (or viewer's) focus. The commentary breaks "the spell of identification"[32] that we think we saw between the familiar figures of veristic author and conventional lover, drawing attention to the poem's own conceit. It is, if ironically, this gloss that leaves the author's presence intact.

Copying Gower's Voices

No matter how assertive the text's explanation of its own devices, the surgical division between author and subject failed to restrain the editorializing impulses of manuscript producers. In Oxford, Bodleian Library MS Ashmole 35, for example, the scribe who translated all of the Latin glossular headings into English substituted the following for the heading to Book I:

> This booke is dyvyded into viii partes whereof þe ffirst parte specifieþ of pride and of þe braunches of pride and a parte of the v wittes þat towchen to loves cause. And also Iohn Gower whiche was maker of þis boke made & devysed it to be in maner of a confession þat þis said Iohn Gower was confessid yn unto a prest whiche was called Genius whom venus þe goddesse of love sent unto þe said Gower to conffesse hym þat he had trespast a yenst venus & hir courte and calleþ hym self a lover & Genius venus clerk is called confessor.[33]

As Siân Echard has observed, according to this glossator Gower is the author of the work, its producer ("maker" here can mean both author and the person physically responsible for the book), and its main subject.[34]

Some scribes' interventions are even more revisionist, and it seems hardly a co-incidence that these revisions co-occur with pictorial representations of Amans's confession.[35] When Venus demands that the narrator identify himself, the scribes of two manuscripts that portray Amans as a youth replaced the author-narrator's oblivious response, "a caitif that lith hiere," with "Ma dame I sayde Iohn Gowere."[36] The scribe of London, British Library Royal MS 18 C xxii, simply omitted the line, maybe inadvertently; but then again, in this manuscript, the image of Amans's confession is placed on the first folio of the poem, where an image of the author is typically found: an indication the scribe was at least somewhat invested in assigning Amans's identity to the author and may have had second thoughts about the response that Gower-Amans offers.[37]

Conventionally, images are provided after the text has been copied, but a number of instances of scribal indecision appear to have emerged from the scribe's knowledge that the provision of such an image would produce a moment of pictorial reckoning for which he would be held to account. The scribe of Oxford, Bodleian Library MS Arch Selden B 11, left a blank, as did the scribe of Cambridge, University Library MS Dd.8.19.[38] The blank space left by the latter mirrors the vacancy in the adjacent column, where, above the beginning of Amans's confession, a small note records "hic imago" (Figure 33). Gower's (or Amans's) response to Venus is also lacking in Oxford, Bodleian Library MS Bodley 693, where the interruption to the rhyme scheme that this omission causes is visible directly across from the adjacent image of Amans's confession (Plate 9). Likewise, across the page from the image of Amans's confession in Bodleian Library MS Laud Miscellaneous 609, the amnesiac narrator's response to Venus completes the couplet but evades her demand for his identification, reading, "And I answered wiþ ful myld chere / what wolde ȝe wiþ me my lady dere" (Figure 34), a revision also appearing across from the miniature in New York, Morgan Library and Museum MS M.126, which I discuss in detail later in the chapter (Figure 45). Oxford, Corpus Christi College MS 67, similarly completes the couplet, "And I answerde wiþ drery chiere," on the recto of same leaf.

In other instances, readers gloss over the author's identity in ways that divulge their inability to condense a persona so complex into a single pithy line. In the table of contents appended to the Princeton manuscript with which I opened, no mention of the author, Gower, or even the lover is made, and subsequent readers are only notified that "Here begynyt the prologe and that Contenyth vii levys . . . Next begynyth the confesion þe viii leff."[39] Similarly, the tabulator of another manuscript (Oxford, Magdalene College MS 213) omits any mention of the narrating voice or protagonist of the prologue, waiting until the entries for Book VIII to mention, "The Complaynt of Iohan Gower wyth a Supplicacio to venus Cort and of the asemble of that dans and what the End of loue is A good Exortacion of the autor the End."[40] Jeremy Griffiths argued that manuscript producers failed "to distinguish between the author and the fictional persona,"[41] but their failure is not one of literacy or intellect so much as it is a failure of cultural precedent to provide a bibliographic context for Gower's English innovations.[42]

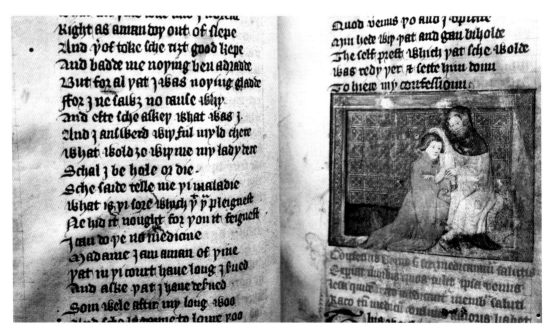

I have dwelt on the poem's two prologues in order to make clear how elusive the "author" of the *Confessio* is. Complication of the authorial persona is a common feature of Middle English poetry, a feature that, perhaps, derives from the origins of much late medieval vernacular literature in translation.[43] Taking responsibility for a text that originally issued from a different "I," Middle English poets such as Chaucer and Gower experienced the first person as an estranging and counterfeit form of diction. If the thread of a singular ego is difficult to pick out from the fabric of the *Confessio Amantis*, it is because the ego that wrote it was formed, in part, by the ventriloquism that is endemic to the intertextual poet and translator. Gower is and he is not: the prophetic voice of the Latin epigraphic verses, the London poet of the prologue, Daniel the exegete of visions, a new Arion, the lovelorn Amans, and even the Latin commentator whose often opaque glossular-headings color while marking out the proairetic code of the poem. If we imagine the introductory material to a Middle English poem to be a surrogate for the portraitist's sitter, then the two prologues to the *Confessio Amantis* don a different mask for numerous sittings: neither one of them indexes the mind of the man who wrote them, but both of them play out visibly on the manuscript's page the artifice of authorial self-fashioning.[44]

Gower's Many Faces

It is this interpenetration of divergent personae—and the divergent contexts that each suggests—that composed the larger cultural background to the limner's art. Scholars who have examined the miniatures of Amans's confession have concentrated on the difficulties the subject posed, difficulties similar to those that attended the representation of Chaucer in manuscripts of *The Canterbury Tales* (see Chapter 2). In his discussion of the confession miniatures, for example, Jeremy Griffiths summarizes these difficulties: "Would one illustrate the historical Gower, the *auctor* of the extrinsic prologue (that is, the *Prologus*), or the 'John Gower' who identifies himself in response to Venus' questioning at the end of the poem (VIII.2320–21), the fictional persona introduced by the intrinsic prologue?"[45] In what follows, I review how scholars have responded to these questions, offering some refinements along the way.

Furthermore, what I will suggest is that this scholarship overlooks a more pressing problem with which illuminators had to cope: it is not simply that limners were taxed in deciding whether or not Amans is John Gower; in addition, the difficulty was in deciding how to show that the person responsible for the text (whether Gower or not) appears in order to renounce his agency over it, to pronounce his authorial death. Among all of the illuminated copies of the *Confessio*, only a single one features an image of Gower composing his work (Plate 10)—a bizarre scene of a man writing (implausibly) while seated on a bed, and an exception that proves the rule of limners' reluctance to depict the English author in the act of composition.[46] I demonstrated in Chapter 1 that the London limner of the fifteenth century played an integral role in the production of books. Whether or not the limner was deeply attuned to the intricacies of the *Confessio Amantis*, he cannot have been ignorant of the broader preoccupations and thematic cruxes of what was, in Gower's own words, "som newe thing," and in our own words, a new kind of book. The variation that we find in representations of the confessional moment betrays limners' attempts to come to grips with Gower's repression of his authorial self in deference to the larger political implications of his poem.

The majority of the fourteen extant confession miniatures portray Amans as a youth and, in this respect, record what might have come to an illuminator's mind when he was cued by the word "Amans." Representative of this group is the image in Oxford, Bodleian Library MS Bodley 294 (Figure 35),[47] which John Burrow found

FIGURE 35. *Amans's confession*. John Gower, *Confessio Amantis*, London, c. 1400–1425. Oxford, Bodleian Library MS Bodley 294, fol. 9r (detail). By kind permission of the Bodleian Libraries.

to be "the right pictorial equivalent . . . for Amans' verbal portrait of himself as a lover."[48] One could also argue that this image is drawn from the stock of imagery representing such young lovers as they appear in manuscripts like the *Roman de la Rose*.[49] Yet, significantly, as I mentioned previously, the scribe of this manuscript has Amans calling himself "Iohn Gower." The miniature is a framed column picture placed immediately before the Latin head to the tale, "Having confessed to Genius, I will try to discover whether that is the healing medicine."[50] The figures of Amans and Genius are pushed up close to the picture plane, placed over a green, tiled ground and a red backdrop with gold filigree. Amans, kneeling on the left, wears a pink robe with ocher collar, the lower hem of which spills over the miniature's frame. His face is clean shaven, and he has a head of closely cropped light brown hair. He nods his head slightly and crosses his hands over his chest. Immediately to the right, Genius sits on a carved stone bench, while resting his right hand just over Amans's shoulder. He wears a blue cowl and undergarment, on top of which is a white alb and a red stole. He looks directly at Amans's face, and his lips are parted to indicate that he is in the midst of speaking—underscored by the active pose of his left hand, raised above his knee, with fingers animated as if in mid-gesture. In other miniatures, Genius may be pointing at his other hand as if enumerating, or he may have his hand over Amans's head in the gesture of absolution. The ten miniatures of Amans as a youth largely represent the scene in this manner.

While the renditions of Amans as a fresh-faced youth contain subtle suggestions that their illuminators were uncomfortable with the scene (more on which later), other versions are far more explicit in documenting the difficulties that the Amans persona posed for illuminators. Two miniatures depict the confessant as an old man, a third identifies Amans explicitly with John Gower, and a fourth depicts him as a figure of indeterminate age who is identified textually as "Gowere."[51] In Oxford, Bodleian Library MS Bodley 902 (Figure 36), almost every element from the images of Amans as a youth is retained: the patterned red backdrop, the green ground, and the composition of a kneeling Amans to the left with a seated confessor to the right. Beyond changes in color, the only alteration here is in Amans's face, which, though still rosy-cheeked, now features a head of graying hair and a long white beard. The illuminator of Cambridge, Pembroke College MS 307, offered a similar rendition of an aged Amans (Figure 37). In Oxford, Bodleian Library MS Fairfax 3 (Figure 38, Plate 11), Amans is of an indeterminate age, but he wears a collar of "SS" on his robe, which has been linked to the same livery collar given to Gower by Henry IV.[52] All of these instances perform a visual compromise by modifying the stock figure of the youthful lover.

A number of scholars have argued that these images portray Amans as the senescent Gower whom he discovers himself to be at the end of the poem. In the

FIGURE 36. *Amans's confession* with note to the illuminator. John Gower, *Confessio Amantis*, London, c. 1400–1425. Oxford, Bodleian Library MS Bodley 902, fol. 8r (detail). By kind permission of the Bodleian Libraries.

closing scenes of the poem, Amans implores Genius for "an ende,"[53] begging for some final advice that will cure him of his lovesickness. Rejecting the counsel that he divert himself from earthly love and devote himself instead to piety, Amans appeals to the authority of Venus and Cupid by taking up a pen and writing them a plaintive epistle.[54] The letter that follows, comprising twelve rhyme-royal stanzas, is the only deviation in rhyme scheme in the entire poem.[55] As such, it draws attention to itself as a composition. Amans, in writing a more complex poetic form than rhyming octosyllabic couplets, is rediscovering himself as an author. And when his epistle comes to a close, he is finally able to answer Venus's interrogation with the confidence he lost at the poem's beginning: "Sche axeth [asked] me what is mi name / Ma dame, I seide, John Gower."[56] This reawakening, however, is only an initial stirring that precedes the "painful and humiliating recognition of aging" that Matthew Irvin tracks across "several phases" in the final book of the poem.[57] The lover dead, he resumes himself as both an old man and an author.

Although representations of Amans as an elderly man would seem to preempt the poem's denouement, knowledge of the conclusion is entirely unnecessary for

I wol zow telle it on a rou.
Boy allo þi þozt z allo þi werk
A gounis upii oiuuo clerk
Come forþ z here þis manys shrift
Quod venus þoo z j vplift
Myne heued wiþ þat z gan byhold,
Þo self preest whiuf as she wold,
was redy þere and sette hy doun
To here my confession

Cofeffio domo fi fit medicina falutis
Expiar morbis. pios uufit ipa venus
lefa. quidem ferro medicauit. meb' faluti
Raiv tii medicui amluus amoris habet.

His worþi preest þ' Holy man
To me spekynge þ') bygan
And seide Benditto
My sone of þe felicito
Of loue and eke of þe uuo
wine oshalt. ne oðriue of Bon tuo

FIGURE 37. *Amans's confession*. John Gower, *Confessio Amantis*, London,
c. 1400–1425. Cambridge, Pembroke College MS 307, fol. 9r (detail).
By permission of the Master and Fellows of Pembroke College, Cambridge.

FIGURE 38. *Amans's confession*. John Gower, *Confessio Amantis*, London, c. 1400–1410. Oxford, Bodleian Library MS Fairfax 3, fol. 8r (detail). By kind permission of the Bodleian Libraries.

illuminators to have conceived of the lover in this way.[58] The final revelation only clouds what is already a vague distinction between author and protagonist within the poem. By and large, scholarship on these miniatures has been troubled by the conflation. While previous criticism held these depictions in low regard as pre-emptive cues detracting from the poem's climax, Thomas Garbáty argues that *most* miniatures of the poem, regardless of how they represent Amans's age, align him with Gower. Noting that the majority of the miniatures portray Amans in a red robe, Garbáty surmises it derives from the tomb effigy of Gower in Southwark Cathedral, where the poet "is not a feeble old man but a chestnut-haired individual in the prime of life, dressed in a flowing red gown."[59] This recourse to the tomb (as a substitute for the archive) is questionable. There is even the—to my mind distinct—possibility that the tomb effigy was produced at a considerable remove from Gower's death, possibly even inspired by the miniatures: the highly unusual "pillow" of books underneath his head recall the *Quia unusquisque* colophon found in many manuscripts of the *Confessio*, at once an enlarged epitaph and curriculum vitae. And the Latin poem above his effigy appears in a copy of Gower's Latin and French works.[60] Nevertheless, no matter which direction the line of influence flowed, Garbáty's point is that rather than misguided attempts to influence the reader in violation of the poem's narrative mechanisms, the vision of a *senex amans* represents only one variation among numerous attempts throughout many confession miniatures to conflate persona and author.

The argument that some illuminators were working toward a more perfect conflation of persona and author gains support from other manuscripts that feature the scene in a different position in the manuscript. The artist of London, British Library Royal MS 18 C xxii, chose not to age Amans, but he did locate the scene of confession in the introductory initial to the entire poem, the customary position for an author portrait (Figure 39). And in a previously unremarked feature of Cambridge, University Library MS Mm.2.21, a rare note to the limner remains in red ink in the margin, directing "hic fiat Gowere" [make here Gower] (Plate 12).[61] The placement of the miniature alone betrays the vexed priorities experienced by those tasked with planning and illuminating it: while the first miniature in the manuscript, depicting Nebuchadnezzar's Dream, was part of the original plan, accommodated by framed space within the text column, the representation of the confession was shoehorned into the margin, evidently an afterthought, but not one so late that it required the services of a different limner. What that limner portrayed likewise hedges on the identity of the confessant: the indeterminate age of the resulting figure (he is blond-haired with rosy cheeks and a touch of red on his lips, but he is bearded rather than clean shaven) depicts Amans as neither fully himself nor fully the aged author he discovers himself to be at the poem's conclusion: he is a visual compromise evidencing the very real problems faced by the very real limners commissioned to picture this poem. That the miniature was wedged into the margin reflects its perceived necessity, but this perception was only arrived at after reflection.

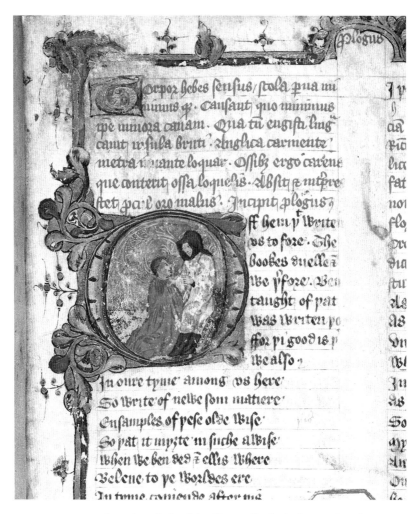

FIGURE 39. *Amans's confession*. John Gower, *Confessio Amantis*, London,
c. 1400–1425. London, British Library Royal MS 18 C xxii, fol. 1r (detail).
© British Library Board.

Amans *in Humilitatio*

Given the variations in the depictions of Amans's age, it is clear why attention to the miniatures has focused on this figure. At the same time, other aspects of this scene and the importance of the confession it stages have been overlooked. This neglect for a long time extended to the poem itself, which, as one scholar remarked, likely arose "from the assumption that confession is a known entity, a traditional language, and therefore that the authors' use of it is unproblematic."[62] In other words, it is the very routineness of confession and the supposed naturalism of its portrayal that has allowed this feature of the poem and the miniature to recede into oblivion. But, if we draw our attention back to what we take for granted, we might appreciate the aggravations involved in representing an extraecclesiastical scene of sexual confession within the functional frame of authorial representation. Kathryn A. Smith has shown in vibrant detail the degree to which the illuminations of profane narratives in a book of hours "contribute fundamentally to the experience and effectiveness of . . . [the] devotional artifact" in which they appear, affirming the convergence of sacred and secular in medieval manuscript culture.[63] I would like to push these suggestions one step further by submitting that illuminators alluded to templates from a range of religious art, seemingly unrelated to the subjects they depicted, in order to query the very subjects they were assigned to depict.

Auricular confession is widely regarded as an inseparable adjunct to the construction of subjectivity in the West. For centuries, it was a principal vehicle of authoring the self, and since Foucault championed this idea, confession has featured as a perennial centerpiece in discussions of selfhood.[64] The notion itself is simple: we bring ourselves into being by relating stories of our selves to an authoritative interlocutor.[65] The corollary to this notion is the inextricable link between confession and sexuality: confession "compel[led] individuals to articulate their sexual peculiarity—no matter how extreme," thereby rendering sex one of its "privileged theme[s]."[66] In what remains the classic study of late medieval confessional practice, Thomas Tentler notes that "while it is true that the medieval church could excoriate all kinds of vices and all kinds of sins, it was inordinately concerned with the sexual."[67] By the end of the fifteenth century and throughout the sixteenth, the Penitential Psalms were frequently illustrated by the scene of David espying Bathsheba bathing and receiving his summons. As one scholar argues, "the astonishing proliferation of images of David and Bathsheba in sixteenth-century Books of Hours must be seen as a new development that organized penitential practice around sexuality."[68] But rather than an entirely "new development," these images consummate late medieval attitudes toward sexual sin and confession. Confessional practice demanded that individuals define themselves as sexual beings in order to renounce this very aspect of themselves, reclaim it and then renounce it in regular attendance to the sacrament.

While a text lends itself congenially to the narrative process of confession, an image must collapse it into a single visual event. Medieval images of confession—which occur, almost without exception, in manuscripts containing scriptural, liturgical, and devotional content, as well as on liturgical furnishings—tend to enshrine the moment of renunciation as a synecdoche for the entire narrative of sin and confession.[69] Often in an initial preceding the Penitential Psalms (usually Psalm 6), the scenes typically consist of a seated confessor and kneeling penitent. The confessor either leans forward, listening to the penitent speak, or is in the pose of absolution, placing his hand over the head of the penitent, who holds both hands together in prayer out in front of his or her chest. Similar to this staging is the image of David kneeling in penitence before God—another favorite subject in the illustration of Psalm 6. In all of these images—particularly those that show the penitent speaking into the confessor's ear and those that show David's harp at his side—the narrative of sin is present, but it is neutralized by the controlling frame of the religious text and the penitent's pose of submission.[70]

The moment of renunciation in the *Confessio Amantis* occurs as a physical and visible metamorphosis in Book VIII, thousands and thousands of lines after the confession has begun. The challenge for illuminators of the confession scene may not have been whether or not to depict John Gower, or the aged author who calls himself that at the poem's end; rather, the challenge may have been in making the moment of renunciation legible while simultaneously communicating the narrative of sexual sin that underwrites the entire poem of the *Confessio Amantis*. Complicating all of this is the fact that what we are reading is not, strictly speaking, a Christian confession but instead one to Genius, the priest of Venus and erstwhile god of (pro)creation.[71] The difficulty of attending to these complex predicates can be read in images of Amans's confession.

A key detail in seven representations of Amans's confession records limners' uneasiness with the nature of the scene and its relationship to the figure responsible for the text—that is, Gower.[72] Oxford, Bodleian Library MS Bodley 902 is one of only three *Confessio Amantis* manuscripts that contain descriptive notes to the limner: in this case, the note remains in pristine condition in the margin, directing, "Hic fiat confessor sedens et confessus coram se genuflectendo" [Make here a confessor sitting and a confessant kneeling in his presence].[73] The limner followed these directions but editorialized by aging the confessing Amans. Moreover, he added a subtle change to the stereotypical gestures of confession: here, the elderly lover crosses his hands over his heart while pointing at the confessor with his right (Figure 36). A further six miniatures in other manuscripts closely replicate this gesture, even when they tinker with other aspects of Amans's appearance.[74] The artists' addition of this gesture enlivens the language of the confessant's body, but it is nevertheless out of place here. There is no precedent for the hands folded over the chest in representations of or written protocols for confession.[75] Yet it does not alter the iconography enough to usher it away from confession.

What, then, is this gesture? Garbáty noted it but mistakenly identifies it as a standard component in the choreography of confession. In normalizing its presence here, he fails to acknowledge the common performance of this gesture by one figure in particular across later medieval art: the Virgin.[76] Specifically, the Virgin is consistently depicted crossing her arms over her chest, and she is most often displayed doing so in images of the Annunciation.[77] Posing in what Fra Robertus Caracciolus categorized in a 1489 sermon as *humilitatio*, the hands placed over the heart represent the fourth Laudable Condition of the Blessed Virgin: "Lowering her head she spoke: *Behold the handmaid of the Lord*. She did not say 'Lady'; she did not say 'Queen.' Oh profound humility! Oh extraordinary gentleness! 'Behold,' she said, 'the slave and servant of my lord.' And then, lifting her eyes to heaven, and bringing up her hands with her arms in the form of a cross, she ended as God, the Angels, and the Holy Fathers desired: *Be it unto me according to thy word*."[78] Similar is the description of the scene detailed in a fifteenth-century Middle English lyric on the Annunciation:

> Mary, on bryst here hand che leyd
> Stylle xe stod, and thus xe seyd:
> "Lo, me here, Godes owyn handmayd,
> With herte and wil and body fre."[79]

In written accounts of the Annunciation, this gesture precedes Mary's willing submission of her own self—her very body—to God, and it is in this moment that she conceives the Christ child. Hand on heart, the Virgin empties herself so that she might make the purest vessel for God's son. The hands crossed over the chest should not be understood simply as a sign of humility but also as a token of willing self-sacrifice, the object of which is the creation of another being and the re-creation of the self.

Language plays an indispensable role in this episode. In every one of these accounts, the gesture of self-abnegation is followed by the Virgin's powerful declaration: "Ecce ancilla domini" (Luke 1:38). It is in this moment that the Word becomes flesh. Discussing this motif in Middle English versions of the Annunciation, Laura Saetveit Miles writes, "Within late medieval vernacular devotional traditions, the transformative powers of speech and stillness combine as key access points for contemplation on the Incarnation. In these examples of Middle English verse, Mary's model of meekness is subtly developed into a more sophisticated model of meditation, wherein her silence and speech become conduits for the individual soul's transformation."[80] The Virgin's gesture is the fulcrum around which past and present revolve: effacing her past self, she crosses hands over heart, then speaks the words that declare her new identity.

By the later Middle Ages, visual representations of this gesture came to encapsulate the Virgin's willing self-debasement.[81] Beginning in the fourteenth century, French, Netherlandish, and English artists all reworked older compositions to show the Virgin placing either a single hand or crossing both hands over her heart.

FIGURE 40. *Annunciation*. John Lydgate, *Life of Our Lady*, England, c. 1450–1475. Oxford, Bodleian Library MS Bodley 596, fol. 104v (detail). By kind permission of the Bodleian Libraries.

In a manuscript of Lydgate's *Life of Our Lady* now in the Bodleian Library, a miniature just above the rubric, "how Gabriell was sente to oure laday," shows the Virgin kneeling before an open book, with both her hands crossed over her chest (Figure 40).[82] And in the decaying fourteenth-century wall painting at Gisleham in Suffolk, Mary's hand is still slightly visible, placed delicately over her heart. The renowned Beaufort-Beauchamp Hours includes this gesture, as do numerous other Books of Hours made in England throughout the fifteenth century.[83] The east window at Gloucester features the willowy figure of the Virgin enthroned, with her arms crossed over her breast;[84] the Virgin Annunciate on the city gate to Lincoln (the "Stone Bow") and on the reredos in Henry V's chantry at Westminster both pose in the same manner.[85] As the prevalence—ubiquity, even—of these examples indicates, the gesture had become a virtual attribute of the Virgin.

Although the Virgin is commonly shown making this gesture, it also featured as shorthand for humility and self-abnegation elsewhere in late medieval art.[86] Occasionally occurring in images of obeisance, the gesture is assumed by a subordinate figure as he or she kneels before the subject of homage (Figure 41). Augmenting the subservience of genuflection, the crossed arms signal a renunciation of one's own will in the interests of a superior. But perhaps the most proximate use of the gesture to Amans's pose in manuscripts of the *Confessio* is its performance by Chau-

Irst twenty knyhtes he ches out off his Rellm
That Wern in Wisdam/and knyhthod most notable
And other twenty/that fro Iherusalem
kam with knyt Offa/famous and honurable
And a mong alle/a knyht off port most stable
Assigned Was the story is fful kouth
ffor to gouerne Edmund in his youth

FIGURE 41. *Alkmund and Edmund in court*. John Lydgate, *Lives of Saints Edmund and Fremund*, Bury St. Edmunds, c. 1434–1439. London, British Library Harley MS 2278, fol. 25r. © British Library Board.

cer's Parson in the Ellesmere manuscript of *The Canterbury Tales*. In the margin, beside the opening lines to his tale, the Parson crosses his hands over his chest—an improbable pose while astride a horse (Figure 42). Over the course of the first three hundred lines, the Parson enjoins his audience to contrition, professing that only penitence and honest confession will secure one's place in heaven. But, of course, the Parson is not the confessant here. Instead, a paragon to those who hear him (a "good ensample"),[87] the Parson models the humility he preaches, divesting himself

FIGURE 42. *The Parson*. Chaucer, *Canterbury Tales*, London, c. 1400–1405. San Marino, Huntington Library MS EL 26 C 9, fol. 206v (detail).

of all vanity, all sin, all thoughts of immediate self-gratification.[88] Humility, in other words, is a necessary *interior* precondition of penance—of which confession was a part—but its *externalization* in gesture was standard in neither written protocols nor visual representations of confession.

In retrospect, it seems almost logical that, during this same period, artists availed themselves of this gesture to encapsulate the recognition of death's approach. The only illumination in a late copy of Hoccleve's *Lerne for to Die* (Oxford, Bodleian Library MS Selden Supra 53) casts the narrator—whom we are invited to read as its author—in the role of a youth gazing on his own expiring body. Startled by the confrontation with his perishing form, the youth crosses his arms over his breast (Plate 13). Ashby Kinch has argued that both text and image here "propos[e] that the very foundation of authorship is a willingness to confront one's own negation in death," a willingness that has "political implications" for the poet who, in death, becomes "malleable to the workings of power."[89] Likewise, a sensitivity to these ideas courses through illuminators' understanding of Gower's metamorphosis for the purpose of his poem. A Book of Hours from circa 1500 generalizes this confrontation by illustrating Psalm 114 in the Office of the Dead (Figure 43). Above the prayer, "Dilexi quoniam exaudi / et Dominus vocem orationis meæ" [I have loved, because the lord will hear the voice of my prayer],[90] is a decaying corpse holding up a mirror before the face of a lusty youth, exhorting him to "penitent self-examination."[91] The young man crosses his arms over his breast as he looks into the mirror to find his despairing reflection. Trussing the erotics of the Office of the Dead with the Virgin's gesture of surrender and assent, this macabre scene envisions the conclusion projected in the author's confessional repudiation of his amatory self.

I have remarked on the struggle illuminators had in reconciling several features of Amans's confession: the narrative of sexual sin with renunciation, the identification of the lover with the elderly author, and the questionable orthodoxy of its proctor. One artist appears to have had the greatest reservations about the last of

FIGURE 43. *Youth before a mirror held by a decaying corpse.* Office of the Dead. Book of Hours, Use of Tours, France, c. 1500. Bibliothèque mazarine MS 507, fol. 113r. © Bibliothèque mazarine.

these three concerns: rather than turning to the pose of *humilitatio*, the limner of Cambridge, St. Catharine's College MS 7 included the face of God peering down from the heavens, perhaps in an effort to neutralize the potential heterodoxy of the scene (Plate 14). Moreover, the miniature he painted appears in the lower margin of the page and "seems to have been an afterthought without space provided."[92]

Signs of scraping in a horizontal strip just above Genius's head likewise betray second thoughts about the propriety of the scene, although the individual who executed the scraping could have been a viewer rather than the limner. Perhaps—and this is admittedly speculation—there were once words of absolution floating above his head. Beyond this example, numerous limners found in the gesture of *humilitatio* a tractable sign that expresses the sheer overabundance of content and conflict in Amans's extended confession to Genius. In the image of the confessant before his confessor, Amans must lay out his thoughts so that they may be redacted; he must lay open his sexual desire only to become chaste; and he must lay to rest his deluded vision of himself in order to author himself anew. In folding Amans's hands over his heart, illuminators channeled these seemingly paradoxical components through allusion to the Virgin's promise of her body to God, the vassal's dedication of his will to his lord, and the dying man's renunciation of his bodily desires. This single gesture captures the repudiation and regeneration of the self within a frame of votive sexual abstention. The youthful lover with arms folded over his chest in London, British Library Egerton MS 1991 (Figure 44), might appear to our eyes as a bland stereotype available to the limner, but directly across from the

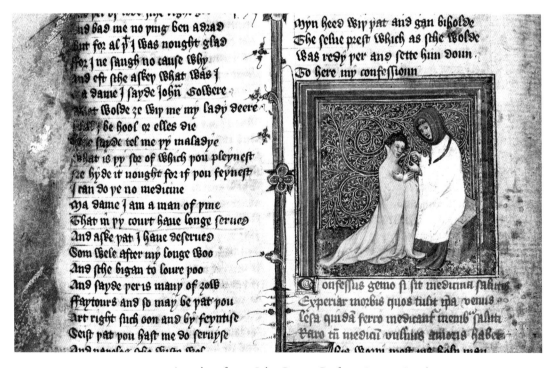

FIGURE 44. *Amans's confession*. John Gower, *Confessio Amantis*, London, c. 1400–1425. London, British Library Egerton MS 1991, fol. 7v (detail). © British Library Board.

image in the adjacent column, the young Amans who explicitly refers to himself as "Gower" is at once the author of the poem and the one who kneels to resign his control over it.[93] Whether young or old, conventionally anonymous or labeled with extratextual biographical detail, the confessant announces, with his chiastic pose, a break with himself and a renunciation of his own authorial agency, not in spite of his identity as author but because of it. Far from defusing the volatile admixture of these elements, the confession miniature is a crucible for the poem's conflict, pushing the protagonist-poet's confrontation with death, sex, and authorship of the self into the foreground.

But I want to suggest here that this image of confession does not need to indicate a close and hermeneutically engaged reading of the *Confessio Amantis*—which is not to say that it is wrong or misses the point of the text or that limners did not read it—rather, that the operations of the book trade were perhaps more responsible for the illuminator's thought process than was a vigilant reading of Gower's poem. It is not that illuminators were extraordinarily sensitive to Gower's entangled aliases; rather, illuminators, like Gower himself, were working through the fundamental conundrum of what exactly an English poet is, a conundrum that appears to have plagued the early copying and dissemination of Middle English poetry. Even a passing knowledge of the contours of the poem would have been enough to set in motion the thought processes that these miniatures disclose.

Furthermore, the visual similarities between the choreographies of confession and book presentation may have proved enticing to the professional image maker, giving further impetus to the conflation of Gower and Amans. In the next chapter, I comment in greater depth on the peculiarities of presentation iconography at this time, but for the present, it is worth recalling Joyce Coleman's opinion that "while the English came to presentation iconography much later than the French, they did interesting things once they got there."[94] Conversely, the same artists did interesting things with presentation iconography even in scenes that do not portray presentation. Common to these images are three essential elements: a kneeling donor, a standing or enthroned recipient, and a book stationed between the two.[95] A final image of confession from New York, Morgan Library and Museum MS M.126, a late copy of the *Confessio Amantis*, bears out well how a comparison between the acts of confession and presentation could be made. This manuscript, which is the subject of Chapter 6, was produced in the 1470s for Edward IV and includes the standard scene of confession but alters its setting enough to produce momentary confusion at what exactly is being portrayed. A unique depiction, the scene transforms the personal moment of solace into a public display (Figure 45). Here, a young chestnut-haired man in red tunic and modish, pointed shoes kneels on a dais before his confessor. The latter, in secular garb, wears a blue and mauve

FIGURE 45. *Amans's confession.* John Gower, *Confessio Amantis*, London, c. 1470.
New York, Morgan Library and Museum MS M.126, fol. 9r (detail).
Purchased by J. Pierpont Morgan (1837–1913), 1903.

robe lined with ermine. He points at Amans while placing his right hand over the
lover's head, in absolution. Behind these two, to the right of the image, are two
witnesses whose presence is at odds with the conventionally private meeting between confessor and confessant.[96] Both observers are young men in brightly colored stockings and short tunics, who seem only to be paying cursory attention to
the activity before them. The conjunction of these elements—kneeling figure,
seated figure, chatty audience, lavish surroundings—suggests at a glance that this is
both ambiguously and appropriately a visualization of the book's envoi.

The construction of this scene articulates the phenomenological and thematic
associations already shared by the acts of confession and book presentation. Both
occasions required the writing or speaking subject to humble himself, on bended
knee(s) to a figure of higher authority, before issuing his offer. In the case of confession, the offer was of an inner book of the self, or a "book of the conscience," as it

came to be known.[97] In the *Cursor Mundi*, a fourteenth-century universal history combined with religious instruction for the laity, the poet writes, "Scrift agh be made wit god for-thoght / þat þou þi dedis sua for-lok / Als þou þam written had in bok"[98] [Confession should be made with good preparation / So that you consider your deeds / As if you had written them in a book], perhaps prompted by the etymological affinity between shriven and scriben [to write].[99] The idea, of course, received early force from Augustine himself, who explicitly referred to his thirteen books as his *Confessiones*,[100] and Gower's colophon to the *Confessio* intimates the deliberateness with which this analogy is deployed, declaring,

> The third book, which is fashioned in the English language . . . distinguishes the ages according to Daniel's prophecy concerning the transformations of the world's kingdoms, from the period of King Nebuchadnezzar up to our own. It also discourses following Aristotle about those matters in which King Alexander was taught, both for his governance of himself and for his instruction elsewhere. But the principal subject of this book has its basis in love and the infatuated passions of lovers. And the name specifically chosen to be applied to it as a title is the *Confessio Amantis* (*Confession of a Lover*).[101]

While Gower summarizes his poem as a virtual encyclopedia of politically useful information and lore, the confession is the organizing principle that converts this compendium into a book.

Like the title, stipulated by the poem's author, the scene of confession does not merely illustrate the moment that Amans "doun falle / On knees" (I.212–13) to make his shrift but stands as an advertisement for the entire work. The organization of figures within the interior space, the lay—practically royal—garb of the confessor, and the presence of talkative spectators all liken the scene to a book presentation. Common in depictions of book presentations is the occurrence of this event among members of the recipient's entourage. The examples are numerous, and the accounts—both poetic and documentary—of book presentations testify to the semipublic nature of the proceedings. It is clear enough, by virtue of the central characters' gestures and the absence of a book, that we are looking at a confession. However, the visual implication is that the lover's confession presented here is also the *Confessio Amantis*.

Surveying the corpus of confession miniatures, we catch sight of limners confirming and denying the right of some vaguely defined notion of the author's "real" self to encroach upon his own work. The subject matter of this miniature demands a confrontation with interiority, a confrontation made more urgent by its contextualization within the most explicitly self-reflective portion of the work, the prologue. Yet in this portion Gower hands over himself, then snatches himself away, placing proxies in his stead, blinking into and out of view. Whatever one's opinion about the postmodernist resonance of late medieval metafiction, Gilles Deleuze and Félix Guattari sound a little like Gower when they write, "The two of us wrote *Anti-Oedipus* together. Since each of us was several there was already quite a crowd. . . . We have been aided, inspired, multiplied."[102] How might an artist represent the men who authored these words? Across the fourteen confession miniatures, illuminators grappled with precisely this question, arriving at diverse answers. In conflating the identities of creator and creature, and in mobilizing visual allusions to the Virgin Annunciate, the humbled retainer, the dying devout, and the officious donor, illuminators endowed the author of the *Confessio Amantis* with a body whose most consistent characteristic is its subjection, its availability to the dictates of someone else.

Returning to the image with which I opened this chapter, we are now in a better position to appreciate one limner's symphonization of the poem's thematic underpinnings with its authorial origins. Before we even begin to read the text, the Taylor folio confronts us with a trio of authorial figures (see Figure 32). This triad does not so much identify the author as they pictorialize, fictionalize, and historicize the sources of writing. The column picture leading the prologue features the lone Statue of Precious Metals, but this body does not speak for itself. To the right, superimposed over the crag is an inscribed—though now illegible—banderole. It is not *of* the statue's world, but it is not completely divorced from it either. The banderole's upper point twists down and in the direction of the statue, while its lower point flips upward and to the right, suggesting that it issues from the mouth of the man posed in the miniature's border. The man, with hoary hair and beard, wears a soft cap and heavy gown, both in the same shade of blue. He glances in the direction of the statue but otherwise remains immobile atop a pink pedestal and beneath the arches of a tabernacular canopy. Although the figure has been identified as an image of Gower, the visual setting indicates a different individual, whose lapidary counterpart stands as witness on the façades and the interiors of Wells, Rochester, Exeter, and countless other cathedrals stamping the landscapes of England and France. He is the prophet Daniel.[103] He is the exegete of signs. Moving our eyes down the page, we come upon the image of a man within the introductory initial to the English text. Set in an ambiguous space, at once interior and exterior, he stands on a grassy ground while motioning with his left hand toward a book-cupboard to the right. His head is no longer present because of a hole in the folio, but it is possible to see the hints of budding flowers that might once have crowned it: a wreath for a laureate? No other features identify the man, although volumes to which he points are probably those identified by the text that this initial begins: "Of hem þat writen us tofore." Here is an image of Gower, without a pen in hand but learned enough to resemble such venerable figures as Jerome and Bartholomeus Anglicus, often accompanied by well-stocked bookcases in late medieval representations.[104]

Arguably the most significant feature of this group is the triangulation envisioned among its constituents. Far from acting as independent performers on the folio's stage, each refers to and participates in a conversation with the others. The inverted S-curve of the banderole links the statue with Daniel, who gazes in its direction. Gower, in the historiated initial, wears a gown of the same blue tone as the prophet, while the green ground and washed pink backdrop replicate the setting in the miniature above.[105] Collected in pictorial congress, the conversation of the three—four, if we count the books that metonymize "hem þat writen us tofore"—contributes to our sense of the origins of the three textual bodies that fill this page: the Latin verses and Middle English poetry in the column, and the Latin prose gloss in the outer margin. And yet, the Taylor folio still does not satisfy. In heaping up specifics, in giving three faces to the voices of poetry,[106] the Taylor folio only obscures the one face we want to attach to the ego of the text. If there is one thing that these representations of authors reveal about Gower-the-author, it is just that: that he is representation. The Taylor folio distorts our perception of the author's a priori existence as author, insisting that where this figure stands in relation to the text depends on the vantage point we choose to assume or, even more likely, the vantage point with which manuscript producers furnish us.

CHAPTER 4

Lydgate *ex Voto*

While Chaucer and Gower are evasive figures in the pictorial records of their major English works, the identity of their much younger contemporary John Lydgate (circa 1371–circa 1449) has more substance in the manuscript corpus of his own poetry. Best known as the poet propagandist, or at least "regal ideologue,"[1] of Lancastrian England, Lydgate was a Benedictine monk of Bury St. Edmunds, with social contacts at the highest levels.[2] His productivity—spurred by the patronage of luminaries like Henry, Prince of Wales, and Humphrey, Duke of Gloucester—was staggering, amounting to over 140,000 lines of verse distributed across histories, hagiographies, a mirror for princes of epic length, short devotional works, occasional pieces for public performance, a popular treatise on health, advice to laundresses, and so on. Essential to his establishment as poet laureate (albeit *avant la lettre*) was Lydgate's habitual self-promotion, executed in frequent references to himself throughout his poetry, often in the voice of a writer consulting his own poetic process: begging the saints or muses for the inspiration he insists he lacks, crediting the *auctores* in whose footsteps he plods, or elevating the dignitaries who condescend to commission his work. Because Lydgate almost always locates himself in an extraliterary position, standing outside of his work's fictive world and admitting responsibility for its facture, his authorial persona never really consolidates in his "I" the pleasing ambiguities that Gower and Chaucer stimulate. And so, despite the prolixity, tedium, and mechanical didacticism alleged against him,[3] scholars pressed to identify the figure who most anticipates the modern author in his public capacity and vaunted valorization have awarded this distinction (if sometimes begrudgingly) to Lydgate.[4]

Still, the manuscript history of Lydgate's works offers an account not quite as confident in its articulation of his authority or even in his relationship to the texts he composed. In her important work on Lydgate's construction as author, Alexandra Gillespie has observed that within manuscript copies of his works, he is often "concealed by his own strategies of bibliographic self-effacement and obfuscation, and by scribal failure to bestow authorizing rubric on his text or to preserve that text's representations of his authorship intact."[5] Gillespie later softened this argument by submitting that there were also some "professional scribes and decorators who preserved 'tracis' and images of Lydgate" as well as "customers willing to spend money on these books [who] ensured that the poet's text was widely known as his 'werke.'"[6] Yet the manner in which this "werke" belonged to him—emerged from him—is not straightforward.

In what follows, I would like to add texture to recent assessments of Lydgate's poetry by examining how visual depictions of Lydgate equivocate on his relationship to the poetry he authored. Like his poetry itself, the images that preface it are, superficially, extraordinary only in quantity: they appear to comprise stock compositions of well-worn iconography, mostly of the "presentation" type. These images are so seemingly innocuous that they have occasioned little analysis.[7] But this putative insipidity is only the product of hindsight. As I will argue here, their classification as author images is proleptic, a label we can only apply in retrospect now that Lydgate's place in literary history has been secured. Although targeting specifically the identification of objects as inaugural (such as the "first" portrait of a king of France), Stephen Perkinson's comments on anachronistic taxonomy are apt here: he cautions against the "difficulty [that] arises when one wishes to identify the first member—the prime image—in a sequence known otherwise through its later manifestations. In order to classify an object as a part of a series of similar objects, an observer must possess an understanding of the criteria that allow those objects to be grouped together, and must be aware of other previously existing objects belonging to that series."[8] In the case of Lydgate, our posterior knowledge of his stature along with a modern category of representation have been mapped onto images that only in retrospect appear uncomplicated: a scene of the author preceding his work. Yet, in none of these images is Lydgate positioned explicitly as an author, and a contemporary audience would not necessarily have perceived him in this role. Just as Perkinson has asked us to reconsider the modern classification as portraiture of images only seen as such in the light of their successors—and in turn has devised a nuanced understanding of medieval portraiture itself—I propose here that we reconsider the modern classification as authorial of Lydgatean representation. I would like, therefore, to put forward a revised generic alignment for depictions of Lydgate that is attuned to "the conceptual horizon that was available to [its] creators"[9] and viewers: namely, as votive. Seeing these images in this light involves only a subtle adjustment but alters dramatically our understanding of the prestige that Lydgate's poetry accrued, the means by which it accrued it, and—as I will explore in the next chapter— the value this prestige had for reading audiences.

Initially, it would seem that there is no better index of Lydgate's success at putting into circulation a stable, historical figure of himself—in other words, an idea of him as author—than the fifteen illuminations that represent him (Figures 46–56, Plates 15–18).[10] In all of these images, Lydgate appears with tonsured head and in the characteristic black habit of the Benedictines. And in all but two of these, he kneels in respect before an authority figure or object of devotion. These images amount to a virtual portrait gallery unmatched by the pictorial record of any of his contemporaries, and it is distributed across a range of different texts, including his *Troy Book*, *Fall of Princes*, *Secrets of the Philosophers*, a hagiography of Saints Edmund and Fremund, and (possibly) the *Fifteen Joys and Sorrows of Our Lady*.[11] Like that of Christine de Pizan, his identity in manuscripts is as "a persona with . . . a very well defined and recognizable, repeatable visual image."[12] The consistency of Lydgate's portrayal across these images is a testament to the early development of the idea "Lydgate," in the Foucauldian sense of authorial coherence: not simply as a proper noun referring to a person but as a descriptor arising from a textual corpus unified in its style, outlook, and preoccupations.[13] This consistency conforms with Robert Meyer-Lee's assertion that "the representation of the *author* as both first-person *speaker* and authoritative, historically specific *person* becomes a normative formal feature" of fifteenth-century poetry.[14]

To be sure, Lydgate's appearance in genuflection aligns well with the nature of his self-promotion, the efficacy of which arose not only from the frequency with which he refers to himself throughout his oeuvre but also from the derogatory language in which these references are couched. Lydgate's routine apologies for his inadequacies alibi the vanity of his self-promotion, and, as Meyer-Lee has argued, it is this paradoxical position that most characterizes his authorial stance—high profile on bended knee, legitimized through the sponsorship of others.[15] Sponsorship is perhaps the most fitting word to describe the motivation behind Lydgate's output—at least as he himself characterizes it. Derek Pearsall once described Lydgate's poetry as "determined by outer needs and pressures,"[16] a view he later affirmed in the even stronger judgment that "there can be no other English poet whose poetic career was so dictated by the circumstances of patrons and commissions. Lydgate can hardly ever have written a poem because it had occurred to him independently to do so."[17]

Exemplifying Lydgate's reliance on sponsorship are the prologue and accompanying prefatory miniatures to his *Troy Book*, which survives in eight illustrated copies.[18] Composed between 1412 and 1420, at the behest of Henry, Prince of Wales (by 1413, Henry V), the extended poem recounts the history of the Trojan

War as a series of exemplary episodes particularly suited to royal education. An early copy of the *Troy Book* opens with a column miniature that depicts a presentation of a book from a kneeling figure in a black habit to a crowned king, enthroned and with a long white beard. In the background, two attendants—one old, one young— observe the proceedings and lend a subtle ceremonial quality to the exchange (Figure 46).[19] This miniature precedes an extended prologue that cuts lofty bombast

FIGURE 46. *Lydgate kneels before Henry V.* John Lydgate, *Troy Book*, London, c. 1420s. Oxford, Bodleian Library MS Rawlinson C 446, fol. 1r (detail). By kind permission of the Bodleian Libraries.

FIGURE 47. *Lydgate kneels before Henry V.* John Lydgate, *Troy Book,* England, c. 1425–1440. London, British Library Cotton MS Augustus A iv, fol. 1r. © British Library Board.

FIGURE 48. *Lydgate kneels before Henry V*. John Lydgate, *Troy Book*, London, c. 1450–1475. Cambridge, Trinity College MS O.5.2, fol. 38r (detail). By permission of the Master and Fellows of Trinity College Cambridge.

with abject humility, by turns invoking the pagan gods and muses to support the narrator's endeavor and excusing his own incapacity for the task. Likewise, in his visual representation Lydgate is at once servile and elevated, kneeling in deference before the king yet welcomed into the privileged royal ambit. Whether indebted to this original scheme, as in this manuscript, or independent of it, illuminators of the *Troy Book* cleaved closely to this composition and iconography, representing Lydgate as a man aligned with royal patronage (Figures 47–49).

It has been observed that it was precisely this royal sponsorship of Lydgate that made his works "desirable cultural commodities."[20] Yet as far as the visual portfolio

FIGURE 49. *Lydgate kneels before Henry V*. John Lydgate, *Troy Book*, London, c. 1420s. Oxford, Bodleian Library, MS Digby 232, fol. 1r (detail). By kind permission of the Bodleian Libraries.

of his output is concerned, this observation is only partially true, and recognizing the limited equivalence between Lydgate's textual self-fashioning and illuminators' visual depictions of him is an important step toward reclassifying Lydgatean representation. In what follows, I trace an alternative tradition of Lydgatean representation, which emerged not in London but rather in Bury St. Edmunds, the site of the abbey where Lydgate was housed and quite possibly a commercial shop that appears to have specialized in the dissemination of the poet's works. This detour offers an alternative framework for the illuminations of Lydgate presenting his work, one that extends beyond the courtly images of presentation to which they have been compared.

While Lydgate is shown unanimously in a pose of deference across all of the illustrated manuscripts of his poems save one, the two major loci for production of illuminated manuscripts containing his works—Bury St. Edmunds and London— are in near-complete disagreement about the identity of the poet's Maecenas.[21] With one or possibly two exceptions (Figures 50 and 52), manuscripts originating in Bury St. Edmunds portray in their opening leaves a monk, presumably Lydgate,

AUTHORS

FIGURE 50. *Lydgate kneels before Humphrey, Duke of Gloucester*. John Lydgate, *Fall of Princes*, Bury St. Edmunds, c. 1450–1460. Montreal, Rare Books and Special Collections, McGill University Library MS 143, fol. 4r (detail).

humbling himself before Edmund, the patron saint of his abbey, and in one case before God (Figures 51, 53, and 54).[22] Although the provision of a holy or divine sponsor is entirely in accord with the devotional and hagiographic works that emerged from this milieu, a manuscript of his nondevotional work, *The Fall of Princes*, positions Lydgate not before Humphrey, Duke of Gloucester, the named patron of the poem, but rather with a fellow Benedictine monk, both abasing themselves before the feet of Saint Edmund (Plate 16). The devout orientation of these Bury manuscripts is evidenced further in another manuscript that shows Lydgate kneeling in supplication to God in the historiated initial to his *Secrets of the Philos-*

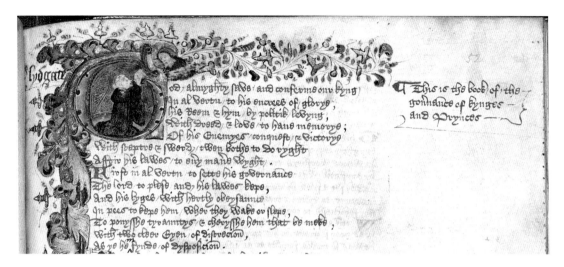

FIGURE 51. *Lydgate kneels beneath God.* John Lydgate, *The Secret of the Philosophers,*
Bury St. Edmunds, c. 1450–1460. London, British Library Harley MS 4826, fol. 52r
(detail). © British Library Board.

FIGURE 52. *Presentation of a book to Henry VI; Henry VI's induction into confraternity.*
John Lydgate, *Lives of Saints Edmund and Fremund,* Bury St. Edmunds, c. 1434–1439.
London, British Library Harley MS 2278, fol. 6r (detail). © British Library Board.

Vpon my knees / riht thus J gan to fere
To the holi martir and meekly gan to preie

D precious charboncle / of martirs alle
O heuenly gemme / saphir of stabilnesse
Thyn heuenly dewh of grace / let Vou falle

FIGURE 53. *Lydgate kneels before the shrine of Saint Edmund.* John Lydgate, *Lives of
Saints Edmund and Fremund,* Bury St. Edmunds, c. 1434–1439. London, British
Library Harley MS 2278, fol. 9r (detail). © British Library Board.

ophers (Figure 51).[23] The opening invocation, "God almyghty save and conserve our
kyng"[24] availed itself to the representation of either God or king, but, in accordance with the pictorial tradition of Lydgate manuscripts originating in Bury, the
illuminator represented God.

Taken together, images of the monk before the king, God, and Saint Edmund
parallel both the piety and opportunism of Lydgate's self-debasing rhetoric. In his
deft analysis of Lydgate's manuscript representations, Sebastian Sobecki argues
that "these manuscripts appear to have made an effort to reconcile the religious and
secular dimensions of Lydgate's identity as a monk-poet," a reconciliation that Lydgate himself attempts in his late poem *The Testament.*[25] Not only does Lydgate appear across copies of his work kneeling before holy figures and royals, Sobecki argues, but he also appears universally in genuflection rather than on a single bent
knee: "Just as kneeling on both legs before Henry turns the king into a saint, so the
fact that there is no distinction in Lydgate's manner of kneeling . . . collapses the

FIGURE 54. *Lydgate kneels before the Shrine of Saint Edmund.* John Lydgate, *Lives of Saints Edmund and Fremund*, Bury St. Edmunds, c. 1450–1460. London, British Library Yates Thompson MS 47, fol. 4r. © British Library Board.

distinction between worldly and spiritual iconography. The secular and the religious pose have become one in a Lydgatean gesture."[26] This account of Lydgate's pictorial self is, in large measure, in line with the poet's self-fashioning and with the reputation he established. Yet, as Gillespie points out, many of these Bury manuscripts efface the poet, naming him in neither text nor rubric, although representing a stereotyped monk who could be him in image.[27] What is more, it is only a minority of these images that show Lydgate with a book in hand and never writing in it. And when Lydgate does depict himself textually, he is "knelyng on my knee" (singular).[28] In other words, it is not certain that the illuminators responsible for these images and their fellow manuscript producers were reverential to Lydgate's self-portrayal or concerned with fashioning Lydgate as an author—that is, the efficient cause of the work.

One way in which Sobecki's analysis and Gillespie's observations can be brought into alignment is to lay aside two assumptions. The first is the assumption that an illuminator would have been engaged in reconciling aspects of Lydgate's career and that he then extrapolated this reconciliation onto the images across the poet's works. In other words, the assumption is that these images are primarily *about* Lydgate. In a detailed examination of presentation iconography in late medieval manuscript culture, Dhira Mahoney concludes that "text and image work together in the function of authorial self-presentation, acting as a double-pronged vehicle by which the author can fashion an identity and a role appropriate to the political or cultural purpose of the work."[29] This statement is certainly applicable to the situation in France at the time, but as I discussed in the Introduction and in Chapter 1, there is little indication of authorial participation in manuscript production in this period in England. While it has been argued that Lydgate had a hand in devising the manuscript copies of his works, no direct evidence supports this claim, while similar evidence for French authors abounds. So, however aptly the images rhyme with the priorities voiced throughout Lydgate's oeuvre, there was little precedent in this period for projecting anything of the author's personal preoccupations onto the images that purport to represent him. Instead, as I will discuss in detail, these images are about the social arrangements that produce literature.

The second assumption to lay aside is the identification of Lydgate as an author in the images. This is not to say that the images do not purport to represent Lydgate, simply that they do not identify him as an author. It has been argued, for example, that the image of Lydgate kneeling in prayer before Saint Edmund (Plate 16), which I discuss in further detail later, "creat[es] an interpretative framework that uses author portrait conventions to construct an authorial narrative and add literary value to the manuscript book."[30] Yet there is nothing in this image that hints at an authorial occupation, activity, or identity. Even Psalter images of David often show him

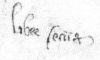

FIGURE 55. *Lydgate and Boccaccio*. John Lydgate, *Fall of Princes*, Bury St. Edmunds (?), c. 1450. San Marino, Huntington Library HM 268, fol. 18r (detail).

with an instrument in his hands or by his side while he implores God.[31] But for Lydgate, the visual trappings of authorship have been eschewed. This point is not merely a matter of pedantry but one of semiotics. The image provides the data with which its viewers are given permission to work, and there are no data on display here that point to the monk's authorial activities. Rather, in these manuscripts, the audi-

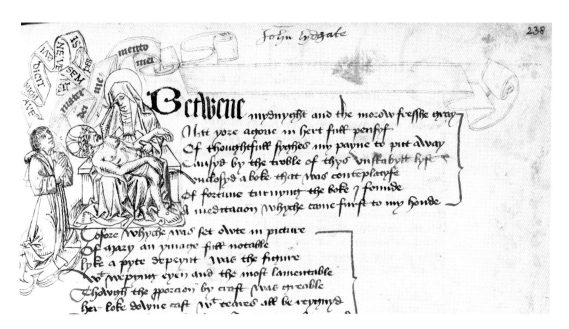

FIGURE 56. *A man kneels before the Pietà*. John Lydgate, *Fifteen Joys and Sorrows of Our Lady*, London, c. 1471–1483. Cambridge, Trinity College MS R.3.21, fol. 238r (detail). By permission of the Master and Fellows of Trinity College Cambridge.

ence encounters an image of a black-habited monk, in accordance with the figure who occasionally names himself as responsible for the work's production and who, at other times, would only have been known to the reader as such through extratextual means. For those who lacked access to this knowledge (and I show later that readers did lack this access), these poems open with either a visual guarantee of the book's acceptability to royal patrons or a reminder to honor God and one of England's premier saints. These are arguments I will now take up in detail.

Lydgate *ex Voto*

These two facts—the representation of the figure who is known to be the author and the visual configuration of him in a nonauthorial guise—present an opportunity to monitor the visual formulation of the English poet in the moments of his construction. A number of examples walk us with halting and tentative steps through vacillating notions of Lydgate's relationship to his works. And although I am for the most part preoccupied with the production of English poetry in London, observing Lydgate's formulation by provincial manuscript producers in Bury St. Edmunds is essential to gaining a more nuanced understanding of the images of

Lydgate before secular authorities, which were produced in the metropolis. In cross-referencing these two traditions of Lydgatean manuscript production, a point of contingence emerges, and it is in this contact zone where we encounter the essence of vernacular literary causation for fifteenth-century illuminators: namely, in the act of self-donation.

An extensively illustrated manuscript of *The Fall of Princes*, produced roughly ten years after Lydgate's death, exhibits almost point for point the indeterminacy of the English poet's condition (Plate 16).[32] As a translation of Laurent de Premierfait's *Des cas des nobles hommes et femmes* (circa 1409)—itself a French translation of Boccaccio's *De casibus virorum illustrium* (circa 1355)—the *Fall* aggravates any attempt to define the nature of Lydgate's responsibility for its content and form. Furthermore, it is, like the *Troy Book*, one of Lydgate's major Lancastrian commissions, in this case, from Humphrey, Duke of Gloucester,[33] and in this respect receives its impetus (its primary efficient cause) from someone other than Lydgate himself.[34] Moreover, Jennifer Summit has pointed out that "Humphrey not only commissioned the work but actively involved himself in its production. . . . Indeed, the poem everywhere registers Humphrey's influence, as he repeatedly interjected himself into the writing process . . . playing the role less of distant patron than of collaborator."[35] Finally, the poem's profile as a compilation disperses its authorial origins, relating in effect a digest of world history as a series of exemplary (and well-known) tragic episodes, from Adam and Eve down to the capture of King John of France by the English in 1356. On the first folio to the poem proper in this manuscript, a half-page miniature precedes the opening lines:

> He that whylom did his dilligence
> the book of bochas in frenssh to translate
> out of latyn he callyd was laurence
> the tyme trewly remembryd and the date
> yeer whan kyng John thorugh his mortal ffate
> was prisowner brought to this regioun
> whanne he first gan on this translacioun.[36]

So the poem inaugurates itself by crediting its originator (Boccaccio) and first translator (Laurent de Premierfait). And although Lydgate does not yet introduce himself into this chain of transmission, he gestures toward his own identity in assuming an English audience in which he includes himself ("to *this* regioun").[37] Yet nothing of these preoccupations is evident in the miniature above.

Rather, the opening illumination sits squarely within the conventions of devotional imagery. For medieval artists and audiences alike, the image of an individual in double genuflection was, first, supplicatory, and the configuration is instantly recognizable: "The venerator or venerators, their hands raised in prayer, knelt to the left and/or right of a central image of Christ, the Madonna and Child, or a hieratically composed narrative scene."[38] In the miniature, two monks in black habit kneel on a grassy mound, flanking the saint to whom they direct their prayers. The saint—Edmund, identifiable by his royal garb and the arrow of his martyrdom, which he holds—is enthroned and frontal, bearing the compositional qualities one would expect from a devotional image, and those which marked "by far the most widespread mode of [Edmund's] representation."[39] Emerging from each monk is a (once-blank) text scroll that floats upward toward the saint. Now, however, the banderole beside the monk to the right bears the words "dan Iohn Lidgate," added by a later hand.[40] Compounding the miniature's allusion to supplicatory iconography is the long history of donative imagery between monastics and the figures of their devotion or allegiance, with the former holding a book in their hands. While Lydgate's position on both knees differentiates him from the lay individuals shown presenting their works to kings and nobles in presentation iconography, he is no different from his religious counterparts, whether it is Matthew Paris at the feet of the Virgin; John Capgrave before Humphrey, Duke of Gloucester; or Giles of Rome before an unidentified prince.[41] Likewise, examples of religious genuflecting while offering books of Scripture to saintly and secular figures are legion. In short, the sight of someone kneeling with a book in hand did not necessarily indicate that the kneeling person was responsible for composing the work inside of the book, and audiences would not have taken this association as read.

But if this is not an author or a patronal or donor portrait—and I think it is uncontroversial to say that it is none of these—then what exactly is it?[42] It seems to me that the miniature models itself most closely on votive portraiture. Like the range of objects and actions that had a donative function, the votive portrait was a commemorative object given to redeem a vow or attest to its fulfillment, beseech favor or simply to pledge one's self to a deity, and the fourteenth and fifteenth centuries in particular saw the "coming of age of the votive portrait."[43] There is no evidence in the image of the saint's thaumaturgic powers, but there need not be. Edmund's fame as a miracle-working saint was indisputable, and additions to his miracles were composed—in Lydgatean style—for later copies of his hagiography.[44] Kathleen Scott has remarked on the paucity of illuminations in England at the time representing supplicants at the feet of a saint, but this is arguably because manuscript illumination was an extraordinary context for *ex votos*, the function of which was, in part, public testimony to a saint's efficacy.[45] Yet this is the closest analog one might find to Lydgate's role here.

Everything about this image confers on the monk a secondary, even instrumental function. Like so many devotional Christian images, this one is recursive, in which "the beholder . . . is offered a target of attention, and at the same time sees attention modeled."[46] Like the images to which Christopher Wood is referring, this "picture theorizes itself through embedded analogons of itself."[47] In this case, the monks offer a guide to contemplative viewing practice and, in their position before Edmund rather than Christ himself, bear witness to the saint's intercessory or thaumaturgic powers and perhaps even his responsibility for the successful completion of the book in which his image appears. The image is not "about" Lydgate in any dedicated sense. It is about the target of his vows. It is more than merely incidental that Lydgate is not the only monk to attend the opening of the poem and that he is not distinguished from his companion. Although the other monk is not identified, and although the illuminator's intentions here are unclear, the image itself diminishes the poet's exceptionality, whichever of the two monks he may be.[48] Without features that allude to his responsibility for the poem at hand, each monk appears exclusively as a supplicant, and it is not at all certain which of the two was originally intended to represent Lydgate. What is more, the presence of two figures who arrange their bodies identically with respect to the enthroned saint ensures the ease of emulation, encouraging the viewer to likewise adopt (if mentally) the same pose. Meditation on these features reduces the possibility that we are gazing on a portrait of the author.

The original blankness of the scrolls arising from the monks also equivocates on the precise function of this image.[49] What could possibly be the significance of something whose primary purpose is to label or to convey a prayer but here does neither?[50] The blankness of the scrolls seems to subvert their deeper function to make visible the word. Here, the artist has not only deprived the viewer of that visible word but has also evidenced his own refusal to effect this conversion. If the votive portrait is a surrogate that enables the individual to achieve the perfection of perpetual devotion to a holy figure, then a portrait with a blank scroll not only fails to achieve its purpose but also admits its own failure.[51] More than anything, this image seems to be the product of vigorous indecision, the kind of reluctance that led the producers of another illustrated copy of *The Fall of Princes* with its initial folios intact to provide no image of Lydgate at all.[52] Instead, the prologue is unillustrated, and the first book is prefaced by a frontispiece medley of vignettes illustrating a variety of tales related in the poem.[53] In the case of the Harley manuscript, the image of the royal Saint Edmund enthroned is perhaps a counter-model to all of the fallen and failed princes described and depicted in the folios to follow, but absent any legitimate reason to place him here, the illuminator conjured a devotional pretext. What if the producers of *The Fall of Princes* simply could not fathom an appropriate posture for the man who was both the originator and not the originator of its content? In one instance the problem is glossed over; in another, a compromise is made.

Yet the inscription that was added to this miniature indicates the rapidity with which a discourse of authorial precedence crystallized at the end of the Middle Ages, and this exemplifies the crux of my argument.[54] Although the miniature was not illuminated to individualize the two monks beyond their age, the later hand that inscribed "dan Iohn Lidgate" on the banderole by the younger monk betrayed a discomfort with the apparent absence of an authorial presence from the scene. In other words, at the time of the manuscript's production, the illuminator was indifferent to the monk's identity, while a later individual—one who appears to have lived within one hundred years of the book's creation—so craved the stamp of validity that the author's name provides that he inscribed it himself, this despite the fact that the banderole emerges from the body of the monk and was initially meant to give him a voice, not a name.

Still, it would be disingenuous to maintain that Lydgate was evicted from his poem. To the contrary, the manuscript opens with a quire containing a table of contents that accords him pride of place, declaring,

> This famous werk to putte in remembraunce
> the sodeyn chaunge tretyng of many estat
> The pedegre and thabbyaunce
> newly translatyd by the poete laureat
> monk of bury namyd John Lydgat
> ffrom lyne of Adam evene distendyng doun
> This table doth conveye with oute varyacioun.[55]

There is a lot to chew on here. Not only does the table open with an assurance of the work's value by dint of its fame; it also aims to impress with the recentness of its Englishing. Its first line also echoes the opening to another work by Lydgate, *Lives of Saints Edmund and Fremund* ("the noble stoory to putte in remembranuce / off Seint Edmond mayde martir and kyng"), a subtle nod to the poet with whose other work the table's author appears to be familiar (Plate 17).[56] And, of course, there is the laureation of Lydgate. Read alone, this opening salvo would appear to stake the kind of claim against which I have been arguing up to this point: specifically, that Lydgate's stature did indeed precede and authenticate the currency of his works. However, the vocabulary of authorship throughout the table of contents counters this claim. For one, the remainder (meaning, from this point on, the entirety) of the table of contents forgets Lydgate, recalling repeatedly instead the *auctor* Boccaccio from whom his secondhand translation derives. To a degree, this representation of the poem is unsurprising: the entries in the table derive in part from the rubrics throughout the manuscript, which themselves issue from Lydgate's text, which tracks its own progress via Boccaccio's movements from story to story.[57] Yet one entry in particular clarifies the distinction between the kinds of authority invested in Lydgate and Boccaccio. In it, the tabulator describes "a chapitle that laurence petrark the laureat poete seying to bochas as it makith mencyoun in this book."[58] Using the same honorific for Petrarch as was used for Lydgate in the opening rubric, the tabulator scores a more granular gradation between the categories of literary authority: while Boccaccio is an *auctor*, Petrarch and Lydgate—that is, poets who wrote in the vernacular—merit the different, though still estimable title of laureate. This distinction (which is perhaps obvious) deserves a fuller study, but it is suggestive here of lingering uncertainties.[59] Together, the table of contents and miniature that usher the reader-viewer into the poem present a confounding cast of characters: there is Boccaccio as *auctor*, Laurent de Premierfait as translator, John Lydgate as laureate, and two anonymous monks kneeling before Saint Edmund.

While it might seem to us now that the relationships between these characters were not especially obscure to reading audiences at the time, scribal additions and reader annotations divulge the confusion they could stir. In another manuscript of *The Fall of Princes*, a final envoi appended to the poem by its scribe conflates the identities of Boccaccio and Lydgate: in deploying ambiguous syntax, the scribe attributes to Boccaccio the black habit that only Lydgate was known to wear.[60] And, whether a result of this envoi, inattention, or any number of other paratextual ambiguities, a sixteenth-century hand noted the following alongside Lydgate's account of his poem's commission: "Bocas translated this book at the commandement of the Duke of Glouc[ester] who was uncle unto henri the syxthe" (Figure 57).[61] Tipped into yet another *Fall of Princes* manuscript is a parchment slip that was a part of the book's original or early binding, identifying its contents as "Bockas in Inglyshe writyn on parchme[n]t."[62] David Lawton is of course right to assert that abrogation of his poetic status is an important tactic that Lydgate deploys throughout his work, and the astute reader may find in Lydgate's deference a decorous strategy for self-promotion. But others took Lydgate at his word and forgot his name.[63]

Even more compelling evidence of Lydgate's precarious relationships to his works are the copies that expunge his presence from the illuminations where one would be expected to find him—particularly in cases where he is present in analog copies. A copy of *Lives of Saints Edmund and Fremund* follows the habits established in other manuscripts produced at Bury by opening with an image of Saint

Edmund (Plate 19). Yet in this manuscript, Saint Edmund is alone, with Lydgate present only on a later folio, in prayer at the saint's tomb. As I have argued elsewhere, this absence was only one element in the manuscript producers' campaign to reconceptualize the hagiography as a surrogate relic for the devout reader.[64] Surrendering to the demands on her piety, the reader placed herself in the space where Lydgate usually is represented, and the paint that has flaked off Edmund's shins and feet divulge her tactile reply. Her interaction with this miniature raises an important question: should we assume that because Lydgate is the (otherwise unacknowledged) author of the work at hand, his image in other manuscripts was intended to convey something different from the reader's vision of herself at Edmund's feet? I think not. The reader's physical engagement with the book urges us to reconsider Lydgate's function before Saint Edmund and God in the images that do include him. Far from constructing him as an author condoned by the patron saint of his abbey, the miniatures station him as a perpetual votary and witness to the saint's miraculous interventions. In an important way, then, the image of Saint Edmund without Lydgate turns the metaleptic situation of Gower-as-Amans (see Chapter 3) out on the devout reader of Lydgate's text. Earlier, it was Gower the author who threatened the insularity of narrative fiction with his ambiguous entrance into the tale from the frame. Now, the reader performs this service, displacing the monk at the feet of the saint whose biography unfolds over the subsequent pages. The author as the (possible) protagonist of his own work is not at all replaceable, but the author as supplicant sanctions his own dismissal. And in this case, the illuminator dismissed him in no uncertain terms.[65]

This dismissal was not relegated to Lydgate's devotional works nor to the manuscripts of his poetry produced in Bury St. Edmunds. A late copy of his *Troy Book* and *Siege of Thebes*, which is the subject of the following chapter, opened originally with an image of an enthroned king surrounded by attendants and supplicants just above the lines "O mighty Mars . . . " (Plate 20).[66] Commissioned by Sir William Herbert and Anne Devereux, the manuscript was possibly a gift of thanksgiving from subjects pardoned by the king they had recently betrayed: on the original opening folio to the manuscript, the married couple appear on both knees at the feet of a king, their hands raised in gestures of supplication.[67] Such pious attention to royals was not so unusual or beyond the powers of popular imagination, and Henry VI attracted it both posthumously and, to a lesser degree, during his own lifetime. A woodcut print in the Bodleian Library, for example, attests to the growing cult of Henry VI at the end of the fifteenth century (Figure 58).[68] In it, the king stands surrounded by pendant votive offerings and genuflecting subjects of a weird array: several bear the instruments of their cured maladies and averted deaths, such as the woman with a dagger through her neck in the foreground. While the wood-

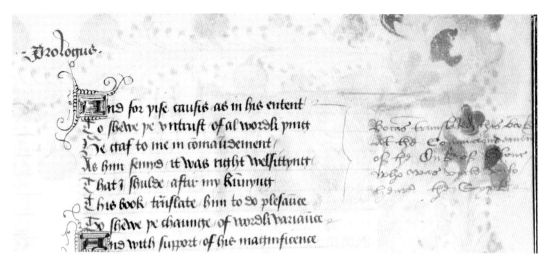

FIGURE 57. Marginal note. John Lydgate, *Fall of Princes,* London, c. 1450–1475. Manchester, Rylands Library MS English 2, fol. 3r (detail). © University of Manchester.

cut is an extreme case, it only carries to a logical culmination the near-apotheosis of kings that was expressed with regularity in public processions and entry ceremonies. Henry VI in particular was likened to Christ before the eyes of Parisians and Londoners, and public participation in these civic events might even have habituated the public—or, as Gordon Kipling has argued, evinced their alacrity to be habituated—to assuming a pose of pious deference before their king.[69] Similarly, in a manuscript presented to an English queen (probably Elizabeth Woodville), the frontispiece features a book passing between the donor and queen, but everything else echoes the conventions of pious representation: the woman genuflects on both knees and the scroll issuing from her contains a phrase from a hymn to the Guardian Angel, "with everlasting joy" (Figure 59).[70] Like the Herberts and the donor before the queen, the figure of Lydgate on both knees before Henry V issues no claims about the monk's contribution to the words contained in the book he presents; it does, however, inform the reader that deference to orthodox, royal authority is a prerequisite to reading the feats and travails of Trojan heroes, a beatified king's hagiography, and tales of princes' downfalls.

Lydgate's displacement and replacement in the images preceding the poems he authored demands that we reconsider the role he plays in the six images that do represent him kneeling before royals. Again, our taxonomization of images according to an iconography categorized as such in modernity blunts our receptiveness to their nuances and points of unfamiliarity to fifteenth-century audiences. It is generally assumed that "presentation" miniatures narrate visually the moment when

FIGURE 58. *Henry VI surrounded by devotees*. Woodcut tipped into a Bible, England,
c. 1490–1500. Oxford, Bodleian Library MS Bodley 277, fol. 376v.
By kind permission of the Bodleian Libraries.

the one kneeling gives something to the one seated. Yet images that represent gift giving in the opposite direction are common in English illumination. Numerous charters show the king enthroned presenting the desired document to the genuflectors by his feet (Figure 60), a tradition visible in English art from at least the fourteenth century.[71] Conversely, the earliest manuscript containing an English

FIGURE 59. *Woman presents a book to Queen Elizabeth Woodville. Hours of the Guardian Angel*, England, c. 1464–1483. Liverpool, Cathedral of Christ MS 6, fol. 5v. By courtesy of Liverpool Cathedral Radcliffe Collection held by Liverpool Hope University.

text that illustrates the presentation of the book to an enthroned king was produced in 1409, one of only a handful of such representations that precede the production of Lydgate's poetic corpus.[72]

Illuminators of such images may even have been keen to play up uncertainties about who is presenting the gift to whom. The Lovell Lectionary features a re-

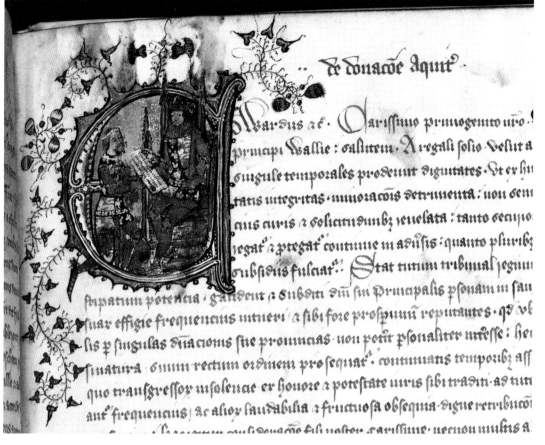

FIGURE 60. *Edward III enthroned presenting a charter to the Black Prince*. Documents relating to the Black Prince's Principality of Aquitaine, England, c. 1375–1400. London, British Library Royal MS 20 D x, fol. 28r (detail). © British Library Board.

nowned scene that shows Lord Lovell himself joined by a canon or book producer, with a book passing between their hands (Figure 61). Yet scholars have puzzled over the direction in which the book moves.[73] Surely the parties involved in the actual gifting and receipt of a book knew exactly which way the book was moving and exactly who was represented in the image. But a certain hedging in the image—a deliberate lack of precision—endows each party, in theory, with as much power to give as to accept. Likewise, even so seemingly transparent an image as the representation of a man kneeling and presenting a book to Henry V in a copy of Hoccleve's *Regiment of Princes* (Figure 62) has precipitated doubt as to the identity of the kneeling man and the direction in which the book passes. Does the scene portray the author Thomas Hoccleve presenting his work to Prince Henry? Or does it represent Prince Henry gifting the book to John Mowbray, second Duke of

FIGURE 61. *Lord Lovell and a monk.* Lovell Lectionary, Glastonbury(?), c. 1400–1410. London, British Library Harley MS 7026, fol. 4v (detail). © British Library Board.

Norfolk, whose arms appear in an illuminated initial beneath the scene?[74] Again, the point is not that the manuscript's contemporaries could not identify the people in the scene; rather, the point is that the scene was produced in a visual environment in which viewers were as accustomed to seeing kneeling figures as donors as they were to seeing them as recipients. In other words, the scene has more resonance than we give it credit for, and it is enunciating in a frequency we have not tuned in to hear.

Another image of Lydgate himself has stimulated similar confusion (Figure 55). In a lavish copy of *The Fall of Princes* (San Marino, Huntington Library HM 268), a miniature illustrates Lydgate in his characteristic black habit, seated beside Boccaccio at his desk. A book passes between the two, and while Seth Lerer asserts that the image imagines the moment when Lydgate presents his work to his "patron" (i.e., Boccaccio), logic suggests to me that the book is passing in the opposite direc-

FIGURE 62. *Book presentation.* Thomas Hoccleve, *The Regiment of Princes*, London, after 1411. London, British Library Arundel MS 38, fol. 37r. © British Library Board.

tion: from the long-dead *auctor* to his follower to translate.[75] Picayune as my correction might seem, it compromises the foundation of Lerer's belief that the image elevates Lydgate and by extension "his status in the poem."[76] Extending this suspicion to the representations of Lydgate at the knees of Henry V and Humphrey, Duke of Gloucester, we might even surmise that the images celebrate the moment not when the poet offers his finished work to his patron but rather the occasion when the patron passes source material to the poet to translate.[77]

All of these questions and observations affirm, with some qualifications, Joyce Coleman's observations regarding the novelties apparent in English images of book presentation. English presentation iconography was not a foreign import; it is in evidence in manuscripts produced in the British Isles for centuries. Instead, its newness to vernacular poetry (because English poetry attributed to named authors in prestige manuscripts was itself new) gave illuminators a reason to ponder its visual semantics and suitability to a new category of literary work. I am not debating what is plainly on view in the miniatures of Lydgate kneeling with a book in his hands; what I am debating is the plain view that what these miniatures narrate is unanimous with what they express. Attempts to infer what these images think about Lydgate-the-author will fail to satisfy because the images are not really about him as an author—not in any conventional sense anyway. Instead, the images are about the social arrangements that generate literature, guarantee its value, and predicate its reception. Lydgate is never once shown independent of a legitimating party. It is always someone else who occasions Lydgate, and illuminators appear to have been unable to imagine his existence independent of the authorities on which the authority of his texts rest. Seen en masse, the images argue that the poems at hand are the product of a willing donation of the monk to others. What is remarkable about this assertion is that the identity of Lydgate's sponsor was more important than his own. Lydgate does not authorize the value of his own works, no matter how august he was as laureate *avant la lettre*; rather he is a perpetual placeholder for the values of submission to those who authorize the act of engaging with the written, vernacular word.[78]

Lydgate: A Coda as Codicil

What happened when the poet lacked explicit sponsorship? Arguably the poem that most compelled the illuminator to consult his own opinions on textual ontology is Lydgate's *Siege of Thebes*, described variously as either a masterful or bungling sequel to *The Canterbury Tales*.[79] Believed to have been written circa 1421–22 without patronage, the *Siege* stages an encounter between the self-named monk of Bury and a group (*the* group) of pilgrims in Canterbury on the evening before they embark on their return to Southwark.[80] Coerced by the host to take a hiatus from his prayers and turn to a different kind of verse, Lydgate is pressed to join the pilgrims' competition and contribute the inaugural tale of their return journey. The *Siege* is, in this sense, an odd free agent of a poem, written at the command of no one real, set in motion by someone fictional, and informed by the unfinished brief of someone dead. Even more playfully, in this sequel Lydgate stages himself as one of Chaucer's creations, yet he also precedes Chaucer by recounting the historical prequel to "The Knight's Tale," the first of the Canterbury suite. Scholars have focused largely on the relationship between Lydgate and Chaucer that the prologue to this poem forges, whether as one of slavish and childlike emulation, Oedipal rivalry, or adroit and self-aggrandizing homage.[81] Rather than add to this lively conversation, I focus instead on what manuscript producers, and in particular two illuminators, made of Lydgate's pilgrim. Two related points emerge from my analysis: the first is that, unanchored by a patron, Lydgate took on a mutable nature and was easily subsumed by his own text, disappearing from it as its author; the second is that, absent a governing agent, the text itself became similarly labile, assuming a variety of generic guises.[82]

A critical moment in the prologue has Lydgate's historical person occupy the place where, initially, only an anonymous pilgrim persona once stood. The narrator first introduces himself to the reader as the stock figure of an ascetic monk, a type antithetical to his hedonistic counterpart in *The Canterbury Tales*. His initial anonymity is advertised by the Host's first words to him, "Daun Pers, Daun Domynyk, Dan Godfrey, or Clement, Ye be welcom newly into Kent."[83] Like Tom, Dick, or Harry, Lydgate could be anyone in orders, a point the Host mocks with his roster of pious names. He proceeds to flesh out the narrator's piteous appearance in a catalog of lack: the monk's bridle has neither studs nor bells, and his face is not just pale but "devoyd of blood."[84] Only then, after establishing that this monk is a no one who could be anyone, does the Host ask his name and where he is from. What follows is an abrupt reversal of the monk's anonymity:

> I answerde my name was Lydgate,
> "Monk of Bery, nygh fyfty yere of age,
> Come to this toune to do my pilgrimage,
> As I have hight. I ha therof no shame."
> "Daun John," quod he, "wel broke ye youre name."[85]

Two notable things have happened here: first, the monk not only provides his surname (Lydgate) and his origin (Bury St. Edmunds), but he also offers his age (nearly fifty years), giving the Host more than he solicited; second, although Lydgate only provides his surname, the Host shortly thereafter refers to him by the first name (John) that he never tendered. The earliest modern editors of the *Siege* noticed this episode, an "inadvertency...of slight importance,"[86] but the opposite has to be true. In a prologue that traces so precisely a silhouette of anonymity only to color it in with the specifics of a fully realized person, the Host's knowledge of Lydgate's first name is a stunning admission that this monk's reputation has preceded him. What other reason could the Host have for knowing that this monk does a credit to his own name ("wel broke ye youre name")? As with the combined prologues and prefatory miniatures in which Lydgate kneels in deference, the historical author has come visiting the world of the text of his making.

This little exchange anticipates precisely the trouble that manuscript producers had in deciding where to place Lydgate in relation to the *Siege of Thebes*. Of the thirty-one extant manuscripts of the *Siege*, only two contain figural illumination of the fifteenth century (although numerous others contain lavish decorative borders and initials), and of these, only one features an image of a monk, presumably Lydgate (Plate 18). The manuscript (London, British Library Arundel MS 119) was copied circa 1425 for William de la Pole, first Duke of Suffolk, whose arms appear after the prologue in a historiated initial at the start of the tale proper.[87] In the first historiated initial of the manuscript—before the first words, "Whan briȝt Phebus"—a simply clad monk in black habit and hat sits astride a pathetic nag that lacks any embellishment beyond its harness and reins: "a complementary visual addition and giving a visage to Lydgate's virtual self."[88] In this, a rare portrayal of John Lydgate that diverges from the conventional image of the man in genuflection, the monk is figured as both character and author following the pretext of the poem and Chaucer's template.

The historiated initial raises a number of questions about Lydgate's relationship to the *Siege of Thebes*. Does the image replace Lydgate's historical integrity with a fictionalized self produced by Chaucer? Does it, alternatively, stake a claim for his autonomy, taking up where his predecessor left off? Another way to think about this would be to ask whether the image signifies its own indexicality to an external referent or whether it is discernibly self-reflexive. Both the mise-en-page and choice of iconography are entirely ambivalent on this point. On the one hand, the monk Lydgate is shown at the opening to the manuscript preceding its prologue. This position distinguishes the Lydgate-pilgrim from his counterparts, including Chaucer, in manuscripts of *The Canterbury Tales*: whereas the latter appear consistently just before their tales and never in the "General Prologue," the Lydgate-pilgrim precedes the imagined world internal to the tale. Nevertheless, Lydgate is in costume, like the pilgrims into whose company he wrote himself. In venturing to depict a pilgrim at the inauguration of this book, the illuminator intensified the ambiguities generated by the poem's account of its own genesis.

Yet other features of this manuscript insist that the miniature was not conceived as a supplement to Lydgate's conceit but rather emerged from the same indecision that was on display in the representations of Lydgate kneeling before Saint Edmund. In her important work on manuscripts of the *Siege of Thebes*, Jane Griffiths has identified the experimental nature of their glosses, particularly in their "rather idiosyncratic interest in questions of authorship."[89] In the case of this copy, the four rubrics that parse the tale are so inconsistent in their treatment of the author as to suggest that the pretext for the *Siege of Thebes* was too effective in its assimilation of Lydgate to his fictional persona. Although Griffiths does not discuss these rubrics, they fit in well with her overarching argument. Appearing between each of its sections, they are

1) Explicit prologus. Incipit pars prima per & c[etera][90]

2) Explicit prima istius codicilli. Incipit secunda pars eisdem[91]

3)   Explicit secunda pars

   John   Lydgate

          Incipit pars tercia[92]

4) Explicit. Here endeth the destruction of Thebes[93]

In the first of these rubrics, the "et cetera" reports on the rubricator's indecision by refusing to specify exactly *who* wrote the first part. The "et cetera" pretends that the identity of the author is common knowledge, so common as to obviate the expenditure of more ink, but its ellipsis only exposes uncertainty on precisely this point. In the second rubric, the deictic phrase "istius codicilli" is explicit in its conception of the manuscript as a supplementary object, a little codicil, appended to something larger to which it owes its legitimacy. As a result, the reader is directed elsewhere in his or her search for the origins of this book. It is only in the third rubric, deep into the book, where Lydgate's name finally appears, oddly positioned and lacking a relationship to the "explicit" and "incipit" that his name flanks. There is something noncommittal in the scribe's concession to an authorial presence, buried as it is deep into the book, fractured, and lacking any syntactical relationship to the explicit and incipit. John Lydgate's name is here, but how it relates to the end of the second part and the beginning of the third is not articulated. Finally, the concluding "explicit" leaves off abruptly without any gesture toward the book's author. The linguistic switch into English—the only "explicit" in the manuscript not in Latin—confuses matters further. If the Latinity of rubrics and marginalia suggests the presence of a compiler or commentator who exerted an organizing presence over the manuscript, then the reversion to English—the language of the body text and marginalia throughout the manuscript—allows for the possibility that it was composed (if not written) by the author himself.

In other cases, manuscript producers simply reduced Lydgate to the character of a tale told by someone else. A manuscript (London, British Library Additional MS 18632) that combines both the *Siege* and Hoccleve's *Regiment of Princes* treats Lydgate through and through as a product of fiction.[94] Although the manuscript is beautifully illuminated, it opens with neither an image of Lydgate, whether as a pilgrim or otherwise, nor a rubric mentioning him. Perhaps more interestingly, the scribe made a telling edit to the opening line of the tale proper. In other manuscripts, John Lydgate acts as the narrator to his own encounter with the Canterbury pilgrims, recalling, "'Sirs,' quod I, 'sith of your curtesye I entred am into your companye.'"[95] In the case of this copy, however, the first person is swapped out for a third-person pronoun: "'Sirs,' quod he."[96] Here, it is not Lydgate recounting his own history as a pilgrim at Canterbury; rather it is some unidentified narrator who relays the words of Lydgate-the-pilgrim. Similarly, the subsequent item in the manuscript, Hoccleve's *Regiment*, contains no announcement of authorial presence at its start.

What the manuscript lacks in authorial presence, it recompenses with an elaborate pictorial and textual colophon on its final folio, amounting to a palimpsest of participants in the book's facture (Plate 21). After the final lines of the *Regiment* is written "Explicit Hoccleve in Aristotele et Egidio de Regimine Principum et Jacobo de Cicele, scilicet Chesse."[97] Hoccleve's *Regiment* is indebted in different ways to the *Secretum secretorum* (believed to have been written by Aristotle for Alexander the Great), Aegidius Romanus, and Jacobus de Cessolis, but the vague preposition "in" does not specify exactly how.[98] Immediately beneath these lines is a small framed miniature of a man seated at a desk with an open book and two other closed volumes tucked away in the cupboard below. Adjacent to the miniature are the words "verba compilatoris ad librum," followed by the envoi "O litil book, who yaf the hardinesse," which is typically found in manuscripts of the *Regiment*.[99] Finally, following the envoi, on the verso, the scribe appended his own verse: "Explicit & cetera / Nunc finem fixi penitet me si male scripsi" [Explicit and so forth / Now the end is composéd; I'm sorry if I poorly wrote it].[100] Of all the figures present on this final folio—Hoccleve, Aegidius, Jacobus, the compiler, and the scribe writing in the first person—it is only the compiler who is endowed with a visual form. Since an "explicit" precedes the envoi, and since the envoi receives its own heading, the question of whether the compiler and Hoccleve are one and the same remains open. Certainly, the scribe's final "explicit et cetera" refuses to answer it, and if it applies to the entire volume, then its evasion shirks the matter of Lydgate's contribution to the *Siege* as well. It seems that the credit being given here is to the judicious compiler assembling an apt collection of texts on good governance. This final equation is complicated even further by the illuminator's unexpected intrusion on to the page. As a "pictorial foil to the scribal colophon," the illuminator's presence "coloniz[es] the written surface of the colophon page" and presents by implication the artist's membership among the manuscript's producers.[101]

Other manuscripts are more brazen in their treatment of Lydgate as Chaucer's creation. Oxford, Bodleian Library MS Bodley 686, is a collection that brings together an altered and abridged text of *The Canterbury Tales* with works by Lydgate, but along the way it forgets momentarily who Lydgate is.[102] Among the text is, unremarkably enough, "The Manciple's Tale" of the crow, which opens with the words "When phebus dwelt."[103] Like all of the other Canterbury tales in this manuscript, this one is accompanied by a running, rubricated head that names its respective teller. But unlike the other instances, the header here is wrong, naming not the Manciple but rather "Lydgate" across the entirety of the tale (Figure 63).[104] David Boyd has remarked that this misattribution "questions an author's status as maker and controller of meaning," the origins of which arise instead from its "collaborative creation and use."[105] In this case, the reliably pious monk Lydgate is a neutralizing presence that lends an overarching orthodoxy to the volume as a whole and in particular demands from the reader a moral response to the scandals related in the tale of the crow. Interestingly enough, scholars have allowed the centrality of Chaucer today to guide their analyses of this manuscript (asking what the inclusion of Lydgate here does for our understanding of Chaucer's text), although it has as much to reveal about Lydgate as it says of his predecessor. It seems to me an extraordinary coincidence that the rubricator appended Lydgate's name to the narrative that opens similarly to Lydgate's own Canterbury tale, the *Siege of Thebes*. Like "The Manciple's Tale," which begins "when phebus dwelt," the *Siege of Thebes* opens with the words "whan bright Phebus." Did the scribe think he was rubricating the *Siege of Thebes*, placed here, among the other *Canterbury Tales*? This is unlikely since the same hand that named Lydgate above also added the incipit, "and bygynneþ a lytel tretis of þe crowe."[106] What is most likely is that the rubricator came across a manuscript containing Lydgate's *Siege of Thebes*, possibly one of the many that includes it along with *The Canterbury Tales* and recalled that Lydgate was responsible for a tale that begins with a reference to Phebus. However coincidental, Lydgate's "inadvertency" in the prologue to the *Siege*, which I discussed earlier, anticipated precisely this scribal infelicity, acknowledging that to be a poet was to send one's name into the world. Whether an honest mistake by a scribe who genuinely took Lydgate for a pilgrim or a shrewd calculation that his reader would be none the wiser, this misattribution attests to the amorphousness of Lydgate's extratextual reputation, as easily recalled as a pilgrim as not.

FIGURE 63. "The Manciple's Tale" ascribed to Lydgate. Chaucer, *Canterbury Tales*, London, c. 1425–1450. Oxford, Bodleian Library MS Bodley 686, fol. 173v (detail). By kind permission of the Bodleian Libraries.

Released from the patron's ballast and rather loose on the facticity of its own author, the *Siege of Thebes* was reinterpreted according to the other texts to which it was variously yoked. It found a home not only with the other tales of Canterbury or mirrors for princes; it was also featured alongside a travel narrative, which frames the Theban story as a part of the description of an exotic locale. Cambridge, Trinity College MS R.4.20, originally contained two texts: *The Travels of John Mandeville* and Lydgate's *Siege*. The former opens with a historiated initial of a knight with sword and armor, presumably Mandeville, whose identity as a knight is reinforced in the explicit to the narrative: the illuminator was obviously not uninterested in the knightly protagonist of the text.[107] In contrast, the historiated initial that introduces the *Siege* frames a walled city, a tiny emblem for the starring location (Figure 64).[108] The centrality of place is reiterated in the final explicit to the poem, which pronounces, "here is now eendid the fynal distruccioun of myghty Thebes. that strong & royal toun."[109] Similar to Lydgate's omission from miniatures preceding his other works, this historiated initial dispenses with him in order to redraft a new generic alignment for the poem. In this case, the walled city of

Thebes moves from its place in the background of a tragic history to the fore-ground, like one of the many distant lands to which the knight pictured on the manuscript's opening page journeyed. As a pilgrim, Lydgate is a traveler just like Mandeville, but not to the location in which his tale is set. Lacking the credibility of an eyewitness, Lydgate is made to retreat into the pages of the manuscript, a pilgrim like the others noted in the margins.

Compared with the manuscripts that omit an image of Lydgate or otherwise obscure his authorship of the *Siege*, the depiction of him astride a horse riding into his own text (Plate 18) looks more ambitious than "a complementary visual addition [that gives] a visage to Lydgate's virtual self."[110] If we assume that our task is only to evaluate whether the historiated initial conforms to Lydgate's self-presentation as a Canterbury pilgrim, then our task ends in a simple "yes." But if instead we are curious about manuscript producers' larger enterprise to negotiate the place of the English author within a culture undecided as to how authoritative he is, then the historiated initial of a monk astride his horse takes on far greater significance. The manuscript was made for William de la Pole, husband to Chau-cer's only granddaughter. We can only guess what his personal motivations were in commissioning it, and there is even the possibility that it was the presentation copy from Lydgate to him. There is no evidence either way, so speculations on the mean-

FIGURE 64. *Thebes as a walled city*. John Lydgate, *Siege of Thebes*, England, c. 1450. Cambridge, Trinity College MS R.4.20, fol. 89r (detail). By permission of the Master and Fellows of Trinity College Cambridge.

ings of its presentation or commission will fail to have any payoff. What is certain is that someone paid for the *Siege* to be illuminated and disposed elegantly with an apparatus that included headers, explicits, incipits, and ample glossing. Given this directive, the producers of the manuscript strained under its impositions. And the placement of the pilgrim Lydgate and the arms of William de la Pole may be the most revealing sign of this challenge. Although the owner's arms can occupy a number of positions in a manuscript, placement somewhere on the opening page is the most common for obvious reasons. Yet here, representation of the pilgrim Lydgate took priority and occurs before the start of the prologue. If the illuminator had been indifferent to Lydgate's responsibility for the *Siege*, then the second initial that opens the tale proper would have made for an entirely appropriate space for his image, particularly since the initial letter *S* precedes a first-person account of indirect speech ("'Sirs,' quod I"). Instead, locating a monk astride a haggard nag on the opening folio to the manuscript, the illuminator figured Lydgate as both continuator and initiator, creator and creature, refusing to answer the question of who the "I" of the text really is. Neither embodying the pose and dignity of an *auctor* nor displaced from the space where an *auctor* might be seen composing his work, Lydgate occupied the indeterminate position that, as I have been arguing, defined the English poet of this period.

I have advanced in this and the preceding two chapters that limners—far from elevating the status of the English poet by portraying him in image—formalized equivocality as the English poet's defining feature. But the consequence of this argument is not to dispute the fact of canon formation in this period nor the fact of its formation on the backs of three particular authors: the sheer number of manuscripts and early attempts even to collect Chaucer's, Gower's, and Lydgate's works together in compilations indicate that indeed manuscript producers and audiences found worth, value, and more important, cultural coherence in the English poetry of these three men—whether they were aware of the names of the authors responsible for them or not. Instead, the consequence of this argument is that the wellspring of these books' authority lay not with the authors responsible for composing the texts copied into them. And because of this, the source of each poem's claims to cultural value lay in copy-specific features that cannot be generalized in the way that the author's name as a guarantor of authenticity can be extrapolated onto all copies of his works. In the chapters to follow, I offer two case studies that explore the means by which limners redrafted the terms in which poetry by Gower and Lydgate was to be read in the second half of the fifteenth century.

PART III

HISTORIES

CHAPTER 5

History in the Making
Lydgate's *Troy Book*

Representational practices encoded in works of art continue to be
encoded in their commentaries.
—HOLLY, *Past Looking,* xiii

Each book is an expression of the modes of production that produced it,
which it in turn reproduces across time as its own production.
—KUSKIN, "The Archival Imagination," 85

Illuminations of John Lydgate seize on the aporia that energizes his poetry. The aporia, as I laid out in the previous chapter, is Lydgate's flamboyant derogation of himself. Visibly absent, the author is a tenuous point of consolidation within his works, at once anchoring them to the moments of their production and releasing them to later use. Maura Nolan expresses well the forces of these two poles in Lydgate's verse, which "simultaneously demands to be read in topical terms . . . and resists topicality by asserting its status as a distinctively literary object."[1] In short, every one of Lydgate's major poems services a momentary need and forecasts its future use.

In this and the following chapters, I elucidate the implications of arguments staked out in the earlier parts of this book by examining these incidents of future use. In the preceding chapters, I showed that the illuminator was integral to the rising prestige of English verse, not only as a figure who endowed manuscripts with the cachet afforded by lavish illumination but also as a figure who processed and gave visual form to one of the central challenges posed by the composition of the first major works of Middle English verse by named authors—that is, defining the identities of these authors for reading and viewing audiences and, by extension, defining the terms on which their words were to be read. As illuminators had it, in the literary economy of late medieval London, it was not the author who guaranteed the currency of his works. To the contrary, the English poet was often a symptom of the text rather than its cause. If the author was shown, it was in situations of his departure or in conditions that question his relationship to the text of his making. Made apparent in order to be dismissed or absorbed into the fictions of their texts, English authors, as portrayed by illuminators, licensed the adaptability and exploitation of their verse.

This dismissal had real stakes. The cultural project to establish a national, vernacular literature was, by many accounts, a political one, set against the background of two defining conflicts with lasting impact: the Hundred Years' War (1337–1453) and the domestic conflicts that eventually culminated in the Wars of the Roses (1455–1485).[2] Literary scholars have examined expertly the political engagement of the *Confessio Amantis* and Lydgate's "mega-compositions," the *Troy Book* and *The Fall of Princes*, in the moments of their production and early reception.[3] But the recruitment of these works into the factional conflicts that cleaved England in the second half of the fifteenth century has occasioned little comment.[4] Gower and Lydgate may have addressed directly Kings Richard II and Henry IV, and Henry V and Henry VI, respectively, but later manuscript producers redacted these conversations to speak on behalf of different interlocutors. As the Hundred Years' War limped to its ruinous conclusion for the English, and as the domestic conflict over the throne known as the Wars of the Roses gathered momentum, the aristocracy and gentry who participated in both enlisted English verse and in particular the objects that mediated it for self-aggrandizing purposes.

It is an obvious point—but one worth articulating—that in a manuscript culture, poetry is not merely a product of the moment in which the text was composed but is equally a product of the subsequent moments of its reinscription, no matter how distant they lie from textual inception. In the belief that these subsequent moments of inscription are as important to the history of Middle English poetry as are the moments of textual conception, I will, in this chapter and the one that follows, translate the political preoccupations written into Lydgate's *Troy Book* and Gower's *Confessio Amantis* to the objects that transmitted such preoccupations in the second half of the fifteenth century and move away from the limited ambits of their original composition. This maneuver is sanctioned by the manuscripts themselves (which were produced in this later period), by the poets who wrote themselves and their dismissal into the copies of their works, and by the illuminators who made this dismissal a foregrounding aspect of their authorial identities. Visible to make apparent their own self-negation, Lydgate and Gower licensed a succession of future readers to find in their poetry—and exploit—"a privileged aesthetic zone for the encounter of past and present, sameness and difference."[5]

The coincidence of timely utility and timeless adaptability is a conspicuous feature of this chapter's central object of focus: a majestic manuscript containing Lydgate's *Troy Book* and *Siege of Thebes*, begun in London and left incomplete between roughly 1457 and 1461, continued around 1490, and complemented with further texts and illuminations in one or possibly two separate stages between circa 1516 and 1530 (London, British Library Royal MS 18 D ii).[6] Each of these components is visible as a stratum within the book, predicated on the contours of the layers that preceded it. Attentiveness to stratigraphy is essential to understanding manuscripts in general, but this attentiveness is particularly apposite to the Royal volume because it was, for so long, a permeable object that "grew in stages and/or was put together from originally separate pieces."[7] In its stratigraphic profile, the Royal manuscript demands the archaeological approach that I take here, with some qualifications.[8] While the "archaeology of the book" proceeds with faith in the forensic candor of the physical book, I recognize that history and the archive—textualized bodies themselves—offer at times salutary agitations to an overly positivistic habit of thought. My purpose in excavating this manuscript is not to uncover the lapidary facts of its original program and intentions. Rather, I want to chart the "rhetorical mandates"[9] of the manuscript's original plan, mandates that produced a sequence of productive acts within the manuscript itself. The Royal *Troy Book* and *Siege of Thebes*, in this respect, realizes literally the operational strategy of reuse, which I described in the Introduction as essential to manuscript production in this context. Because my primary interest is in one of the strata, that is, the manuscript's fifteenth-century core, part of what I will be doing here is examining the later layers for what they reveal about the first layer's dictates and demands.

Both Michael Ann Holly and William Kuskin offer, from the perspectives of their different disciplines, congenial frameworks for achieving this goal. Holly—in her salve to art history's existential crisis in the wake of poststructuralism—argues that images prefigure their receptions and legislate the statements that can be said plausibly about them.[10] Similarly, Kuskin, in an account of what he terms "symbolic bibliography" has shown that material texts dictate and archive the contours of the objects that mediate them across time.[11] As a succession of commentaries on itself—of bibliographical autoexegesis—the Royal manuscript repeatedly reifies inflections of its natal self, the germ of which lay in both the Lydgatean verse it channels and the first manuscripts that materialized it. Future readers of this manuscript were also future producers, and in the act of production, they poached from the field of possibilities circumscribed by the Royal manuscript's earliest shape.[12] My understanding of these additions to the manuscript, then, builds upon revisionist accounts of miscellaneity in manuscript production, by vesting the organizing agency and impulses not only in the individuals responsible for gathering together the components of or commissioning a book but also in the suasions of the manuscript's earliest material.[13]

My aim in this chapter is to dislodge Lydgate's verse from the occasion of its production (1412–1420) and immediate reception, and instead install it in the subsequent moments that it imagines, gauging a manuscript's submission and resistance to the text's predicates. While the text of the *Troy Book* stages itself as an address from Lydgate to his patron, Prince Henry (by the time of the poem's conclusion eight years later, Henry V), its manuscript copies orchestrate conversations between different groups of people, groups that Lydgate could have projected only hazily might be the audience for his poem. This orchestration climaxes in the Royal manuscript. When spouses William Herbert, first Earl of Pembroke (d. 1469),[14] and Anne Devereux (d. circa 1486) commissioned this manuscript for the king (either Henry VI or Edward IV), they induced a number of different historical moments to speak both to the present and to the future. In its later additions, the future responded so that this manuscript remakes over and over again both history and current events. By the time of its abortive production between the late 1450s and 1461, Henry V was dead, Lydgate was deceased, Henry VI was deposed, and Edward IV was crowned: everything about this manuscript is buffeted by unexpected scenarios and the kind of change about which its text warns. Within Lydgate's *poem* is a confrontation between the protracted moment of its composition and the ancient moments of the history it relates. But within the *manuscript* is an imbrication of epochs that proves the rule of historical utility that the text advocates and that the dismissal of its author authorizes.

The Megacomposition and the Manuscript

There are risks in reading the works of Lydgate without a sensitivity to the objects that represent them and the circumstances of their circulation. One of these risks is a wan return on the investment of time in reading such long poems, and centuries of this insensitivity consigned Lydgate to the trash heap of literary history. Since the tail end of the last century, critics have carried out a formidable salvage operation of Lydgate's works, but it is still routine to advertise one's own hard-won mastery of the poet by relishing his defects.[15] Derek Pearsall is arguably the most enthusiastic contributor to the genre of Lydgate-contumely, the modern champion of Lydgate who resurrected the study of his corpus only to pummel it at every opportunity. Early in his career, Pearsall opined that when Lydgate "has to select for himself, he is undiscriminating, and the result is flatulence."[16] Forty years of scholarly devotion have not changed his mind, so that in 2005 he condemned "Lydgate's halting versification, his turgid syntax, his repetitiveness, his long-windedness and verbosity . . . [as] not matters of debate."[17] With friends like these . . .

Yet these slanders lose their purchase when Lydgate's works are brought into contact with circumstance and situation. Lydgate, like so many poets of the fifteenth century, demands a historicist approach because his works are so explicitly anchored to the events of their commission and publication. Helen Cooper has gone so far as to observe that peculiar to fifteenth-century poetry is its "active and often fully conscious participation in the moment of its own production."[18] New Historicist reclamations of Lydgate by David Lawton, Nigel Mortimer, Lee Patterson, and Paul Strohm all express, in a variety of flavors, the political interventions of the poet's work, often straining under the mercurial demands of the Lancastrian regime it was conscripted to serve. What emerges from these studies is a poet who is either cleverer than previous scholars have thought or cleverer than even Lydgate himself thought, but one infinitely less dull than earlier generations alleged.[19]

Complementing this historicist approach are materially engaged studies that examine Lydgate's words on the walls, in the performances, and even adorning the edible confections that mediated them. Both Maura Nolan and Claire Sponsler, in what the latter called a "provocation to literary history," recover Lydgate's shorter and dramatic compositions as an exhilarating body of work, as rich in its "situatedness" as it is bland in modern printed volumes.[20] Likewise, Amy Appleford reads Lydgate's *Daunce of Poulys* (circa 1430)—a *Danse Macabre* combining text and image on painted panels hung in the cemetery cloister of St. Paul's Cathedral—as a canny commentary on London's structures of authority, a reading dependent on its monumental placement and presentation.[21] Similarly, Jennifer Floyd's recovery of the extracodical life of Lydgate's works on textiles for patrons like the Armourers Guild shows the poet participating in corporate bodies' "transformations in power and social relations within their own real, local communities."[22] Lydgate frequently disparages, if disingenuously, the insipidity of his rhetoric, as bereft of color and in shades of "white and blak."[23] But in their earliest habitats, Lydgate's works were rarely encountered in so drab a habit.

Curiously, interest in "material Lydgate" has not extended to the illuminated copies of his works. This neglect is especially surprising in light of the centrality of the manuscript in medieval literary studies today. In 1983, A. S. G. Edwards implored scholars to attend to the manuscripts of Lydgate's poetry, drawing special attention to the significance of their illumination.[24] Yet in the decades since this plea was issued, precious little has been written about the illuminated copies of his works.[25] Perhaps the reason for this neglect is our resistance to the idea that illumination is anything but a supplement to the manuscript page in English literary culture. Where royals, merchants, and civic bureaucrats (i.e., patrons) can be counted on to infuse the tedium with the meaningfulness of its exertions, illuminations "may . . . come out of a richly indeterminate verbal culture of complete ignorance. Their sole function may indeed be to heighten the value of the book as a saleable product and an object of prestige to the owner."[26] This statement echoes, if with an added edge of condescension, Stephen Nichols's characterization of illumination as "important supplements": important, but nevertheless supplemental to text.[27] It is not that the *Troy Book* and *Siege of Thebes* require programs of illumination and pages of sprawling proportions in order to be read, and there are certainly medieval copies of both poems that are neither lusciously adorned nor commodiously disposed; but if we are to pursue Lydgate's literature with any degree of interest in its relationship to the audiences who read it and—notably—whom Lydgate invokes and forecasts, what is required is the recognition that neither illumination nor any other aspect of the physical book is supplemental to its meaning.

The manuscript that is the central object of this chapter (London, British Library Royal MS 18 D ii) is a case in point. It is a hulking volume of 395 by 280 millimeters with a sumptuous opening page (Plates 20 and 22). As such, it is a semipublic object that demands to be read from a lectern or propped on a table, an object that announces its gravitas in its dimensions alone.[28] Judging by the style of its earliest illuminations, it appears to have originated in London and engages fully with the iconographic repertoire that dominates nondevotional, London-produced manuscripts of the time. Its two original, core texts (*Troy Book* and *Siege of Thebes*) appear to have been copied by one scribe, who wrote out the text in a hybrid Anglicana hand, combining both formal textura and secretary elements.[29] Cadels wrapped around an ascender on folio 87v contain letters that spell out the word "boswelle," which could be the scribe's name,[30] and the ascenders of other letters on folio 133v appear to spell out "SVBEEM," possibly an error for the dictaminal acronym "SVBEEV."[31] No further information about the manuscript's scribe is known, but whoever he was, he copied the text into a manuscript that was designed to contain twenty-five miniatures: twelve miniatures to accompany the *Troy Book* and thirteen miniatures to accompany the *Siege of Thebes*. Only five of these miniatures were painted during this first campaign.[32] It was not until the end of the century that a further three were painted[33] and the first quarter of the sixteenth century that all of the remaining spaces for miniatures were filled and further texts were added.[34] In its intellectual rigor and programmatic coherence over seventy years of production, this megamanuscript makes history several times over.

What we encounter in the Royal manuscript is a multigenerational project to take up the invitation to adaptive reading practices that both the *Troy Book* and *Siege of Thebes* tender. This invitation is extended first in the prologue to the *Troy Book*, which telegraphs the overlapping temporalities that readers find repeatedly throughout the poem. Even from its opening lines, the distant, sweeping past and the precise, momentary now make startling contact. First, the narrator channels a Virgilian spirit, invoking Mars as the masculine muse to galvanize his labors.[35] And after several dozen lines appealing to a cast of pagan deities, he then reveals that their help is solicited not to inspire a song of ancient myth but rather to assist him in fulfilling a recent brief.

> The eldest sone of the noble kyng,
> Henri the firþe, of knyȝthood welle and spryng,
> In whom is schewed of what stok he grewe;
> The rotys vertu þus can the frute renewe—
> In euery part the tarage is the same,
> Lyche his fader of maneris and of name,
> In sothefastnesse, this no tale is,
> Callid Henry ek, the worthy prynce of Walys,
> To whom schal longe by successioun
> For to gouerne Brutys Albyoun,
> Whyche me comaunded the drery pitus fate
> Of hem of Troye in englysche to translate,
> The sege also, and the destruccioun,
> Lyche as the Latyn maketh mencioun,
> For to compyle and after Guydo make,
> So as I coude, and write it for his sake,
> By-cause he wolde that to hyȝe and lowe
> The noble story openly wer knowe
> In oure tonge, aboute in euery age,
> And y-writen as wel in oure langage
> As in latyn and in frensche it is;
> That of the story þe trouthe we nat mys
> No more than doth eche other nacioun:
> This was the fyn of his entencioun.[36]

While sowing the virtues of his patron, Lydgate plants in this encomium the seed of his historiographic method. In describing Henry, he draws out the irruption of the past in the present, embodied and inscribed in the form of the prince. Henry, Prince of Wales, shares both his father's manners and his name. But this inheritance extends far beyond the ligature joining two generations. In addition to his name and his manner, Henry IV will bequeath to his son the ancient realm of Brutus's Albion, and this is, in one sense, the raison d'être for this book. From the twelfth century, the legend of Troy was favored reading among Europe's nobility, who traced their descent back to the exiled heroes of Troy.[37] But through the alchemy of Lydgate's allusion, England is more than the heir of an ancient founder; it remains to this day consubstantial with the land that Brutus founded.

Furthermore, the past takes up residence in Lydgate's own activities as translator and poet. In the *Troy Book*'s best-known example of periphrasis, Lydgate piles diverse systems for measuring time on one another, all to tell us that he began his work at exactly four o'clock in the afternoon on Monday, October 31, 1412:

> And of the tyme to make mencioun,
> Whan I be-gan of this translacioun,
> It was the ȝere, sothely for to seyne,
> Fourtene complete of his fadris regne,
> The tyme of ȝere, schortly to conclude,
> Whan twenty grees was Phebus altitude,
> The hour whan he made his stedis drawe
> His rosen chariet lowe vnder the wawe
> To bathe his bemys in the wawy see,
> Tressed lyche gold, as men myȝte see,
> Passyng the bordure of oure occian;
> And Lucyna, of colour pale and wan
> Hir cold arysyng in Octobre gan to dyȝt,
> Tenchace the dirknesse of the frosty nyȝt,
> In the myddes of the scorpion;
> And Esperus gan to wester dovn,
> To haste hir cours ageyn þe morwe graye;
> And Lucifer, the nyȝt to voyde awaye,
> Is callyd than, messanger of day,
> Our emysperye to put out of affraye
> Wyth briȝt kalendis of Phebus vpryst schene
> Out of the boundis Proserpina the quene,
> Wher Pluto dwelleth, the dirke regioun,

And the furies haue her mansioun;
Til after sone Appollo lyst nat tarie
To take soiour in the Sagittarie.[38]

Mustered in this calculation is a parade of metrics, from the regnal year, solar elevation, and the seasonal clock to the Julian calendar and the zodiac's time of myth.
Lydgate may be flexing his vocabulary here, but he is also giving us a digest of his
historiographic method. On this passage, Karen E. Smyth remarks that a "poly-
phonic time discourse is clearly operating throughout this text, at once insisting on
precise moments and dates, on clear demarcations of historical periods, yet also
blurring temporal boundaries, enlarging timescales and moments, forcing and en-
abling past and present times to synthesize. . . . Such a layered perspective in Lydgate's text promotes more of a focus on the mediation of history than the authenticity of it."[39] This attitude to time is one that James Simpson detects throughout
Lydgate's oeuvre, referring to it as a reformist textual practice, which "is a sufficiently wide and complex dispersal of jurisdictional power as to disallow any cultural monopoly."[40] In other words, none of the temporal regimes is prioritized over
another, to the effect that each cultural matrix invoked has as much authority as
any other to inform the reader's experience and interpretation of any given passage,
chronology be damned. In his exorbitance, Lydgate was expressing what Georges
Didi-Huberman, Alexander Nagel, Christopher Wood, and others refer to alternatively as anachronistic or anachronic history, where "deliberate anachronisms, juxtapositions of historically distinct styles in a single picture and stagings of historical events in contemporary settings, fed back into the symbolic machinery of the
pictures."[41] The *Troy Book*, declaredly about a specific set of events in ancient time,
has all the labile requisites to resonate infinitely with future scenarios.

In addition to offering an account of the Trojan War, Lydgate's *Troy Book* (and
the *Siege of Thebes*) situates itself within the conventions of the *Fürstenspiegel*, or
Mirror for Princes genre, a genre that, in its late medieval iteration, was designed to
appeal to such adaptive practices.[42] The typical format, beginning with their earliest
iterations in the fourth century, is a catalog and description of moral traits pre-
scribed to a king for the benefit of the common weal. A commonplace in these
works is the admonition to study the examples of one's forebears. For example, the
anonymous translator of a Middle English version of the *Secretum secretorum* advises his reader to "haue in thy remembraunce the deedys of thy forefadirs, and how
they haue lyued. And therby shalt thou see and lerne many good ensaumples which
shall yeue the vndirstandinge of diuers thinges that may falle in tyme comynge."[43]
Still, these treatises offer few concrete illustrations of moral behavior and are largely
generalized commendations of such values as largesse, magnanimity, pity, and so on.

It was in the fifteenth century that the *Fürstenspiegel* genre underwent a profound change, under the influence of Boccaccio's *De casibus virorum illustrium*—a compilation of exempla recounting the catastrophic fates of princes subject to the rotation of Fortune's wheel. During this period, translators of Boccaccio's *De casibus* strove to offer their patrons strategies to avert the ends that befell their historical protagonists. Incorporating the hortatory elements of the *Fürstenspiegel* into their translations, authors such as Laurent de Premierfait and John Lydgate counseled that by keeping the examples of past princes in mind and by implementing proper countermeasures in the realm of political action, one might forestall his own fall.[44] In contrast to the recommendation cited above, which only advises that by learning from past examples a king might *understand* or come to terms with his future, these new works intimate that one might have the power to evade the cycle of misfortune. It is in this new, "*Des cas* genre" of Mirrors—or "*Des cas* Mirrors"— where the two discourses of politics and history effect a stable marriage. As a genre, it "is effectively Janus-faced, looking back respectfully at the predecessors to whom a debt is owed, and looking for opportunities to resituate its admonitions in a new political context."[45] Yet resituations did not occur simply because readers colluded with the text to adapt its admonitions to personal circumstance. Such resituations were aided by the manuscript production process, which provided opportunities for adaptation and renewal each time a new copy was produced. Committing an act of resituation is precisely what the patrons of the Royal manuscript did when they commissioned a copy of the *Troy Book* and *Siege of Thebes*.

The *Troy Book* for the King

The opening page to the Royal *Troy Book* initiates through an imbrication of visual allusions the process of personal adaptation that became the hallmark of this manuscript (Plate 22). Dovetailing both the precision and capaciousness of the *Troy Book* itself, the page confronts the viewer with a moment in time not accounted for in—but certainly solicited by—the introduction to the poem. Set above the first line is a large column miniature that frames the image of a king in majesty. He sits on a throne covered in blue damask and with a fringed canopy above, and he wears the accessories of state: a large golden crown, an orb in one hand, and a scepter in the other. Flanking the throne are three attendants on either side, one carrying the king's sword and the other a thin white staff. At the king's feet are two kneeling figures, identifiable by the coats of arms that adorn their garments, the heraldic escutchons in between the text columns, and the mottos that garnish the page: William Herbert and Anne Devereux, whom he had married in 1449.[46] Of course, neither William, nor Anne, nor the king before whom they kneel has any direct relationship to Lydgate's poem.

It is the choreography of the couple's supplication that lends this image both its specificity and a vagueness that betrays the politically erratic moment in which this manuscript was produced. Like Lydgate himself in other introductory initials to the *Troy Book*, both Herbert and Devereux kneel before the feet of the king. But, as others have pointed out, there are a number of features that make this image unusual as a prefatory miniature to the poem: the Herberts' genuflection on both knees, the position of their hands, the absence of a book, the hierarchically enlarged figure of the king, and the hieratic gold background. Together these features persuaded Lesley Lawton to remark that the scene represents "an act of homage, an affirmation of loyalty," which Kathleen Scott sees as "fit[ting] well with the historical circumstances of Howard's [sic] change from the Lancastrian (Henry VI) to the Yorkist (Edward IV) cause at this period."[47] But whether the king represented on this page is Henry VI or Edward IV is not straightforward.

What the heraldry and mottos provide in specifics about the patrons of this manuscript, the throne, crown, orb, and scepter contribute to uncertainties about their intended recipient.[48] And this brings me to the matter of the manuscript's patronage and commission. The arms with which Herbert's and Devereux's surcoats and gown are emblazoned give the miniature a *terminus post quem* of 1449, the year in which William Herbert and Anne Devereux were married; and the absence of the Garter, which Herbert received in 1462, gives it a probable *terminus ante quem*. In contrast to the attributes that guarantee our knowledge of the manuscript's donors, an absence of denotative accessories characterizes the depicted king. Furthermore, our ability to identify the king as Henry VI or his opponent and successor Edward IV is aggravated by the vexed relationship that William Herbert had with both of these kings. Knighted by Henry VI in 1452, Herbert went on with his brother-in-law, Sir Walter Devereux, to attract allegations of treason in 1456.[49] Long tied to the Yorkist retinue, both Herbert and Devereux were viewed by the Lancastrians as critical sources of support worth courting. Consequently, on June 7, 1457, Henry VI pardoned Herbert, while freeing Devereux from jail a year later.[50] And while in February 1460, Herbert was raised to the offices of sheriff of Glamorgan and Morganno, four months later he drew another indictment, which yet again culminated in Herbert's pardon in June 26, 1460.[51] Herbert may have fallen off the Lancastrian wagon too often to convince us that he would have invested in a lavish manuscript to guarantee his loyalty, but it is possible that during this turbulent period precisely this sort of investment was necessary.[52]

Like the stereotyped features of the enthroned king, the postures of William and Anne admit alternate readings. In one reading, the scene assumes all of the features of devotional imagery I described in the previous chapter, displacing Christ in Majesty with the new king and substituting the Herberts for Lydgate. In another reading, which hangs on the specifics of current events, it is the moment of Herbert's and Devereux's pardon, cast as an actual meeting between king and subjects, which is presented on this page—even if an actual meeting between them is unlikely ever to have occurred.[53] This identification relies on both the Herberts' pose as well as the configuration of the king as the embodiment of justice and distributor of mercy. Textual and visual representations of royal pardon are not often explicit about the physical conditions or actions of the accused, but they do often imagine—whether through a fictional encounter between king and subjects in literature or through the use of performative language in actual petitions—a direct address to the king. As one might expect, the parties seeking pardon present themselves in attitudes of abjection, certainly in line with the poses of the Herberts on the Royal manuscript's page.[54] When, for example, Sir Bors begs his brother for mercy in *Le Morte d'Arthur*, he "kneled downe tofore hym to the erthe, and cryed hym mercy, holdyng up both hys hondis."[55] Like Sir Bors, Herbert kneels in perpetuity, suppliant to and pardoned by the king he may have betrayed, while Anne Devereux, in her family's arms, deputizes the brother who also received the king's grace.

In accordance with the Herberts' posture, which couches the ritual gestures of humility within the visual language of supplication, the king's accessories and attendants enframe the image within the conventions of legal procedure. Not long before the Royal manuscript was produced, images of the king in manuscripts of the *Nova Statuta*, all produced in London or possibly Westminster, began to endow him not only with a floriated scepter but also with an orb (Figure 65).[56] Likewise, the king can be seen holding both scepter and orb on the first membrane to the Common Plea Rolls from 1463.[57] Rosemarie McGerr has posited that these images "might be read as highlighting the king's sovereignty as lawgiver," while Anthony Musson has pointed to such unindividualized, "a-historical" images of kings as promoting "continuity of the monarchy and of the common law tradition itself and thereby provide legitimacy not only for their rule, but their judicial policy."[58] If, as I suggested in Chapter 1, the idiosyncrasies of English literary illustration in this period were informed in part by the institutional documents that scriveners–cum–literary scribes and limners were accustomed to copying and adorning, then there may be some logic from the production side of things to the ways in which this miniature ushers the visual standards of book presentation in the direction of the petitionary process. Just as fifteenth-century authors appropriated the political languages found in parliamentary records and polemic—as Sarah Peverley has shown—limners, too, interpolated the visual topoi of institutional documents into their literary work.[59] Both the appearance of the Herberts and the king enact the procedures of supplication and pardon that limners would have been more than capable of supplying and that would have been in the Herberts' interest to bring before the eyes of the king.

More important than the king's identification is his notional presence in the book. Whether the king portrayed on this page is Henry VI or Edward IV, and whether the scene reports an affirmation of devotion or entreaty for pardon, the manuscript never made it to the intended target of this pledge or plea. Not only was it left incomplete, but it also bears signs of a hasty and unexpected cessation: in addition to the incompletion of the majority of its miniatures, the large initials on the final three folios of the *Siege of Thebes* were not decorated until later.[60] The apparent suddenness of its incompletion gives an impression of the manuscript's engagement in real time with the political culture that its opening miniature acknowledges. Deposed in March 1461, Henry VI was no longer a necessary font of grace to tap; crowned in June but confronted by a number of challenges in the first year of his reign, Edward IV may have communicated his distaste for or inability to accept such literary gifts at the time. Of course, any number of other reasons could have arrested work on the manuscript before 1462.

FIGURE 65. *Edward I enthroned. Cartae Antiquae*, London or Westminster, c. 1475. London, Metropolitan Archives COL/CS/01/007, fol. 37r (detail).

Reckoning the date of the manuscript's production, far from offering an answer, only produces questions. What does this act of pardon or affirmation of loyalty have to do with the *Troy Book*? Why would this book be an appropriate vehicle for such a commemoration? What were an illuminator and scribe to make of the brief to tack such a targeted statement on to Lydgate's opening verses? As these questions insinuate, establishing a more precise dating of the manuscript's original production is not, in itself, the point here. The point is that the opening page embodies a pictorial mode of address that generates these questions. In furnishing an image that at once contains the particular (Herbert and Devereux) and the type (king), the miniature stages a strange convergence that exemplifies the usefulness of both Kuskin's and Holly's formulations, outlined at the beginning of this chapter. The "representational practices encoded" in the manuscripts of the *Troy Book*, its "bibliographical elements [that] operate in concert with its rhetoric"[61] implore commentators and book producers—who in this case are one and the same—to file yet another moment in time in the temporal dossier that Lydgate opened. To put an even finer point on it, if Lydgate and his manuscript producers could and did intercalate contemporary figures and preoccupations both textually and visually into the relation of history, then so could subsequent patrons and producers of *Troy Book* manuscripts.

Whereas miniatures that preface other texts are often tautologous, the specifically commemorative function of this opening page in the Royal manuscript introduces a disjunction. In what I am calling tautologous scenes of book presentation, the image of a book passing between two parties contains within it a reminiscent, or aspirational, portrait of the object that is its own support (i.e., the book). Similarly locking the text in a specific moment, frontispiece or prefatory miniatures are often, from the perspective of the book, biographical. They are about the moment the book traveled between donor and recipient (if a presentation miniature), the instance of the book's conception (if an author portrait), or the time of an event that the book itself recounts (if a narrative scene). The frontispiece "really belongs there, as it sets up the reasons for the book's existence."[62] But here, in the Royal manuscript, is an image in which the book, its contents, and its author are moot, supplanted by the patrons and their own agenda. In supplanting the author, it defies the basic premise of the frontispiece, what Kathryn Rudy has called "the most intentional of illuminations."[63]

This exploitation is not so much opportunistic on the Herberts' part as it is attentive to the long-term expectations written into the poem by Lydgate and instilled in its form by producers of earlier *Troy Book* manuscripts. While it may seem like the Herberts had this image placed here in spite of Lydgate's text, the image itself pays reverence to other images of Lydgate in *Troy Book* manuscripts. I commented at length in the previous chapter on the construction of Lydgate as a figure who donates himself to his clients. The illuminator of the Royal manuscript appears to have assimilated the precedent that these earlier images set, finding in Lydgate's *ex voto* inspiration for the Herberts' perpetual submission. The Herberts' humble self-promotion here is savvy, then, committed in a literary environment in which it was appropriate for personal dispatches to piggyback on the messages of someone else's text.

The Royal manuscript is not unique in this regard. Most illuminated manuscripts of the *Troy Book* feature some token of individualization or an invitation to it, which wrests the book from the narrow compass of its origins. It may be the roughly drawn and added arms of the vintners in one manuscript,[64] the blank space for arms in another,[65] the arms of Sir Thomas Chaworth (d. 1458) and Isabella de Ailesbury in another copy,[66] or the full-page display of arms of the Carent family at the back of yet another.[67] An additional copy is so prodigious in escutcheons—included in illuminated borders, added to the margins of pages, and even painted on the manuscript's fore-edge—that they have daunted attempts at identification.[68] The addition or accommodation for personal marks of rank and pedigree may not sound like a noteworthy feature of any illuminated book, but it is the common *absence* of heraldry that distinguishes deluxe manuscripts of Middle English verse. A. I. Doyle and M. B. Parkes note that "the incorporation or addition of such insignia in the illumination of vernacular manuscripts in England seems to have been less common than might be expected when one considers that a significant portion of potential customers must have been armigerous."[69] Manuscripts of the *Confessio Amantis* and *The Canterbury Tales*—the two other major works of concern in this study—are notably poor in heraldry.[70] The consistency with which illuminated *Troy Book* manuscripts feature the arms of their owners suggests that the work itself encouraged personal appropriation.

The Royal manuscript, then, does nothing less than to follow Lydgate's recommendation to contravene the linear movement of time and to interject one's self and one's preoccupations into it. Even in its original form, the Royal manuscript organized history out of chronological order. With the *Troy Book* preceding the *Siege of Thebes*, the latter, though prehistory, is presented as a sequel (this despite the fact that Lydgate weaves into the *Troy Book*'s prologue events recounted in the *Siege*).[71] There is nothing gratuitous or inappropriate about this arrangement. Throughout the *Troy Book*, history zigs and zags in erratic maneuvers. Lydgate interrupts himself at times to provide sneak previews of the conclusions to the stories he is in the midst of recounting, sometimes inserting into these nested accounts references to earlier events that preceded them both. Despite the poem's plodding pace, one gets whiplash from its reversals of chronological direction. It is a coincidence that a similarly abrupt revolution of Fortune's Wheel—precisely that which the *Troy Book* advertises as a historical principle—resulted in the deposition of Henry VI by Edward IV (either of whom was its intended recipient) and the initial incompletion of the Royal manuscript. But, as I will now go on to discuss, it was by no means serendipitous that subsequent owners of the book augmented it repeatedly, tangling the book's already complicated reticulation of past and present.

The Best-Laid Plans

As a series of accretions, the Royal manuscript comments on itself and offers an archive of its own production history. In considering the manuscript as a form of bibliographical autoexegesis, my purpose is to continue in my deployment of Holly's and Kuskin's theses and to evaluate the degree to which later additions to the manuscript respond with sensitivity to the plan that was prospected by its producers in the middle of the fifteenth century, which in turn was predicated on features of Lydgate's own verse. That plan, as I argued above, was to aggrandize the utilitarian view of history that characterizes both the *Troy Book* and the *Siege of Thebes*, redirecting both their blandishments and commendations toward a royal recipient different from the one they originally targeted. But since this plan was disturbed and only resumed in two separate stints several decades later, we have the rare opportunity to monitor its success in foregrounding later responses, embodied in the manuscript's additions.

The concept of the plan is a useful one for conceptualizing these outcomes because it accounts for the decisiveness or agency of makers in plotting future activity, while circumventing the vexations of intention. I do not know what the producers of the Royal manuscript intended—that is, what they willed or desired—but I can infer from material evidence what they planned. Moreover, a plan is a cross-temporal act: when one plans to achieve something, one has to take the imaginative leap of envisioning that future conditions will accommodate a particular action. In its cross-temporal nature, the plan (as a concept) coheres thematically with the overarching concerns of both the *Troy Book* and the *Siege of Thebes* with the ability of the past to exert a decisive impact on future scenarios—and for those future scenarios to engage meaningfully with the past. Plans are also useful because they imply, more than does intention, an empirically observable effort—apart from desire or will—made in the present to facilitate a future action. To adopt a framework from Stephen Murray, who proposes that a "*plot* . . . implies control and manipulation of space," a *plan* implies control and manipulation of time (and the events that occur within it).[72] Embedded in the Royal manuscript's mid-fifteenth-century plan is a form of prospecting, a predictive act that is unsettled in its outcomes but adequately scoped to bear on future results.

This first campaign departs from earlier traditions of illumination for both the *Troy Book* and the *Siege of Thebes*, but this departure is prefigured by a modest pictorial divergence from the poem's organization in these earlier manuscripts. On the one hand, all pre-1450 manuscripts of the *Troy Book* (with figural illumination) were designed to contain one miniature at the head of the prologue and one in each of the five books, as, for example, in London, British Library Cotton MS Augustus A iv (Figures 66–70); and no manuscript of the *Siege of Thebes* contains a cycle of narrative illustration.[73] So by virtue of the number of miniatures it contains—twelve in the *Troy Book* and thirteen in the *Siege of Thebes*—the Royal manuscript deviates from its predecessors and the *divisio* of the poet's text.[74] On the

FIGURE 66. *Peleus implores the gods to restore the Thessalians*. John Lydgate, *Troy Book*, England, c. 1425–1440. London, British Library Cotton MS Augustus A iv, fol. 2r (detail). © British Library Board.

FIGURE 67. *Priam receives news of Troy's destruction*. John Lydgate, *Troy Book*, England, c. 1425–1440. London, British Library Cotton MS Augustus A iv, fol. 25v (detail). © British Library Board.

other hand, even earlier copies have an odd relationship to Lydgate's system for organizing the *Troy Book*: while most miniatures mark the beginning of each new book, the miniatures that precede Book II in three manuscripts appear two hundred lines into it, in order to precede immediately the first narrative it relates.[75] Lesley Lawton suggested that "the miniatures were primarily used as visual indices, a means of dividing the text up into units in the manner suggested by Laurent de Premierfait" (and by extension Lydgate), but the placement of the miniature in Book II rather than at its commencement suggests that *divisio* was not the only determinant.[76]

The Royal manuscript moves even further away from the organizational priorities of Lydgate's text while remaining deferential to the ideas of opportunistic reading practices it encourages. The number of miniatures allocated to both the

FIGURE 68. *Hector slays Patroclus*. John Lydgate, *Troy Book*, England, c. 1425–1440. London, British Library Cotton MS Augustus A iv, fol. 69r (detail). © British Library Board.

Troy Book and the *Siege of Thebes* may be telling. Presumably, when the Herberts commissioned this manuscript, they stipulated that they were willing to pay a particular price, and this price was sufficient to pay for twenty-five miniatures. Yet the distribution is odd: at roughly four times the length of the *Siege of Thebes*, the *Troy Book* ought, by rights, to have a greater number of miniatures. That this is not the

FIGURE 69. *Hector's tomb.* John Lydgate, *Troy Book,* England, c. 1425–1440. London, British Library Cotton MS Augustus A iv, fol. 98v (detail). © British Library Board.

case points less to a personally or patronally motivated desire to have certain episodes illustrated than to the mechanics of a commercial transaction. In other words, the number of spaces for miniatures that were allotted to each looks very much like the patrons put in an order for a specific number of images, the distribution of which was left to the book's producers to interpret.

I am stressing the decisiveness of the producers here because, in its unfinished state after 1461, the manuscript featured five completed miniatures that betray signs of an illuminator who attempted to coordinate a thematically coherent program but who, perhaps owing to the nature of his profession, ultimately buckled under pressures that this brief presented. The five miniatures completed during the first campaign introduce the prologue and all but one of the five books of the *Troy Book.*

FIGURE 70. *Ajax complains to Agamemnon.* John Lydgate, *Troy Book*, England,
c. 1425–1440. London, British Library Cotton MS Augustus A iv, fol. 135r (detail).
© British Library Board.

In other words, the miniatures that were painted are those that appear as part of the
program of illumination in other, earlier manuscripts of the *Troy Book*. Unfinished
were the additional miniatures that had never before been represented in other
manuscripts of the *Troy Book* and the entire cycle of miniatures for the *Siege of Thebes*, which had never before been illuminated. Effectively, I think the illuminator
went through the manuscript, completing images that appeared in his exemplar and
leaving for later the others, which would require more thought and planning.[77]

Yet even the images that were painted by 1461 do not replicate predecessors
from earlier *Troy Book* manuscripts, which illustrate and punctuate the narrative
progression of the war. Instead, at work in this initial cycle of illustrations is an
endeavor to centralize the role of a singular monarch in history and suggest the
invulnerability of royal institutions to larger political strife—an endeavor that signals the illuminator's awareness of the manuscript's intended, royal recipient. Here,

Lydgate's "mirror" was initially planned to reflect a reassuring image back at the king, softening the text's hortatory profile. This endeavor materializes in both programmatic differences as well as in the illuminator's adjustments to the form of similar scenes in earlier manuscripts. As far as programmatic differences are concerned, the Royal manuscript does not contain—nor was planned to contain—a miniature before the start of Book I. The four earlier manuscripts that do precede the first book with a miniature all depict the first episode in the book, as in London, British Library Cotton MS Augustus A iv (Figure 66).[78] In it, the entire race of Thessalians—save their king, Peleus—is exterminated by the gods. Devastated, King Peleus retreats to the woods, where he implores the gods to restore his people by transforming the ants swarming on a nearby tree into warlike men. This, the gods abide. It is easy to speculate that this episode was omitted in the Royal manuscript—designed as a gift for the king—because it portrays not only genocide but also a king we later learn is rotten to the core. Naturally we cannot visit the intentions of the individuals who decided to omit this scene. What is important is that this omission itself betrays the manuscript producers' liberal attitude toward exemplars and the organization of the poem.

Similarly, larger differences in composition across the remaining four miniatures contribute toward an inflection of the poem's identity. Earlier manuscripts of the *Troy Book* include a miniature not at the beginning of Book II but rather before line 203, which shows King Priam besieging a town and receiving the news of Troy's destruction from a messenger (Figure 67).[79] Instead, the Royal manuscript features a representation of Fortune's Wheel before the first line of the book (Figure 71).[80] The Royal manuscript is not alone in this respect, and the two other illuminated manuscripts of the *Troy Book* from the second half of the fifteenth century also contain the image of Fortune (Figures 72 and 73).[81] These other two images innovate the iconography of Fortune's Wheel, showing a crowned female personification of Fortune who sweeps up a multitude of kings and other members of the social order in the indiscriminate rotation of her wheel, flinging them from its rim. In contrast, the miniature in the Royal manuscript reduces Fortune's compass to the institution of the monarchy and is in this respect a far more traditional image. While warning against the susceptibility of individual kings to the vicissitudes of Fortune, the image insists regardless on the perpetuity and stability of the royal office—only a single man clings to each sixth of Fortune's wheel, either ejected from his seat at its pinnacle or waiting his turn to reign, but nevertheless affixed to an everlasting cycle of singular rule. In opting for this more conventional image, the Royal illuminator augmented the *Troy Book*'s profile as a Mirror for Princes.

In addition, all of the miniatures from the first campaign—with one exception—portray a single king as the protagonist of the scene's action, even when ear-

FIGURE 71. *Wheel of Fortune.* John Lydgate, *Troy Book*, London, c. 1457–1461.
London, British Library Royal MS 18 D ii, fol. 30v. © British Library Board.

FIGURE 72. *Wheel of Fortune*. John Lydgate, *Troy Book*, London, c. 1450. Manchester, Rylands Library MS English 1, fol. 28v. © University of Manchester.

Their shippes were with gold and tress lade
Wherof in hert ther wer woundir glade
And for thei had ont so wele them born
To conquer Troye and so few I lorn
Of their meneye then thank their godes all
And of the grace that to them is befall
ffor with the tress that thei hane w them brought
full many poer was made vp of nought
Thruthout the lond ther was such abundance
So moch goode and so moch suffisaunce
that no wyght had amongs them no nede
And many a day this blissful lyfe thei lede
ffrom yere to yere by resolucion
And for their manhode and their hygh renoun
their honour ran round the world about
ffor their knyhthode i for thei were so wyse
And till the stoun list agayn deuise
In this mater forther to procede
Shath the fauour of wyse godhede
I Wolle me rest for a litell space
And than vpbon with support of w grace
forth accomplissh ne of I subietoke
And her and ende of the first boke

make nott with quaking hond for drede
Wonse for fere oft yon that shal it rede
lift ye allas oft hastie morion
ne Wol nat haue noo compassion
Pitee ne ronthe vpon my richnesse
Poslie besechinges to yonpe gentilnesse
Of mercy wonke both me and fair
Wher that ye finde that I faule ae eyn
fforto coriect oe ye fiythir flitt
fforto yonpe grace I Wolle al comitt

An isto loco presenti liber modo plenariam
petit suam finem Et immediate de secundo
St Aliquid Dicendum

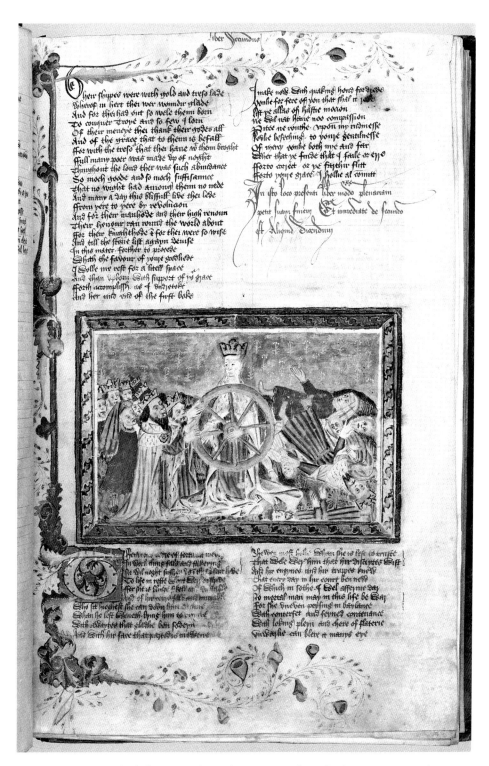

Fortunes a werre oft fortunal mev
in Work thing fals and slithering
he Wil nought suffre i til tal lastie lese
To life in rest Wont hay destined
ffor she is slivde skell ar oo haste
i of hir coucion his mvianhl
Who it hiesthest she can doun hni i thine
When he left Beneth lying him to reyne
With Wherher that slastie his redeyn
hir with hir face that paytchis misvenve

The Wer most hulle: Whan she is lese to rruse
that Wele Wey him thei hir Inserrtes list
Ass hir engynes and hir traytes knens
that every day in hir court ben ness
Of Which in sothe I Wel affermie day
No mortal man may in this life be Way
for she euen perfsing in barlaunce
With conterfet and feyned contenaunce
Will loking pleyni ans chere of flaterie
Sinkeslie can blere a maupis eye

FIGURE 73. *Wheel of Fortune.* John Lydgate, *Troy Book,* England, c. 1450. New York,
Morgan Library and Museum MS M.876, fol. 6r.

FIGURE 74. *Hector slays Patroclus.* John Lydgate, *Troy Book*, London, c. 1457–1461.
London, British Library Royal MS 18 D ii, fol. 66v (detail).
© British Library Board.

lier manuscripts populate a scene with more than one crowned figure (Plate 22,
Figure 71, Figures 74–76). What is more, this king is remarkably similar in facial
features to the monarch on the manuscript's original introductory page. As a result,
the frontal figure of an enthroned king, which greeted the audience on opening to
the first page of the manuscript, recurs as a binding visual motif across its illustrative program. But the seven miniatures left unfinished by the manuscript's first illuminator might have scuppered any plan to furnish so coherent a program: installed
before episodes illustrating either the story of Troilus or episodes of Greek treachery, they failed to offer an opportunity for commentary on monarchic constancy.
Perhaps more time would have afforded the illuminator a chance to work out these

FIGURE 75. *Agamemnon in council and Achilles in bed*. John Lydgate, *Troy Book*,
London, c. 1457–1461. London, British Library Royal MS 18 D ii, fol. 95r (detail).
© British Library Board.

compositions or locate suitable models in order to produce a satisfactorily coherent program, but this time was cut short.

Whatever the illuminator's intentions were for the remaining miniatures, the
program he left behind, including the completed miniatures and blank spaces, bequeathed to its later owners a mandate in the form of the manuscript's plan. In other
words, the original producers of this manuscript inflected Lydgate's poem in the ways
I recounted above, and what remains to be shown is how (or whether) this inflection
informed the actions of its later contributors. English manuscripts from this period
commonly hand down blanks to their owners and later readers, some of which were
filled, and many of which were not.[82] Yet so far as we can tell, these blanks did not

FIGURE 76. *Ajax complains to Agamemnon*. John Lydgate, *Troy Book*, London,
c. 1457–1461. London, British Library Royal MS 18 D ii, fol. 128r (detail).
© British Library Board.

register as such a failure as to impede the book's use and passage into circulation, and
often blanks offered opportunities for elaboration. Just as the lack of closure in so
much literature of this period accommodated expansion and "play" by successive
writers, so the incompletion and permeability of the manuscript accommodated material additions that enhanced its meaningfulness to subsequent generations.[83]

The portions of the Royal manuscript that were completed and augmented in
the later fifteenth and early sixteenth centuries resume the personal appropriation
of literature encouraged by the manuscript's opening page. After they suspended
work on the manuscript, the Herbert family appears to have done what anyone
who has sunk money into a stalled project would do. They kept the investment for
themselves, retaining as their own the manuscript that was originally intended for

FIGURE 77. *Calchas and the Brass Horse.* John Lydgate, *Troy Book*, London, c. 1490. London, British Library Royal MS 18 D ii, fol. 74r (detail). © British Library Board.

the king. Yet the manuscript did not slumber on a shelf or molder away in the attic only to be forgotten. Rather, three of the remaining twenty miniatures that were incomplete were painted by a professional illuminator, and based on their style, this continuation appears to have been carried out by an illuminator working (or trained) in London around the last decade of the fifteenth century (Figures 77–79).[84] Also at this time, the emblem of Henry Percy, fourth Earl of Northumberland (d. 1489),[85] was appended to the final page of the *Siege of Thebes*—at the time, the final page of the manuscript that contained text (Figure 80).[86] The completion of the three miniatures in particular is odd. For one, they were not contiguous. Although they were (mis)bound together in the sixteenth century (more on which I discuss later in the chapter), in the manuscript's original state, these three minia-

FIGURE 78. *The Trojan Horse*. John Lydgate, *Troy Book*, London, c. 1490. London, British Library Royal MS 18 D ii, fol. 75r (detail). © British Library Board.

tures were folios apart from one another and are not, sequentially, the first three miniatures left unfinished. The illuminator jumped around, and it is possible that the manuscript's owners directed him to do so, although this is not at all certain. All that we can extrapolate reasonably is the general context in which the miniatures were painted.

Treating the added emblem as both an artifact of archaeological interest and as a historical document provides this general context, while dissuading us from attempting a contextual analysis of what these miniatures mean. Around 1476, Henry Percy married Maud (d. circa 1485), the daughter of the manuscript's original patrons, William Herbert and Anne Devereux. So, like Maud herself, the Royal manuscript probably migrated to the Percy household around 1476, after which the emblem was

FIGURE 79. *The Greeks' tents toppled*. John Lydgate, *Troy Book*, London, c. 1490.
London, British Library Royal MS 18 D ii, fol. 82v (detail). © British Library Board.

added to the final page, bookending the manuscript with the insignia of the Herbert family at the introduction and the Percy family at the conclusion. Because of the emblem's misalignment with the text block on the left side, it seems likely that the illuminator painted it without first unbinding the manuscript and was therefore prevented from executing his work so closely to the gutter.[87] The distinctions in pigments and possibly even hands across the three added miniatures supports this hypothesis: working with a bound book, the illuminator (or illuminators) would have had to wait for each image to dry before moving on to paint the next one, a period in which he (or they) might have mixed or procured new paints while carrying out other work. In other words, since these circa-1490 contributions toward finishing the illustrative cycle were carried out while the manuscript was intact, they are not un-

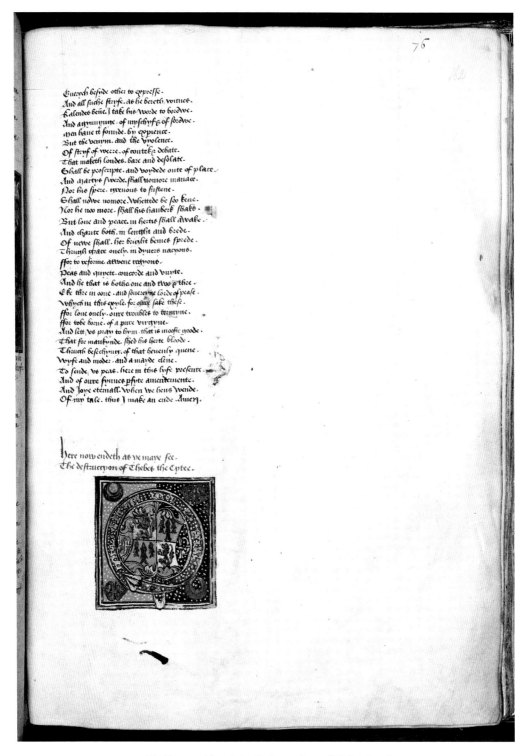

FIGURE 80. *The Percy emblem*. John Lydgate, *Siege of Thebes*, London, c. 1490.
London, British Library Royal MS 18 D ii, fol. 162r. © British Library Board.

contiguous because of a binding error at this stage or simply because the illuminator(s) approached unbound quires in a haphazard order. They are uncontiguous probably because these particular spaces for miniatures were chosen for completion.

This uncertainty—all of the probables and likelihoods—is disappointing, surely. But I think the nature of these additions, similar to the opening miniature, should discourage us from cherry-picking historical events in an attempt to track down precisely the right one that would seem to have spurred these additions.[88] The exercise would amount to nothing more than speculation not at all warranted by the narrative content of the scenes. The miniatures *do* seem to share a thematic preoccupation with the Greeks' treachery and its consequences. The first miniature portrays the storm that was sent to punish the Greeks for waging war on the Trojans.[89] The second two illustrate the story of the Trojan horse, the Greeks' ultimate act of deception and foul play.[90] But this thematic coherence may only be illusory. Rather than focusing on the content of these miniatures, I am much more interested in what the working procedure reveals about the illuminator's or the patrons' entitlement. Was the license to jump around somehow informed by the adaptive reading practices encouraged by the manuscript? Again, the illumination of the manuscript at this stage in its bound form suggests that bias and selection or the availability of models are more responsible than haphazard working practice for the illustration of these three scenes. What is important is that some element of personal agency (whether the illuminator's, illuminators', or the owner's) drove this selection rather than deference to the order of incomplete miniatures as they occur in the book. And like the original program to which these images and emblem were added, the illustrative cycle of the manuscript remained unfinished and perhaps even halted abruptly since one of the three miniatures was painted without a border.

Sometime between circa 1516 and circa 1530, work resumed on the Royal manuscript, and this work gave historical authenticity—artifactual authenticity even— to the relationships between an English family's leading lights, the English language's laureate poet, and the English nation's monarch in ways that the manuscript's original contents and plan permitted. At this stage, all of the remaining miniatures were painted, which is to say the remaining four in the *Troy Book* and the entirety of the cycle illustrating the *Siege of Thebes*.[91] But the Percy family did not simply contract an illuminator to round out unfinished work. In addition, they hired their household secretary, William Peeris, to add a substantial number of texts with decorative and figural flourishing, as well as a singleton image, all in his own hand and all deliberately designed for insertion into the Royal manuscript.[92]

An archaeological approach to the book is particularly useful in revealing the design behind this campaign. When the manuscript was passed down to the next generation of Percys, there remained at the back of the manuscript a final quire of twelve that began with the last page of the *Siege of Thebes* (now fol. 162r) and continued on to numerous pages that had been ruled—like all of the preceding original folios—with brown ink and to accommodate two columns per page of anywhere between forty-six and fifty lines. At some point after 1504, someone copied in a medium brown ink and bâtard hand William Cornish's "Treatise Between Information and Truth" onto one of these ruled pages (now fols. 163r to 164r).[93] The hand used here differs from that used for all of the other added texts, and so it is uncertain who is responsible for copying the Cornish poem. The act may have been responsible for inspiring the entire enterprise to contract William Peeris to expand the manuscript sometime after he began working for the Percys in 1508, since both the script and ink used for the subsequent added portions are all in a uniformly flamboyant variation of bâtard and in a very dark brown ink. Peeris appears first to have recycled the manuscript's remaining blank pages (with their mid-fifteenth-century light brown ruling), copying Lydgate's *Testament* from Pynson's edition (printed circa 1520) on to the three central bifolia from this quire.[94] These three bifolia he moved to the front of the manuscript (now fols iv recto–5v, in the gutters of which old sewing holes are visible). As an autobiographical poem, the *Testament* provides a surrogate for the frontispiece or author image with which the original manuscript never opened.[95] Peeris then copied on to the remaining pages of the quire John Skelton's "On the Death of the Earl of Northumberland," which in one line compares the earl to the Trojan Hector (now fols. 165r–166v).[96] The final leaf in this quire was then cut out, leaving behind a stub between what are now fols. 166v and 167r. Presumably this final leaf was cut because the text of the "Death of the Earl of Northumberland" finished on fol. 166v and Peeris wanted to start copying the subsequent text onto folios with a new ruling pattern, which indeed he did. Next, the remaining parchment for the expansion of the manuscript was found, and each folio was scarfed (extended) using parchment strips to match the size of the original folios. These new folios were all ruled in red and with patterns that are specific to the content copied onto them, which includes the anonymous (although then believed to be by Lydgate) *Assembly of Gods*, copied from the circa-1498 Wynkyn de Worde edition (fols. 167r–180v);[97] Lydgate's "The Reignes of the Kyngis of England," which was continued up to Henry VIII (fols. 181r–183r);[98] a description of arms of various kings (fols. 183v–185v); William Peeris's own chronicle of the Percy family, composed sometime between 1516 and 1523 (fols. 186r–195r); and proverbial and moral verses transcribed from the walls and ceilings of the Percys' houses (fols. 195v–211v).[99] In between two sections of these transcribed proverbs is a singleton containing an elegant pen-drawn emblem combining Latin and English mottos and a man within the Tudor Rose, which showers droplets on an eye set over the Percy badge of a crescent (Figure 81).[100] Finally, one

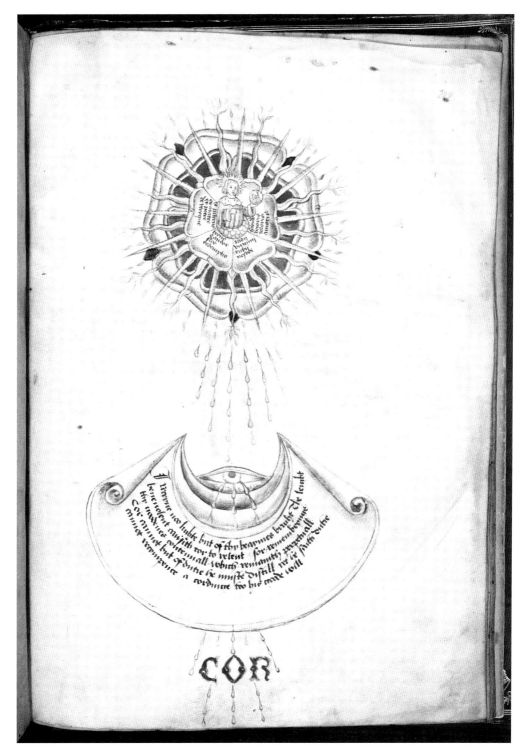

FIGURE 81. *The Tudor–Percy emblem*. John Lydgate, *Troy Book*, England, c. 1525.
London, British Library Royal MS 18 D ii, fol. 200r. © British Library Board.

of the miniatures that was painted around 1490 received an illuminated border (Figure 79), which had not originally been supplied, and two of the miniatures from around 1490 were misbound so that all three late fifteenth-century miniatures are contiguous. The misbinding was noticed by a sixteenth-century annotator, who marked up the errors and directed the reader to the correct sequence of pages.[101] Both the content of these items and their physical features point to their inspiration in and emergence from the original portions of the manuscript rather than their happenstance binding together with these early items.

Indeed, the Percy family had a substantial manuscript collection and sufficient wealth to have any of these new items bound separately.[102] Their library in Wressle Castle was an ambitious space, tricked out with an elaborate shelving system that caused John Leland (d. 1552) to remark, "One thing I likid excedingly yn one of the Towers, that was a study caullid Paradise, wher was a Closet in the midle of 8. squares latisid aboute: and at the Toppe of every Square was a Desk ledgid to set Bookes on . . . Cofers withyn them, and these semid as yoinid hard to the Toppe of the Closet; and yet by Pulling one or al wold cum downe, briste higthe in rabettes, and serve for Deskes to lay Bokes on."[103] We can infer from this description of the Wressle Castle library both the importance of display when it came to the Percy family's books as well as the fact that if they wanted these other texts produced, they certainly had the means to have them bound together or individually as separate volumes. Why have them added to a seventy-year-old manuscript? This accretive impulse was not exclusive to the Royal manuscript either and was directed at another volume owned by the Percy family, who contracted the same scribe (i.e., Peeris) to copy and add Lydgate's *Proverbs* to a circa-1470 manuscript that contains John Hardyng's *Chronicle*.[104] Carol Meale has observed that these additions "reflect a proud heritage and proclaim the family's loyalty to the reigning monarch—an astute enough move, bearing in mind the charges of rebellion which document the reversals of Percy fortunes in the fifteenth century and later."[105] Similarly, Alexandra Gillespie has described both Royal 18 D ii and Oxford, Bodleian Library Arch Selden B 10, as "noble, household miscellanies, sustaining traditional ideas about noble service to the monarch."[106] While agreeing with these assessments, I think that the physical appearance of these additions to the Royal manuscript amount to more.

More than merely a reflection of a proud heritage, it is specifically the compound nature of the Royal manuscript that assembles the archive that testifies to this heritage and evidences its longevity. Documented here are seventy years of a family's proximity to the crown, from William Herbert and Anne Devereux's perpetual submission to the king and a chronicle of the Percy family, to a full-page image of the Percy emblem of a moon receiving rays of light from the Tudor sun alongside verses on the kings of England. Into this latter portion, the scribe inserted a reminder of the family for whom he wrote, including in the cadels of an ascender the word *esperance*, part of the fourth Earl of Northumberland's personal motto.[107] The accretive nature of this manuscript offers a literary counterpart to what Kathryn Smith has called the devotional "family book."[108] These additions do not just reveal the preferences of a family to whom the combined manuscript was greater than the sum of its parts. More important, these additions take up the brief issued on the initial opening page of this manuscript and lodged in the fabric of Lydgate's verse.

The differences in style across the manuscript, from the scribal hands to the three campaigns of illumination, attest visually to the longevity of this archive. Embodied in the sixteenth-century form of the manuscript is what Beat Brenk has referred to as the aesthetics of spolia, which "materializ[e] the innovating principle of *varietas* as well as a traditionalistic, conservative gesture," by combining both old and new.[109] The stylistic incompatibilities between the layers of the Royal manuscript are, to be sure, a product of its protracted and halting production, yet they are also compelling evidence of this protraction. The misbinding that occurred in the sixteenth century was a mistake, but it is a valuable one that evidences a later audience's sensitivity to these incompatibilities and the periodization they signify. When the manuscript was misbound, the three images that were produced at the end of the fifteenth century were (mis)placed in the same quire, producing a sequence out of textual order but both thematically and stylistically coherent. The binder obviously erred, and I doubt that he was attempting to issue some clever commentary by it. Rather, I think he simply looked at three images that appear to have been illuminated during the same period and, with little further thought, misassembled the quire. This error is revealing of the binder's visual sensibility informed by some sense of stylistic periodization. In other words, he—and I believe we can extrapolate reasonably from this, his clients—was aware of the different visual styles enfolded into this manuscript and the pertinence of those styles to different historical periods. The Royal manuscript, in its sixteenth-century iteration, deposits three different stylistic periods into one volume with its audience's knowledge and appreciation of this accumulation. It does not simply parallel Lydgate's own historiographic methodology of cross-temporal contingence; it embodies it.

Keith Moxey has pointed to the ways in which the aesthetic power of the image can "break the boundaries of the historical context in which it was produced."[110] He elaborates that "even if images serve as records of the time and place of their creation, they also appeal to the senses and possess an affective force that allows them to attract attention in temporal and cultural locations far from the horizons in which they were created."[111] The Royal manuscript is a prime example of an object that extended beyond the horizons of its originary moment, and it did so literally by compelling successive generations to engage with and modify it. It seems unlikely, however, that it behaved in this way through the magnetism of its images or the affective charge of its form. Scholars who examine the anachronistic or anachronic charisma of the image have tended to privilege works of art that compel veneration or achieve a dazzling aesthetic excellence, the power of which derives from the scintillating illusions of their virtuosic forms.[112] Nothing quite so scintillating or virtuosic is on offer here. The Royal manuscript was, it seems to me, able to break through history by appealing to a pragmatic, even tactical inclination that compelled its owners to respond or act. It moved audiences over half a century to interact with it because of the gestures toward adaptation extended in the text it contains and the images that composed its earliest illustrative program. It was the author's own invitation to use and instrumentalize both that opened his work to the horizons of time in which it would be read and viewed.

CHAPTER 6

History's Hall of Mirrors

Gower's *Confessio Amantis*

Over sixty years after Gower's death in 1408, a lavish manuscript of the *Confessio Amantis* was produced for Edward IV and his queen consort Elizabeth Woodville (New York, Morgan Library and Museum MS M.126).[1] Commissioned probably after Edward's deposition and subsequent return to power in 1471, the Morgan *Confessio* emerged from what has been called a period of "political instability without parallel in English history since 1066."[2] The throne had changed hands twice in half a year, the king's brother and his closest adviser were in league with the enemy house, and upstart nobles were fomenting intermittent rebellions that threatened to oust the king a second time. To restore the public's faith in the vigor and validity of their reinstated king, his Yorkist supporters unleashed an avalanche of written and visual advocacy, including new chronicles, positive "eyewitness" accounts of Edward's victorious return to London, and newsletters of his success, in addition to staging spectacles in celebration of his venerable lineage. At the same time, the royal couple embarked on a campaign to reshape the king's own image through the patronage of manuscripts and tapestries—almost all of which were imported from the Low Countries—with an almost exclusive focus on historical content.[3]

The Morgan *Confessio*, the subject of this chapter, is a deluxe volume tailored to the purposes of advocacy. It was copied by the "vogue scribe,"[4] Ricardus Franciscus, whose elegant and conspicuously individualized hand has been traced to over a dozen manuscripts produced in England from 1447 to the 1470s.[5] Both Franciscus's insertion of his initials as well as mottos within cadels that include references to the king and queen (e.g., "vive le roy edward vraie" and "vive la belle") have helped identify him as the scribe and Edward IV and Elizabeth Woodville as the original intended audience for this book.[6] Noteworthy about Ricardus Franciscus's scribal practice is the consistent marriage of his own name with the names or mottos of his clients. This practice finds a parallel in John Lydgate's self-identifying strategy, outlined in Chapter 4, which counterbalances the individualism of self-promotion with deference to a sponsor. Where this scribe does announce his identity, it is to promote the identities of his patrons.

Embellishing the folios of the Morgan *Confessio* are 106 miniatures that elevate the poem's political underpinnings. All of these, with the exception of seven miniatures in a single quire, appear to have been created by one illuminator.[7] Of these, the majority are miniatures that illustrate many of the 140 narrative exempla related in Gower's poem: each of these miniatures is placed between a Latin prose summary and the Middle English verses of an exemplum. The choice of these narratives for illustration is itself remarkable because they neither mark significant structural divisions of the text nor every single narrative told. Rather, in concert with the body of art commissioned by the king, the pictorial cycle of the manuscript is devoted predominantly to history and to the kings who are its protagonists. The illustrations accompany tales that are designated by Gower himself as having been culled from "croniqs" (chronicles)—a body of narrative that Larry Scanlon refers to as "public exempla."[8]

While the previous chapter applied an archaeological approach to the Royal manuscript of Lydgate's *Troy Book* and *Siege of Thebes*, delving into the strata of its manufacture to uncover the recursive structuration of meaning over time, this chapter applies a much more selective approach to a manuscript. The selectiveness, however, is encouraged by the format of the manuscript itself, which compartmentalizes history into a series of excerpts arranged without heed to the progression of time. Here I examine illustrations of "public exempla" in the Morgan *Confessio* alongside its shelfmates in the royal library and within the broader field of pictorial representations of history produced during Edward IV's reign.

For the producers of the Morgan *Confessio*, the charge to create a book filled with narratives of Trojan, Theban, Roman, and biblical provenance for the king and queen placed them in the powerful position of depicting subjects that had seldom or even never before been visualized, creating, in the words of Brigitte Buettner, "objects of cognition rather than mere recognition."[9] In giving visual form to what had been up until this period events known largely in word, the images they produced had a tremendous impact on the reception of various histories. These histories are made to resonate with their contemporary audience: they are set in a discernibly medieval habitat, featuring Gothic interiors peopled with knights in armor, crowned kings in ermine, elegantly dressed ladies flaunting the elaborate headdresses popular in the later fifteenth century, and even the occasional heraldic or emblematic mark of Edward's own court.[10] It is my argument here that far from a temporally ignorant conception of the past, these visions of the historical exempla in the Morgan *Confessio* are at the nexus of the patrons' political preoccupations and the illuminator's artistic practice.

It has been argued frequently that medieval representations of history had an exemplary purpose designed to communicate the transitive property of morals learned from past events.[11] Such images achieved a temporal leveling, uniting all times into a visually consistent field of action—the moment of the image's production. Various phrases have been coined to describe the figurations of history that admit contemporary incidentals into their borders, including "actualization," "visual translation," and "medievalization."[12] Despite the variety of these critical terms, the common position held is that such visions of the past "attest to a specific historiographic conception whereby the scenery of past events was equated with contemporary ones and, by extension, with the world of the onlooker," resulting in scenes "saturated with persuasively didactic intents."[13] More important, this didactic intent has ends beyond itself, serving as an expedient vehicle for conveying the ideologies of a ruling class recruiting English literature into telling narratives favorable to its own aspirations. This exemplary function is certainly operative in the Morgan *Confessio*.[14]

At the same time, there are indications throughout the manuscript—subtle cracks in the mirror of historical exemplarity—that past events (and not just their interpretation) are open to manipulation and reconfiguration. Rather than canvassing the entire corpus of historical images in the manuscript, I focus here at length on a number of scenes that epitomize the Morgan illuminator's opportunistic vision of the past. In addressing these images, I have two related aims. The first is to explore the participation of the Morgan *Confessio* in shaping the Yorkist royal-political identity. By situating it within the context of pro-Yorkist advocacy disseminated by Edward's adherents, I show how the depiction of historical exempla in the Morgan *Confessio* coincided with this political project, and in particular, in its reliance on the revision of history to install Edward IV, both proleptically and retroactively, into a panhistorical gallery of leaders.

The second aim of this chapter is to investigate temporality in the nascent genre of history painting in fifteenth-century manuscripts.[15] In extending the analysis of these select images past their relationship to the text they illustrate, it becomes evident that the Morgan *Confessio*'s pictures of the ancient and biblical past embody a visual rhetoric the force of which derives not only from a refusal to isolate history in the past but also in a refusal to use the present as its only reference point. Images depicting historical events throughout time are cross-referenced here, mixed and matched for comparative purposes. Set against an expansive backdrop of painted histories, the illuminations of the Morgan *Confessio* emerge as effective agents in transforming the past into a collection of visual resources to be plundered by the privileged royal viewer and in transforming Gower's poem in ways its author never could have anticipated, much less countenanced.

Gower's Mirror for a Prince

This privileged royal viewer is very much the target audience of the Morgan *Confessio*, the main features of which call to mind the popular genre of conduct literature. In this section, I observe how the pictorial cycle of the Morgan *Confessio* displaces the Lover's Confession with the Prince's Mirror. But while the illustrative programs for instructional literature of the fifteenth century often feature an incendiary display of monarchic folly and its gruesome repercussions, the pictorial cycle of the Morgan *Confessio* remains committed to a view of monarchic infallibility more radical than the respect for royal authority expressed in Gower's text.[16]

The exemplary utility of history is a defining feature of the *Confessio Amantis* and is arguably the reason for its organization as a repeating alternation of exempla with exegetic dialogues. It is, if unceremoniously, in the *Confessio Amantis* where the word *history* makes its first appearance in the English language.[17] In the course of his confession to Genius, Amans admits that although he has been largely unsuccessful in the pursuit of love, the histories of past lovers give him both hope and solace:

> For whan I of here loves rede,
> Min Ere with the tale I fede;
> And with the lust of here histoire
> Somtime I drawe into memoire
> Hou sorwe mai noght evere laste;
> And so comth hope in ate laste,
> Whan I non other fode knowe.[18]

Gower's inaugural use of *histoire* in this passage is important for what it reveals about the purpose to which history is put by the audience inscribed into the poem. Reading the histories of past lovers, Amans is not interested in learning about the past in any objective or academic sense. Instead, Amans's is an egocentric history, the aim of which is to reframe his own present condition as one iteration in a pattern of recurring incidents throughout time.[19]

Of course, Gower did not invent the idea of history for English-reading audiences, and it would be misguided to lay too much stress on an inaugural moment that is for all intents and purposes lexical. Like his forebears, Gower's interest in history was not in reconstructing an archaeologically accurate picture of the past but rather—and explicitly—in rendering its verifiable events in terms meaningful to current audiences. "This ethical function," Gabrielle Spiegel notes, "ties history to rhetoric, for it is the orator's duty to guide the historian's expression so that he may achieve moral persuasiveness."[20] Gower's anglicization of this word is important, then, for its repeated coupleting with the word *memoire*,[21] which celebrates the uniquely human capacity to integrate the distant third-person past into an immediate first-person experience.[22] It is true, however, that Amans's selection of the narratives that constitute (what is for him) the history of love is determined by his affirmation bias: none of these tales seems to end badly for the lovers involved. And this is Gower's point: when histories are recounted, they are vetted prejudicially and cultivated for their relevance to present circumstances.[23]

This is where the germ of the *Confessio*'s political intervention takes root. From its opening, the *Confessio Amantis* grafts history onto the present, merging "olde worldes with the newe" and rearranging stories from throughout time to fit within the poet's own—decidedly not chronological—schema.[24] To Gower, the "literature of the ancients was very much a source of priceless wisdom. Yet, while antiquity was Gower's study, so his own times were his target: however timeless he might have imagined the lessons of his poetry, it was directly and primarily at the world around him that Gower aimed his verse."[25] Amans is not simply a proxy for the author, but he is also a stand-in for the royal reader who might look to history in the same manner.[26] In the Ricardian prologue—the version contained in the Morgan *Confessio*—the book is explicitly *for the benefit* of the king, "for King Richardes sake," predicating the histories to follow on their political serviceability.[27] Furthermore, the prologue is rife with the language of the *Des cas* Mirror for Princes (see Chapter 5), invoking repeatedly its most potent emblem, the Wheel, to remind the reader of Fortune's caprice. The *Confessio Amantis* may not be, strictly speaking, a Mirror for Princes in the *Des cas* mode, but the political theory advocated in its prologue, and its recourse to historical exempla, invite this comparison.

The producers of the Morgan *Confessio* were sensitive to this reading and were perhaps even under the impression that the poem is a Mirror, commissioned for this very reason.[28] As far as sheer numbers are concerned, the majority of narrative illustrations in Morgan MS M.126 are given over to exempla centered on the sagacity and virtue, or folly and vice, of princes throughout history. Book VII, a *Fürstenspiegel* in its own right, displays a particularly dense concentration of royal characters and is the most heavily illustrated book in the manuscript.[29] A common configuration in the manuscript, depicting a king or emperor enthroned, shows how these images orient a reading of the poem that favors royal exceptionalism. Regardless of the intended moral function of these exempla, an unassailable monarchic authority arises from these scenes, as in the miniatures illustrating the tales of "King Alphonso and the Three Questions" (Figure 82) and "Pompey Restoring the Crown to the King of Armenia" (Figure 83). Figures surrounding or before the king assume poses of subordination, either kneeling or with their palms up in deference, or centralizing the throne as a symbol of inalienable power, regardless of its status as benign or tyrannical. Still other images in the manuscript reinforce the nature of the king as a wise figure (or at least one who pursues wisdom), depicting him interacting with scholars and philosophers, as Alexander before Diogenes, Alexander promenading with Nectanabus (Figure 84), and Athemas and Demephon brought to accord by Nestor. If we can agree with Russell Peck's assertion that "the most single-minded of Gower's themes is the self-governance of the wise man,"[30] then the pictorial program of the Morgan *Confessio* offers up the king as the most adroit practitioner of self-regulation, courting the advice of philosophers when he cannot advise himself. Aligning royal decree with scholarly wisdom, envisioning the king-philosopher (to reverse the ideal), these miniatures expand on the poem's "thorough exploration of the authorizing power of kingship."[31] This expansion appears to be even larger when the Morgan *Confessio*'s program is viewed within the genre of *Des cas* Mirrors in which it positions itself.

FIGURE 82. *King Alphonso enthroned*. John Gower, *Confessio Amantis*, London, c. 1470. New York, Morgan Library and Museum MS M.126, fol. 26v (detail).

FIGURE 83. *Pompey restoring the Crown to the King of Armenia.* John Gower, *Confessio Amantis,* London, c. 1470. New York, Morgan Library and Museum MS M.126, fol. 171r (detail). Purchased by J. Pierpont Morgan (1837–1913), 1903.

In the manuscripts of *Des cas des nobles hommes et femmes* that were produced throughout the fifteenth century, kings, queens, and emperors are embroiled in narrative scenes electric with inflammatory content.[32] These scenes expose in vivid detail the "danger" within the *Des cas* genre, its relentless testimony that histories uncomfortable for incumbents are "subject to unruly and unpredictable revival as an affront to settled arrangements of power."[33] Whereas the textual narratives of falls accommodate the arc of a prince's metabasis and its subsequent recuperation as a cautionary tale for the present reader, the images in these manuscripts capture only its horrid nadir: the assassination of the once *nobles hommes et femmes.* A manuscript of *Des cas* produced for Edward IV (probably between 1479 and 1480), for example, offers a gruesome menu of regicide, including death by decapitation, the rack, severed limb, ejection from a cliff, drowning, mauling, stabbing, dragging behind a cart, pummeling with clubs, inter alia, et cetera, ad nauseam.[34] To appreciate fully the terror of this display requires leafing through this book to find again

FIGURE 84. *Alexander the Great and Nectanabus.* John Gower, *Confessio Amantis,*
London, c. 1470. New York, Morgan Library and Museum MS M.126, fol. 158r
(detail). Purchased by J. Pierpont Morgan (1837–1913), 1903.

and again without respite truly nasty ways to go, an orgy of carnage. Yet it would
be misguided to reduce to sensationalist entertainment this volume, prized for its
scandalous diversions. In a culture that deemed even "imagining" the king's death
a treasonable act,[35] this exposition of regicide flirts with the threat of sedition that
blighted late medieval kingship, retreating from it by displacing its targets.

The *Confessio Amantis* could vie capably with the grisly narratives of the *Des cas,*
perhaps even trumping them in ferocity. One critic has remarked that "Gower . . .
displays in the *Confessio Amantis* a taste for the lurid that might make Stephen
King squeamish—not only incest but adultery, rape, infanticide, parricide, be-
headings, mutilations, and all other manner of violence and brutality" infiltrate the
poem.[36] Many of these atrocities are executed by or committed against kings and
queens. Yet the Morgan cycle is restrained in gory exposition, keeping the violence
to a minimum, even suppressing the macabre climaxes of some narratives in favor
of illustrating less appalling moments. A testament to the program's reserve is the

disjunction between its illuminations and this excerpt from its index, which was possibly composed for the manuscript by its scribe, Ricardus Franciscus:

> Ligurguis prince of Athens how he kepte his laws
> Laude an preisyng of them that first were cause of ordeynyng of the
> laws Iustise
> Leoncuis a tyraunt gifully putte doun meke Iustinian fro his
> empire and in more spite kitte of his nose
> Lychaon a tyraunt madde mannys flessh to be eten in his hous in
> stede of othir flessh.[37]

Only the first of these entries has an accompanying illustration in the manuscript. Moreover, out of the entire program, only two miniatures in the Morgan *Confessio* depict royal assassinations.[38] What I am suggesting here is that in a delicate tight-rope walk, the producers of this manuscript have insinuated their work into a dangerous discourse of advice while limiting its participation in the condemnatory function of that discourse.[39] Instead, enacting the evasive maneuvers in which *Des cas* instructs its audience, they reject the many opportunities Gower furnishes for exposing royal disgrace. It is not that the manuscript's producers censored inflammatory portions from the volume: the text is complete, and the index logs many of these episodes. But by lending pictorial priority to so many scenes of royal sagacity and by manipulating others to equivocate on the represented king's defects, the illuminators achieved a culling of historical exempla tantamount to Amans's self-affirming readings of the past. The Morgan *Confessio* enframes itself as a mirror, schooling its viewer in how to produce a prejudicial reflection to his own liking.

Visual History in the Apostrophic Mode

As a mirror for a prince, the Morgan *Confessio* is less instructive in policy than—to alter Derek Pearsall's formulation—the politics of royal self-representation.[40] Several miniatures in the manuscript make explicit references to Edward's court: the royal arms appear in one scene, badges identify Yeomen of the Crown, Yorkist livery collars are worn by several figures, and tabards contain the initials of what might have been members of Edward's inner circle.[41] Evidentiary as these nuances are with respect to patronage, their appearance *within* scenes of historical action (as opposed to outside of them, in the margins of folios, or in a separate frontis-piece) demand theorization. In one sense, these details personalize the scope of the miniatures, restricting their exemplary value to a specific and exceptional audience in a way that no revision of the text could possibly achieve. In this respect, the Morgan *Confessio* fits comfortably within John Lowden's notion of a royal/imperial book, which bears "an awareness on the part of its makers and users of its royal/imperial connections, an awareness that is made patent by some visual device."[42] The nesting of these "visual devices" within miniatures in the Morgan *Confessio* adds a further dimension to the encoding of kingship with historically received values, which I explore here. In another and less obvious sense, they suggest the complicity of this manuscript in an amorphous propagandistic milieu, a scattered coalition of partisan commentators and collaborators that included artists.[43] The Morgan manuscript takes on increased meaning when it is considered a member of this milieu, informed by strategies common to those that guided outright propaganda.

During the internecine struggles for power between the Yorkists and the Lancastrians between 1450 and 1485, combat between the competing factions was enacted not just in armed encounter but also in the visual and literary culture of a propagandistic "boom."[44] The conflict that came to be known as the Wars of the Roses had its origins over a half-century earlier when in 1399 the Lancastrian Henry Bolingbroke ousted (the heirless) Richard II.[45] The ensuing dynastic succession from Henry IV to his son and grandson, Henrys V and VI, faced a serious challenge by the Yorkists beginning around 1450 when widespread dissatisfaction with Henry VI's rule, his mental instability, and—until the 1453 birth of his son—his lack of an heir made it an advantageous time for Richard, Duke of York, to mount his claim to the throne. After Richard's death in battle in 1460, his son Edward, Earl of March, commanded the torch of the Yorkist claim. Numerous factors made opposition to Lancastrian rule challenging, not the least of which was the entrenchment of the dynasty: Henry VI was, after all, the legitimate heir to the previous king, who was the legitimate heir to the king who preceded him.

These challenges made the proliferation of advocacy a necessary tool in advancing the Yorkist cause. Leading up to and following Edward's successful deposition of Henry VI, a rash of rolls, genealogies, chronicles, proclamations, public poetry, and prophecies were produced and disseminated in order to cement Edward's legitimacy in the eyes of a public weary from dynastic unrest but invested in the outcome of its turmoil.[46] In particular, it was the relation of history that assumed an urgent political utility, as Alison Allan has noted.[47] With two familial branches possessing comparably strong hereditary claims to the throne, the key determinant was not a juridical consensus over the right to rule based on the snarled genetic thicket of a family tree. Rather, the key determinant was control over public perception of this claim's foundation in history—a history extending far beyond the genealogic fork that separated the Plantagenet line into the branches of Lancaster and York. In the emerging tactics of political campaigning of the fifteenth century,

PLATE 1. *Man writing*. John Lydgate, *Fall of Princes*. Bury St. Edmunds (?), c. 1450. San Marino, Huntington Library HM 268, fol. 79v (detail).

PLATE 2. Eton College Consolidation Charter. Westminster/London, 1446. Eton, ECR 39/57 (detail). Reproduced by permission of the Provost and Fellows of Eton College.

PLATE 3. Draft copy of a grant of arms to Louis de Bruges. Westminster(?), 1472.
Kew, National Archives, C 81/1505, number 4 (detail).

PLATE 4. Ironmongers' Grant of Arms. London, 1455. London, Worshipful Company
of Ironmongers Grant of Arms of 1455 (detail). Reproduced by kind permission
of the Worshipful Company of Ironmongers.

PLATE 5. *Chaucer*. Geoffrey Chaucer, *Canterbury Tales*, London, c. 1450–1475.
Beinecke Rare Book and Manuscript Library, Yale University
MS Takamiya 24, fol. 1r (detail).

PLATE 6. *Chaucer*. Geoffrey Chaucer, *Canterbury Tales*, London, c. 1450–1475.
Oxford, Bodleian MS Rawlinson Poet. 223, fol. 183r (detail).
By kind permission of the Bodleian Libraries.

PLATE 7. *The Friar*. Geoffrey Chaucer, *Canterbury Tales*, London, c. 1450–1475.
Oxford, Bodleian MS Rawlinson Poet. 223, fol. 142r (detail).
By kind permission of the Bodleian Libraries.

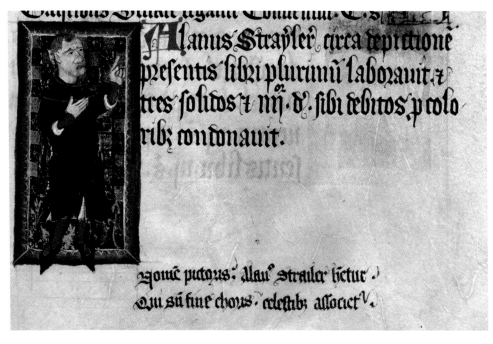

PLATE 8. *Alanus Strayler*. St. Albans Abbey Benefactors Book, St. Albans, c. 1380.
London, British Library Cotton MS Nero D vii, fol. 108r (detail).
© British Library Board.

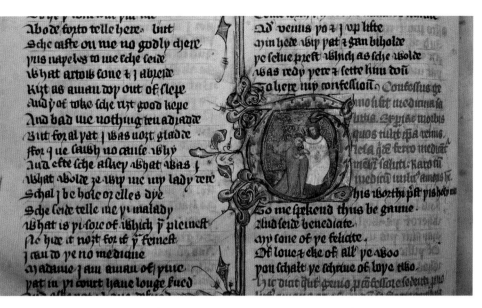

PLATE 9. *Amans's confession* and missing verse. John Gower, *Confessio Amantis*, London, c. 1400–1425. Oxford, Bodleian Library MS Bodley 693, fol. 8v (detail). By kind permission of the Bodleian Libraries.

PLATE 10. *John Gower writing*. John Gower, *Confessio Amantis*, London, c. 1425. Philadelphia, Rosenbach Museum and Library, MS 1083/29, fol. 1r (detail).

PLATE 11. *Amans's confession showing Collar of SS.* John Gower, *Confessio Amantis,*
London, c. 1400–1410. Oxford, Bodleian Library MS Fairfax 3, fol. 8r (detail).
By kind permission of the Bodleian Libraries.

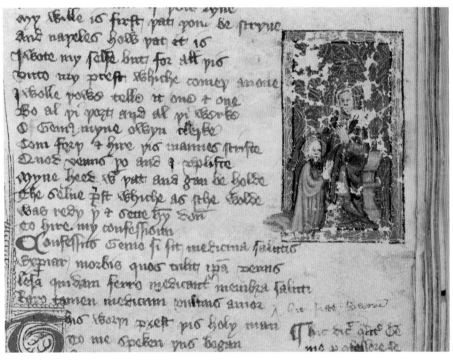

PLATE 12. *Amans's confession* with note to the illuminator. John Gower, *Confessio
Amantis,* London, c. 1400–1425. Cambridge, University Library MS Mm.2.21,
fol. 8r (detail). Reproduced by kind permission of the Syndics
of Cambridge University Library.

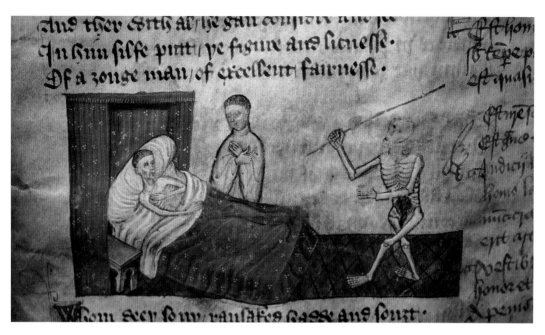

PLATE 13. *The Disciple encounters his dying form*. Thomas Hoccleve, *Lerne to Dye*, England, c. 1425–1450. Oxford, Bodleian Library MS Selden Supra 53, fol. 118r (detail). By kind permission of the Bodleian Libraries.

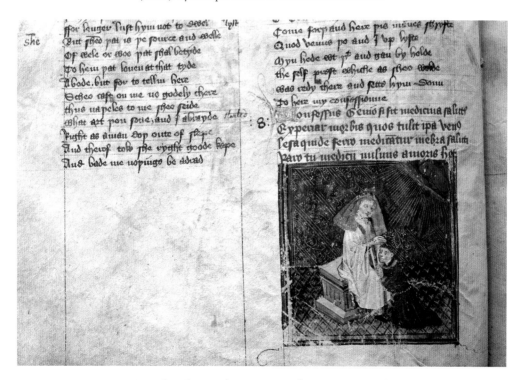

PLATE 14. *Amans's confession*. John Gower, *Confessio Amantis*, London, c. 1450. Cambridge, St. Catharine's College MS 7, fol. 8v (detail).

PLATE 15. *Lydgate kneels before Henry V.* John Lydgate, *Troy Book*, London, c. 1450. Manchester, Rylands Library MS English 1, fol. 1r. © University of Manchester.

PLATE 16. *Two monks kneel before Saint Edmund.* John Lydgate, *Fall of Princes,* Bury
St. Edmunds, c. 1450–1460. London, British Library Harley MS 1766, fol. 5r.
© British Library Board.

PLATE 17. *Lydgate kneels before Saint Edmund enthroned.* John Lydgate,
Lives of Saints Edmund and Fremund, Bury St. Edmunds, c. 1450–1460.
Oxford, Bodleian Library MS Ashmole 46, fol. 1r (detail).
By kind permission of the Bodleian Libraries.

PLATE 18. *Lydgate as a
pilgrim.* John Lydgate,
Siege of Thebes, England,
c. 1425–1450. London,
British Library Arundel
MS 119, fol. 1r (detail).
© British Library Board.

PLATE 19. *Saint Edmund enthroned*. John Lydgate, *Lives of Saints Edmund and Fremund*, Bury St. Edmunds, c. 1450–1460. London, British Library Yates Thompson MS 47, fol. 1r. © British Library Board.

PLATE 20. *William Herbert and Anne Devereux kneeling before the King*. John Lydgate, *Troy Book*, London, c. 1457–1461. London, British Library Royal MS 18 D ii, fol. 6r (detail). © British Library Board.

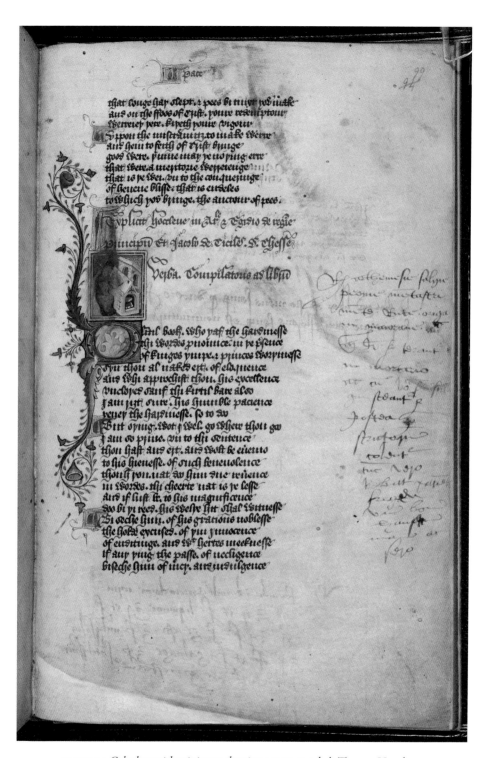

PLATE 21. *Colophon with miniature showing a man at a desk.* Thomas Hoccleve, *Regiment of Princes,* and John Lydgate, *Siege of Thebes,* England, c. 1450. London, British Library Additional MS 18632, fol. 99r. © British Library Board.

PLATE 22. Opening page. John Lydgate, *Troy Book,* London, c. 1457–1461. London, British Library Royal MS 18 D ii, fol. 6r. © British Library Board.

PLATE 23. *Lycurgus enthroned*. John Gower, *Confessio Amantis*, London, c. 1470.
New York, Morgan Library and Museum MS M.126, fol. 169r (detail).
Purchased by J. Pierpont Morgan (1837–1913), 1903.

PLATE 24. *Penelope hands a letter to a messenger*. John Gower, *Confessio Amantis*,
London, c. 1470. New York, Morgan Library and Museum MS M.126, fol. 68v
(detail). Purchased by J. Pierpont Morgan (1837–1913), 1903.

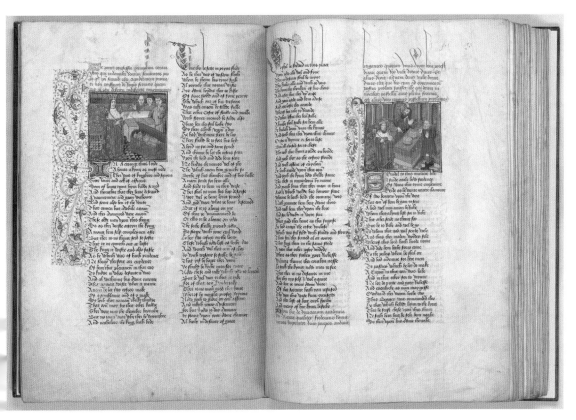

PLATE 25. "The Tale of the Two Coffers" and the "Tale of the Two Pasties."
John Gower, *Confessio Amantis,* London, c. 1470. New York,
Morgan Library and Museum MS M.126, fols. 102v–103r.
Purchased by J. Pierpont Morgan (1837–1913), 1903.

PLATE 26. *Edward escaping to Calais.* Typological Life of Edward IV.
England, after 1461. London, British Library Harley MS 7353 (detail).
© British Library Board.

PLATE 27. *Hand-tinted copy of the pilgrims at table.* Chaucer, *Canterbury Tales,*
London: Caxton, c. 1482. Oxford, St. John's College MS 266, fol. 139r. Reproduced by
permission of the President and Fellows of St John's College, Oxford.

dueling blocs harnessed the commercial forces of a new market for literary and artistic production in the use of language, narrative, and image to promote the historical foundation for their respective claims.[48] Francis Ingledew puts the point trenchantly when he remarks that "the possession of . . . power came to correlate distinctively with ownership of time."[49] In his single-minded patronage of art focused on historical narratives, Edward's ambition to own time is clear.

The political engagement of the Morgan *Confessio* rests in its facilitation of the king's prerogative to envision himself as a "historical actor" and, crucially, to choose the histories in which he is envisioned.[50] One of those histories is the story of Lycurgus. Lycurgus was, as Genius recalls to Amans, a prince of Athens, righteous and endowed with infinite wisdom.[51] He feared, however, that the laws he had established while prince—laws that had shepherded the Athenians to a period of unprecedented peace and prosperity—would be overturned after his death. In order to prevent this potentiality, Lycurgus committed the members of his "parlement" to vow that while he was away from the city, they would protect his laws until his return.[52] The oath taken, Lycurgus departed, never to return again. Lycurgus's greatest deed, according to Genius's interpretation, was to sacrifice his own estate for the common weal. According to at least one commentator, Lycurgus was "Gower's ideal monarch."[53]

When we confront the miniature illustrating this tale in the Morgan *Confessio*, what we are seeing is not a toga-clad dignitary speechifying on the gleaming white plateau of the Acropolis (Plate 23). Instead, Lycurgus is outfitted in the ermine-lined robes of a late medieval king, a bejeweled crown of gold on his head. Before him, three nobles gather around a book, placing their hands upon it to make an oath, while to the right, an attendant observes the proceedings. All of these figures are dressed in textiles of the later fifteenth century, colored hose with doublets, and a long gown. These actors all "move in a mediaeval environment"[54] as well, and like the majority of interior spaces depicted in the Morgan *Confessio*, the environment features a green-tiled floor and a red damask or tapestry with a gold filigree pattern lining the rear wall. These features install the historical episode that is about to be narrated in a current setting—a typical expression of past events, from no matter which era.

What distinguishes the Lycurgus miniature from images that admit a generic contemporary incursion on the past are its pictorial allusions, painted in the dialect of its intended viewers—Edward IV, the queen, and members of their court. The first is the crown badge worn on the sleeve of the outermost figure in the scene. Precisely this sort of livery was worn by the Yeomen of the Crown in Edward's court, attendants whose occupation included supervising the king's books and transporting them between palaces.[55] In keeping with the yeoman's actual status, the figure remains peripheral to the events portrayed, observing but not participating in the oath being taken. What is certain is that no such figure is mentioned in Gower's narrative and that he was invited to the scene by the illuminator. In addition to this figure, lifted from Edward's court and dropped into this scene of historical action, the three members of "parlement" depicted wear livery collars with badges. Two of these three can be identified as Yorkist badges issued during Edward's reign: on the left-most figure is the sun in splendor, perhaps the most ubiquitous royal logo during the twenty-two years of Edward's rule.[56] Similarly, the Lion of March badge hanging from the riband collar of the right-most figure is found both in pictorial representations, as in the depictions of Sir John Donne and his wife in Memling's *Donne Triptych* (Figure 85), and in artifacts.[57] In at least this respect, the artist's reconstruction of Lycurgus's parliament reveals a nuanced familiarity with Edward's court. Like the dove-topped rod identified by Kathryn Smith in the *Queen Mary Psalter*, these badges are "iconographic 'punctuation mark[s],' simultaneously identifying the work's patron and signaling to the reader that he has left the historical past and entered the sphere of contemporary events."[58]

It seems the only figure in this scene whose depiction does not parallel in a specific way the royal milieu is Lycurgus, or the prince himself, who lacks any iden-

FIGURE 85. *Sir John Donne wearing livery of the Lion of March on a chain of suns in splendor alternating with roses.* Detail of Hans Memling, *Donne Triptych*, Bruges, c. 1478. London, National Portrait Gallery.

tifying attributes other than his crown. The refusal to identify Edward IV with this king from the past is something I return to later. For the moment, it should be clear that, taken together, the incidentals of this miniature force history to address not just a general now but also a specific "you." This "you" can only have an implied presence in the narration of history and is, in essence, only capable of inclusion via apostrophe.[59]

Still, my purpose is not to inventory the objects inside the image as imports from the material world beyond it. Identifying them is only an initial, necessary step to grasping the contours of the marriage of past and present in the Morgan *Confessio*. It is salutary to remember, as Georges Didi-Huberman reminds us, that in Aby Warburg's relentless search for identities in Florentine painting, the identification of "a painted face in a fresco makes no sense unless one refers this identification . . . to the process at work . . . which characterises, on the one hand, the particular form of the representation and, on the other, its function in an anthropological web of social relations and symbolic exchanges."[60] In other words, diagnosing the specific reference in a particular artifact can only be a meaningful endeavor so long as it uncovers, first, the operations that render that identification possible and, second, the broader cultural stakes that made that identification efficacious in its own time.

The possibility of identifying the figures in these two miniatures derives entirely from the outward signs of their courtly affiliation and not from any physiognomic specificity. The collars, badges, and liveries that the depicted figures wear are vital to the expression of an individuality—just not necessarily the wearers' own. The Ordinance of 1478, a series of measures taken to improve the daily administration and management of Edward's household, mandates a penalty of a week's wages for any member who neglects to wear his livery.[61] Both the Lion of March and the Sun in Splendor are examples of such liveries, which Edward distributed to acolytes and members of his household. More than that, each of these is the *personal* badge of Edward IV, a portable icon of the king's biography. Regnal analogues to the manufactured crucifix, they are steeped in the residue of presence yet avoid an ontological elision with the individual made present.[62] The sun badge was adopted by Edward as a sign of divine assent for his kingship, after a solar event presided over the sky on the day of a crucial military victory against the Lancastrians.[63] And the Lion of March, whose origins are not entirely clear, was a cognizance that Edward appropriated from his Mortimer lineage, the familial branch crucial to his prosecution of the throne.[64] These badges, then, are not the personal marks of the individuals who wear them, yet neither are they simply the outward signs of a corporate identity.[65] Susan Crane has argued eloquently for the "paradoxical integrity and dispersion in personal devices," describing their distribution of the issuer's individuality to the corpus of his recipients.[66] As the Ordinance of 1478 stipulates,

Edward's individuality is dispersed to followers through royal mandate, a measure ensuring that both in and out of court, the king's self is visible by proxy when he cannot be bodily present.

Presence and absence, or visibility and concealment, commonly figured in the monarch's repertoire of theatrical effects. The appearance of the king to his subjects was long recognized as a political necessity, and we find in various treatises the prescription that a king should regularly present himself to the people—though not so much as to depreciate his aura.[67] To be absent only to appear again—playing out in a civic scale the trauma and alleviation of *fort-da*—was the source of the royal epiphany's mystifications, used to dramatic effect in fifteenth-century pageants and ceremonies.[68] But the absence of the king was an especially charged theme during the Wars of the Roses. During and between Edward's two reigns, anxiety surging from the uncertainty of royal absence ran deep, finding expression both in works critical of the king and in those sponsored by Yorkist supporters. In the play *Mankind*, produced at Bury St. Edmund's during Edward's exile, a mock-court scene is introduced by a pronouncement of doggerel:

> Carici tenta generalis
> In a place þer goode ale ys,
> Anno regni regitalis
> Edwardi nullateni
> On ȝestern day in Feuerere—þe ȝere passyth fully,
> As Nought hath wrytyn; here ys owr Tulli,
> Anno regni regis nulli!
>
> [The reed-grass[69] of the people having been held
> In a place where good ale is
> In the regnal year of King
> Edward By-no-means
> Yesterday in February—the year having fully passed
> As Nought has written; here is our Cicero
> In the regnal year of a nonexistent king!][70]

Jessica Brantley and Thomas Fulton find in the parodic "Edward By-no-means" the flash point for the drama's "shrewd engagement with the absences plaguing the kingship," here subjected to "ludic critique."[71] Edward's absence was a liability with which he and his agents had to reckon upon his restoration in April 1471. But rather than banking on mass oblivion of Edward's flight, Yorkist poetry thoroughly aired this absence, textualizing it to stage Edward's return as a long-awaited elixir, as in a political poem composed after his restoration, "Then aftur kynge Edwarde thay cryed and did wepe / The lacke of his presence made the pepull woo."[72] Absence, so framed, becomes a dramatic prerequisite for a desired return. When staged as overture, it evidences not a dereliction of kingly duty or catastrophe in governance (as in *Mankind*), but rather clears a space necessary for "the pepull" to yearn.

The theme of absence as prerequisite is similarly on view in the Morgan *Confessio*'s illustration to the tale of Penelope (Plate 24). The poem recounts how Penelope, pursued relentlessly by suitors while her husband is away at Troy, sends Odysseus a plaintive letter imploring him to return home.[73] In the miniature accompanying this tale, the moment depicted is not extracted from an episode in Gower's rendition, which is for the most part given over to the content of Penelope's letter and Odysseus's internal strife on reading it. Instead, Penelope, in the ermine and oddly crowned headdress of a queen, is shown with a lady-in-waiting behind her, handing a letter to a messenger who is accompanied by a Yeoman of the Crown.[74] On the one hand, this portrayal cleaves to other manuscript representations of Penelope's tale—as related in manuscripts of the *Heroides*—which show her either in the act of writing or handing her epistle off to a messenger.[75] However, with its admission of the Yeoman of the Crown into the scene, this miniature transforms the home of Odysseus into the Edwardian court and aligns one of the *Confessio*'s four unimpeachable female protagonists with the queen occupying it—Elizabeth Woodville.[76] This conflation of protagonist and viewer may even have been positioned so as to echo the queen's own recent experience. Not long before this manuscript was produced, Elizabeth herself had waited, pregnant and in sanctuary at Westminster, for the return of her husband from his exile in Bruges. A political poem circulated in the 1470s imagines her anxiety, leveraging the emotional intensity of familial rupture to gain support for the newly restored king:

> O quene Elizabeth o blessid creature
> O glorious God what payne had sche?
> What langowr and angwiche did sche endure?
> When hir lorde and sovereyn was in adversité
> To here of hir wepyng it was grett peté.[77]

Whether or not the illuminator is deliberately alluding to his patron's personal travails, the inclusion of contemporary insignia within the miniature invites the possibility for identification: of the king's absence and of the queen's longing for his return.

Given the gravity of the 1478 Ordinance and its enforcement of the king's presence by proxy, it was perhaps an aggravating inconvenience that the king could not likewise render himself temporally ubiquitous. One solution to this problem was the promulgation of genealogical rolls that present Edward as the long-awaited sovereign wished for in history and promised by prophecy. At the lower margin of one of these rolls, a prophecy inscribes Edward and his opponents into both history and historically ancient lineages for this purpose (Figure 86).[78] Here, a brief history of Britain includes the story of an angel's appearance to Cadwaladr, the last Welsh king to have occupied the throne of Britain and a king from whom Edward claimed descent:[79]

And þat tyme þat kynge Cadwaldrus was put out þe Angel professyde & sayde un to hym. Thow ner non of thyn herys of þhy blode shal not inherete þys lande ageyn unto þe tyme þat þo pepyl þat inhabyde it be funde in þe same synnys þat you & thyne ar drewyn out for at þys tyme. Thys fulfyllyde þe heyres of þhi body shal cleyme & recouyr be meritis of theyr feyth all þe landys þe whych theyr antecessowrs have lost beforne & out of mynede. . . . And þe name of hym þat shal conquere shal be callyde Rubius draco. And þe name of hyme þat shal be conquerit shal be callyde Albus draco.

[And at the time that King Cadwaladr was put out [of Britain] the angel professed and said to him, "You! None of your heirs by blood shall ever inherit this land again until the time that the people who inhabit it are found with the sins for which you and yours are being exiled. This fulfilled, the heirs of your body shall recover by the virtue of their faith all the lands that their ancestors have utterly lost. And he who shall conquer will be called the Red Dragon. And he who shall be conquered will be called the White Dragon."][80]

Just above this prophecy is the roundel for Edward IV, the largest on the roll and the only one surmounted by two crowns. Rubricated below this roundel is a gloss labeling Edward as *rubius draco*, the same cognomen the roll assigns to his most ancient forebears, the direct descendants of Cadwaladr. Time thus moves in two directions on this roll: with the deterministic forward progression of genealogy that led to Edward's coronation, and Edward's return to the past as the *rubius draco* to fulfill the promise of an ancient prophecy.

The virtual time travel effected by this roll finds a pictorial analogue in the Lycurgus miniature (Plate 23), in which the insinuation of such details as livery and personal devices cast Edward's presence over the history of the scene depicted. In other words, just as actual livery collars and badges distributed Edward's presence in space, so the cognomens of prophecy and the livery collars and badges included within the visual representation of historical events distributed Edward's presence

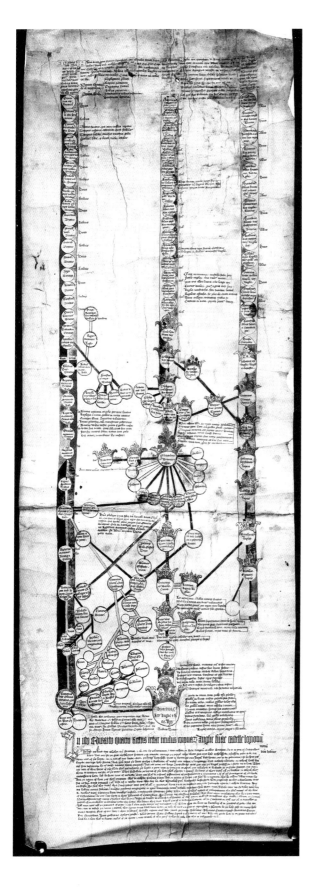

FIGURE 86. Genealogy of
Edward IV. England, after 1461.
London, British Library
Additional MS 18268a.
© British Library Board.

in time. The tale of Lycurgus was a particularly charged subject for the illuminator to tackle, given its direct confrontation with the idea of kingly absence.[81] Other illustrations of the tale present Lycurgus's voluntary exile as the crowning achievement of his reign.[82] In contrast, the Morgan illuminator locates the prince's greatness not in his absence but in the moment of enforcing the perpetuity of his laws, his legacy, and, in effect, himself. The illustration reveals a profound understanding of the subversion of absence that is at the heart of this tale, pictorializing the meeting that extends the king's presence past the moment of his departure. It is significant, however, that the illuminator of this miniature in the Morgan *Confessio* was cautious not to calibrate a flawless alignment between Edward and Lycurgus. Edward is decidedly *not* an alternate for Lycurgus, and it is only a cast of courtly extras who carry the specter of his presence into the scene.

Contemporary accounts of the king's patronage construe it as political in motivation, and there is no reason to insulate the producers of his manuscripts from the characterization. According to the Crowland continuator, in the wake of Edward's abortive military expedition to France in 1475, the king "was not unaware of the condition of his people and how easily they might be drawn into rebellions and strange schemes, if they were to find a leader. . . . He therefore flung himself wholeheartedly into plans to reassemble treasure worthy of his regal estate."[83] The books and the tapestries that Edward commissioned contributed considerably to this effort and include pieces featuring the history of Thebes, the tale of Paris and Helen, Noah's ark, the life of Alexander the Great, the story of Nebuchadnezzar, the history of Tullus Hostilius (third king of ancient Rome), and Publius Horatius.[84] Another set that was probably commissioned by Edward depicted the story of Brutus, legendary grandson of Aeneas and founder of England. Surely, the consistent historical preoccupation of the tapestry and manuscript collections militates against the view that it was through sheer "display of magnificence" that these objects communicated Edward's vigor as sovereign.[85] Rather, the treasury resulting from Edward's patronage—including the Morgan *Confessio*—participated in a campaign to produce a corpus of images and texts that ensconced Edward within a dazzling gallery of historical action.

We might now conceive of personal libraries as restricted enclaves for private property, but in the royal household of the fifteenth century, they were not "exclusive and jealously guarded institutions whose contents were intended more for show than use . . . and [the royal books], whether through public reading or private study [may] have reached a number of courtiers."[86] Given the enormous size and heft of the Yorkist court's newly commissioned volumes in the 1470s and 1480s, it is unlikely they would have circulated freely. Nevertheless, the "open character of the lord's dwelling"[87] ensured that such volumes were seen by many more than the king and queen themselves, perhaps laid out on large tables in the newly refurbished study in Eltham.[88] Designed to be viewed, the pictorial content of these books activated their political impact. The manuscript collection that Edward amassed during his second reign might be understood, then, as the bricks and mortar of a theater of history in which he was to reign supreme over all time.

Specifically, the apostrophic nature of the historical images in the Morgan *Confessio* sponsored an interface between Edward and the tableaux of historical events that surrounded him in his library.[89] Because Edward's presence in the image of Lycurgus is only indirect—that is, through the delegation of his sovereign individuality to anonymous, liveried surrogates—the historical king portrayed is not cognate with him. For this reason, Edward is not under contract to identify with Lycurgus or, for that matter, with any one historical figure in the Morgan *Confessio*. Instead, his personal absence from the scene of historical action allows for plausible deniability. Edward is able to maintain his integrity as himself, while maintaining the ability to claim at any given time historical precedents for whatever posture is, in the moment, most politically expedient.

One official document in particular exposes this retrieval and selective integration of history as a deliberate facet of Edward's royal policy. Along with his patronage of books and tapestries on resuming the throne, Edward embarked on a major reorganization of the royal household in the early 1470s. This endeavor is enshrined in the *Liber Niger*, or the *Black Book*, a set of recommendations for the maintenance of the royal household.[90] The sober technicalities of this manual are garnished with hortatory and descriptive passages and *auctoritates* in Latin, making it something more than a mere household ordinance.[91] This curious composition, the admixture of literary language and historical exempla along with the *Black Book*'s main pragmatic matter, offers an implicit prospectus for the exchange program between past and present that Edward's administration fostered.

A seventeenth-century facsimile of the *Black Book* gives an idea of the formality of this prospectus.[92] Heading the main sections of the text are copies of two drawings that were contained in the original. The first of these precedes the section on the *domus regie magnificencie* and appears under an inscription vouching for its authenticity: "Pictura ista inferius locata uti et symbola cum in hac pagina tum in adversa exacte ab exemplaria in initio *Libri Nigri* limantur" (Figure 87).[93] In the drawing, a king is seated at a long table, accompanied by a bishop and three nobles, all of whom are attended by servants. Over the king's throne are the royal arms of England, which, lacking supporters, suggests that the figure portrayed is a generic king and not Edward IV himself. Three banderoles with sententious statements from Socrates, Seneca, and an uncited *auctor* are superimposed over the scene, the first two of which appear to be "spoken" by depicted figures:

Socrates: It is proper to eat to live, not to live to eat.

The unconquered king will be he whose diet is abundant.

The people require food far more than anything else. Seneca.[94]

The contradictory advice of the two spoken maxims might seem to be the first part of a syllogism, but the lack of resolution offered by the third leaves the contradiction intact. Following this drawing is a long preamble to the technical text proper, which launches into a "strangely florid" description of exemplary royal households throughout history: Kings Solomon, Lud, Casibellan, Hardeknout, Henry I, and Edward III.[95] Like the advice in the frontispiece, these kings offer bizarrely—and explicitly—contradictory exemplars. On the one hand is King Lud, whose "dayly dyet was not muche in sotyle [sophisticated] and delicate vyaunde."[96] On the other is King Hardeknout, who "used for his own table neuer to be serued with ony [any] like metes of one mele in another. And that chaunge and diuersitie was dayly in greate habundaunce."[97] The inclusion of these two models, praised for their respective austerity and gourmandise, seems only to complicate the operational blueprint that the *Black Book* was intended to streamline. More important for my argument is that it exposes, in a technical instance, the variety of exemplars made available to Edward and his perceived prerogative to elect his own precedents. The plethoric exordium coupled with a generic depiction of the *domus regie magnificencie* and its contradictory aphorisms concretizes inconsistency as the king's unique privilege and contracts history as the alibi for his changing postures.

The implied alignments between Edward and Lycurgus, Odysseus, and a number of the other commendable leaders in the Morgan *Confessio* represents the unofficial and imaginative counterpart of the *Black Book*'s official program. If the *Des cas* genre teaches any one generalizable lesson, it is that a favorable historical paragon can, at any given point, become a liability. Edward, like any medieval ruler, must have been aware of this fact, for with every comparison to, say, the heroic Alexander was the potential allusion to his tyrannical and patricidal alter ego. It is probably no coincidence that in the Morgan *Confessio*, Alexander appears in three separate miniatures being counseled by sage figures, but there is no miniature accompanying the exemplum in which his assassination is interpreted as a just end to his career of slaughter and conquest.[98] What appears to have been an innovation with Edward was his deftness in avoiding marriage to any one, single model. Writing on Edward's reign, Paul Strohm has identified an "attitudinal shift of considerable magnitude" in this period, a "new midcentury spirit," in which "deception, temporization, and sharp dealing are understood not as disqualifications but as positive entitlements to the throne."[99] In other words, Edward's prevarications and his frequently overt exploitations of history were not concealed, reconciled, or glossed over but rather were lionized by pro-

Yorkists as evidence of his suitability to rule. It is only within this altered climate that we can appreciate the vision of history that is presented in the Morgan *Confessio*. Part of my argument here is that this manuscript was a member of visual repertoire that reinforced to the king his prerogative to plunder history and advertised the appeal of this tack to a variety of publics, from the courtiers and dignitaries privileged to see Edward's library and tapestries to the masses exposed to outright propaganda.

Mirrored Typologies

The cavalier attitude to history that I outlined previously is encouraged even further in the Morgan *Confessio*, where the past is rendered violable and open to redaction. On numerous occasions throughout the *Confessio Amantis*, exempla with similar narrative scenarios, themes, or motifs are recounted sequentially. Critical reception of this compilational strategy varies, with some scholars finding in it the genius of the poet's art as a didact, while others have found it to detract from the carefully constructed parataxis that allows Gower to, say, revile incest in one tale and condone it in another.[100] Whatever the strategy's purpose, the two illuminators of the Morgan *Confessio* capitalize on these parallels, using the diptychal format of the codex to mirror the text's bilateral poetics. Several moments in time are explicitly thrown into dialogue in the manuscript, in which miniatures are juxtaposed through their position on the page as well as through formal similarities.[101] In exploring these pairs as companion pieces, my aim here is to instigate a deeper understanding of the revisionist nature of the manuscript's historiographic-political project. What appears at first to be a pictorial amplification of a literary conceit turns out to evoke a form of allusive revisionism with real-world stakes.

At roughly the center of the manuscript is an opening that levels two images against one another for a lesson in the visual manipulation of history. On the verso is illustrated "The Tale of Two Coffers" (Figure 88), in which an unidentified king overhears officers of his court complaining that, in spite of their long service, they have not been promoted.[102] In order to prove that their stalled careers owe to their own failures and not administrative oversight, the king devises a proof. He orders two identical coffers made and delivered to his chamber, filling the one with jewels and gold and the other with straw, stones, and rubbish.[103] He then invites the disgruntled knights into his chamber, explaining they must choose which chest to open and explicating the lesson to be derived from this exercise: success is only a matter of personal fortune. As a group, they elect to open the coffer that, it emerges, contains worthless contents. Made to see that their ambitions exceed their fates, the knights abandon their embittered speech and beg the king's pardon. Although nothing within the tale indicts the king for trickery or for teaching by fatuous proofs, the Morgan illumination hints at his fluency in game theory. In a rejection of the—crucial—instructions that the coffers be "of o semblance and of o make," the two trunks are differentiated. In the foreground, a blue trunk opens to reveal a hoard of golden vessels, while in the background a heap of straw is enclosed within a trunk coated in liquid gold. Another manuscript of the *Confessio* with narrative miniatures provides an apt comparison to this scene, showing identical boxes on a board (Figure 89). The discrepancy between the enclosing cases and enclosed goods in the Morgan version not only contradicts the tale but also hints at the king's orchestrations. While the Latin preceding the exemplum outlines its condemnation of grasping individuals, the pictorial focus remains centered on the king as one who dispenses wisdom—if through somewhat disingenuous means.

FIGURE 88. *The King before two coffers*. John Gower, *Confessio Amantis*, London, c. 1470. New York, Morgan Library and Museum MS M.126, fol. 102v (detail). Purchased by J. Pierpont Morgan (1837–1913), 1903.

Across the opening is a miniature that alludes to and then reworks the motifs in its companion piece. In the tale of the Emperor Frederick (Figure 90), two beggars dispute whether it is the king or God who enriches man.[104] Overhearing this debate, the emperor invites the two men to his palace where he has arranged two identical pasties to be served to them: the one filled with gold coins and the other with meat.[105] While the beggar who places his faith in the king is met only with meat inside his pasty, his God-fearing companion finds riches in his. A paradoxical exemplum in which the monarch's subordination to God is enacted by his very ability to distribute divine munificence, it is one that flatters the king for his power and for his reverence. This paradox is parlayed to the advantage of the king in the Morgan illumination. Within a royal hall, three men stand around a table that hosts two pasties, one exposing its rich filling. As with the facing miniature, here, the emperor appears in the foreground left, gesturing to the right with the same hand in which he holds a scepter. On the right, a pauper in ragged garments recip-

FIGURE 89. *The King before two coffers*. John Gower, *Confessio Amantis*, London, c. 1425–1450. Oxford, New College MS 266, fol. 102v (detail). By kind permission of the Warden and Scholars of New College, Oxford.

rocates, indicating back in the direction of the emperor. The second pauper, in the background, points to the treasure-filled pasty and gazes up. His eyes focus on radiant beams of gold that filter through the window in the rear wall, the signs of divine grace. But what confuses the source—or at least the conduit—of this radiance are the royal arms of England, positioned as stained glass in this window. The suggestion, much like that in the text, is that grace has a divine issuance but requires a royal franchise for its allocation. Both this illustration and its companion piece agree on crediting kings with greater agency than their own exegeses admit. That is, they seem to amplify what is already a form of amplification in the poem. From this vantage, it appears the miniatures are redundant, reiterating the same point and implicitly advocating a cyclical view of history.

FIGURE 90. *The King before two pasties.* John Gower, *Confessio Amantis,* London, c. 1470. New York, Morgan Library and Museum MS M.126, fol. 103r (detail). Purchased by J. Pierpont Morgan (1837–1913), 1903.

It is in the miniatures' conversation with one another from across the opening that a far more progressive idea of meliorative history emerges—an idea of history familiar to medieval audiences as typology (Plate 25).[106] In the depiction of "The Tale of Two Coffers," the king's role as didact is enunciated in gesture and pose, and the viewer is not cued to doubt this characterization. Yet his reputation for honesty is diminished by the distinct appearances of the two coffers. The principle of the game remains—it was, as is made clear, the knights' own joint decision to open the golden case—but the king is shown to have given himself a competitive edge. The facing miniature, however, affords the king a mulligan, and on this try, he plays in good faith, without attempting to fix the outcome. The pictorial reward for this behavior is the visual conflation of divine grace and regnal beneficence. It is surely no coincidence that the royal arms of England appear in this second image, aligning the royal viewer of the manuscript with the superior royal model in this quasi-diptych.

A similar typological situation appears again in the manuscript, in the elision of Theban history with that of a vague Hungarian past.[107] Folio 20r contains two

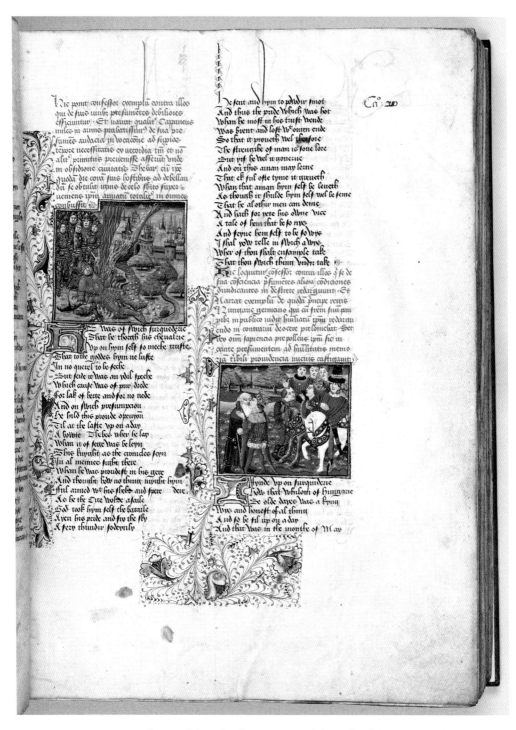

FIGURE 91. Page showing "The Tale of Capaneus" and the "Tale of the Emperor of
Hungary." John Gower, *Confessio Amantis,* London, c. 1470.
New York, Morgan Library and Museum MS M.126, fol. 20r.
Purchased by J. Pierpont Morgan (1837–1913), 1903.

FIGURE 92. *Capaneus struck down*. John Gower, *Confessio Amantis,* London, c. 1470.
New York, Morgan Library and Museum MS M.126, fol. 20r (detail).
Purchased by J. Pierpont Morgan (1837–1913), 1903.

miniatures on the same page, and the narrative moment portrayed in each reveals
an effort to draw the two into conversation with one another (Figure 91). The miniature on the left illustrates the tale of Capaneus's pride (Figure 92): while besieging
Thebes, Capaneus is so boastful that he refuses to beseech the gods' aid. Launching
himself before the fray, Capaneus is suddenly struck down by fire from the sky and
turned to ash.[108] As depicted here, Capaneus lies on his back in the foreground,
gazed upon by a crowd of soldiers to the left. The red and yellow tongues of a fire
cascade from a crease in the heavens, while a pillar of smoke and ash deliver his
cremated remains to the sky. The illustration is a serviceable depiction of the tale,
but its force as an illustration against pride derives from its juxtaposition with the
miniature in the adjacent column.

History's Hall of Mirrors

215

FIGURE 93. *The Emperor of Hungary kisses a beggar.* John Gower, *Confessio Amantis,*
London. c. 1470. New York, Morgan Library and Museum MS M.126, fol. 20r
(detail). Purchased by J. Pierpont Morgan (1837–1913), 1903.

Opposing the illustration of Capaneus struck down in his pride is an image of
the king of Hungary's willing descent for humility (Figure 93). The poem relates
how a king of Hungary was rebuked by his brother for deigning to kiss a beggar in
public.[109] To teach his brother the value of humility, the king commissions the city's
trumpeter to stand before the gates of his brother's house and to blow his trumpet:
the traditional announcement that the inhabitant was to be executed on the following day. In the morning, the brother, his wife, and their five children proceed to
court in nothing but their undergarments, with their eyes full of tears, to plead,
prostrate before the king, for the brother's life. Following the king's lecture on the
ills of prideful behavior, the king then agrees to spare his brother. As at least one
scholar has pointed out, the crux of this story, the "focal point in the narrative,"[110]
occurs at the moment the trumpet is blown, when several lines are devoted to the
brother's confusion and helplessness on realizing his death is imminent but not

FIGURE 94. *The Trumpeter blows the Horn of Death.* John Gower, *Confessio Amantis*, London, c. 1425–1450. Oxford, New College MS 266, fol. 17v (detail). By kind permission of the Warden and Scholars of New College, Oxford.

knowing the cause. In another copy of the *Confessio*, this is precisely the moment chosen for illustration, as the fated brother can be seen cowering with his family within their home, the dreaded trumpeter before their gate (Figure 94).[111] But the Morgan illustration, in contrast, focuses not so much on the brother's disdain but instead on the king's humility. On the left, a crowned king embraces and kisses an elderly man with a long white beard and walking cane. On the right, the head of the same crowned figure is seen beside a horse that is steadied at the reins by an attendant, while with his right hand the king grips the horn of his saddle, indicating he is about to remount. Behind the king's horse, looking on, are three courtiers, while in the foreground the king's brother rests a hand on his chest as he sits astride a richly caparisoned white steed. The two parts of this synoptic composition—the king's physical contact with a peasant and the resumption of his place with those of high estate—dramatize a willing act of self-abasement.

History's Hall of Mirrors

Both text and form collude to draw this image into an allusive relationship with the miniature across the page. The scribe has arranged it so that the first line beneath each miniature recalls the other, underscoring the common thematic pre-occupation of each exemplum: "He was of swich surqederie [arrogance]" and "I ffynde upon surquiderie." As Derek Pearsall has shown, one of the major challenges confronting *Confessio* scribes was coordinating the placement of the Latin prose version of each exemplum with respect to the Middle English exemplum it pre-cedes—especially considering that the earliest manuscripts of the *Confessio* located the Latin prose versions like glosses in the margins, thereby leaving later scribes to grapple with its appropriate relocation in the columns.[112] In this case, the scribe placed the Latin and the miniature immediately above what is, properly speaking, the fifth verse of Capaneus's tale. To determine *who* "was of swich surqederie," the reader-viewer must refer to the preceding leaf in order to discover that it is the "proude knyht Capaneus."[113] The configuration of two miniatures above verses reminiscent of one another results in a syntax of the page that is heightened by a symmetry between the two scenes. In each instance, a main figure (i.e., Capaneus or the king of Hungary) is literally brought low before a crowd of spectators. But whereas Capaneus rises only as a pillar of smoke, the king of Hungary's voluntary humility allows him to return with ease to his elevated station on his steed. The presence of two horses in this scene perhaps accentuates the act of humility we are seeing, an inversion of the fall that comes after pride.[114]

Essential to the rapport between this set of miniatures is their transcendence of time. Without respect for distinctions between places, institutions, and habits, the images collapse different historical periods into a single moment for the purposes of comparative analysis. In doing so, they call a transhistorical congress, in which episodes from throughout history jostle with each other—as well as with current events. The example of this pair suggests that the theories on "visual translation," "actualization," and "medievalization" I described earlier offer only a partial ac-count for their interactions. Much as these miniatures "bridg[e] the cultural gap"[115] and refer to the era of their production through the inclusion of such contempo-rary incidentals as dress, they also converse with each other. In other words, the clothes and setting in which the figures appear are identifiable to the general time in which the miniatures were painted, but such nuances probably passed either unnoticed or as unremarkable to a contemporary audience. Mary Carruthers, in attempting to understand the use of the present tense (i.e., the "historical present") in vernacular narrative has argued that it is in actuality "an unmarked tense-without-time [that] can readily be pressed into the service of all sorts of needs, pragmatically, on a moment-by-moment basis."[116] Because narrative is always pro-duced in some present moment, it is necessary—unavoidable—that it bears the residue of that present moment.[117] The appearance of the present tense in the relation of past events is a linguistic "tic" prompted by history's resurrection in the moment of its retelling, but it is not necessarily experienced by the teller or audience as representing or even making a connection to the actual present (e.g., "I was in the store yesterday, when the clerk says to me . . ."). If we relate this notion of the unmarked present to the images of kings and their coffers and pasties, we could say that the form of their representation—the guise in which the figures appear—is not *medievalized* but *unmarked*. The form of their representation is of the fifteenth-century present, and it is precisely this form that allows these episodes from disparate periods to gloss one another and to play with each other, a form of allusion in its most etymologically faithful sense (i.e., from *alludere*, "to play with").

The difference between the terms *medievalized* and *unmarked* is not, however, a distinction in the illuminator's level of intentionality. The difference is in the point of reference for each image. If we say that the images are medievalized, then we are suggesting that the artist is deliberately subordinating the past to the present, drawing an analogy between the action in the image and the moment of the image's production. But, if we say that the image is unmarked, then we acknowledge the temporal elasticity that is on show in its juxtaposition with other historical images. This unmarking enables a "flattening of historical difference that opens up items of the past to arbitrary and playful citation"[118] not just in relation to the present but in relation to all times. The result is a very different notion of history from the cyclical one embodied in the repetition of narrative scenarios throughout time. Instead, the result is a secular typology in which any historical episode, properly aligned, may be seen as a more perfect enactment or reversal of a preceding or succeeding event.

An astonishing set of propagandistic images from early in Edward's first reign divulges the high stakes in the typological game played out in the Morgan *Confessio*. Shortly after Edward had unseated Henry VI, a roll produced for public consumption compares, across four sets of images, events from Edward IV's life to episodes from the Old Testament (Figure 95).[119] In the lowest pair, for example, Edward's escape across the Channel to Calais after the Battle of Wakefield is compared to Moses's salvation from the pharaoh's infanticidal spree, in a basket set adrift on the Nile (Figure 96, Plate 26). Other scenes compare Edward to King David and to Joshua, commanding the trumpets that crumbled Jericho's walls. What distinguishes the use of typology here from the sacred paradigm on which it is modeled is not just its startling juxtaposition of sacred type with profane antitype. Equally pioneering is its reliance on *formal*—that is, visual—symmetry, made plain to the viewing public. Most biblical typology hinges on allegorical and tropological parallels that are difficult to extrapolate without facility in exegesis but that are often made intelligible to

FIGURE 95. Typological Life of Edward IV. England, after 1461. London, British Library Harley MS 7353. © British Library Board.

FIGURE 96. *Moses in a basket escaping Pharaoh*. Typological Life of Edward IV.
England, after 1461. London, British Library Harley MS 7353 (detail).
© British Library Board.

viewers by (at times tendentious) visual similarities.[120] In contrast, in the spectacular politics of Edward's reign, the representational hierarchy at the core of typological hermeneutics is inverted, allowing surface resonance the priority to dictate the terms in which history is read.[121] The statements issued in this roll are as pictorially enterprising as they are unsubtle. Turning scriptural typology to secular, political use, it forges new and audacious paths in visual persuasion. This all-too-brief discussion of this roll has required a detour from a book owned by the king and stationed in the comparably controlled territory of his library to the more volatile space of public promotion. But part of my aim throughout this chapter has been to suggest how the visual culture of partisan politics and that of semipublic self-assertion can throw light on one another, exposing operations that prowl beneath the more overt signals of iconography and narrative.

Viewed alongside the opportunistic typologies of the Harley roll, the companion pieces in the Morgan *Confessio* appear less deferential to Gower's poetics than

FIGURE 97. *Carmidotirus commits suicide*. John Gower, *Confessio Amantis*, London, c. 1470. New York, Morgan Library and Museum MS M.126, fol. 168v (detail). Purchased by J. Pierpont Morgan (1837–1913), 1903.

receptive to a larger historiographic project motivated by factional politics and realized in the cultural products that scribes and limners produced. The miniature of Lycurgus, which I addressed previously, is not an isolated miniature but is rather part of a pair that similarly invokes a typological framework for revisionist purposes. Across the opening is a miniature that, like the depiction of Lycurgus, accompanies an exemplum praising those who preserve the law (Figure 97). Seated within a shallow space on a curved bench are four men in similar long gowns and tall hats, three of whom are in various poses of conversation. The figure at the far left, however, drives a sword between his own ribs, while the man beside him places a hand on his shoulder, a disconcerting gesture in this grim context. In reading the text that follows, we find that the suicidal figure is Carmidotirus, consul of Rome and steadfast keeper of its laws.[122] After accidentally contravening his own decree that no one bearing weapons may enter the counsel house, he slays himself despite his fellow consuls' insistence on his innocence. The poem praises Carmidotirus for his integrity, but the visual reality of the miniature casts a pall over his methods for preserving the law. He is in this sense very different from Lycurgus, whose protection of order, at least in the miniature, originates in word and in oath. Whereas Carmidotirus wields a sword, Lycurgus gestures with his hands. The similarities between these episodes are elaborated textually, but their differences are embellished in this pictorial collision, made possible by the poem's structure but aggrandized by the manuscript's producers. Although another short exemplum intervenes between the stories of Carmidotirus and Lycurgus, the choice to focus visual attention on the suicidal consul demonstrates the same impulse toward typology embodied in the juxtaposition of the kings with their coffers and pasties.[123] Edward's proxied presence in this latter scene, like his arms in the depiction of the Emperor Frederick, further supports the deliberateness of this typological strategy. In comparing these scenes to the Harley roll, I have sought to show that this strategy has an older provenance, extending back to early in Edward's first reign, when the more overt persuasions of factional politicking dropped him into a typological template to improve on the models of Moses, David, and Joshua.

At the beginning of this chapter, I remarked that the Morgan *Confessio*'s pictorial focus on kingship lies at the intersection of the patron's political concerns and the book artist's professional preoccupations. The typological occasions throughout the manuscript are at the epicenter of this intersection. For the artist, the images suggested opportunities to indulge in that habit of practice I outlined in the Introduction: the use of modified "copies" to produce meaning through pictorial allusion. In this case, the modified "copies" come from within the manuscript itself, from directly across the page. And for the patron, these typologies refine for a privileged audience the brazen methods of persuasion originally devised for urgent needs and broadcast to a large public. Taking a poem as generically diverse as the *Confessio Amantis*, the producers of this manuscript made an appreciable effort to place pictorial emphasis on its royal protagonists and on those stories that relate most closely to royal sagacity. Seen, in this respect, as a coherent work, the Morgan *Confessio* takes the political mission that Gower inculcated into his poem, written in the last decade of the fourteenth century, and revises it for the pressing needs and new political realities of the late fifteenth-century court for which it was made. The Morgan *Confessio* is only one among a corpus of such customized books—launched by illuminators into the moments of their reception—that are the tangible foundation for what came to be the Middle English literary canon.

EPILOGUE

Chaucer's Missing Histories

A question looms over this book, one that I have worried might embarrass its premises: why are there no manuscripts of *The Canterbury Tales* with narrative illumination?[1] If, as I have argued, illuminators were integral to the rising prestige of English verse, if they were coproducers who gave form to some of the most important questions that this body of work raised, and if manuscripts with illustration accommodated audiences' desires to couch exemplary verse within the contexts of personal and often political preoccupations, then how could so rich an omnibus of stories as *The Canterbury Tales* be bankrupt of narrative cycles?

Rather than confront this question at the start, I have decided to close with it, in the hope that this consideration will magnify the main arguments of this book. By way of an epilogue, I gesture toward some answers to this question through a glimpse at the second edition of *The Canterbury Tales*, printed by William Caxton in circa 1482.[2] In concluding on print rather than manuscript, I also want to compensate for the technologically determined periodization to which this book subscribes as a matter of pragmatics but not conviction. To be sure, I agree with Vincent Gillespie in his challenge to the "assumption of a speedy or decisive paradigm shift from one medium to the other."[3] The absence of narrative illustration in printed copies of *The Canterbury Tales* is indeed an important sign of continuity.

Like the illuminators who idealized book production as a consultative process and like the three authors at the center of this study whose works he cast in print, Caxton opens his prologue to the second edition of *The Canterbury Tales* with a commendation of old books. The commendation is only one trope that allies Caxton's contextualization of his second edition with the prologues that Chaucer, Gower, and Lydgate wrote for a number of their own works. After praising Chaucer as a "noble & grete philosopher" who embellished the English tongue, Caxton recounts the genesis of the second edition. A "gentylman," he claims, approached him after the publication of the first edition to report that it was deficient as compared to his own father's manuscript of *The Canterbury Tales*, which "was very trewe / and accordyng vn-to [Chaucer's] owen first book by hym made." After receiving this more accurate copy, Caxton tells us, he produced the second edition that this prologue precedes. This narrative positions the reissue of Chaucer's poem as a story of inheritance stretching from old "noble bokes," to Chaucer, to Caxton, and finally to his fine readers, embodied in the gentleman. But it is also staged as a story of editorial accountability to both the reading public and the author himself, whom this more "trewe" copy would "satysfye."[4]

Conversations about this passage have focused on whether Caxton's report is an earnest account or a clever marketing ploy. Not only, the latter argument goes, would this appeal attract new buyers, but it would also entice repeat customers by convincing them of the obsolescence of their first purchase. Much of the momentum behind both sides of this argument is the degree to which Caxton *did* edit the first edition. Opinions regarding the extent of Caxton's revisions range from N. F. Blake's agreement with Thomas Dunn that "the revision of the text for the second edition is perfunctory and superficial"[5] to Barbara Bordalejo's more recent computer-assisted analysis, which she argues shows that "unequivocally, Caxton was not careless in his preparation of his second edition of the *Tales* and we should take his claims in its prologue as truthful."[6]

The most obvious difference between the two editions has figured little in this debate: the twenty-three woodcuts—many used more than once, amounting to a total of forty-seven illustrations—that were added to the second edition.[7] It is entirely possible that these pictures—which are similar but not identical to the illustrative cycle represented in the Oxford fragments now divided between Philadelphia and Manchester—were part of what the (real or rhetorical) gentleman's father felt to be "very trewe" about his copy of the poem.[8] Caxton does include among the flaws of the manuscripts he consulted for his first edition "many thynges left out," in addition to textual corruption and abridgment. In other words, it is plausible that those things later perceived to have been "left out" of some manuscripts and, as a result, of Caxton's first edition, were the pictures. Indifference to the place of images in this account parallels the history of neglect for the illuminations in manuscripts of Middle English verse that this study has attempted to redress.

In the opening and first part of this book, I demonstrated that illuminators were intrinsic participants in the book trade and in turn the production of English literary culture. For the elite culture makers who owned manuscripts of their works, Chaucer's, Gower's, and Lydgate's verse was illuminated. Moreover, I argued, the nature of limners' profession and participation elevated images above the supplementary status they are often accorded, particularly since they emerged from the hands of men whose involvement in the book trade and literary culture extended beyond the contribution of illumination. What is important about Caxton's second edition is that a prominent feature of the printed edition of *The Can-terbury Tales* that directed its reception for more than a century carried on the legacy of the limner's work. That copies with figural illustration make up less than 10 percent of the total number of extant manuscripts is immaterial. Whether or not the exemplar used to inform Caxton's second edition had illuminations, after circa 1482, when readers encountered *The Canterbury Tales* in the latest version, they encountered a book with pictures, a book that was pronounced to be truer to the author's making than the preceding, unillustrated edition. The woodcuts were commissioned specifically for this edition and were not recycled from another context, meaning that Caxton could have had the artist produce an entirely new series based on the content of each pilgrim's tale.[9] Instead, the woodcuts follow the convention that remains in three other manuscripts of the *Tales*, providing each pilgrim with an iconic representation of his or her physical form.[10]

Still, there are some differences. Unlike the manuscript cycles, the printed edition of circa 1482 inserts each pilgrim portrait both before his or her description in the "General Prologue" and before his or her tale. In addition, toward the end of the "General Prologue," another woodcut print gathers the twenty-three tale-telling pilgrims and host in a congenial environment around a table set with food (Plate 27).[11] The choice of pilgrim images and the "group portrait" around a table was canny enough to have convinced printers to retain them through 1602, even as the blocks grew old. Economy is probably more than anything else responsible for their retention; but Pynson did commission a new set of blocks in 1492, which, while different in form and detail, nevertheless reiterate the format of pilgrim portraits.[12]

Even if these woodcuts are nothing more than derivative—a common allegation against Caxton's body of work—they sat comfortably enough with the truth claims that Caxton issued in his prologue and rang true enough to the tenor of the *Tales* to promote their preservation and reuse for well over a hundred years.[13] In other words, they seem to capture and magnify what it is that made *The Canter-bury Tales* appeal not only to the people who owned the more than eighty copies and fragments that survive but also to the numerous customers whom the printed editions attracted sufficiently to warrant nine separate editions between circa 1482 and 1602. This essence is what at once likens *The Canterbury Tales* to and differentiates it from the *Confessio Amantis* and Lydgate's "megacompositions." Like the *Confessio Amantis* and *The Fall of Princes*, *The Canterbury Tales* gathers together stories reaped from a range of sources; and even the *Troy Book* recounts Trojan history as a series of discrete, exemplary episodes so that it has the flavor of a compilation. But unlike Gower's and Lydgate's works, each of the tales is anchored to a specific, speaking subject whose vitality addresses the reader directly rather than through Chaucer's mediation.[14] Lee Patterson characterized the pilgrims "less as objects whose particularity is to be detailed than as subjects caught in the very process of self-construction," and I think Caxton, a shrewd entrepreneur whom we should credit with at least some literary perspicacity, capitalized on this as the unique selling point of the *Tales*, even if only in its second edition.[15]

The illustrative cycle of this edition doubles down on the principle that illuminated copies of the poem pronounce, and in this respect reports with an amplified voice the source—or at least one source—of the poem's allure. In addition to prefacing each tale with an image of its pilgrim-teller, the second printed edition also mounts an image of each pilgrim above his or her description in the "General Prologue." Lotte Hellinga cautioned that "the success of the progress of pilgrims throughout the volume should not obscure the fact that they were inserted by the printer primarily to offer a guide to the reader."[16] But I think this arrangement achieves more. For one, if the images had only offered guides to the reader, then the inclusion of them in the "General Prologue" would have been unnecessary. Furthermore, the second edition also includes a consistent series of running heads throughout the main text, which are arguably more useful in locating the desired tale than are the woodcuts. Like so many manuscript copies of the *Tales*, these headers name each tale's speaker and not its content or number in the order of the poem.

Rather than merely providing a visual index to the poem, the series of portraits imbues the pilgrims with an authenticity that, like Chaucer himself, both stands apart from and resides within the *Tales* itself. Poised in a static parade in the "General Prologue," the pilgrims appear as we or any third-person observer might encounter them at the Tabard Inn, as the objects of our vision. Prefacing each of their own stories, they reappear in the second person, as subjects who speak directly to us rather than through the poet's filtration. Their features are generalized—even to the extent that some pilgrim portraits from the "General Prologue" are used to represent other pilgrims before their tales—which resists the iconic value that modernity assigned to portraits. But their appearance before and then within the tales proper vouches for their authenticity, if not as real, live historical actors, then certainly as subjects. Occupying the prologue's frame, the pilgrims have a visible presence before fiction conjures them, a presence that helps to consolidate them as credible interlocutors.

In the central chapters of this book, I lingered on the complexities of what only in hindsight appears to be a straightforward form of imagery: the author portrait. Resistant to such easy categories, the illuminators who depicted Chaucer, Gower, and Lydgate grappled not only with the identity of the figures they portrayed but also, and more important, with defining in visual terms the precise nature of the relationship between these men and the texts they authored. Acting as translators, compilers, commentators, protagonists, and subjects to patrons' commissions, these men seemed apt to be seen in any guise but that which might most easily define their literary vocation and unite them with a lineage of *auctoritas* extending back to the Evangelists: writing at a desk. Instead, illuminators communicated via allusion to stake out the indeterminacy that defined the English poet's identity in the moments of his bibliographic formation.

Whatever reservations about authorial imagery I ascribed to these illuminators should, however, not be confused with indifference. To the contrary, illuminators were engaged enough to be vexed by questions about authorship. And their engagement is paralleled in Caxton's decision to illustrate *The Canterbury Tales* with portraits of its tellers rather than simply with an image of Chaucer preceding the entire work, as Thomas Speght did in his edition of 1598 (Figure 31).[17] Like its Ellesmere counterpart, Caxton's second edition multiplies the source of literature and disperses it across the body of its text. This dispersal is not altogether different from the allusive acts committed by the limners who gave a face (or faces) to Gower and Lydgate. Their allusions exposed the English poet's authorial act as an overdetermined enterprise, whether because of its discomfiting multivocality, as in the case of the *Confessio*, or because of its sponsorship, as in the case of Lydgate's long poems, *The Fall of Princes* and the *Troy Book*. In woodcut array, the presence of so many speakers minimizes Chaucer's governance over the poem, something for which Caxton—unlike his scribal predecessors—compensates in the effusive tribute to Chaucer that precedes it.

At the same time, the repeated coupling of faces (even fictional ones) with narratives within *The Canterbury Tales* offers a radically different take on the social contract between a work of literature and its audience from that which manuscripts of Gower's and Lydgate's works endorse. In the third part of this study, I moved on to examine how illuminators and other manuscript producers fostered contact between the historical narratives in both the *Confessio Amantis* and the *Troy Book* and the moments in which they were produced for later fifteenth-century audiences. Illuminators exploited the opportunities offered by the narratives they illustrated to instrumentalize Lydgate's and Gower's verses, recasting their admonitions in terms compelling to viewing and reading audiences who were forecast but unimagined in their particularities by either poem. In the Royal *Troy Book* and *Siege of Thebes* commissioned by William Herbert and Anne Devereux, the illuminator capitalized on the invitations offered by the text and envisioned in earlier manuscript copies of the poem to supplant Lydgate and his original sponsor with these later patrons and the king they wished to court. And while current events intervened to prevent the book from reaching its intended destination, later generations, informed by the original program, resumed the Herberts' enterprise and made their own history a part of national history several times over. In the Morgan *Confessio*, history was not so much made as it was distorted to reflect visual modes of political discourse about the past. History was here opened up by images to admit current figures into the scenes of its action and to authorize its exposure to prejudicial use. The ability to fracture the mirror of history depended in part on manuscript producers' conception of the verse they illuminated as unmoored from the moment of its composition but moored to the moment of its manuscript's making. This making is integral to the history and identity of Gower's and Lydgate's works; not a form of reception, but one of constitution.

The occasions for prejudicial production that the *Confessio Amantis* and the *Troy Book* afford are foreclosed by *The Canterbury Tales*, a point that Caxton's circa-1482 edition focalizes. For one, each tale is the property of its own speaker, whose face precedes it and whose name brands the head of each page. Moreover, concluding the "General Prologue" is an image of twenty-four people sitting around a table (Plate 27). Before reaching this image, however, we get a vision of individual subjects differentiated in form, attribute, and description. And after we greet them as individuals, we witness them come together to inaugurate their journey as a collective enterprise. This image gives a face, or faces, to what David Wallace terms the associational ideology of the "General Prologue." This ideology "proposes that adults representing (almost) every profession, cultural level, age, and sexual orientation can come together under one roof, form themselves into a corporate unity and regulate their affairs without reference to external authority."[18] While, as Wallace goes on to discuss, Chaucer scrutinizes this proposal and submits it to a variety of stresses throughout the *Tales* themselves, the woodcut of the "Pilgrims at Table" lends associational ideology a weight that overrides whatever hierarchical or authoritarian leanings are articulated in later portions of the poem.

Even the table around which the pilgrims sit is egalitarian, lacking the ceremonial stratification of the lord's long board. The woodcut lays out in the frankest terms the redundancy of authors with audience who populate the poem as protagonists, and with centripetal force draws together the possibility for multiple interpretations that has floated *The Canterbury Tales'* canonicity for six hundred years. While the *Confessio Amantis* and the *Troy Book* accommodate the operations of power that the makers and patrons of later manuscripts sought to exploit, *The Canterbury Tales* refuses to take port at any political harbor. Factionalism itself—never mind factions—is glossed over and given no foothold for purchase. And part of the source of this elusiveness is the diversity of its quasiauthorial subjects, who deny the poem a center of origin or singular point of view and whose candid subjectivity thwarts whatever exemplarity their stories might retail.

Of course, there is no empirically demonstrable answer to the question "Why are there no manuscripts of *The Canterbury Tales* with narrative illumination?" But if I had to extrapolate one reason, apart from anything to do with the practicalities of manuscript production, I would say that illustrations of the content of each tale could never achieve the level of idiosyncratic inflection that is already provided by the pilgrim characters who recount it. This is perhaps another way of saying that because the pilgrim-tellers are themselves protagonists, their representation *is* a form of narrative illustration. What could possibly be more effective at creating a coherent narrative cycle than to portray each protagonist marking the progress of pilgrimage to Canterbury across the manuscript's or printed book's pages? Ultimately, the answer to the question posed above is that, to the contrary, there are.

Mooting the question with which I opened is not meant to be subtle; instead, I mean to propose, as I have done throughout this book, that in order to deepen our understanding of England's emerging literary canon at the end of the Middle Ages, we should accord the illumination within the books that fashioned it the discursive and generic capaciousness that we allow the texts that they join. Gazing on the pilgrim representations in both manuscript and print not as (or not only as) portraits—itself a complex category of representation in the later Middle Ages—but rather (or also) as segments of a narrative cycle opens discussion to avenues of inquiry that depart from the stable center of the text. Similarly, declining to think of images of Chaucer, Gower, and Lydgate as straightforward author portraits and extending the horizon of reference points for narrative illustrations beyond the texts they accompany can activate a more nuanced appreciation for how the books that contain these images and their adjoining texts produced meaning for their owners and audiences. For these audiences, it was not just poets and scribes who made literature; it was illuminators too.

NOTES

All abbreviations in quoted text have been expanded silently. All translations are mine unless stated otherwise.

INTRODUCTION

1 For a description of the manuscript, see Scott, *Later Gothic Manuscripts,* 2:229–33.

2 San Marino, Huntington Library HM 268, fol. 79v. Bergen, ed., *Fall of Princes,* 4:1–7.

3 The analogy between writing and plowing has a long history, and English-Latin word lists translate the words *arator* and *exarator* (literally, *plowman*) as *writer*. See Griffiths, "Book Production Terms."

4 *Parliament of Fowls,* 22–25. All quotes, unless stated otherwise, are from Benson and Robinson, eds., *The Riverside Chaucer.*

5 *Confessio Amantis,* Prol. 1–7. Unless otherwise stated, all quotes are from Macaulay, ed., *The English Works of John Gower.*

6 Comprising what Derek Pearsall called the "conventional triad of praise," Chaucer, Gower, and Lydgate were repeatedly invoked by fifteenth- and sixteenth-century writers as the cornerstone of the English literary canon. Pearsall, *John Lydgate,* 1.

7 In his revisionist account of canonization, Prendergast provides a helpful summary of the standard narrative: "The narrative goes something like this: Chaucer emerged shortly after his death as the exemplar of a laureate poetics. Within a decade of Chaucer's death, John Gower was being mentioned along with him as one of the great poets. By the midpoint of the fifteenth century John Lydgate had joined Chaucer and Gower in a kind of medieval triumvirate. The popularity of these three poets continued into the sixteenth century as evidenced by the fact that all three were represented in printed editions." Prendergast, "Canon Formation," 242. With a broader focus on the institutions that supported this development, Jennifer Summit argues that there occurred "a major reorganization of vernacular literacy and literate institutions in England in the face of several interrelated key events: the emergence of a highly literate, book-owning aristocracy in the fifteenth century, the Lancastrian promotion of English as a national language, and the development of print in the 1480s by William Caxton and his followers, all of which helped to establish a secular, English culture of the book." Summit, *Lost Property,* 62.

8 Pearsall, "The Idea of Englishness," 23.

9 Important exceptions are Kerby-Fulton, Olson, and Hilmo, *Opening up Middle English Manuscripts*; Driver and Orr, "Decorating the Page"; and Scott, "Design, Decoration, and Illustration."

10 Horobin, "The Professionalization of Writing," 57. Edwards and Pearsall claim that "even the most cursory comparison of the seventy-five years . . . on either side of 1400 reveals a spectacular transformation: in broad figures, one is speaking of the difference between a rate of production that leaves about thirty manuscripts and one that leaves extant about six hundred." Edwards and Pearsall, "The Manuscripts of the Major English Poetic Texts," 257. Scott estimates roughly one-sixth of these are illuminated, although, as Hilmo notes, this count is low. Scott, "Design, Decoration and Illustration," 32–33; Hilmo, *Medieval Images, Icons, and Illustrated English Literary Texts,* 4–5.

11 Scott, *Later Gothic Manuscripts*, 1:33.

12 Boffey and Edwards, "Middle English Literary Writings," 390.

13 French remained the language of the elite, and Latin the language of scholars and religious, and any number of objections could be raised to the larger point about the "arrival" of English. For an important account of the hold French had over England's cultural landscape, see Butterfield, *The Familiar Enemy*. Opinions regarding the emergence of English nationalism or nationhood remain divided. See Turville-Petre, *England the Nation*; Lavezzo, ed., *Imagining a Medieval English Nation*; and Ruddick, *English Identity and Political Culture*. For a brief extension of this conversation into the fifteenth century, see Pearsall, "The Idea of Englishness." The idea of French "influence" on English manuscript production is usefully complicated by Sandler in "Illuminated in the British Isles." See also Bovey, "Introduction: Influence and Illumination."

14 Buettner, "Profane Illuminations, Secular Illusions," 80.

15 Scott, *Tradition and Innovation*, xi. Regarding the participation of Continental artists in English manuscript production and the import of foreign books into England, see Alexander, "Foreign Illuminators"; Wright, "Bruges Artists"; and Driver, "'Me fault faire,'" which contains further references to the scholarship that has dealt with this matter.

16 Coleman, "The First Presentation Miniature," 429.

17 Jessica Brantley identifies a similar technique for image production—what she refers to as "borrowing"—in the frontispiece to a work by Chaucer that I will not address in this study. See Brantley, "Venus and Christ."

18 Irwin, "What Is an Allusion?" 289. I discuss later in this chapter why I prefer allusion to "intervisuality," a term that is generally attributed to Camille, "Gothic Signs and the Surplus."

19 Hamburger, "The Medieval Work of Art," 406.

20 Many of these are listed in Scott, "Representations of Scribal Activity." At the beginning of the essay, Scott remarks on the increased number of author images produced during this period (115). For an extended consideration of the ideas addressed in this section, see Drimmer, "Visualizing Intertextuality."

21 Meier notes the appearance of these images, associating them with the act of compilation and a desire to display the author's knowledge. Meier, "Ecce auctor," 351–53.

22 Innumerable studies of individual Evangelist portraits have been published, but for a particularly useful survey, see Friend, "The Portraits of Evangelists." For a relevant study of scribal self-conception in image, see Hamburger, "The Hand of God and the Hand of the Scribe." See also Sandler, "'Written with the Finger of God.'"

23 Friend, "The Portraits of Evangelists," 134.

24 London, British Library Cotton MS Nero D iv, fol. 25v.

25 For a survey of literature on the relationship between the *Lindisfarne* Matthew and the *Codex Amiatinus* Ezra, see Henderson, "Cassiodorus and Eadfrith Once Again." See also Meyvaert, "Bede, Cassiodorus, and the Codex Amiatinus," 880–81.

26 Camille, "Visual Signs of the Sacred Page," 117.

27 On the transition from dictation to copying, see Saenger, "Silent Reading."

28 London, British Library Yates Thompson MS 26, fol 2r. The manuscript was produced at Durham in the last quarter of the twelfth century. See Morgan, *Early Gothic Manuscripts*, 1:57–60.

29 Minnis, *Medieval Theory of Authorship*, 9, 12. For an engaging application of these ideas to the production of architecture, see Binski, *Gothic Wonder*, 57–63.

30 Tilghman, "Pattern, Process, and the Creation of Meaning," 21.

31 "It would appear that the influence of Aristotle's theory of causality as understood by late-medieval schoolmen helped to bring about a new awareness of the integrity of the individual human *auctor*. Henceforth each and every inspired writer would be given credit for his personal literary contribution." Minnis, *Medieval Theory of Authorship*, 84.

32 "Quadruplex est modus faciendi librum. Aliquis enim scribit aliena, nihil addendo vel mutando; et iste mere dicitur scriptor. Aliquis scribit aliena, addendo, sed non de suo; et iste compilator

dicitur. Aliquis scribit et aliena et sua, sed aliena tamquam principalia tamquam principalia, et sua tamquam annexa ad evidentiam; et iste dicitur commentator, non auctor. Aliquis scribit et sua et aliena, sed sua tanquam principalia, aliena tamquam annexa ad confimationem; et talis debet dici auctor. Talis fuit Magister, qui sententias suas ponit et Patrum sententiis confirmat. Unde vere debet dici auctor huius libri. 'In primum librum sententiarum,'" in Bonaventure, *Opera omnia*, I *Sententiae*, proem, quaestio iv. Translation from Minnis, *Medieval Theory of Authorship*, 94. I have altered one word in his translation (*mere*, which I have translated as "purely" as opposed to the cognate "merely," as it is in Minnis, for reasons explained in n. 33 below).

33 This passage ("et iste mere dicitur scriptor") is almost universally translated as "and he is *merely* the scribe." However, Elizabeth J. Bryan has argued that Bonaventure's language does not prize any act over the over but rather concerns degrees of mixture and combination: it is more likely that the sense is one of purity, since the scribe adds or changes nothing ("nihil addendo vel mutando"). Bryan, *Collaborative Meaning in Medieval Scribal Culture*, 19.

34 Burrow, *Medieval Writers and Their Work*, 31.

35 See Minnis, *Medieval Theory of Authorship*; and for the impact of scholastic discourse and practice on book production, see Parkes, "The Influence of the Concepts of *Ordinatio* and *Compilatio*."

36 Minnis explores this transition (*Medieval Theory of Authorship*, 73–117). His work was supplemented substantially by Wogan-Browne et al., eds., *The Idea of the Vernacular*, which assembles prologues expressing vernacular authors' notions of authorship.

37 "In the middle ages the copying of books was not regarded as a menial task. . . . The art of handwriting was developed in books, where the versatile nature of the medium not only recorded texts but also reveals the individuality, as well as the skills, of those who handled a pen." Parkes, *Their Hands Before Our Eyes*, 145. Studies on the scribal labor of authors have appeared since the 1970s, focusing more on authors who copied their own works, for example, Edwards, "The Author as Scribe"; Lucas, "An Author as Copyist of His Own Work"; and David Watt, *The Making of Thomas Hoccleve's Series*. More recently, studies have appeared that focus on scribes whose additions and revisions to others' work places them in a more authorial or editorial role. See Matthew Fisher, *Scribal Authorship*; and Wakelin, *Scribal Correction and Literary Craft*.

38 See n. 20 above. For more studies related to the representations of French authors, see Chapter 2, n. 12. Significantly, a similar change in the iconography of reading occurred at this time. See Amtower, *Engaging Words*, 5.

39 Scott discusses this image and proposes that for a variety of reasons, it cannot document fifteenth-century writing practice but rather is about "authorial possession." Scott, "Representations of Scribal Activity," 120. For a similar argument with respect to author portraits in manuscripts of the *Roman de la Rose*, see Hult, *Self-Fulfilling Prophecies*, 79–80.

40 The most thorough study to date of medieval model books remains Scheller, *Exemplum*. See also Müller, ed., *The Use of Models in Medieval Book Painting*; and Alexander, "Facsimiles, Copies, and Variations," in which he notes that "medieval art seems almost incapable of direct copying. Variations of style and content are constantly introduced" (61). Exact or "literal" replication could even have negative spiritual implications. See Smith, "The Monk Who Crucified Himself."

41 Early images explicitly portrayed illuminators as letter painters. Of one such early image, depicting the self-described "pictor" Hugo, Alexander writes, "It is significant that [Hugo] represented himself dipping a pen in an inkwell and holding a knife in his other hand—that is, as a scribe. This may partly be explained in terms of the power of the scribal image so often shown in early medieval art. It also emphasizes how the two activities have now drawn together, are complementary, and in practice are often done by the same person." Alexander, *Medieval Illuminators and Their Methods of Work,* 10. See also, on the "pictorial self-consciousness" of late medieval illuminators, Camille, *Mirror in Parchment*, 309–50.

42 Cerquiglini, *In Praise of the Variant*; Zumthor, *Essai de poétique médiévale*. For a particularly penetrating study of variation in Middle English texts, see Machan, *Textual Criticism and Middle English Texts*. The literature on translation and translation theory is enormous, but for an overview,

see Batt, "Translation and Society." See also Di Bacco, Plumley, and Jossa, eds., *Citation, Intertextuality and Memory in the Middle Ages and Renaissance*, 2 vols.

43 Luxford, review of *Tradition and Innovation*, 804.

44 Scott, *Later Gothic Manuscripts*; and Kerby-Fulton, Olson, and Hilmo, *Opening up Middle English Manuscripts*.

45 Pearsall, "Beyond Fidelity," 197.

46 Noteworthy monographs include Kerby-Fulton and Despres, *Iconography and the Professional Reader*; and Hilmo, *Medieval Images, Icons, and Illustrated English Literary Texts*. See also Kolve, *Chaucer and the Imagery of Narrative* and Kolve, *Telling Images*. Kolve's studies examine contemporary images from an array of sources to illustrate the mental images raised by Chaucer's verse and to use "pictures as a means of recovering the meaning of literary texts." Kolve, *Chaucer and the Imagery of Narrative*, 3. For an important study that extends analysis of illumination that accompanies Chaucer's verse beyond the text it accompanies, see Brantley, "Venus and Christ."

47 See Steinberg, *The Sexuality of Christ*, 386.

48 See Emmerson, "Middle English Literature and Illustrated Manuscripts"; and Alexander, "Art History, Literary History."

49 Hamburger, *Nuns as Artists*; Hamburger, *The Visual and the Visionary*; Brantley, *Reading in the Wilderness*.

50 For example, Sandler, *Psalter of Robert De Lisle*; Sandler, *Illuminators and Patrons*; Smith, *Art, Identity, and Devotion*; Smith, *Taymouth Hours*; Kumler, *Translating Truth*; Sand, *Vision, Devotion, and Self-Representation*; Camille, *Mirror in Parchment*.

51 Smith, "Accident, Play, and Invention," 364. On the complications of apportioning agency in medieval art, see Caskey, "Whodunnit?"

52 Buettner, *Boccaccio's "Des cleres et nobles femmes"*; Buetter, "Profane Illuminations, Secular Illusions"; Hedeman, *The Royal Image*; Hedeman, *Translating the Past*; Hindman, *Christine de Pizan's "Epistre d'Othéa"*; Inglis, *Jean Fouquet*; Sherman, *Imaging Aristotle*.

53 The arms included in a copy of the *Confessio Amantis* (Oxford, Christ Church College MS 148, fol. 1r) indicate that it was almost certainly produced for one of the sons of Henry IV, but not for Henry IV himself. The ownership of Huntington Library MS EL 26 A17 is a matter of debate. See Harris, "Ownership and Readership," 123–34.

54 Claire Sherman is believed to have been the first to use this term with respect to medieval manuscript illumination in *Imaging Aristotle*. Aden Kumler presents a compelling, revisionist conception of visual translation different from the kind I am addressing here. For Kumler, images within devotional manuscripts for the laity translated not word but rather truth itself. See Kumler, *Translating Truth*. Likewise, Anne D. Hedeman conceptualizes visual translation differently from Emmerson. For a consideration of Hedeman's application of the term, see Chapter 6.

55 Emmerson, "Visual Translation in Fifteenth-Century English Manuscripts." See also Emmerson, "Translating Images" and Emmerson, "Visualizing the Vernacular."

56 Emmerson, "Visual Translation in Fifteenth-Century English Manuscripts," 21 (emphasis in original).

57 Kristeva, *Desire in Language*, 65.

58 Jeffrey Hamburger uses the term *reinscription* to encapsulate a number of ideas to which I am gesturing here. See Hamburger, "Rewriting History."

59 Genette, *Palimpsests: Literature in the Second Degree*, 2.

60 See n. 18 above.

61 Camille, "Gothic Signs and the Surplus," 151.

62 Binski, *Gothic Wonder*, 65.

63 Irwin, "What Is an Allusion?" 292.

64 Binski, *Gothic Wonder*, 50.

65 Alexander, "Facsimiles, Copies, Variations," 62–63.

66 Sandler issues an important plea for attending to the significance of makers, writing, "we are so accustomed in present-day scholarly study to focusing on medieval illuminated manuscripts in terms of their reception, that is, how the user used or was supposed to use or be affected by a book, that I think we sometimes lose sight of the makers of manuscripts, that is, those who produced the impact on the reader/viewer." Sandler, "'Written with the Finger of God,'" 282.

67 Burrow, *Medieval Writers and Their Work*, 30.

68 Nolan, "Historicism After Historicism," 64.

CHAPTER 1

1 London, St. Bartholomew's Hospital, St. Nicholas Shambles Churchwardens' Account, SNC/1, fols. 36r–v.

2 The manuscript is London, Westminster Abbey MS 37. James and Robinson, *The Manuscripts of Westminster Abbey*, 7. Backhouse discusses the details of this commission and surmises that the scribe Thomas Preston, who was housed in the abbey and paid to write out the missal over the course of two years, subcontracted the illumination. Backhouse, *The Sherborne Missal*, 9–12.

3 I am distinguishing here between the patronage of a text and the commission of a physical book. For an overview of the former, see Meale, "The Patronage of Poetry."

4 Hanna, *Introducing English Medieval Book History*, 135. A number of publications have been particularly important in offering a picture of medieval London's book trade. As I will be returning to them throughout this chapter, it should be helpful to cite them here: Griffiths and Pearsall, eds., *Book Production and Publishing in Britain 1375–1475*; Christianson, *A Directory of London Stationers and Book Artisans*, which was recently supplemented by Mead, "Printers, Stationers, and Bookbinders"; Hellinga and Trapp, eds., *The Cambridge History of the Book in Britain*; and Gillespie and Wakelin, eds., *The Production of Books in England, 1350–1500*. For an excellent overview of commercial manuscript production in a number of English urban centers (including London) up to 1400, see Michael, "Urban Production of Manuscript Books."

5 McKenzie, "Printers of the Mind." For a critique, see Tanselle, *Bibliographical Analysis*, 27–28.

6 Scott, *Later Gothic Manuscripts*, 1:33.

7 Alexander, "Art History, Literary History," 55.

8 Gillespie, "Books," 92.

9 Ibid. See also Gillespie and Wakelin, "Introduction," 1–11.

10 On the explosion of vernacular manuscript production after 1400, see Edwards and Pearsall, "The Manuscripts of the Major English Poetic Texts," 257.

11 For the prehistory of the Company of Stationers, up to 1501, see Blayney, *The Stationers' Company*, 1:1–67. In the book, Blayney issues some important corrections to the influential essay by Pollard, "The Company of Stationers."

12 "Misterie: (a) Ministry, office, service; (b) a handicraft, an art; (c) a guild." McSparran, gen. ed., *Middle English Dictionary*. Scott asserts that "undoubtedly the merger reflects the reality of daily operations in a limner's shop: a limner must have had continual dealings with copyists of books and of documents, and, like a book binder or text writer, he might have acted as an organizing entrepreneur in the production of a book" (*Later Gothic Manuscripts*, 1:27).

13 There also remain eleven records of the presentation of the company's wardens between 1403 and 1492, kept in the City's Letter Books I and K (London Metropolitan Archives, COL/AD/01/009 and 010). Interestingly enough, nine of these entries occur at various times between 1403 and 1441, and the other two instances occur in 1491 and 1492. The three entries from 1441, 1491, and 1492 refer to the company as the "Stationers." It is unknown how the company referred to itself in the fifty years between 1441 and 1491. See Christianson, *Directory*, 16.

14 London Metropolitan Archives, COL/AD/01/009, fol. 25r. Translation from Blayney, *The Stationers' Company*, 5. The original petition was in Law French, which was repeated in Latin in the

document recording the mayor's and aldermen's consent to grant the petitioners their request on July 12, 1403.

15 London Metropolitan Archives, COL/AD/01/010, fol. 195r. Although I do not address here book producers working for monastic institutions, there is an interesting parallel seen in the inventories of Westminster Abbey, which, according to a record of 1398–99, show a clear division of labor between a named scribe and a named illuminator (Westminster Abbey, *Liber Niger Quaternus*, fol. 92r), but by 1489 refer to one Edward Bottiler, who is a "faire writer, a fflorissher and maker of capitall letters" (Westminster Abbey, Register A, fol. 30v). Both texts are cited from James and Robinson, *The Manuscripts of Westminster Abbey*, 9 and 12, respectively.

16 Blayney, *The Stationers' Company*, 7.

17 Ibid., 13. Anyone who had the freedom of the City could practice any trade he or she desired. It is worth remarking that the company in which limners merged was one devoted to the production of books, because it illustrates their investment in this profession. In contrast, illuminators in Bruges could be required to join both the Guilds of Painters and Saddlers and the Guild of Book Producers. See Farquhar, "Identity in an Anonymous Age," 372.

18 Blayney, *The Stationers' Company*, 10–13, at 10. The term presumably derives from the Latin *stationarius*. See "stationarius" in Latham et al., eds., *Dictionary of Medieval Latin from British Sources*, s.v.

19 London Metropolitan Archives, COL/AD/01/010, fol. 195r.

20 Christianson, *Directory*, 25; Scott, *Later Gothic Manuscripts*, 2:384.

21 Doyle and Parkes state that manuscripts of Middle English literary texts show only "sporadic" "evidence for supervision." Doyle and Parkes, "The Production of Copies," 166.

22 See n. 17 above.

23 Gillespie, "Books," 91.

24 Christianson's *Directory of Stationers* is the most extensive work in this regard, and a glance at its contents and those of Mary Rouse and Richard Rouse's magisterial volumes on the book trade in Paris illustrates well not only the differences between the two cities but the paucity of documentation for London's trade as compared with Paris's. See Rouse and Rouse, *Manuscripts and Their Makers*. Another important source of information—this, devoted exclusively to limners but across England rather than simply London—is Michael, "English Illuminators c. 1190–1450."

25 Christianson, "Evidence for the Study of London's Late Medieval Manuscript-Book Trade," 96. Similarly, for Paris, "the booktrade's loose structure functioned only because its members were concentrated on adjoining streets." Rouse and Rouse, *Manuscripts and Their Makers*, 1:15.

26 Gillespie and Wakelin, "Introduction," 3.

27 Christianson, *Directory*, 32; Driver and Orr, "Decorating the Page," 119.

28 Edwards, "Beinecke MS 661," 188.

29 Scott, "Limning and Book-Producing Terms," 160. See also Scott, "Instructions to a Limner in Beinecke MS 223." And in the rare cases that illuminators did receive instructions, they were as likely as not to disregard them. See Sandler, "Notes for the Illuminator." Significantly, some inscriptions that look like they may be instructions could instead be captions added by a reader. See, for example, London, British Library Arundel MS 109. Also useful for book production terms are Gould, "Terms for Book Production in a Fifteenth-Century Latin-English Nominale"; and Jeremy Griffiths, "Book Production Terms in Nicholas Munshull's *Nominale*."

30 See Williams, "An Author's Role in Fourteenth-Century Book Production"; Hindman, *Christine de Pizan's "Epistre Othéa"*; Hindman, "The Role of Author and Artist"; Hedeman, "Making the Past Present: Visual Translation"; Hedeman, *Translating the Past*, 61–67; 251; Hedeman, "Making Memories"; Earp, "Machaut's Role"; and Leo, "Authorial Presence." Significantly, Alexander's survey of instructions to illuminators contains many examples from France, Italy, and the Low Countries, but only three examples (two of which are from the thirteenth century) for English books. See Alexander, *Medieval Illuminators and Their Methods of Work*, 52–71.

31 Cambridge, University Library MS Dd.8.19, fol. 8v. There are ample manuscripts that contain notes the scribe wrote to himself or herself, often for rubricated headings, but also to indicate the need for correction. See Wakelin, *Scribal Correction*, 71–98. Rouse and Rouse refer to such notes as "instructions or reminders." *Manuscripts and Their Makers*, 1:12.

32 Rouse and Rouse, *Manuscripts and Their Makers*, 1:30–31. For example, in an account from St.-Jacques-aux-Pèlerins from 1408 to 1409 for four antiphonals, they find the following: "Jean Briquede bound the volumes. She also directed the addition of two quires' worth of new feasts, to the winter portion of the confraternity's breviary; Jean (Yvonenet) Riout the binder did the necessary cleaning and binding to insert the quires. . . . Guillaume Paternostre painted the vignettes for the antiphonals. Joce painted the *histoires*, Yolent contracted with Gilles Crudel to do some of the remaining writing and notating. . . . Jean de Caen helped finish the notation." Ibid., 2:139–40.

33 Christianson, "A Community of Book Artisans," 212. Kathryn A. Smith has recently discussed the commercial conditions of London manuscript production in relation to devotional manuscripts of the fourteenth century, tracking similarly flexible arrangements and collaboration. Smith, *Taymouth Hours*, esp. 27–34.

34 Scott, *Later Gothic Manuscripts*, 1:25. Compare this paucity of signed manuscripts in London to the abundance of signed books in Paris. While the majority of these examples are scribes, illuminators did also on occasion sign their work. For Parisian illuminators who signed their works, see, for example, Rouse and Rouse, *Manuscripts and Their Makers*, 2:31, 55, 57, 60, 66, 79, 91, etc.

35 Canonical monuments and masterpieces have performed the same function as the artist's name in other subfields where anonymity prevails or the names of artists have been lost. Jeffrey Hamburger cites names as "the Holy Grail of medieval art history," and he critiques the practice of searching for them. Hamburger, "The Hand of God and the Hand of the Scribe," 63.

36 Alexnder, *Medieval Illuminators and Their Methods of Work*, 139–40. Criticizing Millard Meiss, Alexander wrote, "This project seems to be connected with the values ascribed in our present Western society to individualism, and consequently with the need to ascribe achievement to a single, individual talent. It does not reflect contemporary, that is late medieval, preoccupations" (ibid.). Both Alexander and Michael Camille challenged the practice of ascribing names to unknown artists whose work could be detected in numerous manuscripts or whose work was judged to be of exceptional quality. See Camille, review of *Medieval Texts and Images*.

37 The Consolidation Charter dates to March 5, 1446, and is Eton, ECR 39/57. The record of payment is Eton, ECR 61 AR/A/3. See Ker, ed., *Eton College, Quincentenary Exhibition*, 13.

38 See Alexander, "William Abell 'lymnor'"; Christianson, *Directory*, 59–60; Scott, *Later Gothic Manuscripts*, 2:264; Combes, "William Abell: Parishioner, Churchwarden, Limnour, Stationer." For the court records I located, see n. 46 below.

39 In the first part of his article, Alexander mentions that the manuscripts he associates with Abell are identified as such "by comparison with the Eton charter," yet the longer, discursive part of the article that characterizes Abell's style opens, "In considering Abell's style, we may start with a mature work." Alexander, "William Abell, 'lymnour,'" 166 and 168.

40 Eton College Consolidation Charter of 1446 (Eton, ECR 39/57); Cambridge, King's College Charter of 1446, (King's College Archives KC/18); Worshipful Company of Haberdashers, Grant of Arms of 1446 (no shelfmark); Statutes of London, copied in 1447 (San Marino, Huntington Library HM 932); the first miniature in a copy of Stephen Scrope's *Epistle Othea* (Cambridge, St. John's College MS H.5); Bible Concordance (Cambridge, King's College MS 40); Prayer Roll for Margaret of Anjou, after 1445 (Oxford, Jesus College MS 124); Genealogical Chronicle Roll c. 1447–55 (London, Society of Antiquaries MS 501); *Polychronicon* with a historiated initial added c. 1446–48 (Eton, College Library MS 213). To this list Scott adds tentatively a manuscript of Rolandus Ulixbonensis, *Reductorium phisionomie* (Oxford, St. John's College MS 18). See Scott, *Later Gothic Manuscripts*, 2:264. From this list I exclude the *Polychronicon* because it is damaged and difficult to assess on

this basis, and the prayer roll because its figures do not contain the high level of contour in facial features seen in the Eton College Consolidation Charter. On this latter manuscript, see Drimmer, "Beyond Private Matter."

41 I refer to the belief that Abell worked repeatedly with Ricardus Franciscus, the scribe who signed a 1447 copy of the Statutes of London, ornamented with two historiated initials (San Marino, Huntington Library HM 932) attributed by Scott to Abell; the other manuscript is Cambridge, St John's College MS H.5. On this manuscript, see Drimmer, "Failure Before Print." The two most recent considerations of Ricardus Franciscus's work contain comprehensive bibliographies: Thorpe, "British Library MS Arundel 249"; and James-Maddocks and Thorpe, "A Petition Written by Ricardus Franciscus."

42 "De Willelmo Abelle, lymnour, pro uno gardino ibidem per annum -iii s." (for Morelane in the Parish of St. Egidius extra Cripplegate in 1447). Recorded in Jefferson, *The Medieval Account Books of the Mercers of London*, 1,024. The rental payment was not known to Combes, who has written the most extensive account of Abell's life (Combes, "William Abell"). And for the consolidation charter, Abell was paid "Et sol' Willo Abell Illuminanti act[us] p[ar]liamenti xxvi s viij d" (Eton, ECR 61/AR/A/3). I am grateful to Eleanor Cracknell for sending me an image of the receipt.

43 Cambridge, King's College Archives KC/18. See Marks and Williamson, eds., *Gothic: Art for England*, 162. The Eton Charter is signed by "Broke," but whether Broke is the clerk who copied the document or simply the supervising official is unknown. See Danbury, "The Decoration and Illumination of Royal Charters," 164.

44 London, Guildhall Library MS 9171/5, fol. 8v. Text of the will is printed in Christianson, *Directory*, 110.

45 Scott, *Later Gothic Manuscripts*, 2:265. While Rouse and Rouse remark that evidence for the activities of apprentices in Paris's book trade is slim, it is far more revealing than the records regarding apprenticeships in London's book trade. For London, I am aware of a few records, in Christianson, that specify only that someone was an apprentice; whereas for Paris, there are, for example, manuscripts that contain the names of both master and apprentice responsible for illumination, records that indicate a given manuscript was passed off to an apprentice for completion, and even some records that specify the nature of the work parceled out to the apprentice. Rouse and Rouse, *Manuscripts and Their Makers*, 1:311–14. And for some examples of apprentices who were tasked with completing or complementing a master's work, see ibid., 2:43, 91, 119. See also van Buren, "Collaboration," 90–93. I am grateful to Nick Herman for this reference.

46 The wardens' accounts are London, St. Bartholomew's Hospital SNC/1. By the early 1470s, Abell's income was sufficient that he could donate to his church an altar cloth stained with images of the piéta and signs of the Passion. Business dealings may have been behind a court case in 1461 in which Abell—named as a citizen and stationer of London—sued Richard Veyland of Stoke Sudbery for 9 pounds, 5 shillings, a high sum (Kew, National Archives CP 40/802). This case has not, to my knowledge, been known previously. Another court case from 1467 also named William Abell, Stationer, as an executor plaintiff, but it is unrelated to his work in the book trade (Kew, National Archives CP 40/823). On this latter case see Mead, "Printers, Stationers, and Bookbinders," 14. Documentation of the first case can be seen at http://aalt.law.uh.edu/AALT1/E4/CP40no802/aCP40no802 fronts/IMG_0080.htm and http://aalt.law.uh.edu/AALT1/E4/CP40no802/bCP40no802dorses /IMG_1094.htm; the second case can be seen at http://aalt.law.uh.edu/AALT2/E4/CP40no823 /aCP40no823fronts/IMG_0230.htm

47 London, St. Bartholomew's Hospital SNC/1, fol. 102r. The second of the two items is ambiguous on whether Abell paid for the reparative work or whether he himself executed it.

48 Christianson, *Directory*, 59–60. Henry Edwards was another limner who likewise rented several shops, which he deeded to Guildhall clerks John Marchaunt and Richard Osbarn (ibid., 101).

49 For a similar revision to previous Master-centric studies of French manuscripts, see Andrews, "The Boucicaut Masters."

50 Scott, "A Mid-Fifteenth Century Illuminating Shop," 172.

51 Doyle and Parkes, "The Production of Copies," 203.

52 For an alternative approach, see James-Maddocks, "The Illuminators of the Hooked-G Scribe(s)."

53 Likewise Lucy Freeman Sandler has, at times, advocated an approach that does not attempt to parse individual hands. See Sandler, "One Hundred and Fifty Years," 257. See also Michael, "Oxford, Cambridge and London."

54 *Records of the Worshipful Company of Carpenters,* 2:70.

55 Two guildbooks contain the signatures of their sixteenth-century limner-cum-scribes, not included in Christianson's directory, and which I mention only as notes because the first was not produced in London and both lie outside of the chronological scope of this chapter. Museum of Luton, Luton Guild Register, fol. 121 (Thomas Shrppey [*sic?*]), and the Skinners' Company Register for the Fraternity of the Assumption of the Virgin contains the name of Thomas Wygg, who signed it in 1529 (London, Guildhall Library MS 31692, fol. 52r). Both are cited in Marks, "Two Illuminated Guild Registers," 123 and 137, n.10.

56 "Johanis Genycote pro scriptura & lymnynge vi balades porrecto regine nove aduento suo, iiis." Bridgehouse Accounts, 1460–1484 (London, Metropolitan Archives CLA/007/FN/02/003, fol. 94r). Christianson, *Directory,* 111.

57 Cox, ed., *Churchwardens' Accounts,* 106.

58 Christianson, *Directory,* 115–16.

59 Mackman and Stevens, eds., *Court of Common Pleas,* s.v.

60 "Thomas Elbrigge in propria persona sua opponet se iiii^to die versus Johanem Bradley de London lymnour de placito quod reddat quadraginta solidos quos eodem debet et iniuste detinet et quendam librum precii quadraginta solidos quem ei iniuste detinet." Kew, National Archives CP 40/647. My thanks to Nigel Ramsey for discussing the case with me. The case can be seen at http://aalt.law.uh.edu/AALT1/H6/CP40no647/bCP40no647dorses/IMG_0477.htm

61 I am grateful to Kathleen Kennedy for sharing this information with me and for providing me with a photograph of the binding. London, Lambeth Palace Library MS 560 is a book of hours and is possibly from London, c. 1500.

62 Habits varied. Kwakkel suggests that itemization accords with the person who carried out each piece of work. While some invoices do record each line item by individual, others only specify material or activity. See Kwakkel, "Commercial Organization and Economic Innovation," 175–76.

63 London, St. Bartholomew's Archives SNC/1, fol. 34r.

64 Ibid., fols. 134–135r.

65 Littlehales, ed., *Medieval Records of a London City Church: St Mary at Hill,* 131.

66 London, Metropolitan Archives P69/DUN1/B/001/MS04887, fol 8v. And in the churchwardens' account for St. Martin Orgar, "payed for a masse boke and the olde legend xiii s. iiii d. / payed for the byndyng of them vi s. viii d." London, Metropolitan Archives P69/MTN2/B/001/MS00959/001, fol. 7v. Richard Rider is another individual who was paid for multiple activities, including mending, writing in, and providing clasps for books. Littlehales, ed., *Medieval Records of a London City Church: St Mary at Hill,* 131.

67 In contrast, there is ample evidence in Paris of manuscript producers taking on specialized roles. See n. 32 above.

68 For the earliest application of Scott's working methods, see Scott, "A Mid-Fifteenth Century Illuminating Shop." She also offers a detailed description of her methods and principles in "Dated and Datable Borders in English Books;" and *Dated and Datable,* 7–16. Berenbeim has recently expressed hesitation about current practices in partitioning manuscripts into discernible hands and workshops. See Berenbeim, *The Art of Documentation,* 115–20.

69 Stanton, "Margaret Rickert (1888–1973)."

70 Rickert, "Herman the Illuminator."

71 Rickert, *The Reconstructed Carmelite Missal*, 59–90; see also Rickert, *Painting in Britain*. The *Carmelite Missal* is British Library Additional MSS 29704–5, 44892.

72 The *Sherborne Missal* is British Library Additional MS 74236. For an examination of the *Sherborne Missal* (with comprehensive bibliography) see Berenbeim, "Art of Documentation," 44–85. The *Great Bible* is British Library Royal MS 1 E ix. On the division of hands in the *Great Bible*, see Scott, *Later Gothic Manuscripts*, 2:100–106; and *Royal Manuscripts*, 142–43.

73 Farquhar, "Identity in an Anonymous Age."

74 A good overview of the situation can be found in Mooney, "Vernacular Literary Manuscripts and Their Scribes," which should be paired with Mooney, "Locating Scribal Activity." Important works that argue for the importance of civil servants and scriveners in the dissemination of literary manuscripts include A. I. Doyle, "The Work of a Late Fifteenth-Century English Scribe"; Hanna, "The Scribe of Huntington HM 114"; John Fisher, "*Piers Plowman* and the Chancery Tradition"; and Kerby-Fulton, "Langlandian Reading Circles." See also, Sandler, *Omne Bonum*, 1: 20–26 for her discussion of a fourteenth-century scribe of the Exchequer who similarly performed extracurricular work.

75 On the origins of the Scriveners' Company, see Green, "The Early History of the Scriveners' Company Common Paper." See also (but with caution owing to errors of transcription and translation) Steer, ed., *The Scriveners' Company Common Paper*; Ramsay, "Forgery and the Rise of the London Scriveners' Company"; and Ramsay, "Scriveners as Notaries and Legal Intermediaries."

76 On Scribe D (*qua* Scribe D), see Doyle and Parkes, "The Production of Copies"; Kerby-Fulton and Justice, "Scribe D and the Marketing of Ricardian Literature"; Horobin and Mosser, "Scribe D's SW Midlands Roots"; and Thaisen, "The Trinity Gower D Scribe's Two *Canterbury Tales* Manuscripts Revisited."

77 The manuscripts are Cambridge, Trinity College MS R.3.2; London, British Library Egerton MS 1991; New York, Columbia University, RBML Plimpton MS 265; Oxford, Bodleian Library MS Bodley 294; Oxford, Bodleian Library MS Bodley 902; Oxford, Christ Church College MS 148; Oxford, Corpus Christi College MS 67; and Princeton, University Library MS Taylor 5. Only Trinity College MS R.3.2 contains no figural illumination, but its opening folios (the likeliest to have been illuminated) are lost; Oxford, Christ Church College MS 148 contains only a decorated initial with the royal arms.

78 Mooney and Stubbs, *Scribes and the City*, 38–65.

79 Horobin remarks on these engagements between clerks and members of the Stationers' Company and surmises the financial disadvantages to specialization in particular kinds of books. Horobin, "Thomas Hoccleve: Chaucer's First Editor?" 245–46.

80 Doyle and Parkes. "The Production of Copies."

81 On the Guildhall, see Barron, *The Medieval Guildhall of London*. More generally on guilds in England, see Rosser, *The Art of Solidarity in the Middle Ages*.

82 Mooney, "Chaucer's Scribe." In her article, she identifies Adam Pinkhurst as the scribe responsible for the renowned Ellesmere and Hengwrt manuscripts of *The Canterbury Tales*, among others, and that he was Chaucer's "own scriveyne." For arguments against this identification see n. 83 below. For further work on Pinkhurst and the identification of London scriveners as copyists of Middle English poetry, see Stubbs, "'Here's One I Prepared Earlier'"; Horobin, "Adam Pinkhurst and the Copying of British Library MS Additional 35287"; Horobin, "Adam Pinkhurst, Geoffrey Chaucer and the Hengwrt Manuscript"; Mooney, "A Holograph Copy of Thomas Hoccleve's *Regiment of Princes*"; Mooney and Stubbs, *Scribes and the City*; and Horobin, "Thomas Hoccleve: Chaucer's First Editor?"

83 A number of scholars have voiced varying degrees of skepticism about the viability of relying on paleographical evidence when features of a scribe's own writing could vary considerably. See Roberts, "On Giving Scribe B a Name"; Hanna, review of *Scribes and the City*; and Edwards, review of *Scribes and the City*. For an admirably balanced review that gives due credit to the book's strengths

while remarking on its less convincing aspects, see Kerby-Fulton, review of *Scribes and the City*. Most recently, Lawrence Warner stated definitively that "Adam Pinkhurst and Scribe B were not the same man." Warner, "Scribes, Misattributed," 98.

84 Warner, "Scribes, Misattributed," 58.

85 On the impact of the naming of "Chaucer's" scribe, see Gillespie, "Reading Chaucer's Words to Adam."

86 Neer, *The Emergence of the Classical Style*, 9.

87 Hui, "The Many Returns of Philology," 143–44.

88 Neer, "Connoisseurship and the Stakes of Style," 1. In this article, Neer provides comprehensive references to the historiography of connoisseurship.

89 Morelli, *Italian Painters*, esp 1:74–82

90 Scallen, *Rembrandt, Reputation, and the Pratice of Connoisseurship*, 96.

91 See n. 83 above.

92 Wollheim, tellingly, uses paleography (which he calls graphology) to illustrate this flaw in the Morellian method, writing, "it is not that the tails of the gs are always the same length or the loops of the ls the same shape, but the interrelations between these forms remain constant." Wollheim, *On Art and the Mind*, 198. For a similar critique as it relates specifically to the study of English manuscripts, see Sandler, "One Hundred and Fifty Years," 259.

93 Hanna, "Auchinleck 'Scribe 6,'" 215, n. 17. It should be noted that in this case Hanna endorses the effort to ascribe works to individual hands, accepting "an allowable degree of variation" (217).

94 Feldman, *Communities of Style*, 18.

95 Wittgenstein, *Philosophical Investigations*, 204–18; Freedberg, "Why Connoisseurship Matters," 34.

96 Parkes, *Their Hands Before Our Eyes*, 149.

97 Neer, "Connoisseurship and the Stakes of Style," 19.

98 Feldman, *Communities of Style*, 36.

99 On general versus individual style, see Neer, "Connoisseurship and the Stakes of Style," 11–12. The concepts originate with Wölfflin's famous discourse on the "double root of style" (originally delivered in 1911 and published in 1915) in *Principles of Art History*, 1–13, which was criticized by Panofsky in "Das Problem des Stils." Neer refers usefully to Richard Wollheim's refinement and critique of Wölfflin in Wollheim's "Pictorial Style: Two Views." See also Holly, *Panofsky and the Foundations*, 46–68. I am replacing here "general" with "communal" or "group" so as not to embrace the baggage of immanence and determinism that was central to Wölfflin's theory.

100 Mosser and Mooney, "The Case of the Hooked-*g* Scribe(s)."

101 Feldman, *Communities of Style*, 37.

102 London, Guildhall MS 5370, p. 72. It is not my intention to suggest that Pumfrey was responsible for this manuscript. Mooney and Mosser refer to the scribe of Rawl. Poet 223 as "the Hooked-g Scribe 2." See Mosser and Mooney, "The Case of the Hooked-*g* Scribe(s)."

103 For a discussion of the decorative features that appear in documents written by clerks and scriveners, see Jenkinson, *The Later Court Hands*; Danbury, "The Decoration and Illumination of Royal Charters in England"; and Danbury and Scott, "The Plea Rolls of the Court of Common Pleas." I am grateful to Elizabeth Danbury for sending me an advance copy of this article.

104 For example, Knapp, *The Bureaucratic Muse*; and Steiner, *Documentary Culture*. For an excellent discussion of the discursive convergence that characterizes London literature of the late fourteenth and early fifteenth centuries, see Lindenbaum, "London Texts and Literate Practice."

105 Danbury, "The Decoration and Illumination of Royal Charters," 160. This is almost certainly the same Kirkby who signed the Inspeximus Charter for Eton College from 1442 (Eton, ECR 39/8). Christianson lists John Carswell as a professional scrivener, text writer, and limner (*Directory*, 84–85). And, as Kerby-Fulton and Despres argue, the only fully illustrated copy of *Piers Plowman* (Oxford, Bodleian Library MS Douce 104) was created by a civil servant they refer to as the scribe-illustrator.

Because the manuscript was made in Dublin it cannot necessarily shed light on the London scene. See Kerby-Fulton and Despres, *Iconography and the Professional Reader*. On the illumination of documents, see Berenbeim, *Art of Documentation*.

106 Christianson (*Directory*, 106–7) lists Frampton as a clerk and scribe. For the most recent work on Frampton, see Stubbs, "Richard Frampton and Two Manuscripts in the Parker Library"; and Parkes, "Richard Frampton, a Commercial Scribe."

107 Christianson, *Directory*, 106–7.

108 Stubbs, "Richard Frampton and Two Manuscripts in the Parker Library," 243. See also Somerville, "The Cowcher Books." Doyle even ventures that "flourishing must have been learned together with writing or limning (being a cheaper alternative to illumination)." Doyle, "Penwork Flourishing of Initials," 68.

109 Kew, National Archives C 81/1505, number 4.

110 The fair copy is London, British Library Egerton MS 2830.

111 London, Guildhall Library MS 12112.

112 Sutton, "An Unfinished Celebration," 135. See also Scott, "The Decorated Letters of Two Cotton Manuscripts."

113 Ironmongers' Company Wardens' Accounts, London, Guildhall Library MS 16988, fol. 21r.

114 The manuscript is kept in the hall of the Worshipful Company of Ironmongers. Its illumination is rather different from that on its later grant, from 1463, which is strongly reminiscent of that found in books. I am grateful to Teresa Waller-Bridge, assistant clerk of the Worshipful Company of Ironmongers, for welcoming me to the hall to inspect the grants. Other grants of similar quality to the Ironmongers' survive, such as that made for the Carpenters' Company in 1466 and the Brewers in 1469. The Carpenters' Company Grant is located at the Hall of the Worshipful Company of Carpenters, and I am grateful to Julie Tancell, archivist, for her assistance while I examined the grant. The Brewers' Company Grant is London, Guildhall Library MS 5436. While the inclusion of a helm surmounting the arms here is unusual in fifteenth-century company grants, it could compared to the Parish Clerks' Company grant (London, Guildhall Library MS 39293) from 1482 and the Tallow Chandlers' Company grant from 1456. The Tallow Chandlers' grant is kept in the Hall of the Worshipful Company of Tallow Chandlers, and I am grateful to Nicholas Baker, beadle, for welcoming me to the hall to examine it.

115 The Grant of Arms (1439) is the earliest surviving company grant. I am grateful to Penny Fussell, archivist of the Worshipful Company of Drapers, for welcoming me to the hall to inspect it.

116 London, Worshipful Company of Drapers, WA/1, fol. 44r. John Daunt included this same notarial mark adjacent to his name registered in the Scriveners' Company Common Paper (London, Guildhall Library MS 5370, p. 66).

117 Kew, National Archives E 361/6. On Daunt, see Drimmer, "The Painters," 446 and 447.

118 Sutton, "An Unfinished Celebration." From between 1426 and the end of Henry VII's reign, the first membranes of Common Plea Rolls typically feature some form of pen elaboration, with figural historiation appearing in roughly one-tenth of the rolls. Kew, National Archives CP 40/660 is from 1426. Danbury and Scott, "The Plea Rolls of the Court of Common Pleas," 206. The same is true for the King's Bench rolls, starting in 1439 (Kew, National Archives KB 27/714). See also the pen-drawn ornamental letters and figures in the Bridge House Accounts, addressed in Christianson, *Memorials of the Book Trade*, 41–42.

119 Scott, *Tradition and Innovation*, ix. For an excellent overview of methodological and intellectual trends in the study of late medieval manuscript illumination, see Sandler, "One Hundred and Fifty Years."

120 Alexander, "Painting and Manuscript Illumination for Royal Patrons," 162.

121 Smith, *The Taymouth Hours*, 2. These two epithets appear frequently in descriptions of English manuscript illumination from nineteenth-century catalogs and essays to today. Paul F. Reichardt discusses the ubiquity of these terms in "'Several Illuminations, Coarsely Executed,'" 119. See also Sandler, "Illuminated in the British Isles." The accumulation of these judgments seems to have been

enough to establish a mythology of the "badness" of English art, on which see Richmond, "The Visual Culture of Fifteenth-Century England," 187.

122 Backhouse, "Illuminated Manuscripts Associated with Henry VII," 177.

123 Scott, *Later Gothic Manuscripts*, 1:43–52. Rickert, *Painting in Britain*, 180–85.

124 This criticism was aimed at the 2003–2004 exhibition at the Victoria and Albert Museum, *Gothic: Art for England*. Crossley, "Between Spectacle and History," 150.

125 Scott, *Later Gothic Manuscripts*, 1:43–47. The oft-cited case of Oldcastle's heretical tracts found with a limner ("cum uno Lymnore in 'Pater-Noster Rowe,' London ad aluminand") is interesting both for its singularity and for the fact that he specifically states these tracts were left with a limner to ornament. See Wilkins, ed., *Concilia Magnae Britanniae et Hiberniae, a Syndo Verolamiensi*, 3:352.

126 Major studies that address, from a variety of different perspectives, the centrality of the devotional image in late medieval England and responses to Lollardy include Duffy, *Stripping of the Altars*; Marks, *Image and Devotion*; Kamerick, *Popular Piety and Art in the Late Middle Ages*; Stanbury, *The Visual Object of Desire*; and Gayk, *Image, Text, and Religious Reform*.

127 Kennedy, *The Courtly and Commercial Art*.

128 See, for a similar methodological recommendation as applied specifically to changing styles, Henk van Os's revision to Millard Meiss's thesis in "The Black Death and Sienese Painting," 242.

129 Rouse and Rouse, *Manuscripts and Their Makers*, 1:259.

CHAPTER 2

1 The image of Chaucer in the Ellesmere Manuscript of *The Canterbury Tales* (San Marino, Huntington Library MS EL 26 C9) has occasioned extensive commentary and debate focused on the degree to which it records his physiognomic likeness, whether it presents him as a venerable *auctor*, how it compares to Chaucer's self-representation as a Canterbury pilgrim, and how it compares to the representations of the other pilgrims in the manuscript. Scholars, notably Martin Stevens and Richard Emmerson, have also offered differing views on the "fidelity" between the illuminations and the descriptions of the pilgrims (and Chaucer's descriptions of himself). See Seymour, "Manuscript Portraits of Chaucer and Hoccleve"; Stevens, "The Ellesmere Miniatures as Illustrations of Chaucer's *Canterbury Tales*"; Gaylord, "Portrait of a Poet"; Emmerson, "Text and Image in the Ellesmere Portraits"; Olson, "Marginal Portraits and the Fiction of Orality"; Hardman, "Presenting the Text"; Hilmo, "Illuminating Chaucer's *Canterbury Tales*."

2 The pilgrims are believed to have been illuminated by three limners, and I follow the scholarship on these attributions here. The first limner was responsible for the first sixteen pilgrims and the final pilgrim, the second illuminated Chaucer, and the third illuminated the remaining five pilgrims. The dimensions of the figures painted by the first artist range between 45 and 95 mm in height and 45 and 65 mm in width. Chaucer's figure measures 102 × 73 mm. And the dimensions of the figures painted by the third limner measure between 70 and 100 mm in height and 45 and 80 mm in width. See Emmerson, "Text and Image in the Ellesmere Portraits." Kathleen Scott identifies work in other manuscripts by the illuminators who provided the borders in Ellesmere. See Scott, "An Hours and Psalter by Two Ellesmere Illuminators."

3 The object is identified as a penner (a case for a writing implement) in Brosnahan, "The Pendant in the Chaucer Portraits."

4 Astell, "Chaucer's 'Literature Group,'" 269–70.

5 Emmerson, "Text and Image in the Ellesmere Portraits," 152. Similarly, the first limner placed the Prioress, the Shipman, the Franklin, the Squire, the Merchant, the Friar, and the Man of Law on the left-hand side of the page, paralleling Chaucer's placement.

6 Evans, "An Afterword on the Prologue," 375.

7 Hilmo, "Illuminating Chaucer's *Canterbury Tales*," 250.

8   The frontispiece to Cambridge, Corpus Christi College MS 61 has been discussed elsewhere extensively. For two recent studies, see Carruthers, "The Sociable Text of the Troilus Frontispiece"; and Helmbold, "Chaucer Appropriated."

9   Burrow, *Medieval Writers and Their Work*, 30.

10   On this choice of iconography, Kathleen Scott writes, "The frequent selection for representation of an author, narrator or main character over an event from a story or life is of singular importance for an understanding of the late medieval approach to narrative materials. . . . It was a state of mind which perceived the speaker as more significant than the marvels of which he spoke." Scott, "Design, Decoration and Illustration," 47. While Scott's insistence on the primacy of speaker over speech is not entirely accurate, she is right in noting the extreme consistency with which author images appear in later medieval manuscripts.

11   For a discussion of the *auctor*, see the Introduction. The image appears in Philadelphia, Rosenbach Library MS 1083/29, fol. 1r. The manuscript contains John Gower's *Confessio Amantis* and portrays Gower seated on a bed with an open book in his lap while dipping his pen into an inkhorn at his side. I discuss this image further in Chapter 3. *Pace* Anthony Bale, Chaucer's position holding an open book in London, British Library Lansdowne MS 851, fol. 2r, is not tantamount to the image of someone writing; the image of Sir John Mandeville (London, British Library Add. MS 24189, fol. 4r) as an author in the style of the Evangelists was illuminated in Bohemia and therefore does not reflect English ideas about authorship at the time; and there is no extant image of John Lydgate writing in his study, although one manuscript of *The Fall of Princes* (San Marino, Huntington Library HM 268, fol. 79v) does depict a man (not Lydgate) writing. See Bale, "From Translator to Laureate," 922 and 929. I recently noted an overlooked image in a historiated initial to a manuscript of *The Fall of Princes*, but, for reasons I discuss in detail, it is unlikely the figure represented is Lydgate. See Drimmer, "Unnoticed and Unusual." Also *pace* Mooney and Stubbs (*Scribes and the City*, 62), Gower is not shown in the act of writing in Princeton, University Library Taylor MS 5, fol. 1r. He is, rather, depicted standing and gesturing toward a two-tiered cupboard full of books, presumably a reference to "hem that writen ous tofore." I discuss this image in Chapter 3.

12   Krochalis, "Hoccleve's Chaucer Portrait," 235. Guillaume de Lorris and Jean de Meun, Jean Gerson, Guillaume de Machaut, Jean de Courcy, and such Italian authors as Brunetto Latini and Dante are all represented commonly in the act of writing. Author images in *Roman de la Rose* "usually [show] a figure seated at a desk with a book open before him, either writing in the book or simply looking at it" (Hult, *Self-Fulfilling Prophecies*, 77); Deborah McGrady discusses at length images of authors in the act of writing in "Constructing Authorship in the Late Middle Ages," 39–41, 48–49, 59–79, 87–102. On the representation of Dante as an *auctor*, and for images of him writing, see Fugelso, "Dante as 'Auctor' in Musée Condé MS 597." For an overview of the differences between the invention of the vernacular author in England and France as seen in the levels of authorial control maintained over manuscript production of their works, see Taylor, "Vernacular Authorship and the Control of Manuscript Production."

13   There is a large body of literature on medieval portraiture and the visual construction of identity. Especially useful for the twelfth and thirteenth centuries are Bedos-Rezak, *When Ego Was Imago*; and Dale, "The Individual, the Resurrected Body, and Romanesque Portraiture." For the later Middle Ages, Stephen Perkinson's extensive scholarship is essential. See esp. Perkinson, "Rethinking the Origins," *The Likeness of the King*, and "Likeness." See also for a concise synthesis of scholarship on late medieval portraiture, Sand, *Vision, Devotion, and Self-Representation*, 12–14.

14   Conrad of Hirsau, "Dialogue on the Authors," 41. See also Sears, "Portraits in Counterpoint," 71.

15   Salter and Pearsall, "Pictorial Illustration of Late Medieval Poetic Texts," 116.

16   Peters, *Das Ich im Bild*.

17   Foucault, "What Is an Author?" See also Barthes, "The Death of the Author." Foucault's essay was written as an implicit response to Barthes's. For a useful historiography of authorship studies, see Haynes, "Reassessing 'Genius' in Studies of Authorship."

18 A translation of "semantisch bedeutendes Bildschema" (Wenzel, "Autorenbilder: Zur Ausdifferenzierung von Autorenfunktionen in mittelalterlichen Miniaturen," 3).

19 For a discussion of this issue, see the Introduction.

20 Koerner, "Confessional Portraits," 125.

21 See Berger, "Fictions of the Pose"; and Didi-Huberman, "The Portrait, the Individual and the Singular." Both critique what the latter derides as the "Miss Marple" kind of art historical investigation of portraiture, in which the historian tracks down clues to the painted person's juridical or "actual" identity.

22 Spearing, *Medieval Autographies*. Spearing defines *autography* as "first-person writing in which there is no implied assertion that the first person either does or does not correspond to a real-life individual" (7).

23 For an account of the known manuscripts of *The Canterbury Tales* and their affiliations, see Owen, *The Manuscripts of* The Canterbury Tales. Stephen Partridge provides a brief overview of current thinking on Chaucer's relationship to the manuscript copies of *The Canterbury Tales* and notes that "hypotheses that Chaucer may have overseen a few of the earliest surviving manuscripts of some works has yet to be laid out in detail or to gain general acceptance." Partridge, "'The Makere of This Boke,'" 140, n. 20; see also 110–14. In addition, see Horobin, "Compiling the *Canterbury Tales*"; da Rold, "Textual Copying and Transmission," esp. 47–50; and Mooney and Stubbs, *Scribes and the City*, 67–85.

24 London, British Library Lansdowne MS 851; Oxford, Bodleian Library MSS Rawlinson Poet. 223 and Bodley 686; New Haven, Beinecke Library MS Takamiya 24 ("The Devonshire Chaucer"); San Marino, Huntington Library MS EL 26 C 9 ("The Ellesmere Chaucer"); Cambridge, University Library MS Gg.4.27; and the "Oxford MS," of which illuminated fragments survive in Philadelphia, Rosenbach Library MS 1084/2, and Manchester, Rylands Library MS English 63. The manuscripts that lack the Chaucer image are Cambridge University Library MS Gg.4.27 and the copy represented in the fragments in Philadelphia, Rosenbach Library MS 1084/2, and Manchester, Rylands Library MS English 63.

25 Hardman, "Presenting the Text."

26 Compare his pose here to images of authors, often identified by name, positioned frontally, and presenting a book to the reader, found commonly in Italian manuscripts of the period. See Alexander, *The Painted Book in Renaissance Italy*, 213–17.

27 London, British Library Lansdowne MS 851 once enjoyed an illustrious reputation among *Canterbury Tales* manuscripts. See Furnivall, ed., *The Lansdowne MS 851 of Chaucer's Canterbury Tales*. Thomas Prendergast posits that the motivation to reproduce it arose, in part, from the appeal of this opening illumination. Prendergast, *Chaucer's Dead Body*, 92. See also on this manuscript Scott, *Later Gothic Manuscripts*, 2:87, 111, 141.

28 This manuscript has attracted scholars' attention because of its scribe's particularly aggressive editorial hand. I discuss this manuscript at greater length in Chapter 4.

29 Oxford, Bodleian Library MS Bodley 686, fol. 1r.

30 On the gesture of removing one's cap in medieval literature and culture, see Burrow, *Gestures and Looks*, 30–31.

31 For example, Maidie Hilmo detects a sexual subtext to this image, seeing in the red cap a phallic emblem. See Hilmo, "Illuminating Chaucer's *Canterbury Tales*," 256–59.

32 New Haven, Beinecke Library MS Takamiya 24. On the scribe responsible for copying this manuscript (whom Mooney and Mosser designate as "Hooked-g Scribe 2"), see Horobin, "The 'Hooked G' Scribe"; and Mosser and Mooney, "The Case of the Hooked-*g* Scribe(s)."

33 Kelliher, "The Historiated Initial in the Devonshire Chaucer."

34 Pearsall, *The Life of Geoffrey Chaucer*, 291.

35 Hilmo, "Illuminating Chaucer's *Canterbury Tales*," 259–61.

36 This oversight is entirely understandable: for years the manuscript was held in private collections and has only recently been made available for public inspection by the generosity of its owner,

who has given it to the Beinecke Library. On this collection, see Takamiya, "A Handlist of Western Medieval Manuscripts in the Takamiya Collection"; and Clemens, Ducharne, and Ulrich, *Gathering of Medieval English Manuscripts*.

37 See Horobin, "The 'Hooked G' Scribe"; and Mooney and Mosser, "Hooked-G Scribes and Takamiya Manuscripts."

38 The following manuscripts all depict pilgrims on horseback: San Marino, Huntington MS EL 26 C 9 ("The Ellesmere Chaucer"); Cambridge, University Library MS Gg.4.27; and the "Oxford MS," of which illuminated fragments survive in Philadelphia, Rosenbach Library MS 1084/2 and Manchester, Rylands Library MS English 63.

39 Hardman, "Presenting the Text," 47–49.

40 Oxford, Bodleian Library MS Rawlinson Poet. 223, fol. 142r.

41 Ibid., fol. 183r.

42 For an extended comparison between the two, see Gaylord, "Portrait of a Poet."

43 Ethan Knapp examines the paternalistic model of literary inheritance in Hoccleve's *Regiment*, arguing that Hoccleve deploys this trope in order to challenge its validity. See Knapp, "Eulogies and Usurpations."

44 For a biography and concise introduction to Hoccleve's works, see Burrow, *Thomas Hoccleve*. Ethan Knapp explores the impact of Hoccleve's profession on the nature and thematic preoccupations of his works in *The Bureaucratic Muse*.

45 Doyle and Parkes, "Production of Copies," 164, 182–85. See Chapter 1 for a discussion of clerks' and scriveners' participation in the dissemination of English verse.

46 The most extensive study of the *Regiment* is in Nicholas Perkins's *Hoccleve's* Regiment of Princes. Some have argued that this poem was an artful commission from the prince. See Pearsall, "Hoccleve's *Regement of Princes*." Paul Strohm presents a similar line but argues that Hoccleve reveals inadvertently the tendentiousness of Lancastrian claims. Strohm, *England's Empty Throne*, 141–48.

47 On the bifurcated structure of *The Regiment*, see Greetham, "Self-Referential Artifacts"; and Scanlon, *Narrative, Authority, and Power*, 299–321.

48 Burrow, "Autobiographical Poetry in the Middle Ages"; Burrow, "The Poet as Petitioner"; Simpson, "Madness and Texts"; Lee Patterson, "'What Is Me?'" Rory Critten has noted more recently that the apparent autobiographical features of Hoccleve's works held far less appeal for their medieval readers than they do for modern critics. See Critten, "'Her Heed They Caste Awry.'"

49 On this effect in Hoccleve's works, see Spearing, *Medieval Autographies*, 129–70.

50 Blyth, ed., *Regiment of Princes*, 4,982–5,012.

51 There are forty-three extant manuscripts of the poem. London, British Library Harley MS 4866, fol. 88r, contains the best-known image of Chaucer, and London, British Library Royal MS 17 D vi, fol. 93v, contains another. Two other manuscripts once contained images of Chaucer, but they were later excised (London, British Library Arundel MS 38 and Harley MS 4826, fol. 139r, which retains several centimeters of its width, showing that it was a standing image of Chaucer, similar to the one in London, British Library Royal MS 17 D vi). For descriptions of the manuscripts, see Seymour, "Manuscripts of Hoccleve's *Regiment of Princes*"; and Edwards, "Hoccleve's *Regiment of Princes*."

52 On the rosary see Rubin, *Mother of God*, 332–38.

53 The other scribe, designated "Scribe B" by A. I. Doyle and M. B. Parkes ("Production of Copies") has been identified as Adam Pinkhurst by Linne Mooney ("Chaucer's Scribe"). For a more detailed discussion of Scribe B and Adam Pinkhurst, see Chapter 1. See also Thompson, "Thomas Hoccleve and Manuscript Culture." Simon Horobin discusses Hoccleve's status as Chaucer's "literary executor" in "Thomas Hoccleve: Chaucer's First Editor?"

54 David R. Carlson argues most forcefully for its authenticity as a portrait based on Chaucer's actual likeness, claiming that Hoccleve sought to prove his personal acquaintance with Chaucer by providing an image that would tally with the viewer's recollection of Chaucer's appearance. Carlson,

"Thomas Hoccleve and the Chaucer Portrait." For the opposing view, see Seymour, "Manuscript Portraits of Chaucer and Hoccleve."

55 Knapp, "Eulogies and Usurpations," 263–68. Thomas Prendergast makes a similar argument within a psychoanalytic framework in *Chaucer's Dead Body*, 33–37.

56 Simpson, "Nobody's Man." For a revisionist view of patronage as a collaborative enterprise in Hoccleve's work (albeit focused on the *Series*), see Vines, "The Rehabilitation of Patronage in Hoccleve's *Series*."

57 Perkins, *Hoccleve's* Regiment of Princes, 118–21.

58 Gaylord, "Portrait of a Poet."

59 Galloway, "Fame's Penitent," 117.

60 Pearsall, "Hoccleve's *Regement of Princes*," 402.

61 "The image of the old person was not unequivocal. The old man was believed to possess wisdom, an accumulated experience of life, cooler passions.... At the same time, the old person was held to have feebler mental faculties and to tend to irascibility, melancholy, miserliness." Shahar, *Growing Old in the Middle Ages*, 70.

62 See Lerer, *Chaucer and His Readers,* 147–75.

63 Krochalis, "Hoccleve's Chaucer Portrait," 241. See also McGregor, "The Iconography of Chaucer."

64 Blyth, ed., *Regiment of Princes*, 248.

65 Burgess, "'Longing to Be Prayed For,'" 57.

66 Fehrmann, "Politics and Posterity," 86.

67 Ibid., 87.

68 Badham and Oosterwijk, "'Cest endenture fait parentre,'" 191, 235.

69 Weatherley, ed., *Speculum Sacerdotale, Edited from British Museum MS Additional 36791*, 228. See also Badham and Oosterwijk, "Introduction."

70 "Many men ben disseyved in founding of chauntries, in coostli sepulcris, and in solempne sepulturis; and alle þes feden þe world, and done no profit to þe soule; but as þei harmen men lyvynge, so þei done harm to þe soul." Arnold, ed., *Select English Works of John Wyclif*, 2:213. For an engaging analysis of Hoccleve's defense of images, see Gayk, *Image, Text, and Religious Reform*, 46–54. See also Pearsall, "Hoccleve's *Regement of Princes*," 403–5.

71 Blyth, ed., *Regiment*, 4,995–96.

72 Spearing, *Medieval Autographies*, 164–70.

73 Perkins, *Hoccleve's* Regiment of Princes, 118.

74 For a discussion of scribes' and illuminators' responses to this passage in other manuscripts, see Drimmer, "The Manuscript as an Ambigraphic Medium." http://www.tandfonline.com/toc/yexm20/current.

75 See Oexle, "Memoria und Memorialbild," esp. 394–407; Geary, *Phantoms of Remembrance*, 81–114; and Freed, "The Creation of the *Codex Falkensteinensis* (1166)."

76 London, British Library Cotton MS Nero D vii. See Sandler, *Gothic Manuscripts 1285–1385*, 2:178; Scott, *Later Gothic Manuscripts*, 2:237–39.

77 Blyth, ed., *Regiment*, 1,973–74.

78 See Meyer-Lee, *Poets and Power from Chaucer to Wyatt*, 88–124.

79 Wood, *Forgery, Replica, Fiction*, 119–20.

80 York Minster Library, L1(2), fol. 56r; and Northamptonshire Record Office, Stopford Sackville Collection no. 4239. Quote and translation from Badham and Oosterwijk, "Cest endenture fait parentre," 198 and 218, emphasis added. See n. 13 above, for scholarship on medieval notions of identity and the importance of the "type."

81 Wood, *Forgery, Replica, Fiction*, 136, 139.

82 It is important here to acknowledge that the portrait type did not immediately give way to physiognomic likeness in the fifteenth or sixteenth century. Stephen Perkinson offers a nuanced dis-

cussion of the coexistence of the two conventions of portraiture (the "fantastic" and the mimetic) into the sixteenth century. Perkinson, "From an 'Art De Memoire' to the Art of Portraiture."

83 Wood, *Forgery, Replica, Fiction*, 139–40.

84 No inventory or will that includes a *Canterbury Tales* manuscript mentions Chaucer's name until 1540. See Manly and Rickert, eds., *The Text of the* Canterbury Tales, 1:606–45. In a frequently cited article, Sylvia Wright argues that stereotyped heads within the historiated initials of the Bedford Psalter-Hours (London, British Library Add MS 42131) represent Chaucer, Gower, and Hoccleve. However, as can be seen on fol. 209v in the fully digitized manuscript (available online at http://www.bl.uk/manuscripts/), the minims exceed the number required to spell out "Gower." Moreover, the premises underlying the claim that other figures represent Chaucer and Hoccleve are unsupported by the practices of identification within late medieval England's visual culture. These premises are, first, that figural types lacking identifying attributes like heraldry or textual labels would be apprehended by viewers as historically recognizable individuals unrelated to the content or circumstances of production of the book in question, and, second, that a (labeled) figure of a poet licenses the identification of other (unlabeled) poets in the same manuscript. In addition, the manuscript is filled with historiated initials that label their inhabitants as biblical figures. For example, "David Proph" appears on fol. 141v. It seems that any figure in the manuscript, when it is not a stereotyped representation of some social station, is a biblical figure. See Wright, "The Author Portraits in the Bedford Psalter-Hours"; and, for a critique, Harris, "Ownership and Readership," 149, n.233.

85 Strohm, "Chaucer's Fifteenth-Century Audience." See also, for an argument that supports the tight circle of Chaucer's original Southwark audience, Sobecki, "A Southwark Tale."

86 See Chapter 3 for a discussion of similar measures taken by Gower.

87 See Drimmer, "The Manuscript as an Ambigraphic Medium."

88 Minnis, *Medieval Theory of Authorship*, 12.

89 The only exception is London, British Library Lansdowne MS 851, discussed above. Helen Barr has compared Chaucer's hand to a manicule. Barr, *Transporting Chaucer*, 109–18. For an imaginative interpretation of Chaucer's hands as sign language for his monogram, "GC." Bragg, "Chaucer's Monogram and the 'Hoccleve Portrait' Tradition."

90 Bryson, *Vision and Painting*, 88–89, emphasis in original.

91 See Ziolkowski, "Do Actions Speak Louder Than Words?"

92 Quintilian, *Institutio Oratoria*, XI. iii. 94. See Butler, ed. and trans., *The Institutio Oratoria of Quintilian*, 4:295.

93 Houston, *Shady Characters*, 177.

94 Sandler, *Omne Bonum*, 1:64.

95 William Sherman, *Used Books*, 25–52, at 52.

96 Slights, *Managing Readers*, 75. Similarly, John King notes, "The manicule constitutes a common inward reference, whose deictic force requires the reader to attend to nothing outside of the specific textual site." King, *Foxe's* Book of Martyrs *and Early Modern Print Culture*, 64.

97 See Nagel and Wood, *Anachronic Renaissance*, 123–34.

98 Pearsall, *The Life of Geoffrey Chaucer*, 279.

99 Driver, "Mapping Chaucer," 228. See also, on a hand-tinted version of this image and the history of the manuscript in which it was tipped, Cook, "Joseph Holland and the Idea of the Chaucerian Book." It is interesting to note that in the sixteenth century and later, images of John Gower, Thomas Hoccleve, John Hardyng, and others were either drawn on to the blank leaves of or cut out from printed editions and pasted into earlier manuscripts of their works, which lacked images of the authors. See, for example, New York, Morgan Library and Museum MS 690, fol. 1r–v; Oxford, Bodleian Library MS Ashmole 34, fol. 1v; and Oxford, Bodleian Library MS Douce 158, flyleaf iii verso.

100 Koerner, *The Moment of Self-Portraiture in German Renaissance Art*, 175.

1 See Echard, "Designs for Reading"; Emmerson, "Reading Gower in a Manuscript Culture"; Echard, "Dialogues and Monologues"; Butterfield, "Articulating the Author."

2 Princeton, University Library Taylor MS 5. See Fleming, "Medieval Manuscripts in the Taylor Library," 113–15; Jeremy Griffiths, "*Confessio Amantis*: The Poem and Its Pictures"; Fredell, "Reading the Dream Miniature in the *Confessio Amantis*," 74–75; Scott, *Later Gothic Manuscripts*, 2:109, 146. On Gower's auto-exegesis, see Copeland, *Rhetoric, Hermeneutics, and Translation*, 179–221; and Minnis, "De Vulgari Auctoritate."

3 The poem survives in a number of versions, and the date by which it was completed is generally believed to be c. 1393. The earliest textual history of the *Confessio Amantis* was established between 1898 and 1901 by G. C. Macaulay, who devised a theory regarding the differences among the texts in the copies he surveyed, breaking them up into three "recensions." See Macaulay, ed., *The English Works of John Gower*, 1:cxxvii–clxvii. Beginning in the late 1970s, scholars began to question Macaulay's model, and debates about the persons responsible for the revisions continue. See Doyle and Parkes, "The Production of Copies"; Nicholson, "Gower's Revisions in the *Confessio Amantis*"; Nicholson, "Poet and Scribe in the Manuscripts of Gower's *Confessio Amantis*"; Parkes, "Patterns of Scribal Activity"; Lindeboom, "Rethinking the Recensions of the *Confessio Amantis*"; Fredell, "The Gower Manuscripts: Some Inconvenient Truths"; Jones, "Did John Gower Rededicate His 'Confessio Amantis' Before Henry IV's Usurpation?"; Nicholson, "Gower's Manuscript of the *Confessio Amantis*." An abandonment of the recension model was proposed by the participants in a roundtable at the Early Book Society conference in summer 2017, who advocated a division of the manuscripts according to the dedication (Ricardian and Henrician).

4 Daniel 2:19–45.

5 The *Confessio Amantis* survives in forty-nine manuscripts. Nineteen of these contain prefatory miniatures for the poem, and one manuscript (Oxford, New College MS 266) contains an illustrative cycle without prefatory miniatures. The manuscripts with prefatory miniatures are Cambridge, Pembroke College MS 307; Cambridge, St. Catharine's College MS 7; Cambridge, University Library MS Mm.2.21; London, British Library Egerton MS 1991; London, British Library Harley MS 3869; London, British Library Royal MS 18 C xxii; New York, Columbia University, Rare Book and Manuscript Library Plimpton MS 265; New York, Morgan Library and Museum MS M.125; New York, Morgan Library and Museum MS M.126; New York, Morgan Library and Museum MS M.690; Oxford, Bodleian Library MS Bodley 294; Oxford, Bodleian Library MS Bodley 693; Oxford, Bodleian Library MS Bodley 902; Oxford, Bodleian Library MS Fairfax 3; Oxford, Bodleian Library MS Laud Misc. 609; Oxford, Corpus Christi College MS 67; Philadelphia, Rosenbach Museum and Library MS 1083/29; Princeton, University Library Taylor MS 5; San Marino, Huntington Library MS EL 26 A 17. A further seven have blanks where miniatures were to have been painted: Private Collection (formerly Mount Stuart, Rothesay, Marquess of Bute MS I.17); London, British Library Egerton MS 913; Cambridge, St. John's College MS B.12; Nottingham, University Library Middleton Collection MS Mi LM 8; Geneva, Bodmer Library MS 178; London, Society of Antiquaries MS 134; Cambridge, University Library MS Dd.8.19. One manuscript had a miniature, presumably (based on placement) of Nebuchadnezzar's Dream or possibly of the Statue, which was cut out: London, British Library Additional MS 22139; and the leaves where the miniatures of Nebuchadnezzar's Dream and Amans' Confession would have appeared have been cut out of Oxford, Christ Church College MS 148. Scholars have tended to emphasize the "standardization" of this illustrative program, as well as the fact that only two copies contain full cycles of illustration (Oxford, New College MS 266 and New York, Morgan Library and Museum MS M.126). However, among the manuscripts with the "standard" prefatory images are copies with one-off figural illuminations, such as San Marino, Huntington Library MS EL 26 A 17, which features the hybrid figure of an armed knight with the hind

legs of an ass (personifications of wrath and sloth) marking the transition between Books III and IV (fol. 56r); or Oxford, Bodleian Library MS Bodley 693, which contains a crowned lion's head sticking out its tongue on fols. 1r and 86v.

6 There seems to be confusion on this point, which led Ralph Hanna to write that "manuscripts of Gower's *Confessio* already in circulation placed an 'author-portrait' at the head," which is false (Hanna, *Introducing English Medieval Book History*, 163).

7 Debates about Gower's participation in the creation of the manuscripts of the *Confessio Amantis* continue. See n. 3 above. Currently, the only manuscripts that have been associated with Gower's hand and ownership are the Trentham Manuscript (London, British Library Additional MS 59495), containing a collection of Gower's texts in Latin, Anglo-Norman, and English but not the *Confessio Amantis*; and London, British Library Cotton MS Tiberius A iv, which contains his *Vox clamantis* and other Latin poems. For a thorough discussion of these issues, see Sobecki, "*Ecce Patet Tensus*: The Trentham Manuscript."

8 Emmerson, "Reading Gower in a Manuscript Culture," 170.

9 Eleven of these miniatures are placed near the beginning of the confession, while Oxford, Bodleian Library MS Fairfax 3, fol. 8r, and London, British Library Harley MS 3869, fol. 18r, place the confession miniature at the head of Book I; and London, British Library Royal MS 18 C xxii, fol. 1r, places the scene in a historiated initial to the first Middle English line of the poem.

10 Derek Pearsall describes this standard as follows: "There is a type of manuscript of the *Confessio* which is so frequently found among the surviving copies that it can almost be characterised as 'standard.' Such a manuscript was copied during the first quarter of the fifteenth century, or just before, by a good professional London scribe. It consists of about 180–200 folio-size parchment leaves of good quality, in quires of eight with catchwords, and the text is spaciously written, almost always by one scribe only, in double columns, with forty-six lines per column. The manuscript has two miniatures and the decoration is organised according to a regular hierarchy, with vinets (full floreate borders) or demi-vinets (two- or three-sided borders), decorated initials (champs) of different sizes, pen-flourished coloured initials, and decorated or undecorated paraphs, used to mark out different elements in that hierarchy and to indicate the divisions of the text for the reader." Pearsall, "The Manuscripts and Illustrations of Gower's Works," 80.

11 Polyvocality is a popular topic in Gower criticism, most recently taken up in detail in Matthew Irvin, *The Poetic Voices of John Gower*. Opinions have tended to fall into two distinct camps: those who believe the voices either unite to espouse a singular (moral) viewpoint or are reined into reconciliation by the domineering superego of Genius, and those who argue that the voices remain in irreconcilable contention throughout the poem. See Strohm, "A Note on Gower's Persona"; Minnis, *Medieval Theory of Authorship*, 177–90; Pearsall, "Gower's Latin in the *Confessio Amantis*"; Yeager, *John Gower's Poetic*; Olsson, *John Gower and the Structures of Conversion*; Wetherbee, "Latin Structure and Vernacular Space"; Aers, "Reflections on Gower as 'Sapiens' in Ethics and Politics"; Echard, "With Carmen's Help"; Diane Watt, *Amoral Gower*; Barrington, "Personas and Performance in Gower's *Confessio Amantis*."

12 "Torpor, ebes sensus, scola parua labor minimusque / Causant quo minimus ipse minora canam: / Qua tamen Engisti lingua canit Insula Bruti / Anglica Carmente metra iuuante loquar / Ossibus ergo carens que conterit ossa loquelis / Absit, et interpres stet procul oro malus" (unless otherwise specified, all Latin translations by Andrew Galloway, in Peck, ed., and Galloway, trans., *John Gower, Confessio Amantis*).

13 This allusion and its biblical sources are explained Echard and Fanger, eds. and trans., *The Latin Verses in the* Confessio Amantis, xxxvii, 2–3, n.2.

14 A version of the prologue removed this scene on the barge and dedicated the poem to Richard II's rival, Henry Bolingbroke, eventual Henry IV. The revisions occur between lines 24 and 92.

15 *Confessio Amantis*, Prol. 51, in the version dedicated to Richard II.

16 Ibid., Prol. 79–80, in the version dedicated to Richard II.

17 Ibid., Prol. 591–92.

18 That Gower hopes to see himself as this new Arion is a point not unsubtly made here. See Yeager, *John Gower's Poetic: The Search for a New Arion*.

19 *Confessio Amantis*, Prol. 49. According to McSparran, ed., *Middle English Dictionary*, "A task or enterprise; work done or to do; one's job or duty; (b) an occupation or business; (c) affairs."

20 The fictional quality of Gower's meeting with Richard II on the Thames is accentuated by its allusion to the tale of Arion and the Pirate in Ovid, *Fasti*, Book IV. See Astell, *Political Allegory in Late Medieval England*, 73–93; and Grady, "Gower's Boat, Richard's Barge, and the True Story of the *Confessio Amantis*."

21 De Man, *Rhetoric of Romanticism*, 81.

22 Simon Meecham-Jones explores the use of the autobiographical mode in the *Confessio Amantis*, arguing that it "strives to establish the poet in a position simultaneously within and outside the texture of his poem." Meecham-Jones, "Prologue: The Poet as Subject," 17.

23 Simpson, *Sciences and the Self in Medieval Poetry*, 139.

24 *Confessio Amantis*, I:8–16.

25 See "stile," in McSparran, ed., *Middle English Dictionary*.

26 *Confessio Amantis*, I:46, I:61–63.

27 "Anacoluthon: a grammatical term for a change of construction in a sentence that leaves the initial construction unfinished." Baldick, ed., *Oxford Dictionary of Literary Terms*, 11.

28 Burrow, "The Portrayal of Amans," 21, emphasis in original.

29 *Confessio Amantis*, I:154–63.

30 Twenty-five manuscripts contain the Latin prose in the text column, eleven place them in the margin, and a further seven have a mixed format. Six manuscripts excise all Latin passages. See Echard, "With Carmen's Help," 18.

31 Hic quasi in persona aliorum, quos amor alligat, fingens se auctor esse Amantem, varias eorum passiones variis huius libri distinccionibus per singula scribere proponit (*Confessio Amantis*, near I: 59). See Minnis, "De Vulgari Auctoritate"; and Minnis, "The Author's Two Bodies?" On the use of the Latin persona in Gower's work and its semantics in late medieval legalese, see Irvin, *Poetic Voices of John Gower*, 14–17, and on this gloss in particular, 82–84.

32 Moxey, "Mimesis and Iconoclasm," 66.

33 Oxford, Bodleian Library MS Ashmole 35, fol. 4v. An edition of the English apparatus of this manuscript can be found in Harris, "Ownership and Readership," Appendix I.

34 Echard, "Glossing Gower," 253–55. For a consideration of the valence of the term *maker* in Middle English, see Partridge, "'The Makere of This Boke.'"

35 For an extended consideration of my remarks here, see Drimmer, "The Disorder of Operations."

36 Oxford, Bodleian Library MS Bodley 294, fol. 8v, and London, British Library Egerton MS 1991, fol. 7v. Cited in Macaulay, ed., *The Complete Works*, 40. The relationship between these two copies is uncertain, as a stemma of the *Confessio* manuscripts has not been published since John Fisher's attempt. Fisher (*John Gower*, 304–5) includes MS Bodley 294 among the second-version manuscripts and MS Egerton 1991 among the first-version unrevised manuscripts, indicating they were probably not copied from one another or from the same parent.

37 I discuss this image below. The verses with the omitted line read, "And eft sche askiþ what was I / What wolde ȝe wiþ me my lady dere." London, British Library Royal MS 18 C xxii, fol. 9r, which interrupts the scheme of rhyming couplets.

38 Oxford, Bodleian Library MS Arch Selden B 11, fol. 8v, and Cambridge, University Library MS Dd.8.19, fol. 8v. In both of these cases the order of the verses is reversed (i.e., "what wolde ye with me my lady dere" was written first), and so it is possible that the blank was simply a result of eye skip. Nevertheless, the Cambridge University Library manuscript is on parchment, and so the scribe could easily have scraped the verse and inscribed it in its correct position.

39 Princeton, University Library Taylor MS 5, flyleaf iv. For an edition of this table of contents, see Harris, "Ownership and Readership," Appendix V. See also Echard, "Pre-Texts."

40 Oxford, Magdalen College MS 213, end flyleaf recto. For an edition of this table of contents, see Harris, "Ownership and Readership," Appendix IV. See also Echard, "Pre-Texts."

41 Griffiths, "*Confessio Amantis*: The Poem and Its Pictures," 175.

42 The qualification "English" is essential here because French poets had been playing with personas some time before Gower and Chaucer decided to do the same in English, developing the form of what Michel Zink refers to as the *roman du moi* (Zink, *La subjectivité littéraire*). See also McGrady, "The Rise of Metafiction in the Late Middle Ages." Butterfield addresses specifically the ways in which Gower is indebted to Guillaume de Lorris and Jean de Meun, Guillaume de Machaut, and Jean Froissart in "*Confessio Amantis* and the French Tradition."

43 A tremendous amount has been written on this topic. Two classic considerations of this issue are Spitzer, "Note on the Poetic and Empirical 'I' in Medieval Authors," and Donaldson, "Chaucer the Pilgrim." Reuben Sánchez gives an excellent overview of twentieth-century scholarship on persona in *Persona and Decorum in Milton's Prose* (35–40), and for more recent, revisionist accounts, see Spearing, *Textual Subjectivity* and *Medieval Autographies*.

44 I am influenced here by Harry Berger Jr.'s idea that the sitter plays a significant role in founding his representation in the performance of a sitting—which is itself, as opposed to the living individual, the subject of a portrait—as he argued in "Fictions of the Pose." Annabel Patterson makes a similar argument with respect to writers in "'The Human Face Divine.'"

45 Griffiths, "*Confessio Amantis*: The Poem and Its Pictures," 174.

46 Philadelphia, Rosenbach Museum and Library MS 1083/29, fol. 1r. Presumably Gower is placed on a bed in order to identify the poem as a dream vision, a point on which it is ambiguous. See Lynch, *The High Medieval Dream Vision*, 163–200.

47 Of these ten miniatures, there are six that bear a close resemblance to one another. This group includes Oxford, Bodleian Library MS Bodley 294; London, British Library Royal MS 18 C xxii; London, British Library Egerton MS 1991; Oxford, Bodleian Library MS Bodley 693; Oxford, Bodleian Library MS Laud Misc. 609; Oxford, Corpus Christi College MS 67. On the Bodleian Library manuscripts, see Spriggs, "Unnoticed Bodleian Library Manuscripts."

48 Burrow, "The Portrayal of Amans in *Confessio Amantis*," 11.

49 For a good comparison of Gower's Amans to French precedents see Butterfield, "*Confessio Amantis* and the French Tradition," 172–78. Many of the over three hundred extant *Roman de la Rose* manuscripts have been digitized and can be searched online at http://romandelarose.org.

50 Confessus Genio si sit medicina salutis / experiar morbis quos tulit ipsa Venus (*Confessio Amantis*, I:202). The miniatures are variously placed before, after, or next to this heading in the different manuscripts.

51 Respectively, Oxford, Bodleian Library MS Bodley 902; Cambridge, Pembroke College MS 307; Oxford, Bodleian Library MS Fairfax 3; Cambridge, University Library MS Mm.2.21.

52 The wardrobe accounts from Henry, Earl of Derby (later Henry IV), list, c. 1393, the gift of a collar of SS to be given to "un Esquier John Gower." See Fisher, *John Gower*, 68, 341–42 n.5. This collar seems to have originated with the Lancastrians, although the precise meaning of the "SS" has yet to be determined. See Fletcher, "The Lancastrian Collar of Esses"; and Morgan, "An SS Collar in the Devotional Context of the Shield of the Five Wounds." Macaulay noted the SS collar in the Fairfax miniature, remarking that it has "somewhat the appearance of having been added after the original painting was made" (*Complete Works*, 2:clvii).

53 *Confessio Amantis*, VIII:2,059.

54 Ibid., VIII:2,186.

55 See Dean, "Gower, Chaucer, and Rhyme Royal."

56 *Confessio Amantis,* VIII:2,320–21.

57 Irvin, *Poetic Voices of John Gower,* 277–86.

58 Although most scholars tend to disagree, Donald Schueler argued that the poem telegraphs its final revelation, giving hints throughout to Amans's true age. See Schueler, "The Age of the Lover."

59 Garbáty, "A Description of the Confession Miniatures," 338.

60 University of Glasgow, Hunter MS 59, fol. 129r. Retrospective tombs were common in the Middle Ages and Early Modern period. See Wood, *Forgery, Replica, Fiction*, 118–27; and specifically for England, Lindley, "Retrospective Effigies." That Chaucer's tomb was only later created and placed in what came to be called "Poets' Corner" in Westminster Abbey further suggests a later date for the creation of Gower's effigy, which is no longer in its original location (see Prendergast, *Chaucer's Dead Body*). Gower's will provides only for his interment in the Priory of St. Mary Overeys but does not mention a tomb or effigy. For the will, see W. H. B. "Will of John Gower the Poet, anno 1408"; and for a translation, see Macaulay, ed., *Complete Works of John Gower*, 4:xvii–xviii. The earliest description of Gower's tomb is in Stow, *Survey of London* (2:57–58); and for an in-depth discussion of the tomb, see Hines, Cohen, and Roffey, "Iohannes Gower, Armiger, Poeta." On the manuscript tradition of the *Quia unusquisque*, see Echard, "Last Words"; and on its epitaphic qualities, see Summit, *Memory's Library*, 189–90.

61 Garbáty provides a full description of the miniature but does not mention the marginal note. Garbáty, "A Description of the Confession Miniatures," 322; Macaulay mistranscribed the note as "Hic fiat Garn*imentum*." *English Works*, 1:cxl.

62 Little, *Confession and Resistance*, 101. For another study that redresses this neglect, see Lee, "Confessio Auctoris."

63 Smith, *Taymouth Hours*, 74; and 61–109. Likewise, a devotional book "mediated its owner's experience of other imagery and texts within her/his religious environment," an argument that we can extend outward to nonreligious environments. Smith, *Art, Identity and Devotion*, 4. See, for a similar convergence, Brantley, "Venus and Christ."

64 Chloë Taylor's study on confession, though centered on her thesis that confession is *not*, contrary to common perception, a natural human compulsion, provides a thorough review of modern critical approaches to confession and its history. See Taylor, *The Culture of Confession*.

65 Foucault, *History of Sexuality*, 1:61–62. Kumler describes developments in confessional practice during the twelfth and thirteenth centuries as increasingly focused on dialogue, both in word and image in *Translating Truth*, 45–101.

66 Foucault, *History of Sexuality*, 1:61. See also Jameson, *The Ideologies of Theory*, 534–54.

67 Tentler, *Sin and Confession*, 165.

68 Costley, "David, Bathsheba, and the Penitential Psalms," 1,252. See also King'oo, *Miserere Mei*, 25–61.

69 There are two exceptions of which I know: in manuscripts of the *Roman de la Rose* and the single fully illustrated copy of *Piers Plowman* (Oxford, Bodleian Library MS Douce 104, fol. 11v). In both cases, it is a personification who issues the confession—Natura in the former, and Lady Mede in the latter.

70 See Rogers, "The Location and Iconography of Confession." Costley gives an overview of late medieval representations of David before the Penitential Psalms while illustrating how the focus turned later to representing him gazing on Bathsheba, in "David, Bathsheba, and the Penitential Psalms."

71 On the transmigrations of this complicated figure in medieval literature, see Economou, "The Character Genius"; Nitzsche, *The Genius Figure*; Baker, "The Priesthood of Genius"; Wetherbee, "Genius and Interpretation"; Tinkle, *Medieval Venuses and Cupids*, 178–97; Newman, *God and the Goddesses*, 51–111; Wetherbee, "Classical and Boethian Tradition."

72 Possibly eight: the image in London, British Library Royal MS 18 C xxii, has Amans turned slightly away from the viewer, so it is difficult to ascertain whether his arms are crossed over his chest, although the position of his right arm and elbow do imply this pose. The seven manuscripts are London, British Library Egerton MS 1991; Oxford, Bodleian Library MS Bodley 294; Oxford, Bodleian

Library MS Bodley 693; Oxford, Bodleian Library MS Bodley 902; Oxford, Bodleian Library MS Laud Misc. 609; Oxford, Corpus Christi College MS 67; Cambridge, Pembroke College MS 307.

73 The other two are Cambridge, University Library MS Mm.2.21, fol. 8r (see the discussion of this manuscript earlier in this chapter); and Cambridge, St. Catharine's College MS 7, fol. 4v. For the instructions on fol. 4v, see n. 92 below.

74 Possibly seven. See n. 72 above.

75 "Penitents use two gestures for their hands. They hold them folded palm to palm (for example, at Salle, Cley, and Great Witchingham), or lay them on the priest's lap." Nichols, "The Etiquette of Pre-Reformation Confession," 152. For the visual material, see Nichols, *Seeable Signs*, 224–41; and Rogers, "The Location and Iconography of Confession."

76 Garbáty refers to Gougaud, who claims that "the rubrics of many missals of the Middle Ages ordered the priest to keep this position [the arms placed in the form of a cross over the breast] during the prayer *Supplices te rogamus* of the Canon of the Mass." Gougaud, *Devotional and Ascetic Practices*, 20. Gougaud does make use of several sources for this rubric, only one of which is medieval (the rest are from missals dating from the seventeenth to the nineteenth century). With respect to images, Garbáty refers to middle Byzantine art, in which the crossed hands are a fairly common motif. Garbáty, "A Description of the Confession Miniatures," 340, n.3. As Mosche Barasch points out (see n. 77 below), it enjoyed a broad application in Late Antique art but afterward remained relatively unseen until its reappearance in funerary sculpture in the thirteenth century.

77 Mosche Barasch devotes a chapter to discussion of this gesture, its history in early medieval art and liturgy, and its appearance and meaning in Giotto's oeuvre in *Giotto and the Language of Gesture*, 72–87. In English art of the late fourteenth century to the early sixteenth century, the Virgin is also occasionally shown with her hands crossed over her chest in images of the Presentation of the Virgin, Crucifixion, Pentecost, and Coronation. It is important here to distinguish between the Virgin's pose, which signifies humility, and the iconography of the Madonna of Humility, on which see Williamson, *The Madonna of Humility*.

78 Cited from Baxandall, *Painting and Experience*, 51–55, 164–65. The original Italian (which Baxandall prints in full) appears in Caracciolus, *Sermones de laudibus sanctorum*, lxv recto–lxvii recto, clii recto–cliv recto, cxlic recto–clii recto.

79 London, British Library Sloane MS 2593, fol. 28v. Greene, ed., *The Early English Carols*, no. 236.

80 Miles, "The Annunciation as Model of Meditation." http://merg.soc.srcf.net/journal/05cambridge/miles.php.

81 From the late thirteenth century, this gesture is increasingly included in Italian imaginings of the Annunciation, as in Giotto's fresco in Padua in the Cappella degli Scrovegni nell'Arena. See Levin, "Two Gestures of Virtue," esp. 336–42.

82 For the manuscripts of the poem, see Lauritis, Klinefelter, and Gallagher, eds., *A Critical Edition of John Lydgate's Life of Our Lady*.

83 London, British Library Royal MS 2 A xviii fol. 34. For a description of the manuscript, see Scott, *Later Gothic Manuscripts*, 2: 127–32.

84 Marks, *Stained Glass in England*, 164–65.

85 Prior and Gardner, *An Account of Medieval Figure-Sculpture in England*, 397; Gardner, *English Medieval Sculpture*, 240.

86 In addition to visual representations, it also featured as a performed gesture in the Carthusian Liturgy, immediately following the Consecration. See Nash, "Claus Sluter's 'Well of Moses,'" 732; Levin, "Two Gestures," 336; Hedeman, "Rogier van der Weyden's Escorial *Crucifixion*," 194–95.

87 *The Canterbury Tales*, "General Prologue," 520.

88 His crossed arms here may also be linked to the gesture assumed by the priest at Mass (see n. 86 above).

89 Kinch, *Imago Mortis*, 75–76, 105. For a further discussion of the image, see ibid., 92–96. See also David Watt, *The Making of Thomas Hoccleve's Series*, 193–96.

90 Number 114 in the Latin Vulgate and 116 in the Hebrew Psalms. The Latin differs from the Hebrew in tense so that the sense changes from "I love the Lord, because he has heard my voice and my supplications." Richard Rolle's translations and commentary on Psalm 114 intimate God's responsiveness to man's capacity for love. See Bramley, ed., *The Psalter, or Psalms of David*, 403. The contextualization of Jane Scrope's eroticized lament for Phyllyp Sparrow within the Office of the Dead (*Pla ce bo* / who is there, who? / *Di le xi* / Dame Margery . . .) points to later embellishments on this interpretation of the Psalm. Scattergood, ed., *John Skelton: The Complete English Poems*, 71–106. See the discussion of the poem in Jane Griffiths, *John Skelton and Poetic Authority*, 172–74.

91 Smith, *Art, Identity, Devotion*, 296. Smith is referring here specifically to the association between penitence and moralizing mortality themes present in a personal prayer book. Significantly, in the image of the "Three Living and the Three Dead" in the De Lisle Psalter, one of the skeletons crosses his arms over his chest. See ibid., 153–55. See also Kumler, *Translating Truth*, 45–101; and the image of a woman crossing her arms over her chest while kneeling beside a dying man receiving the Last Rites in New York, Morgan Library and Museum MS M.231, fol. 137r. The image can be found online at http://ica.themorgan.org/manuscript/page/30/77118.

92 Binski and Panayotova, eds., *The Cambridge Illuminations*, 278–79. A note to the illuminator, or aide mémoire, that he wrote for himself (which, to my knowledge has never been noted) accompanies the Nebuchadnezzar miniature in this manuscript, and the miniature appears in the text column. The note reads, "hic fiat ymago vel statua ad modum sentencie praedicte" [Make here an image or a statue according to the preceding sentence] (Cambridge, St. Catharine's College MS 7, fol. 4v). This note is fascinating and enigmatic because it is written in red ink and over the marginal illumination, suggesting it was not meant to be scraped or trimmed. Furthermore, the rubricated verses to which they refer ("the preceding sentence") seem to run over the miniature, suggesting the miniature was painted before the verses in red were copied; and finally, the note to the illuminator mentions only the "image or statue" and says nothing about Nebuchadnezzar, who appears in the miniature.

93 See n. 31 above.

94 Coleman, "The First Presentation Miniature," 429.

95 For a survey of early presentation miniatures, the classic study remains Prochno, *Das Schreiber- und Dedikationsbild*. On late medieval English and French presentation miniatures, see Mahoney, "Courtly Presentation and Authorial Self-Fashioning"; Inglis, "A Book in the Hand"; and Coleman, "The First Presentation Miniature."

96 Scott notes the oddity of the two witnesses and cites several images for comparison in which members other than confessor and confessant are present. Scott, *Later Gothic Manuscripts*, 2:324. These (rare) images, however, differ in that they place the observers behind the confessant, seemingly as they wait their turn.

97 Jager, *The Book of the Heart*, 44–64; Huot, "The Writer's Mirror."

98 Morris et al., eds., *Cursor Mundi*, 26, 727–29. Translation from Jager, *Book of the Heart*, 115.

99 See "scriben" and "shriven" in McSparran, gen. ed., *Middle English Dictionary*.

100 For example, "Thus, my son, take the books of my *Confessions* and use them as a good man should—not superficially, but as a Christian in Christian charity. Here see me as I am and do not praise me for more than I am. . . . As, then, you find me in these pages, pray for me that I shall not fail but that I may go on to be perfected." Outler, trans. and ed., "Letter to Darius," *Augustine: Confessions and Enchiridion*, 25.

101 Tercius iste liber qui. . . . Anglico sermone conficitur, secundum Danielis propheciam super huius mundi regnorum mutacione a tempore regis Nabugodonosor vsque nunc tempora distinguit. Tractat eciam secundum Aristotilem super hiis quibus rex Alexander tam in sui regimen quam aliter eius disciplina edoctus fuit. Principalis tamen huius operis materia super amorem et infatuatas amantum passiones fundamentum habet. Nomenque sibi appropriatum Confessio Amantis specialiter sortitus est (third version). This line differs from the previous books mentioned in the colophon, whose titles are mentioned rather matter of factly: "Titulusque libelli istius Speculum Meditantis nuncupatus

est . . . Nomenque volumina huius, quod in septem diuiditur partes, Vox Clamantis intitulat" (first version); "Titulusque libelli istius Speculum Meditantis nuncupatus est . . . Nomenque voluminis huius Vox Clamantis intitulatur" (third version). Peck, ed., *Confessio Amantis*, 1: the colophons.

102 Deleuze and Guattari, *A Thousand Plateaus*, 3–4.

103 The figure is tentatively labeled as a second author portrait, i.e., a depiction of Gower, in all published sources on the manuscript. See Jeremy Griffiths, "*Confessio Amantis:* The Poem and Its Pictures,"163; Emmerson, "Reading Gower in a Manuscript Culture," 168; Fredell, "Reading the Dream Miniature," 91, n.56; Kerby-Fulton and Justice, "Scribe D and the Marketing," 227; Mooney and Stubbs, *Scribes and the City*, 62. Although many depictions of Daniel portray him as a youth, there are a significant number that depict him as in the Taylor folio, that is, as an older man with a long beard. See, for example, Claus Sluter's sculpture of Daniel on the *Well of Moses*. The figure represented here would have been immediately legible to medieval audiences as a prophet by virtue of the scroll at his side. See Camille, "Seeing and Reading"; Cahn, "Répresentation de la Parole"; and Mâle, *Religious Art*, figs. 114–17.

104 Kerby-Fulton and Justice, "Scribe D and the Marketing," 228.

105 Paul Reichardt addresses color as a device for cross-reference in Middle English manuscript illumination in "'Several Illuminations, Coarsely Executed.'"

106 A distant echo of T. S. Eliot's essay *The Three Voices of Poetry*, in which he writes, "The world of a great poetic dramatist is a world in which the creator is everywhere present, and everywhere hidden" (24).

CHAPTER 4

1 Somerset, "'Hard Is with Seyntis for to Make Affray,'" 261.

2 For biographies of Lydgate, see Pearsall, *John Lydgate* and *John Lydgate (1371–1449): A Bio-Bibliography*. On Lydgate as a poet propagandist and public voice, see Scattergood, *Politics and Poetry in the Fifteenth Century*; Green, *Poets and Princepleasers*, 187–90; Lee Patterson, "Making Identities in Fifteenth-Century England"; Pearsall, "Lydgate as Innovator"; Strohm, "Hoccleve, Lydgate and the Lancastrian Court." Maura Nolan complicates the standard view of Lydgate's role as propagandist in *John Lydgate and the Making of Public Culture*. For a useful overview of recent literature on Lydgate, see Bale, "Twenty-First Century Lydgate."

3 What Pearsall referred to as a "mythology of awfulness" in Pearsall, "Lydgate as Innovator," 5. See Chapter 5 for a further discussion of Lydgate's fortunes.

4 It is a commonplace in Lydgate scholarship to invoke his celebrity, both during his lifetime and in the 150 years following his death. Nigel Mortimer offers a detailed account of Lydgate's early reputation in *John Lydgate's* Fall of Princes, 1–9.

5 Alexandra Gillespie, "Framing Lydgate's *Fall of Princes*," 161. See also Gillespie, *Print Culture and the Medieval Author*.

6 Gillespie, *Print Culture*, 41.

7 The only sustained analysis appears in Sobecki, "Lydgate's Kneeling Retraction." Although Dhira Mahoney does discuss the prefatory discourse embodied in text and image in Lydgate's works, her focus is for the most part on the textual elements (Mahoney, "Courtly Presentation and Authorial Self-Fashioning"). Alexandra Gillespie addresses these images briefly in *Print Culture and the Medieval Author*, 40–43.

8 Perkinson, *The Likeness of the King*, 9.

9 Perkinson, "Rethinking the Origins," 153.

10 *Siege of Thebes*: London, British Library Arundel MS 119, fol. 1r. *Troy Book*: London, British Library Cotton MS Augustus A iv, fol. 1r; Cambridge, Trinity College MS O.5.2, fol. 38r; Manchester, Rylands Library MS English 1, fol. 1r; Oxford, Bodleian Library MS Digby 232, fol. 1r; Oxford,

Bodleian Library MS Rawl. C 446, fol. 1r. *Fall of Princes*: London, British Library Harley MS 1766, fol. 5r; Montreal, McGill University MS 143, fol. 4r; San Marino, Huntington Library HM 268, fol. 18r. *Secrets of the Philosophers*: London, British Library Harley MS 4826, fol. 52r. *Lives of Saints Edmund and Fremund*: London, British Library Harley MS 2278, fols. 6r and 9r; London, British Library Yates Thompson MS 47, fol. 4r; Oxford, Bodleian Library MS Ashmole 46, fol. 1r; Arundel Castle, no shelfmark, fol. 1r. *Fifteen Joys and Sorrows of Our Lady*: Cambridge, Trinity College MS R.3.21, fol. 238r.

11 For editions of the latter three, see Steele, ed., *Secrees of Old Philisoffres*; Bale and Edwards, eds., *Lives of Ss Edmund and Fremund*; and MacCracken, ed., *The Minor Poems*, 1: 268–79.

12 Quilligan, *The Allegory of Female Authority*, 5. See also Peters, *Das Ich im Bild*, 190–240.

13 Foucault, "What Is an Author," 123–24.

14 Meyer-Lee, *Poets and Power from Chaucer to Wyatt*, 3. Emphasis in original.

15 Lydgate's use of the humility topos was prodigious, and although it did not exceed the norms of authorial self-presentation at the time, it did, according to Meyer-Lee, embody a more nuanced and complex form. See Meyer-Lee, *Poets and Power from Chaucer to Wyatt*, esp. 1–12, 43–87.

16 Pearsall, *John Lydgate*, 5.

17 Pearsall, "Lydgate as Innovator," 22.

18 On the tradition of illustration in these manuscripts, see Lesley Lawton, "The Illustration of Late Medieval Secular Texts."

19 Oxford, Bodleian Library MS Rawl. C. 446, fol. 1r. This manuscript is believed to have been copied by the same scribe responsible for another illuminated copy of the *Troy Book* (Oxford, Bodleian Library MS Digby 232).

20 Meyer-Lee, *Poets and Power from Chaucer to Wyatt*, 51.

21 Nine manuscripts of Lydgate's works have been identified as the product of a scribe who was based in Bury St. Edmunds: London, British Library Arundel MS 99; London, British Library Harley MS 1766; London, British Library Harley MS 4826; London, British Library Sloane MS 2464; London, British Library Yates Thompson MS 47, Oxford, Bodleian Library MS Ashmole 46; Montreal, McGill University MS 143; Oxford, Bodleian Library MS Laud Misc. 673; and a manuscript of *The Lives of Saints Edmund and Fremund* at Arundel Castle (no shelfmark). On Bury St. Edmunds as a center for the dissemination of Lydgate's works, see Edwards, "The McGill Fragment of Lydgate's *Fall of Princes*"; Scott, "Lydgate's *Lives of Saints Edmund and Fremund*," 360–63; Edwards, "Lydgate Manuscripts: Some Directions for Future Research"; and Horobin, "The Edmund-Fremund Scribe Copying Chaucer."

22 The first exception is the presentation copy of his *Lives of Saints Edmund and Fremund* (London, British Library MS Harley 2278), made for Henry VI, which contains an image of a monk (presumably Lydgate himself) giving a book to the king. On this manuscript, see Drimmer, "Picturing the King or Picturing the Saint." The second possible exception is a manuscript fragment of *The Fall of Princes* (Montreal, McGill University Library MS 143), which contains an image of Lydgate presenting the book to Humphrey, Duke of Gloucester. What is interesting about this fragment is that it places the presentation image before the envoi in Book IX, 3303–3604 (i.e., not on the initial pages of the manuscript), suggesting a reluctance to promote Lydgate's political patronage if we can assume that the initial folios did not repeat this presentation imagery. This suggestion can only be conjectural because only four leaves of this manuscript are known. Further comparisons cannot, unfortunately, be made because two other manuscripts of the *Fall* lack the initial leaves on which a presentation image would most likely occur (Philadelphia, Rosenbach Library MS 439/16, and San Marino, Huntington Library HM 268).

23 London, British Library Harley MS 4826, fol. 52r. This manuscript also contains a frontispiece (fol. 1*), representing a kneeling pilgrim and monk before a knight, but the date when this frontispiece was added is unknown. See Scott, *Later Gothic Manuscripts*, 2:305–7.

24 London, British Library Harley MS 4826, fol. 52r.

25 Sobecki, "Lydgate's Kneeling Retraction," 288.

26 Ibid., 286.

27 Gillespie, *Print Culture*, 43.

28 Bergen, ed., *Troy Book*, Prol. 370. See also Inglis, "A Book in the Hand," 61.

29 Mahoney, "Courtly Presentation and Authorial Self-Fashioning," 126–27.

30 Pittaway, "The Political Appropriation of John Lydgate's *Fall of Princes*," 90.

31 On the iconography of King David, see Boyer Owens, "The Image of King David in Prayer."

32 London, British Library Harley MS 1766. On this manuscript, see Pittaway, "The Political Appropriation of John Lydgate's *Fall of Princes*"; and Scott, *Later Gothic Manuscripts*, 2:302–4. For an edition, see Bergen, ed., *Fall of Princes*.

33 Bergen, ed., *Fall of Princes*, Prol. 393–448.

34 According to the scholastic application of Aristotle's theory of fourfold causes, the patron could be the means by which a work of literature comes to be (i.e., is its motivating force and therefore its efficient cause). See Minnis, *Medieval Theory of Authorship*, 74–94.

35 Summit, "'Stable in Study,'" 208. Nigel Mortimer discusses in detail the degree to which Humphrey influenced Lydgate's version of the Lucretia story in *John Lydgate's* Fall of Princes, 53–78.

36 London, British Library Harley MS 1766, fol. 5r.

37 Lydgate's participation in the establishment of a self-avowedly English literary culture has been the subject of a number of important studies, beginning with Fisher, "A Language Policy for Lancastrian England." More recently, this view has been articulated by Meyer-Lee, *Poets and Power from Chaucer to Wyatt*; Scanlon and Simpson, "Introduction," 1–11; and Sponsler, "Lydgate and London's Public Culture."

38 Schleif, "Hands That Appoint, Anoint and Ally," 1. On the imagery of donors in English manuscript illumination, see Scott, "*Caveat Lector*"; Sandler, "The Wilton Diptych and Images of Devotion in Illuminated Manuscripts"; and Nigel Morgan, "Patrons and Devotional Images in English Art." For more expansive studies that touch on the Low Countries, France, and England, as well as on other media beyond illumination, see van der Velden, *The Donor's Image*; and Sand, *Vision, Devotion, and Self-Representation*, 1–26, 84–148. Aden Kumler offers an engaging analysis of patron images through the lens of Foucault's author function in "The Patron Function" and she likewise complicates the idea of the donor image as a surrogate in "Translating ma Dame de Saint-Pol."

39 Pinner, "Medieval Images of St. Edmund in Norfolk Churches," 121.

40 The added words were attributed to a sixteenth-century hand in Reynolds, "Illustrated Boccaccio Manuscripts," 143. But it is equally possible that the hand is from the later fifteenth century. At most we can say that it is probably not the hand of the scribe.

41 Respectively, London, British Library Royal MS 14 C vii, fol. 6; Oxford, Bodleian Library MS Duke Humfrey b 1, fol. 3r; and Oxford, Bodleian Library MS Digby 233, fol. 1r.

42 There is a general fluidity—both in medieval practice and modern terminology—between what is variously called votive portraiture, devotional portraiture, donor images, patron images, and owner images. Most of the sources cited above (n. 38), for example, use this terminology either interchangeably or variously, but on the matter of distinctions see the commentary by Sand, *Vision, Devotion, and Self-Representation*, 5–6. Each of these categories does seem to have its own identifiable inflections. For an important study that seeks to refine the vocabulary scholars apply to and that revises our understanding of so-called donor figures in southern Italian wall painting, see Safran, "Deconstructing 'Donors.'"

43 van der Velden, *The Donor's Image*, 235. See also Freedberg, *The Power of Images*, 153–60; and for a useful overview of scholarship on *ex votos*, see Weinryb, "Introduction."

44 On which, see Bale, "St. Edmund in Fifteenth-Century London."

45 According to Kathleen Scott, "English patrons and authors of this period are not often portrayed in an attitude of veneration before saints; this fusion of the (presumably) representational

figure of a patron with an iconic figure of a saint occurs in only three other English manuscripts of ca. 1400 or later known to me at present." Scott, "Lydgate's *Lives of Saints Edmund and Fremund*," 347–49, n. 50. Far more common (and no doubt related to the appendage of a supplicant to the opening of the hours of the Virgin Mary in Books of Hours) are representations of supplicants at the feet of the Virgin and Child.

46 Wood, "The Votive Scenario," 210.

47 Ibid.

48 Scholars have puzzled over the identity of the other monk, but a consensus appears to have gathered around William Curteys, the abbot of Bury St. Edmunds while Lydgate was in residence. See Pittaway, "The Political Appropriation of John Lydgate's *Fall of Princes*," 89. Lacking further evidence, I would not hazard a guess as to the other's identity or whether a specific individual was intended.

49 There is little doubt that they were designed to be blank because two other manuscripts with an image of Lydgate before St. Edmund also feature scrolls emerging from Lydgate, which lack inscriptions (Oxford, Bodleian Library MS Ashmole 46, fol. 1r; and Arundel Castle, *Lives of Saints Edmnd and Fremund*, fol. 1r).

50 On the functions of text scrolls, see Camille, "Seeing and Reading," 29, 38–40; and Flett, "The Significance of Text Scrolls." The ubiquity of text scrolls in English illumination and stained glass is discussed in Nigel Morgan, "What Are They Saying?"

51 Gelfand and Gibson, "Surrogate Selves."

52 The opening folios have been removed from other illustrated copies (Philadelphia, Rosenbach Library MS 439/16; San Marino, Huntington HM 268; and Montreal, McGill University MS 143). I have recently discovered an illustration on the opening page to Chicago, Newberry Library MS 33.3, another *Fall of Princes* manuscript (the illumination is heavily damaged and is referred to elsewhere as merely decorative). See Drimmer, "Unnoticed and Unusual."

53 Oxford, Bodleian Library MS Bodley 263, fol. 7r.

54 The observation parallels William A. Ringler's own about the ascription of printed texts to authors on either side of 1500: whereas, he calculates, only 30 percent of texts are attributed to authors in pre-1500 editions, that percentage reaches 80 percent after the turn of the century. Ringler, *Bibliography and Index of English Verse*, 6–7.

55 London, British Library Harley MS 1766, fol. 1r.

56 Oxford, Bodleian Library MS Ashmole 46, fol. 1r.

57 There are no further references to Lydgate in the table, and entries establish Boccaccio's stature repeatedly, as in "Next in this chapitle folwyng my auctor bochas shortly descryveth the malyce of women in general." London, British Library Harley MS 1766, fol. 1v.

58 London, British Library Harley MS 1766, fol. 2v.

59 Seth Lerer comes closest to noting the distinction: *auctores* seem to be the late *antiqui*, whereas laureates are *moderni*. But this distinction disappears in the estimation of Chaucer's Clerk, to whom, at least according to Lerer, death is also a prerequisite to laureateship. See Lerer, *Chaucer and His Readers*, 26–30. For an important account of laureate self-fashioning in Middle English literature, see Meyer-Lee, *Poets and Power*.

60 Manchester, Rylands Library MS English 2, fol. 184r. Alexandra Gillespie, "Framing Lydgate's *Fall of Princes*," 157–59.

61 Manchester, Rylands Library MS English 2, fol. 3r.

62 London, British Library Royal MS 18 D v, in between fols. 1v and 2r. The slip measures 9-by-4 centimeters and has needle holes around the edges.

63 "In one sense, then, dullness is the mark of a fifteenth-century poet; but, conversely, a true mark of a fifteenth-century poet is to deny being a poet-to abrogate, that is, any specialized status (beyond financial reward) that poetry might bring." David Lawton, "Dullness and the Fifteenth Century," 771.

64 Drimmer, "Picturing the King or Picturing the Saint."

65 Another manuscript containing *The Lives of Saints Edmund and Fremund* opens with a representation of Edmund's martyrdom. London, British Library Harley MS 4826, fol. 4r. Only later was a presentation image added (ibid., fol. 1*), indicating a later audience's expectation of an author portrait at the beginning of a text. This image is fascinating in that it portrays a pilgrim kneeling (beside a monk, also kneeling) and presenting a book to a knight. See n.23, above.

66 The manuscript was supplemented by numerous texts (by Lydgate and others) as well as illuminations in several stages, so that the original opening folio is no longer the first folio in the manuscript. See Chapter 5 on this manuscript.

67 I discuss the questions regarding the identity of the king pictured here (as either Henry VI or Edward IV) in Chapter 5.

68 Ettlinger, "Notes on a Woodcut Depicting King Henry VI." See also Marks, "Images of Henry VI."

69 Kipling, *Enter the King*, 85–99, 143–69.

70 On this manuscript, see Sutton and Visser-Fuchs, "The Cult of Angels in Late Fifteenth-Century England."

71 See, for example, Berenbeim, *Art of Documentation*, 21, 25, 64, which features illustrations from Oxford, Merton College Charter 370; London, British Library Additional Charter 71759; and Oxford, Bodleian Library MS Wood Empt. 1, fol. 20. An opening membrane to the Common Plea Roll for Hillary term, 1477 shows, similarly, the king presenting a document to the kneeling figure of Sir Thomas Bryan (Kew, National Archives CP40/861). See Danbury and Scott, "The Plea Rolls of the Court of Common Pleas," 182, 184.

72 The manuscript (Oxford, Bodleian Library MS Digby 233) contains John Trevisa's English translation of Giles of Rome's *De regimine principum* and an English translation by an unknown individual of Vegetius's *De re militari*. See Coleman, "The First Presentation Miniature."

73 The current catalogue description of this image remarks, "It is not clear whether this is Lovell receiving the book from Siferwas, or Lovell presenting it to a canon of Salisbury." In British Library, Catalogue of Illuminated Manuscripts, http://www.bl.uk/catalogues/illuminatedmanuscripts/IL LUMIN.ASP?Size=mid&IllID=16521.

74 Kathleen Scott originally expressed doubts as to whether the image portrays Hoccleve (*Later Gothic Manuscripts*, 2:159), and Kate Harris argued that the manuscript was not made for Henry V but rather for John Mowbray, second Duke of Norfolk (d. 1432). See Harris, "The Patron of British Library MS Arundel 38." For the two opposing views regarding the identities of the figures represented in the miniature, see Erler, "Hoccleve's Portrait?"; and Burrow, "Hoccleve and the 'Court,'" 74.

75 Lerer, *Chaucer and His Readers*, 40–44. It is possible that this image adapts the model of Boccaccio and Petrarch that precedes Book VIII in some manuscripts of *Des cas*, as in London, British Library Royal MS 20 C iv, fol. 269r.

76 Lerer, *Chaucer and His Readers*, 44.

77 See Summit, "'Stable in Study.'" The Prologue to the *Troy Book* recounts how Prince Henry (later Henry V) commissioned Lydgate to make this translation: "Whyche me comaunded the drery pitus fate / Of hem of Troye in englysche to translate" (*Troy Book*, Prol, 105–6). One illuminated copy's heading to the Prologue of the *Troy Book*, just beneath the miniature depicting Lydgate and Henry V, announces, "here begynneth the boke of the sege of Troye compiled by Daun John Lydgate monke of Bery atte excitatioun and steryng of the moost noble worthi and myghty prynce kyng Henry the fyfthe" (Manchester, Rylands Library MS English 1, fol. 1r).

78 This assessment echoes Jennifer Summit's observations about Stephen Scrope and William Worcester, for whom "the salient facts about a book's authorship concern the relationships of patronage that authorize it. 'The author' as they use the term, then, designates less an individual than an authorizing relationship that is characterized by service and reward." Summit, *Lost Property*, 76–77.

79 For a concise historiography of the *Siege of Thebes* as a form of Chaucerian reception, see Leff, "Lydgate Rewrites Chaucer," 472–73.

80 Andrew Higl proposes that perhaps the poem did have a patron in either William de la Pole, Duke of Suffolk, or his wife, Alice Chaucer, the granddaughter of Geoffrey. One of the most highly regarded copies of the *Siege of Thebes* is a manuscript that contains the arms of William de la Pole, and, as Higl posits, the patronage of either him or his wife would be appropriate in light of the poem's conceit as a "Canterbury Tale." See Higl, *Playing the* Canterbury Tales, 50.

81 For two important revisions to the older, prevailing view of Lydgate's ineptitude in following Chaucer, see Kline, "Father Chaucer and the 'Siege of Thebes'"; and Straker, "Deference and Difference."

82 According to Robert Edwards, "*The Siege of Thebes* circulated in a number of literary contexts. The poem is found with *Troy Book* in three manuscripts (Cambridge, Trinity College MS O.5.2; Bodleian Digby 230; and London, British Library Royal 18. D. ii, which has the only extant cycle of illuminations, added in the sixteenth century). It appears with *The Canterbury Tales* in five manuscripts (London, British Library Additional MS 5140; Oxford, Christ Church MS 152; London, British Library Egerton MS 2864; Longleat MS 257; University of Texas MS 143) and with Chaucer's shorter poems and the Siege of Jerusalem in another (Coventry, Corporate Record Office MS Acc. 325/1). It also appears with Thomas Hoccleve's *De regimine principum* (London, British Library Additional MS 18632) and with Vegetius' *De re militari* (Oxford, Bodleian MS Laud misc. 416, dated 1459). It is the sole text in eleven manuscripts (London, British Library Arundel MS 119; Oxford, Bodleian MS 776; Oxford, Bodleian Laud misc. 557; Boston, Public Library MS f.med.94; Cambridge, University Library Additional MSS 2707, 3137, 6864; Lambeth Palace 742; Oxford, Saint John's College 266; Prince Duleep Singh's MS; and New Haven, Beinecke Library MS 661)." Edwards, ed., *Siege of Thebes*, 11–12. For the manuscripts of the *Siege of Thebes*, see Boffey and Edwards, *A New Index of Middle English Verse*, 262.

83 Edwards, ed., *Siege of Thebes*, Prol. 82–84. All quotes, unless stated otherwise, are from this edition. The joke here is that the Host addressed the Monk of *The Canterbury Tales* similarly, but in that episode, the roster of names began with John, which is, of course, Lydgate's first name ("Wher shal I calle yow my lord daun john, Or daun thomas, or elles daun albon?"). "Prol. Monk's Tale," 1,929–30.

84 Edwards, ed., *Siege of Thebes*, Prol. 89.

85 Edwards, ed., *Siege of Thebes*, Prol. 92–96.

86 Erdmann and Erkwall, eds., *Siege of Thebes*, 97.

87 The tentative attribution of the manuscript to the so-called Petworth scribe, who also copied Cambridge, Pembroke College MS 307 (Gower, *Confessio* Amantis); New Haven, Beinecke Library Takamiya MS 54 (*South English Legendary*); and Oslo and London, Schøyen Collection 615 (John of Walton's translation of Boethius, *Consolation of Philosophy*) appears in Jeremy Griffiths, "Thomas Hyngham, Monk of Bury and the Macro Plays Manuscript."

88 Higl, *Playing the* Canterbury Tales, 64.

89 Jane Griffiths, *Diverting Authorities*, 30.

90 London, British Library Arundel MS 119, fol. 3v.

91 Ibid., fol.17v.

92 Ibid., fol. 42v.

93 Ibid., fol. 79r.

94 The manuscript was given to the prioress and the convent of Amesbury by Richard Wygyngton, a priest, in 1508. Linda Olson implies that this manuscript was produced at a monastic house, but aside from its sixteenth-century provenance, I know of no evidence for its place of production. Kerby-Fulton, Olson, and Hilmo, eds., *Opening Up Middle English Manuscripts*, 316–17. Presumably the guiding impulse here was the *Fürstenspiegel*, and the *Siege* appears in a number of other manuscripts with similar Mirrors for Princes. See n. 82 above. On the *Siege* as an inventive response to the mirror for princes tradition, see Battles, *The Medieval Tradition of Thebes*, 145–49.

95 Edwards, ed., *Siege of Thebes*, 177.

96 London, British Library Additional MS 18632, fol. 6r.

97 Ibid., fol. 99r.

98 Presumably "in" with the ablative here means "on" or "with regard to." On Hoccleve's use of these sources see Perkins, *Hoccleve's* Regiment of Princes, 93–99.

99 London, British Library Additional MS 18632, fol. 99r.

100 Ibid., fol. 99v. My translation.

101 Both quotes are from Rice, "Between the Brush and the Pen," 169 and 158, respectively.

102 For a description of the manuscript, see Manly and Rickert, eds., *The Text of* The Canterbury Tales, 1:64–70; and for further discussion, see Owen, *The Manuscripts of* The Canterbury Tales, 26–27.

103 Oxford, Bodleian Library MS Bodley 686, fol. 173v.

104 Ibid., fol. 173v–176r.

105 Boyd, "Social Texts," 87. Andrew Higl has also remarked that this error and other features of the manuscript reveal "a reader not necessarily concerned with presenting Chaucer's text but rather that of the *res* of the *Canterbury Tales* regardless of whether it was written by Chaucer, Lydgate, or the anonymous redactor responsible for the extensive additions to the *Cook's Tale*." Higl, *Playing the* Canterbury Tales, 167. I am not entirely convinced by this argument because this manuscript not only includes an image of (presumably) Chaucer in its opening initial (Oxford, Bodleian Library MS Bodley 686, fol. 1r), but it also designates the "General Prologue" as "Prologe Chaucers" in running heads (Oxford, Bodleian Library MS Bodley 686, fols. 1v–2r and following).

106 Oxford, Bodleian Library MS Bodley 686, fol. 173v.

107 Cambridge, Trinity College MS R.4.20, fol. 1r.

108 Ibid., fol. 89r.

109 Ibid., fol. 169r.

110 Higl, *Playing the* Canterbury Tales, 64.

CHAPTER 5

1 Nolan, *John Lydgate and the Making of Public Culture*, 2.

2 The degree to which this "project" was coherent and deliberate or diffuse and happenstance is a matter of debate. See Introduction, n. 7 and n. 13, for scholarship on either side.

3 The *Troy Book* is described as "the first of his mega-compositions" in Strohm, *England's Empty Throne*, 187. I refer to the literature on the political commitments of the *Confessio Amantis* throughout Chapter 6, although it should be useful here to cite, as a recent examination of the issue, Carlson, *John Gower, Poetry and Propaganda*. For Lydgate, see n. 19 below.

4 Exceptions include Radulescu, *The Gentry Context for Malory's* Morte Darthur; and Pittaway, "The Political Appropriation of John Lydgate's *Fall of Princes*."

5 Nolan, "Historicism After Historicism," 70. While the topic of visual historiography in English-language manuscripts has not received much attention, there is an important body of scholarship for the French material. See Hedeman, *The Royal Image*; Hedeman "Making Memories"; Hedeman, "Making the Past Present in Laurent de Premierfait's *De senectute*"; Inglis, *Jean Fouquet*. Hedeman (*Translating the Past*, 129–205) provides also a useful model for examining the ways in which illuminations in later copies of a text "fostered . . . new visual translations" of that text (129).

6 The entire manuscript has been digitized and can be found at http://www.bl.uk/manuscripts. The *Troy Book* survives in twenty-three manuscripts and fragments, of which eight contain figural illumination and a further six contain decorative illumination. On most of these manuscripts (not all were known to him), see Bergen, ed., *Troy Book*, IV:1–54. For descriptions of London, British Library Royal MS 18 D ii, see ibid., IV:15–19; Lesley Lawton, "The Illustration of Late Medieval Secular Texts," 66–69; Scott, *Later Gothic Manuscripts*, 2:282–85; Kren and McKendrick, eds., *Illuminating the Renaissance*, 431–32; Doyle, Lowden, and McKendrick, eds., *Royal Manuscripts*, 248–49. See also Gillespie, "'These Proverbes Yet Do Last,'" 226–32. Little else has been written about this manuscript,

but one of the sixteenth-century miniatures in it serves as an emblem of sorts for the central premise of Trigg, *Congenial Souls*, esp. xiii–xvii.

7 Gumbert, "Codicological Units," 18.

8 On the "archaeology of the book," see Delaissé, "Towards a History of the Medieval Book." The positivist nature of the endeavor is encapsulated in Delaissé's comment that "this method guarantees that we are in possession of all the material facts revealing the life of these books and vital for the understanding of their contents: text, writing, and miniatures. Furthermore it will provide the foundation upon which we may build up the history of the medieval book, and from this the philologist, paleographer, and art historian will draw objective information, essential for their individual lines of research" (81).

9 Holly, *Past Looking*, 14.

10 Holly, *Past Looking*.

11 Kuskin, "The Archival Imagination," 90. See also Kuskin, *Symbolic Caxton*.

12 On "reading as poaching," see de Certeau, *The Practice of Everyday Life*, 165–76.

13 See, for example, Nichols and Wenzel, eds., *The Whole Book Cultural Perspectives on the Medieval Miscellany*; and Connolly and Radulescu, eds., *Insular Books*.

14 Ralph Griffiths, "Herbert, William, First Earl of Pembroke (c. 1423–1469)," http://www.oxforddnb.com/view/article/13053. The only other extant manuscript of which I know associated (tentatively) with Herbert's patronage is the Pembroke Psalter-Hours (Philadelphia Museum of Art, Phillip S. Collins Collection, acc. no. 45-65-2). Marrow, "Pembroke Psalter-Hours," 897-98.

15 For a particularly useful historiography of Lydgate studies, see Scanlon and Simpson, "Introduction." See also, for the fortunes of Lydgate, Mortimer, *John Lydgate's Fall of Princes*, 1–24.

16 Pearsall, "The English Chaucerians," 210.

17 Pearsall, "The Apotheosis of John Lydgate," 31.

18 Helen Cooper, "Introduction," 4.

19 Lawton, "Dullness and the Fifteenth Century"; Lee Patterson, "Making Identities in Fifteenth-Century England"; Strohm, *England's Empty Throne*; Strohm, "John Lydgate, Jacque of Holland, and the Poetics of Complicity"; Mortimer, *John Lydgate's Fall of Princes*. John Fisher argued that Henrys IV and V implemented a language policy (i.e., used and encouraged the use of English) as a means of "engag[ing] the support of Parliament and the English citizenry for a questionable usurpation of the throne" (Fisher, "A Language Policy for Lancastrian England," 1,170); and Derek Pearsall, among others, has pointed to the Lancastrians' use of John Lydgate to pen verses in support of their legitimacy. See Pearsall, *John Lydgate*, esp. 169; Mooney, "Lydgate's 'Kings of England.'"

20 Sponsler, *The Queen's Dumbshows*, 6, 15. Nolan, *John Lydgate and the Making of Public Culture*. See also the essays in Denny-Brown and Cooper, *Lydgate Matters*, which deal more broadly with material culture.

21 Appleford, "The Dance of Death in London."

22 Floyd, "St. George and the 'Steyned Halle,'" 157. See also Floyd, "Writing on the Wall."

23 Bergen, ed., *Troy Book*, verba translatoris, 101. All quotes, unless otherwise stated, from Bergen, ed., *Troy Book*.

24 Edwards, "'Lydgate Manuscripts: Some Directions for Future Research."

25 For two overviews of illustrated *Troy Book* and *Fall of Princes* manuscripts, see Lesley Lawton, "The Illustration of Late Medieval Secular Texts"; and Lawton, "'To Studie in Bookis of Antiquitie.'" Studies have also been published on Lydgate's *Lives of Saints Edmund and Fremund*. See Scott, "Lydgate's *Lives of Saints Edmund and Fremund*"; and Drimmer, "Picturing the King or Picturing the Saint."

26 Pearsall, "Beyond Fidelity," 198.

27 Stephen Nichols, "Introduction: Philology in a Manuscript Culture," 7.

28 A similar point about the heft of manuscripts of the *Grandes Chroniques de France* is made in Inglis, "Image and Illustration," 191.

29 The kind of script used here can be compared to the kind of script used by Scribe A in London, British Library Additional MS 59678, which "creates the impression of an Anglicana script. . . . The preponderance of letter-forms, however, indicates an overall definition of very formal secretary." Roberts, *Guide to Scripts*, 240. Although the comparison is silent, Roberts places an image from a page of London, British Library Royal MS 18 D ii, after her transcription and discussion of London, British Library Additional MS 59678, suggesting the similarities between the two.

30 See Chapter 6 for a discussion of the scribe Ricardus Franciscus, who identifies himself in precisely this manner. Interestingly enough, Edward Town does record a family of Boswell painter-stainers working in London from the middle of the sixteenth century. The oldest of these, William Boswell (*fl.* 1558; d. 1595) was attributed with a "table" depicting morally and theologically opposed figures, hanging in the parlor of an inn. Whether this Boswell is related to the person who inserted into the Royal manuscript (or is referred to by) this inscription cannot be determined. See Town, "A Biographical Dictionary of London Painters." It is also remarkable that the insertion occurs on a page where Lydgate praises Chaucer. While this is entirely speculative, if the name refers to the scribe himself, it might suggest that he is installing himself, however modestly, into the English literary lineage that Lydgate is establishing here (Bergen, ed., *Troy Book*, III:4197−4263).

31 "Si vales bene est, ego valeo." I am grateful to Michael van Dussen for suggesting this possibility to me. The two *E*s in the cadel letters, it should be acknowledged, are ambiguous.

32 London, British Library Royal MS 18 D ii, fols. 6r, 30v, 66v, 95r, 128r.

33 Ibid., fols. 74r, 75r, 82v.

34 Ibid., fols. 87r, 93r, two miniatures on 108v, 148r, 151r, 153v, 154v, 157v, 158v, 159r, two miniatures on 160r, 160v, 161r, 161v, 162r. I discuss the added texts later in this chapter.

35 *Troy Book*, Prol. 1−24.

36 *Troy Book,* Prol. 95−118.

37 See Benson, *The History of Troy in Middle English Literature*; Baswell, *Virgil in Medieval England*; Federico, *New Troy: Fantasies of Empire in the Late Middle Ages*.

38 *Troy Book*, Prol. 121−46.

39 Smyth, *Imaginings of Time in Lydgate and Hoccleve's Verse*, 66.

40 Simpson, "Bulldozing the Middle Ages," 238.

41 Nagel and Wood, "Interventions," 403. See also Nagel and Wood, *Anachronic Renaissance*; Didi-Huberman, *Confronting Images*; Didi-Huberman, "Before the Image, Before Time"; Didi-Huberman, "History and the Image," 129.

42 For princely conduct literature in England, see Kleineke, *Englische Fürstenspiegel*; and, specifically on its development in the later Middle Ages, Ferster, *Fictions of Advice*. For the ubiquity of the *De Regimine* on aristocratic bookshelves in the later Middle Ages, see Briggs, "Manuscripts of Giles of Rome's *De regimine principum*."

43 Oxford, University College MS 85, f. 47v. Transcription from Manzaloui, ed., *Secretum secretorum*, 324.

44 This argument was proposed in three books that were published within two years of one another. See Battles, *The Medieval Tradition of Thebes*; Strohm, *Politique*, 87−132; and Mortimer, *John Lydgate's Fall of Princes*, 51−90. Laurent de Premierfait translated *De casibus* as *Des cas des nobles hommes et femmes*, first in 1400 to little success and then again in a completely revamped version in 1409 for the Dukes of Berry and Burgundy. For an edition, see di Stefano, ed., *Boccace "Decameron," Traduction (1411−1414) de Laurent de Premierfait*. John Lydgate translated Laurent de Premierfait's *Des cas* as *The Fall of Princes* for Humphrey, Duke of Gloucester (brother of Henry V and uncle to Henry VI) in c. 1431−38. For an edition, see Bergen, ed., *Fall of Princes*.

45 Strohm, *Politique*, 89.

46 The mottos are "e las sy longuement," and "De toute." London, British Library Royal MS 18 D ii, fol. 6r.

47 Lawton, "The Illustration of Late Medieval Secular Texts," 66–68; Scott, *Later Gothic Manuscripts*, 2:283.

48 Matthew Ward identifies the collars of the men flanking the king as the "suns and roses" of Edward IV (which I discuss in Chapter 6), but they appear more generic to me. See Ward, "The Livery Collar," 200–1. I am grateful to Sarah Peverley for this reference.

49 Ralph Griffiths, *The Reign of Henry VI*, 780–81.

50 For Herbert's pardon, see *Calendar of Patent Rolls, Henry VI*, 6:360.

51 *Calendar of Patent Rolls, Henry VI*, 6:549, 574–75, 594.

52 Herbert was absent at the Battle of Ludford Bridge (where he might have supported the Yorkists) in October 1459, making the years between his pardon in June 1457 and his installment to the office of sheriff in February 1460 an appealing window into which to slot the Royal *Troy Book*'s commission. Herbert's nonattendance at the Battle of Ludford Bridge is attested by the absence of his name among the traitors identified in Given-Wilson et al, ed., *Parliament Rolls*, XII:454–60.

53 Another copy of the *Troy Book* was presented by John Touchet (d. 1558), eighth baron Audley, to Henry VIII for a similar reason (i.e., in gratitude for the king's restoration of him to the royal blood). He also added dedicatory verses to the manuscript (London, British Library Royal MS 18 D vi, fols. 1r–2r).

54 See Koziol, *Begging Pardon and Favor*, esp. 59–70; Ormrod, "Murmur, Clamour and Noise"; and Lacey, *The Royal Pardon*, 38–43.

55 Shepherd, ed., *Le Morte Darthur*, 553. Although this description echoes what we see on the Royal manuscript page, it is important to acknowledge with Geoffrey Koziol that "supplication was less a specific posture than a prayer addressed to a lord accompanied by some physical sign of deference.... It was the attitude that remained essential to supplication, the suppliant gesture only providing evidence of the attitude." Koziol, *Begging Pardon and Favor*, 60.

56 Musson, "Ruling 'Virtually'?" 155–56. Examples include London, British Library Hargrave MS 274; London, British Library Harley MS 644; London, British Library Yates Thompson MS 48; London, Metropolitan Archives COL/CS/01/007; London, Metropolitan Archives COL/CS/01/008. Scott suggests that the origins of this iconography lie with the Royal manuscript itself, but this strikes me as unlikely.

57 Kew, The National Archives CP 40/810.

58 McGerr, *Lancastrian Mirror for Princes*, 48; Musson, "Ruling 'Virtually'?" 168.

59 Peverley, "Political Consciousness and the Literary Mind."

60 Folios 160r to 161v contain decorated initials in a looser, even sloppy, style and were probably executed in the second campaign on the manuscript: while the style of these initials differs from the mid-fifteenth-century style of the illumination elsewhere, the springets that emerge from these initials were also partially painted over by the adjacent miniatures' frames during the sixteenth-century campaign to complete the manuscript's program.

61 Holly, *Past Looking*, xiii; and Kuskin, "The Archival Imagination," 85, respectively.

62 Rudy, *Postcards on Parchment*, 41.

63 Ibid.

64 Oxford, Bodleian Library MS Digby 232, fol. 1r.

65 Oxford, Bodleian Library MS Rawlinson C 446, fol. 1r.

66 London, British Library Cotton MS Augustus A iv, fol. 1r.

67 Manchester, Rylands Library MS English 1, fol. 173r. See Kathryn Warner, "The Provenance and Early Ownership."

68 Cambridge, Trinity College MS O.5.2. See Binski and Panayotova, eds., *The Cambridge Illuminations*, 279–81.

69 Doyle and Parkes, "The Production of Copies," 208.

70 Three of the roughly fifty whole manuscripts and thirty fragments of *The Canterbury Tales* contain heraldry integral to their decorative programs. Harris, "Ownership and Readership," 16. Four of the forty-

nine manuscripts of the *Confessio Amantis* contain integral heraldry. Harris, "Patrons, Buyers and Owners," 168; and Oxford, Corpus Christi College MS 67, has the added merchant's mark of the Crisp family (fols. 2r and 207v). Compare this to six (integral and added) out of twenty-three *Troy Book* manuscripts.

71 *Troy Book*, Prol. 225–44. Cambridge, Trinity College MS O.5.2, similarly arranges the *Troy Book* before the *Siege of Thebes*. In contrast, Oxford, Bodleian Library MS Digby 230, places *Thebes* before *Troy*, that is, in chronological order of the events they recount.

72 Murray, *Plotting Gothic*, 9. See also, on plans, Binski, *Gothic Wonder*, 51–54.

73 On the traditions of illumination in *Troy Book* manuscripts, see Lawton, "The Illustration of Late Medieval Secular Texts."

74 It is possible that the manuscript was designed to contain more miniatures: several leaves are now missing, and an offsetting of green paint can be seen on fol. 92v, which precedes one of these now missing leaves.

75 London, British Library Cotton MS Augustus A iv, fol. 25v, and Oxford, Bodleian MS Digby 232, fol. 29v, illustrate the moment that Priam receives news of Troy's destruction; and Oxford, Bodleian MS Rawlinson C 446, fol. 31r, depicts a besieged city. The leaf on which this scene probably appeared has been cut out of Cambridge, Trinity College MS O.5.2.

76 Lawton, "The Illustration of Late Medieval Secular Texts," 65.

77 In this inference, I differ slightly from Scott (*Later Gothic Manuscripts*, 2:283), who believes that the illuminator sought out blanks at the head of books or quires, leaving the rest for himself or another artist to finish.

78 London, British Library Cotton MS Augustus A iv, fol. 2r; Cambridge, Trinity College MS O.5.2, fol. 40r; Oxford, Bodleian Library MS Digby 232, fol. 3r; Oxford, Bodleian Library MS Rawlinson C 446, fol. 3r.

79 See n. 75.

80 On the Wheel of Fortune in medieval culture, see Werner, "Das Rad der Fortuna"; and Todoroki, "A List of Miniatures of Goddess Fortune." Wheels of Fortune are somewhat rare in English manuscripts, although they probably were a popular subject in monumental painting. Kathleen Scott claims there are only "six known Wheel-of-fortune pictures in English 15th-century book illustration." Scott, *Later Gothic Manuscripts*, 2:284. For a survey of the literary tradition, see Patch, *The Goddess Fortuna in Medieval Literature*.

81 Manchester, Rylands Library MS English 1, fol. 28v; New York, Morgan Library and Museum MS M.876, fol. 6r.

82 Hardman, "Windows into the Text."

83 On the lack of closure and its potentials for successive scribes and authors, see Horobin, "Compiling the *Canterbury Tales*"; Higl, *Playing the* Canterbury Tales; Sklute, *Virtue of Necessity*; and McGerr, "Medieval Concepts of Literary Closure," 149–79. On the "permeability" of the manuscript, see Rudy, *Postcards on Parchment*.

84 London, British Library Royal MS 18 D ii, fols. 74r, 75r, 82v. Stylistically, these miniatures are similar, for example, to London, British Library Arundel MS 66 (dated to 1490); and London, British Library Hargrave MS 274, dated to 1488 or 1489.

85 Ellis, "Percy, Henry, Fourth Earl of Northumberland." The emblem contains the arms of Percy and Lucy flanked by initials "HP," accompanied by badges of a crescent and a shackle bolt, and encircled by the Garter (London, British Library Royal MS 18 D ii, fol. 162r).

86 As I discuss later in this chapter, blank but ruled pages followed this one, and texts were only written on them later.

87 The same procedure appears to have occurred in another Lydgate manuscript (containing *The Fall of Princes*) that Henry Percy, fourth Earl of Northumberland came to own, where the illuminator added a different, more elaborate version of his arms in an empty space meant for a heading that was never provided (London, British Library Royal MS 18 D v, fol. 216v).

88 For a similar caution regarding the search for motivations in completing the miniatures in an unfinished manuscript, see Inglis, "Image and Illustration," 194–200.

89 *Troy Book,* III:3,274–322.

90 *Troy Book,* IV:6,023–275.

91 Scot McKendrick posits two separate campaigns: one between c. 1516 and c. 1523, in which all of the texts that I describe later in this chapter were added to the manuscript, and a final campaign in the late 1520s, in which two miniatures were supplied by Gerard Horenbout (London, British Library Royal MS 18 D ii, fols. 148r and 161v) and the rest were painted by another illuminator working in a "Flemish" style. Kren and McKendrick, *Illuminating the Renaissance*, 431–32.

92 Naylor, "'Scribes and Secretaries of the Percy Earls of Northumberland."

93 The text has never been edited, but it records its composition as happening in the nineteenth year of the reign of Henry VII.

94 Lydgate, *Testament*. Although Scott describes the ruling on these pages as "rose or lavender" (*Later Gothic Manuscripts*, 2:284), it is the same shade of brown used throughout the majority of the manuscript.

95 On the *Testament*, see Sobecki, "Lydgate's Kneeling Retraction."

96 See Scattergood, ed., *John Skelton, The Complete English Poems*, 29–35.

97 Fletcher, "The Textual Tradition of the *Assembly of Gods.*" The Wynkyn de Worde edition is STC 17005.

98 Mooney. "Lydgate's *Kings of England.*" Although an edition was printed by Pynson c. 1518 (STC 9983.3), there are too many differences between this edition and the version in London, British Library Royal MS 18 D ii, to posit a connection.

99 The verses are printed in Flügel, "Kleinere Mitteilungen aus Handschriften," 471–97, and they record six sets of verses in five rooms at Leconfield and a further three sets of verses adorning a room in the garden house at Wressle. For a discussion of them, see Edwards, "Middle English Inscriptional Verse Texts"; and Blatt, "Mapping the Readable Household."

100 Dickens, "The Tudor-Percy Emblem in Royal 18 D II." This image contains all the hallmarks of what Kathryn Rudy has termed the "parchment painting," notably the absence of ruling on either side and the differences in the quality of its parchment from that of the surrounding pages. See Rudy, *Postcards on Parchment*, 14–15.

101 Four leaves of quire ix are transposed with the corresponding leaves of quire xvi. The correct order for the first of these misbound sections is fols. 69, 119, 120, 72, 73, 123, 124, 76; and the correct order for the second misbound section is fols. 118, 70, 71, 121, 122, 74, 75, 125. Reader annotations in a sixteenth-century hand that directs the reader to the correct order appear on fols. 73v, 75v, and 118v.

102 Edwards, "Books Owned by Medieval Members of the Percy Family."

103 Hearne, ed., *The Itinerary of John Leland the Antiquary*, 1:55.

104 The manuscript is Oxford, Bodleian Library MS Arch Selden B 10, a copy of the second version of Hardyng's *Chronicle*, composed for Richard, Duke of York, and later Edward IV. The manuscript is currently being edited by Sarah Peverley. For an edition of the first version of Hardyng's *Chronicle*, see Peverley and Simpson, eds., *Hardyng's* Chronicle.

105 Meale, "Patrons, Buyers and Owners," 213–15.

106 Gillespie, "'These Proverbes Yet Do Laste,'" 229. See also, Boffey, "Bodleian Library MS Arch Selden B 24," 130.

107 London, British Library Royal MS 18 D ii, fol. 182v. The whole motto is "esperance ma comfort," and the words "ma comfort" were inserted into the cadels of an ascender on fol. 4v.

108 Smith uses this term to describe the Neville of Hornby Hours in *Art, Identity and Devotion*, 32, 82–139. See also Smith, "The Neville of Hornby Hours."

109 Brenk, "Spolia from Constantine to Charlemagne," 106.

110 Moxey, *Visual Time*, 28.

111 Ibid., 45.

112 See n. 41, as well as Moxey, "Impossible Distance"; and Moxey, "Mimesis and Iconoclasm."

CHAPTER 6

1 For a discussion of the manuscript's ownership and provenance, see Harris, "Ownership and Readership," 116–19; Driver, "Printing the *Confessio*"; and Drimmer, "The Visual Language of Vernacular Manuscript Illumination," 166–205. See also Eberle, "Miniatures as Evidence of Reading"; Scott, *Later Gothic Manuscripts*, 2:322–25; Driver, "Women Readers and Pierpont Morgan MS M.126"; and Rust, *Imaginary Worlds*, 117–64.

2 Ross, *Edward IV*, 126.

3 On Edward IV's manuscript collection, see Warner and Gilson, *Catalogue of Western Manuscripts in the Old Royal and King's Collections*; Backhouse, "Founders of the Royal Library"; McKendrick, "*La Grande Histoire César* and the Manuscripts of Edward IV"; and McKendrick, "*The Roméléon* and the Manuscripts of Edward IV." For an account of the English objects patronized by or produced for Edward and Elizabeth, see Drimmer, "The Visual Language of Vernacular Manuscript Illumination," 166–205.

4 Harris, "Patrons, Buyers and Owners," 178.

5 The two most recent considerations of Ricardus Franciscus's work contain comprehensive bibliographies. See James-Maddocks and Thorpe, "A Petition Written by Ricardus Franciscus," which lists all manuscripts attributed to his hand; and Thorpe, "British Library MS Arundel 249." Three religious manuscripts have been attributed to him, I believe, in error: London, British Library Harley MS 4012; London, British Library Harley MS 2915; Los Angeles, J. Paul Getty Museum MS 5, 84 ML.723. On these rejected attributions, see Drimmer, "The Visual Language of Vernacular Manuscript Illumination," 192, n.81.

6 Driver, "Printing the *Confessio Amantis*," 282–83, n.27. I only differ with Driver on one cadel phrase on fol. 42r, which she transcribes as "vive le roy Edward Ivme" (presumably, quatrième). The last word is "vraie." The "vraie" here echoes prophecies and genealogies that refer to Edward as "verus et indubitatus" (e.g., Oxford, Bodleian Library MS Bodley 623, fols. 23v and 68v).

7 Scott and I differ on the allocation of miniatures and in the opinion that the main illuminator was "probably trained in the Southern Low Countries." Scott, *Later Gothic Manuscripts*, 2:324. While Scott's assessment is possible, there are enough manuscripts made in England with illumination resembling the style of the miniatures here to render it impossible to say with any degree of certainty where the illuminators originated or were trained; more relevant here is the manuscript's production in London, a point on which scholars agree. The miniatures I ascribe to a second illuminator occur in quire 24, on fols. 176r, 176v, 179r, 179v, 180v, 181v, 183v.

8 Scanlon, *Narrative, Authority, and Power*, 81–134. Of the 141 exempla recounted in the *Confessio Amantis*, just over half are illustrated in Morgan MS M.126. The manuscript contains 106 miniatures, 31 of which are devoted to the scientific excursus in Book VII, while a further 4 depict the prefatory matter to the poem. The remaining 71 miniatures illustrate narrative exempla, and of these, 52 depict historical exempla—that is, tales that recount reputedly authentic events located in the Greco-Roman, biblical, or more recent Christian past—leaving many of the mythological and fabulous tales unillustrated. I discuss the medieval conception of history later in this chapter.

9 Buettner, "Profane Illuminations, Secular Illusions," 80.

10 Kate Harris identified minutiae found within M.126's miniatures that indicate familiarity with the court of Edward IV. Harris, "Ownership and Readership," 116–19.

11 There is a massive body of scholarship that grapples with archaeologically incorrect representations of classical history. It is, in fact, the form taken by such images that was (and to a degree implicitly remains) the litmus test for periodization, a key criterion in determining whether an object "belongs" to the Middle Ages or to the Renaissance. This position was most explicitly articulated by

Erwin Panofsky in several passages from *Renaissance and Renascences* in which he lays out his theory of disjunction as the inability to pair classical form with classical content. See Panofsky, *Renaissance and Renascences*, 86. For reflections on these ideas, see Nagel and Wood, *Anachronic Renaissance*, 45–49.

12 Buettner, "Profane Illuminations, Secular Illusions," 82. See also Buettner, *Boccaccio's "Des Cleres et Nobles Femmes*," 93–99; Driver, "Medievalizing the Classical Past"; Sherman, *Imaging Aristotle*; Hedeman, *Translating the Past*; Hedeman, "Making the Past Present"; Desmond and Sheingorn, *Myth, Montage, and Visuality*; Inglis, *Jean Fouquet*; Inglis, "Image and Illustration."

13 Buettner, "Profane Illuminations," 82, 84. Hedeman offers a similar definition of "visual translation" as "the process by which images helped stories set in the past or in a different culture come alive and be current to a medieval reader." Hedeman, "Presenting the Past," 69.

14 For a study of the exemplary purpose of historical images directed at the king and his circle, see Binski, *The Painted Chamber at Westminster*; and Binski, "The Painted Chamber at Westminster."

15 The scholarship on temporality in Middle English literature is vast. For a survey through the first decade of this century, see Smyth, "Changing Times in the Cultural Discourse." See Dinshaw, *How Soon Is Now?* for a more recent engagement. It is only recently that manuscript representations of historical events have been considered within the genre of "history painting." See Inglis, "History in French Manuscripts."

16 Larry Scanlon presents a compelling argument for the royalism of the *Confessio Amantis*, expressed as a belief in "monarchy's inherently self-regulating character, the paradoxical but inevitable logic whereby absolute prerogative produces its own self-generated restraint." Scanlon, *Narrative, Authority, and Power*, 265.

17 "Historie," in McSparran, ed., *Middle English Dictionary*. It is probable that Gower adopted the term from the French *estoire* (Peck, ed., *Confessio Amantis*, 1:5), which was in its twelfth-century usage taken to mean "a (vernacular) narrative of past events, presented as true, and whose authenticity is attested by an authority" (Damian-Grint, "*Estoire* as Word and Genre," 198).

18 *Confessio Amantis*, VI:883–89.

19 On Gower's belief in the efficacy of narratives to shape experience, see Peck, "The Phenomenology of Make Believe." See also Dean, "Time Past and Time Present"; Olsson, *John Gower and the Structures of Conversion*; and Urban, *Fragments*.

20 Spiegel, *The Past as Text*, 87–88.

21 Peck notes that "five of the six times [Gower] uses the word 'histoire' in the *Confessio* he rhymes it with 'memoire.'" Peck, ed., *Confessio Amantis*, 3:6. Chaucer uses a similar pairing for *storie*, as, for example, in his own abbreviated *Fürstenspiegel*, "The Monk's Tale": "Tragedie is to seyn a certeyn storie / as olde bookes maken us memorie." Prologue to the "Monk's Tale," 1973–74.

22 On the suggestion that Middle English literature encouraged the reader to elide the collective with the personal past, see Carruthers, "Meditations on the 'Historical Present.'"

23 Or, as Russell Peck notes, "Gower is astutely aware that 'history,' whether in old texts or folk experience, is constructed out of 'memory' by individual writers and readers who plot for particular purposes. He knows that all documents of the past, the written and the oral, are open to trial and judgment and are relative to the times in which they were produced as well as the times in which they are heard once again." Peck, ed., *Confessio Amantis*, 3:8.

24 *Confessio Amantis*, VII: 2702. Malte Urban explores how Gower employs "poetics of the past" to advocate an idealized (and conservative) social harmony, founded on carefully selected models from history. Urban, *Fragments*.

25 Yeager, "'Scripture Veteris Capiunt Exempla Futuri,'" 341.

26 Elizabeth Porter refers to Amans as a "surrogate of Richard II" in "Gower's Ethical Microcosm and Political Macrocosm," 147. Both James Simpson and Kathryn McKinley support this view. See Simpson, *Sciences and the Self*, 280; and McKinley, "Lessons for a King."

27 *Confessio Amantis*, Prol. 24.

28 A number of modern scholars have subscribed to this account of the poem's generic profile. See Peck, *Kingship and Common Profit*; Ferster, *Fictions of Advice*; and Allen, *False Fables and Exemplary Truth*. Joel Fredell sees the poem as a "penitential mirror for princes" in "Reading the Dream Miniature," 63.

29 On this portion of the manuscript, see O'Callaghan, "The Fifteen Stars"; and Drimmer, "The Visual Language of Vernacular Manuscript Illumination," 268–341.

30 Peck, "The Politics and Psychology of Governance," 216.

31 Scanlon, *Narrative, Authority, and Power*, 256.

32 It is only the rare pre-fifteenth-century *Fürstenspiegel* manuscript that contains illustrations: these are generally what Claire Sherman has referred to as paradigmatic and diagrammatic illustrations absent of narrative content. See Sherman, *Imaging Aristotle*. Also for studies of illustrated *Fürstenspiegel*, see Camille, "The King's New Bodies"; Michael, "The Iconography of Kingship"; and Hedeman, *Of Counselors and Kings*. On illuminations of *Des cas des nobles hommes et femmes*, see Hedeman, *Translating the Past*.

33 Strohm, *Politique*, 88.

34 London, British Library Royal MS 14 E v. See Doyle, Lowden, and McKendrick, eds., *Royal Manuscripts*, 222–23.

35 Strohm, *England's Empty Throne*, 25–28.

36 Scanlon, *Narrative, Authority, and Power*, 247.

37 New York, Morgan Library and Museum MS M.126, fol. 209v. The index is transcribed in Harris, "Ownership and Readership," 308–28. For another transcription and a discussion of the indexer's technique, see Drimmer, "The Visual Language of Vernacular Manuscript Illumination," 382–93.

38 The tales of Albinus and Rosamond (fol. 23r) and Clytemnestra's murder of Agamemnon (fol. 62r). Two others show kings being slain, but the context and circumstances of battle are very different from that of assassination. The miniatures illustrate the tales of Ahab and Micaiah (fol. 166v) and of Gideon defeating the five Midianite kings (fol. 174r).

39 It is perhaps not a coincidence that the manuscript of Lydgate's *Fall of Princes*, which was copied by Ricardus Franciscus and probably produced for Edward IV (Philadelphia, Rosenbach Museum and Library MS 439/16) likewise avoids the pornography of slaughter in other copies, contributing a pictorial program without illustrations for exempla. See Lawton, "'To Studie in Bookis of Antiquitie,'" 61–77.

40 See Pearsall, "Hoccleve's *Regement of Princes*."

41 See n. 10 above.

42 Lowden, "The Royal/Imperial Book," 239.

43 Paul Strohm makes the important point that medieval propaganda was not issued by a centralized machine. See Strohm, *England's Empty Throne*, 87.

44 Ailes, "Heraldry in Medieval England," 100.

45 For a basic reference on the history of the Wars of the Roses, see Grummit, *A Short History of the Wars of the Roses*.

46 Over seventy genealogical rolls from fifteenth-century England survive (both Lancastrian and Yorkist). See Rajsic, "The English Prose *Brut* Chronicle on a Roll," 115. See also Anglo, "The British History in Early Tudor Propaganda"; Louis, "A Yorkist Genealogical Chronicle"; Phillip Morgan, "'Those Were the Days'"; Allan, "Royal Propaganda and the Proclamations of Edward IV"; Scattergood, *Politics and Poetry in the Fifteenth Century*; Coote, *Prophecy and Public Affairs*; and Radulescu, "The Political Mentality of the English Gentry."

47 Allan, "Yorkist Propaganda," 172. See also Gransden, *Historical Writing in England*, 249–87; Sutton and Visser-Fuchs, *Richard III's Books*, 135–202; and Spiegel, *The Past as Text*, 83–98.

48 Alison Allan notes, for example, that "the extant copies of . . . four types of Yorkist pedigree indicate that their production in considerable numbers was consciously planned. They seem to be the output of a small group of craftsmen, probably from the secular workshops which were becoming an

increasingly important source of manuscript production in the fourteenth and fifteenth centuries." Allan, "Yorkist Propaganda," 174.

49 Ingledew, "The Book of Troy and the Genealogical Construction of History," 669.

50 Strohm, *Politique*, 25.

51 *Confessio Amantis*, VII:2917–3028.

52 Ibid., 2949.

53 Scanlon, *Narrative, Authority, and Power*, 289.

54 Panofsky, *Renaissance and Renascences in Western Art*, 85.

55 On the Yeomen of the Crown, see Myers, ed., *The Household of Edward IV: The Black Book and the Ordinance of 1478*, 116–17.

56 See n. 63 below.

57 The Lion of March is differentiated from royal lions by its upraised forepaw and its cowed tail (a tail that passes between the hind legs and crosses over the flank). Although it is difficult to see in the reproduction, the brushstroke of the tail does indicate that it passes through the hind legs in this manner.

58 Smith, "History, Typology and Homily," 150. For a study of this manuscript see Stanton, *Queen Mary Psalter*. See also, on the inclusion of contemporary heraldry in historical scenes Sandler, "Political Imagery."

59 The use of apostrophe is common in Middle English versions of *De casibus*. In Chaucer's "Monk's Tale," the Monk ends numerous tales by addressing the fallen figure, e.g., "O noble Sampsoun, strongest of mankynde" (2,075). In the *Fall of Princes*, Lydgate uses the same device, e.g., "O Alisaundre, thou ouhtest been ashamed / To slen thi clerk with peynes so horrible / For thi vicis because he hath the blamyd!" (IV, 1353–55).

60 Didi-Huberman, "The Portrait, the Individual and the Singular," 177.

61 Myers, ed., *The Household of Edward IV*, 217. See also Hicks, "The 1468 Statute of Livery"; and Ward, "The Livery Collar: Politics and Identity During the Fifteenth Century."

62 Donal Cooper, "Projecting Presence." See also Belting, *Likeness and Presence*, in which the nature of the cross as icon is discussed throughout.

63 On the morning of the Battle of Mortimer's Cross in 1461, Edward proclaimed the appearance of three suns (a phenomenon known as parhelion) to betoken the Trinity, sanctioning his right to the throne. The episode is portrayed on a long roll (London, British Library Harley MS 7353), which I discuss later in this chapter. The episode is also described in Marx, ed., *An English Chronicle 1377–1461*, 99.

64 On the Lion of March badge, see Siddons, *Heraldic Badges in England and Wales*, 2, part 1:167–69.

65 On the use of clothing to establish both group and individual identities, see Piponnier, *Costume et vie sociale*, 231–59.

66 Crane, *The Performance of Self*, 19.

67 Krynen, *Idéal du prince et pouvoir royal*, 129.

68 Freud, *Beyond the Pleasure Principle*, 8–11. Kipling, *Enter the King*. Specifically, with respect to Edward IV, see Scase, "Writing and the 'Poetics of Spectacle.'"

69 Brantley and Fulton argue that *carici* here is an error for *curia*, as in *curia tenta* ("the court having been held"), a formula used in legal documents. "Mankind in a Year Without Kings," 328. Here, the joke is that Nought, who has written it, is both ignorant in Latin and barely capable of writing legibly.

70 Eccles, ed., *The Macro Plays*, 176. This translation is partly mine, with the translations of the odd Latin verses taken from: Brantley and Fulton, "Mankind in a Year Without Kings."

71 Brantley and Fulton, "Mankind in a Year Without Kings," 345 and 331, respectively.

72 Wright, ed., *Political Poems and Songs*, 2:279.

73 *Confessio Amantis*, IV:147–233.

74 There is an interesting precedent for the Yeoman of the Crown acting in this capacity. In the only surviving account book from the household of Margaret of Anjou (queen consort to Henry VI)

is mentioned a Roger Morecroft, custodian of the queen's books as well as the envoy of her council. See Myers, "The Household Accounts of Queen Margaret of Anjou," 95.

75 For a discussion of some of these representations of Penelope in French manuscripts, see Renck, "Reading Medieval Manuscripts," 56–57, 72.

76 At the end of the poem, the narrator confers his highest praise on four women of antiquity: Penelope, Lucrece, Alcestis, and Alceone. *Confessio Amantis*, VIII:2615–56.

77 Wright, ed., *Political Poems and Songs*, 2:281.

78 London, British Library Additional MS 18268a.

79 On the significance of the Cadwaladr prophecy, see Coote, *Prophecy and Public Affairs*, 195–234.

80 London, British Library Additional MS 18268a.

81 As Russell Peck notes, "That [Lycurgus] has made himself superfluous is his triumph." Peck, "Politics and Psychology of Governance," 221.

82 In a nearly contemporary manuscript of Lydgate's *Fall of Princes* (London, British Library Harley MS 1766, fol. 146r), for example, Lycurgus is depicted not in life but rather in death, his bones cast into the sea.

83 Pronay and Cox, eds., *The Crowland Chronicle Continuations*, 137.

84 See McKendrick, "Edward IV: An English Royal Collector of Netherlandish Tapestry"; Campbell, *Henry VIII and the Art of Majesty*, 45–64.

85 Myers, ed., *The Household of Edward IV*, 48. Also, on "magnificence," see Kipling, *The Triumph of Honour*.

86 Green, *Poets and Princepleasers*, 99. For a history of the royal library, as well as its nonprivate nature, see Kathleen Doyle, "The Old Royal library." See also Stratford, "The Early Royal Collections and the Royal Library to 1461."

87 Eames, "Documentary Evidence Concerning the Character and Use of Domestic Furnishings," 48.

88 On the renovations see Colvin, ed., *The History of the King's Works*, 1:246; 2:935-37.

89 This would not have been so strange given that "across medieval Europe it was common for sovereigns to emulate their literary counterparts and to have events in their own lives presented in terms familiar from literature." Laynesmith, *The Last Medieval Queens*, 25.

90 Myers, ed., *The Household of Edward IV*.

91 Ibid., 26.

92 London, British Library Harley MS 642, made by Sir Simonds d'Ewes. Although the original copy (or copies) of the *Black Book* is now lost, later copies that were independently produced attest to its genuine existence and composition at Edward's court, probably in early 1472. See Myers, ed., *The Household of Edward IV*, 29–34.

93 "This picture located below as well as the supporting contributions to feasting on this page and on the facing page are drawn exactly from the exemplar in the beginning of the Black Book." London, British Library Harley MS 642, fol. 4r.

94 "Socrates: Edere oportet ut vivas non vivere ut edas. Rex erit invictus fuerit cui copia victus. Alimoniam super omnia populi plus requirunt. Seneca." Ibid.

95 Myers, ed., *The Household of Edward IV*, 18.

96 Ibid., 82.

97 Ibid., 83.

98 On Alexander's uneven reputation in medieval literature, see Cary, *The Medieval Alexander*; and Bunt, *Alexander the Great in the Literature of Medieval Britain*. The three miniatures in the Morgan *Confessio* illustrate Alexander counseled by Diogenes (fol. 58r), Alexander counseled by a pirate (fol. 65r), and Alexander counseled by Nectanabus (fol. 158r). The unillustrated exemplum occurs in *Confessio Amantis*, III:2438–468.

99 Strohm, *Politique*, 32.

100 Aers, "Reflections on Gower as '*Sapiens*.'" For the opposing view, see Runacres, "Art and Ethics in the Exempla"; and Olsson, *John Gower and the Structures of Conversion*.

101 Aside from the three sets of miniatures I discuss here, other juxtapositions in the Morgan *Confessio* include the King of Apulia and His Steward (fol. 104v) and Achilles and Deidamia (106v); Gideon defeating the five Midianite kings (fol. 174r) and Saul and Agag, (fol. 175r); Lydians Dancing (fol. 179r) and Hebrews in Amorous Poses (fol. 179r). On the expressive potentials of openings in codices see Hamburger, "Openings."

102 *Confessio Amantis*, V:2273–390.

103 They are "Of o semblance and of o make, / So lych that noman thilke throwe / That oon mai fro that other knowe." *Confessio Amantis*, V:2296–98.

104 Ibid., V:2391–418.

105 They are described as "evene aliche, as man mai gesse, / Outward thei were bothe tuo." Ibid., V:2412–13.

106 For a guide to medieval typology see Wirth, ed., *Pictor in Carmine*. See also the foundational text on typology in Auerbach, *Scenes from the Drama of European Literature*, 11–71. For some qualifications to Auerbach's views, see Emmerson, "*Figura* and the Medieval Typological Imagination."

107 On Thebes as history in Middle English literature, see Battles, *The Medieval Tradition of Thebes*.

108 Gower's Latin version and his Middle English rendition differ. *Confessio Amantis*, I:1977–2020. Whereas, in the Latin version, it is ambiguous whether the fire "descended from the sky" (*ignis de celo subito*), was released by Thebans from the ramparts, in the Middle English version, "Godd tok himselve the bataille / Agein his Pride, and fro the sky / A firy thonder sodeinly / He sende." Ibid., I:2000–2003.

109 Ibid., I:2021–253.

110 Braeger, "The Illustration in New College MS 266," 288.

111 Ibid., 288–89.

112 Pearsall, "The Organisation of the Latin Apparatus."

113 *Confessio Amantis*, I:1980.

114 It was common to portray pride as a man being thrown from his horse. See Reidemeister, *Superbia und Narziss*. Reidemeister describes how the allegorical personification of pride as a figure on a horse came to be merged with narrative images, as, in particular, depictions of Narcissus.

115 Hedeman, *Translating the Past*, 23.

116 Carruthers, "Meditations on the 'Historical Present' and 'Collective Memory,'"144.

117 This idea has been expressed, in various permutations, since the New Historicist turn in the 1980s. On its more general application, see de Certeau, *The Writing of History*. On its relationship to the engagement with the medieval past, see Lee Patterson, *Negotiating the Past*. Gabrielle Spiegel's body of scholarship engages deeply with this idea, at times offering powerful critiques. In particular see Spiegel, "Revising the Past/Revisiting the Present."

118 Strohm, *Theory and the Premodern Text*, 150–51.

119 London, British Library Harley MS 7353. This roll is a fascinating object, the complexities of which I cannot begin to give their due here. I am currently writing a full-fledged study of it and similar objects. Because this roll has never been the subject of analysis, the circumstances of its production remain unknown. The genealogy at its foot suggests a date before the birth of Edward's first daughter in 1466. A segment from this roll is discussed in Strohm, *Politique*, 2–5. Jonathan Hughes discusses this roll in *Arthurian Myths and Alchemy*, 71, 78, 82–84, 91, 140–44, 148–51; however some of his descriptions are inaccurate, and some of his translations are wrong.

120 Important here are Emmerson's modifications to Auerbach's thesis regarding the purely historical dimension of typological parallels. See n. 106 above.

121 Edward's deployment of typology extended to his own actions and subsequent publicization of those actions. On his return to England to reclaim the throne in 1471, Edward disembarked at Ravenspur, the same port where Henry Bolingbroke had landed before deposing Richard II. For an illuminating analysis of this episode and its account in the *Arrivall of Edward IV*, see Strohm, *Politique*, 21–32.

122 *Confessio Amantis*, VII:2845–88.

123 In the subsequent exemplum (ibid., VII:2889–916), Cambises, king of Persia, is held up as yet another guardian of the law, although his methods of safeguarding it are questionable. Discovering one of his judges to be corrupt, Cambises has him flayed alive and then commissions a judicial chair to be made from his carcass. In this chair, the judge's son and successor sits and is made to remember the bad example of his father.

EPILOGUE

1 Emmerson similarly wonders about "a crucial question concerning Chaucer and medieval visual culture: why were the narratives of the *Canterbury Tales* not illustrated in the fifteenth century (as were the poems of Gower and Lydgate)?" Emmerson, Review of *Telling Images*, 443.

2 STC 5083. The first edition (STC 5082) was printed c. 1476. For a concise summary of the scholarship on the dating of the two editions, see Bordalejo, "Caxton's Editing."

3 Vincent Gillespie, "Introduction," 8. See also Boffey, "From Manuscript to Print."

4 STC 5083, fol. a2r–v. For an edition, see Crotch, ed., *The Prologues and Epilogues of William Caxton*, 90–91.

5 Blake, "Caxton's Reprints," 174. See also Blake, "Caxton's Second Edition of the *Canterbury Tales*"; and Dunn, "The Manuscript Source of Caxton's Edition."

6 Bordalejo, "Caxton's Editing," 53.

7 Of course, the woodcuts themselves have received attention. See Carlson, "Woodcut Illustrations of the *Canterbury Tales*"; Blake gives a detailed account of the placement of the cuts and hypothesizes how the compositor disposed them in "Caxton's Second Edition," 143–45. Iconographic studies of individual cuts have also been carried out, as in, for example, Hilmo, "The Clerk's 'Unscholarly Bow.'"

8 Philadelphia, Rosenbach Library MS 1084/2, and Manchester, Rylands Library MS English 63. Martha Driver does note that Caxton does not specify whether the copy he says the gentleman brought to him was illustrated. Driver, *The Image in Print*, 8.

9 Carlson, ""Woodcut Illustrations of the *Canterbury Tales*," 26.

10 Ibid. In addition to the Oxford Fragments (see n. 8 above), the two other manuscripts with images of the pilgrims on horseback are San Marino, Huntington Library MS EL 26 C 9, and Cambridge, University Library MS Gg 4.27. The latter also includes personifications of virtues and vices, which accompany the "Parson's Tale."

11 The "Pilgrims at Table" block was reused in Wynkyn de Worde's c. 1498 and c.1500 editions of the *Assembly of Gods* (STC 17005, 17006, and 17007). See Gillespie, *Print Culture and the Medieval Author*, 94–97.

12 STC 5084.

13 On the consideration of Caxton as derivative, see Driver, *The Image in Print*, 33. Although the blocks were reused, editions varied in their placement and overall format, and many were lost over the years. Carlson, "Woodcut Illustrations."

14 This is a point made well in Mann, *Chaucer and Medieval Estates Satire*, 66.

15 Lee Patterson, *Chaucer and the Subject of History*, 30.

16 Hellinga, "Printing," 103. Betsy Bowden opined similarly that "following precedent set by the Caxton edition, printers insert pilgrim portraits as mnemonic aids to help readers remain aware of which pilgrim is telling each Canterbury tale." Bowden, "Visual Portraits of the Canterbury Pilgrims," 172.

17 STC 5077–5079. Speght includes only one pilgrim portrait, that of the Knight. On the Chaucer frontispiece, see Driver, "Mapping Chaucer."

18 Wallace, *Chaucerian Polity*, 65.

BIBLIOGRAPHY

Primary Sources: Manuscript

Arundel Castle

John Lydgate, *Lives of Saints Edmund and Fremund* (No shelfmark)

Cambridge

Corpus Christi College MS 61
King's College Archives KC/18
King's College MS 40
Pembroke College MS 307
St. Catharine's College MS 7
St. John's College MS B.12
St. John's College MS H.5
Trinity College MS O.5.2
Trinity College MS R.3.2
Trinity College MS R.3.21
Trinity College MS R.4.20
University Library MS Dd.8.19
University Library MS Gg.4.27
University Library MS Mm.2.21

Chicago

Newberry Library MS 33.3

Eton

ECR 39/57
ECR 61 AR/A/3
ECR 39/8
Eton College Library MS 213

Geneva

Bodmer Library MS 178

Glasgow

University of Glasgow, Hunter MS 59

Kew

National Archives C 81/1505
National Archives CP 40/647
National Archives CP 40/660
National Archives CP 40/802
National Archives CP 40/810
National Archives CP 40/819
National Archives CP 40/823
National Archives CP 40/861
National Archives E 361/6
National Archives KB 27/714

Liverpool

Cathedral of Christ MS 6

London

British Library Additional Charter 71759
British Library Additional MS 18268a
British Library Additional MS 18632
British Library Additional MS 22139
British Library Additional MS 24189
British Library Additional MS 29704
British Library Additional MS 29705
British Library Additional MS 42131
British Library Additional MS 44892
British Library Additional MS 59495
British Library Additional MS 59678
British Library Additional MS 74236
British Library Arundel MS 38
British Library Arundel MS 66
British Library Arundel MS 99
British Library Arundel MS 109
British Library Arundel MS 119
British Library Cotton MS Augustus A iv
British Library Cotton MS Nero D iv
British Library Cotton MS Nero D vii
British Library Cotton MS Tiberius A iv
British Library Egerton MS 913
British Library Egerton MS 1991
British Library Egerton MS 2830
British Library Hargrave MS 274

British Library Harley MS 642
British Library Harley MS 644
British Library Harley MS 1766
British Library Harley MS 2278
British Library Harley MS 2915
British Library Harley MS 3869
British Library Harley MS 4012
British Library Harley MS 4826
British Library Harley MS 4866
British Library Harley MS 7026
British Library Harley MS 7353
British Library Lansdowne MS 851
British Library Royal MS 1 E ix
British Library Royal MS 2 A xviii
British Library Royal MS 14 C vii
British Library Royal MS 14 E v
British Library Royal MS 17 D vi
British Library Royal MS 18 C xxii
British Library Royal MS 18 D ii
British Library Royal MS 18 D v
British Library Royal MS 20 C iv
British Library Royal MS 20 D x
British Library Sloane MS 2593
British Library Sloane MS 2464
British Library Yates Thompson MS 26
British Library Yates Thompson MS 47
British Library Yates Thompson MS 48
Guildhall Library MS 5370
Guildhall Library MS 5436
Guildhall Library MS 9171/5
Guildhall Library MS 12112
Guildhall Library MS 16988
Guildhall Library MS 31692
Guildhall Library MS 39293
Lambeth Palace Library MS 560
Metropolitan Archives CLA/007/FN/02/003
Metropolitan Archives COL/AD/01/009
Metropolitan Archives COL/AD/01/010
Metropolitan Archives COL/CS/01/007
Metropolitan Archives COL/CS/01/008
Metropolitan Archives P69/DUN1/B/001/
    MS04887
Metropolitan Archives P69/MTN2/B/001/
    MS00959/001
Society of Antiquaries MS 134
Society of Antiquaries MS 501
St. Bartholomew's Hospital SNC/1
Westminster Abbey MS 37

Worshipful Company of Carpenters Grant of
    Arms of 1466
Worshipful Company of Drapers Grant of
    Arms of 1439
Worshipful Company of Drapers WA/1
Worshipful Company of Haberdashers Grant
    of Arms of 1446
Worshipful Company of Ironmongers Grant of
    Arms of 1455
Worshipful Company of Tallow Chandlers
    Grant of Arms of 1456

Los Angeles

J. Paul Getty Museum MS 5, 84 ML.723

Luton

Museum of Luton, Luton Guild Register

Manchester

Rylands Library MS English 1
Rylands Library MS English 2
Rylands Library MS English 63

Montreal

McGill University MS 143

New Haven

Beinecke Library Takamiya MS 24
Beinecke Library Takamiya MS 54

New York

Columbia University Rare Book and Manu-
    script Library Plimpton MS 265
Morgan Library and Museum MS M.125
Morgan Library and Museum MS M.126
Morgan Library and Museum MS M.231
Morgan Library and Museum MS M.690
Morgan Library and Museum MS M.876

Nottingham

University Library Middleton MS Mi LM 8

Oslo

Schøyen Collection 615

Oxford

Bodleian Library MS Arch Selden B 10
Bodleian Library MS Arch Selden B 11
Bodleian Library MS Arch Selden B 24

Bodleian Library MS Ashmole 34
Bodleian Library MS Ashmole 35
Bodleian Library MS Ashmole 46
Bodleian Library MS Bodley 263
Bodleian Library MS Bodley 277
Bodleian Library MS Bodley 294
Bodleian Library MS Bodley 596
Bodleian Library MS Bodley 623
Bodleian Library MS Bodley 686
Bodleian Library MS Bodley 693
Bodleian Library MS Bodley 902
Bodleian Library MS Digby 230
Bodleian Library MS Digby 232
Bodleian Library MS Digby 233
Bodleian Library MS Douce 104
Bodleian Library MS Douce 158
Bodleian Library MS Duke Humfrey b 1
Bodleian Library MS Fairfax 3
Bodleian Library MS Laud Misc. 609
Bodleian Library MS Laud Misc. 673
Bodleian Library MS Rawlinson C 48
Bodleian Library MS Rawlinson C 446
Bodleian Library MS Rawlinson Poet. 223
Bodleian Library MS Selden Supra 53
Bodleian Library MS Wood Empt. 1
Christ Church College MS 148
Corpus Christi College MS 67
Jesus College MS 124

Magdalene College MS 213
New College MS 266
St. John's College MS 18
St. John's College MS 266
University College MS 85

Paris

Bibliothèque mazarine MS 507

Philadelphia

Philadelphia Museum of Art, Phillip S. Collins Collection, acc. no. 45-65-2
Rosenbach Library MS 439/16
Rosenbach Library MS 1083/29
Rosenbach Library MS 1084/2

Princeton

University Library Taylor MS 5

Private Collection

Confessio Amantis (formerly Mount Stuart, Rothesay, Marquess of Bute MS I.17)

San Marino

Huntington Library HM 268
Huntington Library HM 932
Huntington Library MS EL 26 A 17
Huntington Library MS EL 26 C 9

Primary Sources: Print and Electronic

Augustine. *Confessions and Enchiridion*. Translated and edited by Albert C. Outler. Philadelphia: Westminster, 1955.

The Assembly of Gods. London: Wynkyn de Worde, c. 1498. STC 17005.

The Assembly of Gods. London: Wynkyn de Worde, c. 1498. STC 17006.

The Assembly of Gods. London: Wynkyn de Worde, c. 1500. STC 17007.

Calendar of Patent Rolls, Henry VI. Vol. 6, 1452–1461. London: HMSO, 1910.

Caracciolus, Fra Roberto. Sermones de laudibus sanctorum. Naples, 1489.

Caxton, William. *The Prologues and Epilogues of William Caxton*. Edited by W. J. B. Crotch. EETS o.s. 176. London: Oxford University Press, 1928.

Chaucer, Geoffrey. *The Assemble of Foules*. London: Wynkyn de Worde, 1530. STC 5092.

———. *The Canterbury Tales*. Westminster: Caxton, c. 1476. STC 5082.

———. *The Canterbury Tales*. Westminster: Caxton, c. 1482. STC 5083.

———. *The Canterbury Tales*. Westminster: Pynson, c. 1492. STC 5084.

———. *The Riverside Chaucer*. 3rd ed. Edited by Larry D. Benson and F. N. Robinson. Boston: Houghton Mifflin, 1987.

———. *The Workes of Our Antient and Lerned English Poet, Geffrey Chaucer, Newly Printed*. Edited by Thomas Speght. London: Islip, 1598. STC 5077.

Chaucer, Geoffrey. *The Workes of Our Antient and Lerned English Poet, Geffrey Chaucer*, Newly Printed. Edited by Thomas Speght. London: Islip, 1598. STC 5078.

———. *The Workes of Our Antient and Lerned English Poet, Geffrey Chaucer, Newly Printed*. Edited by Thomas Speght. London: Islip, 1598. STC 5079.

Churchwardens' Accounts from the Fourteenth Century to the Close of the Seventeenth Century. Edited by Charles Cox. London: Methuen, 1913.

Concilia Magnae Britanniae et Hiberniae, a Syndo Verolamiensi. Edited by D. Wilkins. 4 vols. London, 1737.

Conrad of Hirsau. "Dialogue on the Authors: Extracts." In *Medieval Literary Theory and Criticism, c. 1100–c. 1375: The Commentary-Tradition*, edited by A. J. Minnis and A. Brian Scott, 39–64. Oxford: Clarendon, 1988.

The Crowland Chronicle Continuations: 1459–1486. Edited and translated by Nicholas Pronay and John Cox. London: Sutton, 1986.

Cursor Mundi. Edited by Richard Morris, Hugo Carl Wilhelm Haenisch, Heinrich Hupe, Max Kaluza, EETS 57. London: Trübner, 1874–93.

The Early English Carols. Edited by Richard L. Greene. Oxford: Clarendon, 1977.

An English Chronicle 1377–1461. A New Edition. Aberystwyth, National Library of Wales MS 21608, and Oxford, Bodleian Library MS Lyell 34. Edited by William Marx. Woodbridge, UK: Boydell, 2003.

Gower, John. *The Complete Works of John Gower*. 4 vols. Edited by G. C. Macaulay. Oxford: Clarendon Press, 1899.

———. *Confessio Amantis*. Edited by Russell Peck and translated by Andrew Galloway. 3 vols. Kalamazoo, MI: TEA MS and Medieval Institute Publications, 2000–2004.

———. *The English Works of John Gower*. Edited by G. C. Macaulay. 2 vols. London: K. Paul, Trench, Trübner, 1900–1901.

Hardyng, John. *Hardyng's* Chronicle, *Edited from British Library MS Lansdowne 204*. Edited by Sarah Peverley and James Simpson. Kalamazoo, MI: Medieval Institute Publications, 2015.

Hoccleve, Thomas. *The Regiment of Princes*. Edited by Charles Blyth. Kalamazoo, MI: Western Michigan University Press, 1999.

The Household of Edward IV: The Black Book and the Ordinance of 1478. Edited by A. R. Myers. Manchester: Manchester University Press, 1959.

The Lansdowne MS (No. 851) of Chaucer's Canterbury Tales. Edited by Frederick James Furnivall. London: Trübner, 1868.

The Latin Verses in the Confessio Amantis: An Annotated Translation. Edited and translated by Siân Echard and Claire Fanger. East Lansing, MI: Colleagues Press, 1991.

Laurent de Premierfait. *Boccace "Decameron," Traduction (1411–1414) de Laurent de Premierfait*. Edited by Giuseppe di Stefano. Montreal: Bibliothèque de Moyen Français, 1998.

Leland, John. *The Itinerary of John Leland the Antiquary*. 3rd ed., edited by Thomas Hearne. 9 vols. Oxford: Fletcher and Pote, 1768.

Lydgate, John. *A Critical Edition of John Lydgate's* Life of Our Lady. Edited by Joseph A. Lauritius, Ralph A. Klinefelter, and Vernon F. Gallagher. Pittsburgh: Duquesne University Press, 1961.

———. *Fall of Princes*. Edited by Henry Bergen. 4 vols. EETS, e.s. 121–24. London: Oxford University Press, 1924–1927.

———. *Lives of Ss Edmund and Fremund and the Extra Miracles of St Edmund*. Edited by Anthony Bale and A. S. G. Edwards. Middle English Texts 41. Heidelberg: Universitätsverlag, Winter, 2009.

———. *The Minor Poems*, Vol 1. Edited by Henry Noble MacCracken. 2 vols. EETS e.s. 107. London: Kegan Paul, Trench, Trübner, 1911.

———. *Siege of Thebes*. Edited by Axel Erdmann and Eilert Erkwall. EETS e.s. 108 and 130. London: Kegan Paul, Trench, Trübner, 1911–1930.

———. *The Siege of Thebes*. Edited by Robert R. Edwards. Kalamazoo, MI: Medieval Institute, 2001.

———. *Testament*. London: Pynson, 1520(?). STC 17035.

———. *Troy Book*. Edited by Henry Bergen. EETS e.s. 97, 103, 106, 126. London: Kegan Paul, Trench, Trübner, 1906–1935.

Lydgate, John and Benedict Burgh. *Secrees of Old Philisoffres*. Edited by Robert Steele. EETS e.s. 66. London: Kegan Paul, Trench, Trübner, 1894.

The Macro Plays: The Castle of Perseverance, Wisdom, Mankind. Edited by Mark Eccles. EETS o.s. 262. London: Oxford University Press, 1969.

Malory, Thomas. *Le Morte Darthur*. Edited by Stephen H. A. Shepherd. New York: Norton, 2003.

Medieval Records of a London City Church: St. Mary at Hill, 1420–1559. Edited by Henry Littlehales. EETS o.s. 125 and 128. London: Kegan Paul, Trench, Trübner, 1904–5.

Parliament Rolls of Medieval England. Edited by Chris Given-Wilson, Paul Brand, Seymour Phillips, Mark Ormrod, Geoffrey Martin, Anne Curry, and Rosemary Horrox. 16 vols. Woodbridge, UK: Boydell, 2005.

Political Poems and Songs Relating to English History Composed During the Period from the Accession of Edward III to That of Richard III. Edited by Thomas Wright. London: Longman, Green, and Roberts, 1862.

Quintilian. *The Institutio Oratoria of Quintilian*. Edited and translated by H. E. Butler. 4 vols. Cambridge, MA: Harvard University Press, 1979.

Records of the Worshipful Company of Carpenters, Vol II: *Warden's Account Book, 1438–1516*. Edited by Bower Marsh. Oxford: Oxford University Press, 1914.

Rolle, Richard. *The Psalter, or Psalms of David and Certain Canticles, with a Translation and Exposition in English by Richard Rolle of Hampole*. Edited by Rev. H. R. Bramley. Oxford: Clarendon, 1884.

The Scriveners' Company Common Paper, 1357–1628. Edited by Francis W. Steer. London: London Records Society, 1968.

Secretum secretorum: Nine English Versions. Edited by M. A. Manzalaoui. EETS, o.s. 27. Oxford: Oxford University Press, 1977.

Skelton, John. *The Complete English Poems*. Edited by John Scattergood. New Haven, CT: Yale University Press, 1983.

Stow, John. *A Survey of London Reprinted from the Text of 1603*. Edited by C. L. Kingsford. 2 vols. Oxford: Clarendon, 1908.

The Text of the Canterbury Tales Studied on the Basis of All Known Manuscripts. Edited by John Matthews Manly and Edith Rickert. 8 vols. Chicago: University of Chicago Press, 1940.

Wycliffe, John. *Select English Works of John Wyclif*. Edited by Thomas Arnold. 3 vols. Oxford: Clarendon, 1869. *Speculum sacerdotale,* Edited from British Museum MS Additional 36791. Edited by E. H. Weatherly. EETS, o.s. 200. London: Oxford University Press, 1936.

Secondary Sources

Aers, David. "Reflections on Gower as 'Sapiens' in Ethics and Politics." In *Re-Visioning Gower*, edited by R. F. Yeager, 185–202. Asheville, NC: Pegasus, 1998.

Ailes, Adrian. "Heraldry in Medieval England: Symbols of Politics and Propaganda." In *Heraldry, Pageantry, and Social Display in Medieval England*, edited by Peter Cross and Maurice Keen, 83–104. Woodbridge, UK: Boydell, 2002.

Alexander, Jonathan J. G. "Art History, Literary History, and the Study of Medieval Illuminated Manuscripts." *Studies in Iconography* 18 (1997): 51–66.

———. "Facsimiles, Copies, and Variations: The Relationship to the Model in Medieval and Renaissance European Manuscripts." In *Retaining the Original: Multiple Originals, Copies, and Reproductions*, edited by Kathleen Preciado, 61–72. Washington, DC: National Gallery of Art, 1989.

Alexander, Jonathan J. G. "Foreign Illuminators and Illuminated Manuscripts." In *The Cambridge History of the Book in Britain*, Vol. 3, edited by Lotte Hellinga and J. B. Trapp, 47–64. Cambridge: University of Cambridge Press, 1999.

———. *Medieval Illuminators and Their Methods of Work.* New Haven, CT: Yale University Press, 1992.

———. *The Painted Book in Renaissance Italy, 1450–1600.* New Haven, CT: Yale University Press, 2016.

———. "Painting and Manuscript Illumination for Royal Patrons in the Later Middle Ages." In *English Court Culture in the Later Middle Ages*, edited by V. J. Scattergood and J. W. Sherborne, 141–62. London: Duckworth, 1983.

———. "William Abell 'Lymnor' and Fifteenth Century English Illumination." In *Kunsthistorische Forschungen: Otto Pächt zu seinem 70 Geburstag*, edited by Arthur Rosenauer and Gerold Weber, 166–72. Salzburg: Residenz, 1972.

Allan, Alison. "Royal Propaganda and the Proclamations of Edward IV." *Historical Research* 59 (1986): 146–54.

———. "Yorkist Propaganda: Pedigree, Prophecy and the 'British History' in the Reign of Edward IV." In *Patronage, Pedigree and Power in Later Medieval England*, edited by Charles Ross, 171–92. Sutton, UK: Rowman & Littlefield, 1979.

Allen, Elizabeth. *False Fables and Exemplary Truth in Later Middle English Literature.* New York: Palgrave Macmillan, 2005.

Amtower, Laurel. *Engaging Words: The Culture of Reading in the Later Middle Ages.* New York: Palgrave, 2000.

Andrews, Christine Geisler. "The Boucicaut Masters." *Gesta* 41 (2002): 29–38.

Anglo, Sydney. "The British History in Early Tudor Propaganda." *Bulletin of the John Rylands Library* 44 (1961): 17–48.

Appleford, Amy. "The Dance of Death in London: John Carpenter, John Lydgate, and the *Daunce of Poulys*." *Journal of Medieval and Early Modern Studies* 38 (2008): 285–314.

Astell, Ann W. "Chaucer's 'Literature Group' and the Medieval Causes of Books." *English Literary History* 59 (1992): 269–87.

———. *Political Allegory in Late Medieval England.* Ithaca, NY: Cornell University Press, 1999.

Auerbach, Erich. *Scenes from the Drama of European Literature.* Translated by Ralph Manheim. New York: Meridian, 1959.

Backhouse, Janet. "Founders of the Royal Library: Edward IV and Henry VII as Collectors of Illuminated Manuscripts." In *England in the Fifteenth Century: Proceedings of the 1986 Harlaxton Symposium*, edited by Daniel Williams, 23–42. Woodbridge, UK: Boydell, 1987.

———. "Illuminated Manuscripts Associated with Henry VII and Members of His Immediate Family." In *The Reign of Henry VII: Proceedings of the 1993 Harlaxton Symposium*, edited by Benjamin Thompson, 175–87. Stamford, UK: Paul Watkins, 1995.

———. *The Sherborne Missal.* Toronto: University of Toronto Press, 1999.

Badham, Sally, and Sophie Oosterwijk. "'Cest endenture fait parentre': English Tomb Contracts of the Long Fourteenth Century." In *Monumental Industry: The Production of Tomb Monuments in England and Wales in the Long Fourteenth Century*, edited by Sally Badham and Sophie Oosterwijk, 187–237. Donington, UK: Shaun Tyas, 2010.

———. "Introduction." In *Monumental Industry: The Production of Tomb Monuments in England and Wales in the Long Fourteenth Century*, edited by Sally Badham and Sophie Oosterwijk, 1–11. Donington, UK: Shaun Tyas, 2010.

Baker, Denise N. "The Priesthood of Genius: A Study of the Medieval Tradition." *Speculum* 51 (1976): 277–91.

Baldick, Chris, ed. *Oxford Dictionary of Literary Terms.* Oxford: Oxford University Press, 2008.

Bale, Anthony. "From Translator to Laureate: Imagining the Medieval Author." *Literature Compass* 5 (2008): 918–34.

———. "St. Edmund in Fifteenth-Century London: The Lydgatian Miracles of Saint Edmund." In *St. Edmund, King and Martyr: Changing Images of a Medieval Saint*, edited by Anthony Bale, 145–61. Woodbridge, UK: York Medieval Press, 2009.

———. "Twenty-First-Century Lydgate." *Modern Philology* 105 (2008): 698–704.

Barasch, Moshe. *Giotto and the Language of Gesture*. New York: Cambridge University Press, 1987.

Barr, Helen. *Transporting Chaucer*. Manchester: Manchester University Press, 2014.

Barrington, Candace. "Personas and Performance in Gower's *Confessio Amantis*." *Chaucer Review* 48 (2014): 414–33.

Barron, Caroline M. *The Medieval Guildhall of London*. London: Corporation of London, 1974.

Barthes, Roland. "The Death of the Author." In *The Rustle of Language*, translated by Richard Howard, 49–55. Berkeley: University of California Press, 1986.

Baswell, Christopher. *Virgil in Medieval England: Figuring the Aeneid from the Twelfth Century to Chaucer*. Cambridge: Cambridge University Press, 1995.

Batt, Catherine. "Translation and Society." In *A Companion to Medieval English Literature and Culture, c. 1350–c. 1500*, edited by Peter Brown, 123–39. Oxford: Blackwell, 2007.

Battles, Dominique. *The Medieval Tradition of Thebes: History and Narrative in the* OF Roman de Thebes*, Boccaccio, Chaucer, and Lydgate*. New York: Routledge, 2004.

Baxandall, Michael. *Painting and Experience in Fifteenth-Century Italy*. Oxford: Oxford University Press, 1972.

Bedos-Rezak, Brigitte. *When Ego Was Imago: Signs of Identity in the Middle Ages*. Leiden, Netherlands: Brill, 2011.

Belting, Hans. *Likeness and Presence: A History of the Image before the Era of Art*. Translated by Edmund Jephcott. Chicago: University of Chicago Press, 1994.

Benson, C. David. *The History of Troy in Middle English Literature: Guido Delle Colonne's* Historia destructionis Troiae *in Medieval England*. Woodbridge, UK: D. S. Brewer, 1980.

Berenbeim, Jessica. *Art of Documentation: Documents and Visual Culture in Medieval England*. Toronto: Pontifical Institute of Mediaeval Studies, 2015.

———. "The Art of Documentation: The Sherborne Missal and the Role of Documents in English Medieval Art." PhD dissertation, Harvard University, 2012.

Berger, Harry, Jr.. "Fictions of the Pose: Facing the Gaze of Early Modern Portraiture." *Representations* 46 (1994): 87–120.

Binski, Paul. *Gothic Wonder: Art, Artifice and the Decorated Style 1290–1350*. New Haven, CT: Yale University Press, 2014.

———. *The Painted Chamber at Westminster*. London: Thames and Hudson, 1986.

———. "The Painted Chamber at Westminster, the Fall of Tyrants and the English Literary Model of Governance." *Journal of the Warburg and Courtauld Institutes* 74 (2011): 121–54.

Binski, Paul, and Stella Panayotova, eds. *The Cambridge Illuminations: Ten Centuries of Medieval Book Production in the West*. London: Harvey Miller, 2005.

Blake, N. F. "Caxton's Reprints." *Humanities Association Review* 26 (1975): 169–79.

———. "Caxton's Second Edition of the *Canterbury Tales*." In *The English Medieval Book: Studies in Memory of Jeremy Griffiths*, edited by A. S. G. Edwards, Vincent Gillespie, and Ralph Hanna, 135–53. London: British Library, 2000.

Blatt, Heather. "Mapping the Readable Household." In *Spaces for Reading in Late Medieval England*, edited by Mary C. Flannery and Carrie Griffin, 165–81. New York: Palgrave, 2016.

Blayney, Peter W. M. *The Stationers' Company and the Printers of London, 1501–1557*. 2 vols. Cambridge: Cambridge University Press, 2013.

Boffey, Julia. "Bodleian Library, MS Arch. Selden. B. 24 and Definitions of the 'Household Book.'" In *The English Medieval Book: Studies in Memory of Jeremy Griffiths*, edited by A. S. G. Edwards, Vincent Gillespie, and Ralph Hanna, 125–34. London: British Library, 2000.

Boffey, Julia. "From Manuscript to Print: Continuity and Change." In *A Companion to the Early Printed Book in Britain, 1476–1558*, edited by Vincent Gillespie and Susan Powell, 13–26. Cambridge: D. S. Brewer, 2014.

Boffey, Julia, and A. S. G. Edwards. "Middle English Literary Writings, 1150–1400." In *The Cambridge History of the Book in Britain*, Vol. 2, edited by Nigel Morgan and Rodney M. Thompson, 380–90. Cambridge: Cambridge University Press, 2008.

———, eds. *A New Index of Middle English Verse*. London: British Library, 2005.

Bordalejo, Barbara. "Caxton's Editing of the 'Canterbury Tales.'" *Papers of the Bibliographical Society of America* 108 (2014): 41–60.

Bovey, Alixe. "Introduction: Influence and Illumination." In *Under the Influence: The Concept of Influence and the Study of Illuminated Manuscripts*, edited by Alixe Bovey and John Lowden, vii–xiii. Turnhout, Belgium: Brepols, 2007.

Bowden, Betsy. "Visual Portraits of the Canterbury Pilgrims 1484(?)–1809." In *The Ellesmere Chaucer: Essays in Interpretation*, edited by Martin Stevens and Daniel Woodward, 171–204. San Marino, CA: Huntington Library, 1995.

Boyd, David Lorenzo. "Social Texts: Bodley 686 and the Politics of the Cook's Tale." *Huntington Library Quarterly* 58 (1995): 81–97.

Boyer Owens, Margareth. "The Image of King David in Prayer in Fifteenth-Century Books of Hours." *Imago Musicae* 6 (1989): 23–38.

Braeger, Peter C. "The Illustrations in New College MS 266 for Gower's Conversion Tales." In *John Gower: Recent Readings: Papers Presented at the Meetings of the John Gower Society at the International Congress on Medieval Studies*, edited by Robert F. Yeager, 275–310. Kalamazoo, MI: Medieval Institute Publications, 1989.

Bragg, Lois. "Chaucer's Monogram and the 'Hoccleve Portrait' Tradition." *Word and Image* 12 (1996): 127–42.

Brantley, Jessica. *Reading in the Wilderness: Private Devotion and Public Performance in Late Medieval England*. Chicago: University of Chicago Press, 2007.

———. "Venus and Christ in Chaucer's *Complaint of Mars:* The Fairfax 16 Frontispiece." *Studies in the Age of Chaucer* 30 (2008): 171–204.

Brantley, Jessica, and Thomas Fulton. "*Mankind* in a Year Without Kings." *Journal of Medieval and Early Modern Studies* 36 (2006): 321–54.

Brenk, Beat. "Spolia from Constantine to Charlemagne: Aesthetics Versus Ideology." *Dumbarton Oaks Papers* 41 (1987): 103–9.

Briggs, C. F. "Manuscripts of Giles of Rome's *De regimine principum* in England, 1300–1500." *Scriptorium* 47 (1993): 60–73.

Brilliant, Richard. *Portraiture*. New York: Reaktion, 1991.

Brosnahan, Leger. "The Pendant in the Chaucer Portraits." *Chaucer Review* 26 (1992): 424–31.

Bryan, Elizabeth J. *Collaborative Meaning in Medieval Scribal Culture: The Otho Laȝamon*. Ann Arbor: University of Michigan Press, 1999.

Bryson, Norman. *Vision and Painting: The Logic of the Gaze*. New Haven, CT: Yale University Press, 1983.

Buettner, Brigitte. *Boccaccio's "Des Cleres et Nobles Femmes": Systems of Signification in an Illuminated Manuscript*. Seattle: College Art Association in association with the University of Washington Press, 1996.

———. "Profane Illuminations, Secular Illusions: Manuscripts in Late Medieval Courtly Society." *Art Bulletin* 74 (1992): 75–90.

Bühler, Curt F. *The Fifteenth-Century Book: The Scribes, the Printers, the Decorators*. Philadelphia: University of Pennsylvania Press, 1960.

Bunt, G. H. V. *Alexander the Great in the Literature of Medieval Britain*. Groningen, Netherlands: Egbert Forsten, 1994.

van Buren, Anne H. "Collaboration in Manuscripts: France and the Low Countries." In *Making and Marketing: Studies of the Painting Process in Fifteenth- and Sixteenth-Century Netherlandish Workshops*, edited by Molly Faries, 83–98. Turnhout, Belgium: Brepols, 2006.

Burgess, Clive. "'Longing to Be Prayed For': Death and Commemoration in an English Parish in the Later Middle Ages." In *The Place of the Dead: Death and Commemoration in Late Medieval and Early Modern Europe*, edited by Bruce Gordon and Peter Marshall, 44–65. Cambridge: Cambridge University Press, 2000.

Burrow, J. A. "Autobiographical Poetry in the Middle Ages: The Case of Thomas Hoccleve." *Proceedings of the British Academy* 68 (1982): 389–412.

———. *Gestures and Looks in Medieval Narrative*. Cambridge: Cambridge University Press, 2002.

———. "Hoccleve and the 'Court.'" In *Nation, Court, Culture: New Essays on Fifteenth-Century English Poetry*, edited by Helen Cooney, 70–80. Dublin: Four Courts, 2001.

———. *Medieval Writers and Their Work*. Middle English Literature 1100–1500. 2nd ed. Oxford: Oxford University Press, 2008.

———. "The Poet as Petitioner." *Studies in the Age of Chaucer* 3 (1981): 61–75.

———. "The Portrayal of Amans in the *Confessio Amantis*." In *Gower's* Confessio Amantis: *Responses and Reassessments*, edited by Alastair J. Minnis, 5–24. Cambridge: D. S. Brewer, 1983.

———. *Thomas Hoccleve*. Aldershot, UK: Ashgate, 1994.

Butterfield, Ardis. "Articulating the Author: Gower and the French Vernacular Codex." *Yearbook of English Studies* 33 (2003): 80–96.

———. "*Confessio Amantis* and the French Tradition." In *A Companion to Gower*, edited by Siân Echard, 165–80. Cambridge: D. S. Brewer, 2004.

———. *The Familiar Enemy: Chaucer, Language, and Nation in the Hundred Years War*. Oxford: Oxford University Press, 2009.

Cahn, Walter. "Représentation de la parole." *Conaissance des Arts* 369 (1982): 82–89.

Camille, Michael. "Gothic Signs and the Surplus: The Kiss on the Cathedral." *Yale French Studies* 80 (1991): 151–70.

———. "The King's New Bodies: An Illustrated Mirror for Princes in the Morgan Library." In *Kunstlerischer Austauch; Artistic Exchange: Akten des XXVIII. Internationalen Kongresses für Kunstgeschichte, Berlin, 15–20 Juli 1992*, Vol. 2, edited by Thomas W. Gaehtgens, 393–405. Berlin: Akademie Verlag, 1993.

———. *Mirror in Parchment: The Luttrell Psalter and the Making of Medieval England*. Chicago: University of Chicago Press, 1998.

———. "Review of *Medieval Texts and Images: Studies of Manuscripts from the Middle Ages*, edited by Margaret Manion and Bernard J. Muir." *Speculum* 69 (1994): 833–35.

———. "Seeing and Reading: Some Visual Implications of Medieval Literacy and Illiteracy." *Art History* 8 (1985): 26–49.

———. "Visual Signs of the Sacred Page: Books in the Bible Moralisée." *Word and Image* 5 (1989): 111–30.

Campbell, Thomas P. *Henry VIII and the Art of Majesty: Tapestries at the Tudor Court*. New Haven, CT: Yale University Press, 2007.

Carlson, David R. *John Gower, Poetry and Propaganda in Fourteenth-Century England*. Cambridge: D. S. Brewer, 2012.

———. "Thomas Hoccleve and the Chaucer Portrait." *Huntington Library Quarterly* 54 (1991): 283–300.

———. "Woodcut Illustrations of the *Canterbury Tales*, 1483–1602." *Library: The Transactions of the Bibliographical Society* 19 (1997): 25–67.

Carruthers, Mary. "Meditations on the 'Historical Present' and 'Collective Memory' in Chaucer and *Sir Gawain and the Green Knight*." In *Time in the Medieval World*, edited by Chris Humphrey and W. A. Ormrod, 137–55. Woodbridge, UK: York Medieval Press, 2001.

Carruthers, Mary. "The Sociable Text of the 'Troilus Frontispiece': A Different Mode of Textuality." *ELH* 81 (2014): 423–41.

Cary, George. *The Medieval Alexander*. Cambridge, UK: Cambridge University Press, 1956.

Caskey, Jill. "Whodunnit? Patronage, the Canon, and the Problematics of Agency in Romanesque and Gothic Art." In *A Companion to Medieval Art: Romanesque and Gothic in Northern Europe*, edited by Conrad Rudolph, 193–212. Oxford: Blackwell, 2006.

Cerquiglini, Bernard. *In Praise of the Variant*. Translated by Betsy Wing. Baltimore, MD: Johns Hopkins University Press, 1999.

Certeau, Michel de. *The Practice of Everyday Life*. Translated by Steven Rendall. Berkeley: University of California Press, 1984.

———. *The Writing of History*. Translated by Tom Conley. New York: Columbia University Press, 1988.

Christianson, C. Paul. "A Community of Book Artisans in Chaucer's London." *Viator* 20 (1989): 207–18.

———. *A Directory of London Stationers and Book Artisans, 1300–1500*. New York: Bibliographical Society, 1990.

———. "Evidence for the Study of London's Late Medieval Manuscript-Book Trade." In *Book Production and Publishing in Britain 1375–1475*. Edited by Jeremy Griffiths and Derek Pearsall, 87–108. Cambridge: Cambridge University Press, 1989.

———. *Memorials of the Book Trade in Medieval London: Archives of Old London Bridge*. Cambridge: D. S. Brewer, 1987.

Clemens, Raymond, Diane Ducharne, and Emily Ulrich, eds. *A Gathering of Medieval English Manuscripts: The Takamiya Collection at the Beinecke Library*. New Haven, CT: Yale University, 2017.

Coleman, Joyce. "The First Presentation Miniature in an English-Language Manuscript." In *The Social Life of Illumination: Manuscripts, Images, and Communities in the Late Middle Ages*, edited by Joyce Coleman, Kathryn A. Smith, and Mark Cruse, 403–37. Turnhout, Belgium: Brepols, 2011.

Colvin, H. M., ed. *The History of the King's Works*. 6 vols. London: H. M. Stationery Office, 1963–82.

Combes, Helen. "William Abell: Parishioner, Churchwarden, Limnour, Stationer in the Parish of St. Nicholas Shambles in the City of London." *Ricardian* 12 (2000): 120–32.

Connolly, Margaret, and Raluca L. Radulescu, eds. *Insular Books: Vernacular Manuscript Miscellanies in Late Medieval Britain*. Oxford: Oxford University Press, 2015.

Cook, Megan. "Joseph Holland and the Idea of the Chaucerian Book." *Manuscript Studies* 1 (2016): 165–88.

Cooper, Donal. "Projecting Presence: The Monumental Cross in the Italian Church Interior." In *Presence: The Inherence of the Prototype Within Images and Other Objects*, edited by Robert Maniura and Rupert Shepherd, 47–69. Burlington, VT: Ashgate, 2006.

Cooper, Helen. "Introduction." In *The Long Fifteenth Century: Essays for Douglas Gray*, edited by Helen Cooper and Sally Mapstone, 1–14. Oxford: Clarendon, 1997.

Cooper, Lisa H. and Andrea Denny-Brown, eds. *Lydgate Matters: Poetry and Material Culture in the Fifteenth Century*. New York: Palgrave, 2008.

Coote, Lesley A. *Prophecy and Public Affairs in Later Medieval England*. Woodbridge, UK: York Medieval Press, 2000.

Copeland, Rita. *Rhetoric, Hermeneutics and Translation in the Middle Ages: Academic Traditions and Vernacular Texts*. Cambridge, UK: Cambridge University Press, 1991.

Costley, Clare L. "David, Bathsheba, and the Penitential Psalms." *Renaissance Quarterly* 57 (2004): 1235–77.

Crane, Susan. *The Performance of Self: Ritual, Clothing, and Identity During the Hundred Years War*. Philadelphia: University of Pennsylvania Press, 2002.

Critten, Rory G. "'Her Heed They Caste Awry': The Transmission and Reception of Thomas Hoccleve's Personal Poetry." *Review of English Studies* 64 (2013): 386–409.

Crossley, Paul. "Between Spectacle and History: Art History and the Medieval Exhibitions." In *Late Gothic England: Art and Display*, edited by Richard Marks, 138–53. Donington, UK: Shaun Tyas, 2007.

Da Rold, Orietta. "Textual Copying and Transmission." In *The Oxford Handbook of Medieval Literature in English*, edited by Elaine Treharne and Greg Walker, 33–56. Oxford: Oxford University Press, 2010.

Dale, Thomas E. A. "The Individual, the Resurrected Body, and Romanesque Portraiture: The Tomb of Rudolf von Schwaben in Merseburg." *Speculum* 77 (2002): 707–43.

Damian-Grint, Peter. "*Estoire* as Word and Genre: Meaning and Literary Usage in the Twelfth Century." *Medium Aevum* 66 (1997): 189–206.

Danbury, Elizabeth. "The Decoration and Illumination of Royal Charters in England, 1250–1509: An Introduction." In *England and Her Neighbours, 1066–1453: Essays in Honour of Pierre Chaplais*, edited by Michael Jones and Malcolm Vale, 157–79. London: Hambledon, 1989.

Danbury, Elizabeth A., and Kathleen L Scott. "The Plea Rolls of the Court of Common Pleas: An Unused Source for the Art and History of Later Medieval England." *Antiquaries Journal* 95 (2015): 157–210.

De Man, Paul. *The Rhetoric of Romanticism*. New York: Columbia University Press, 1984.

Dean, James. "Gower, Chaucer, and Rhyme Royal." *Studies in Philology* 88 (1991): 251–75.

———. "Time Past and Time Present in Chaucer's *Clerk's Tale* and Gower's *Confessio Amantis*." *ELH* 44 (1977): 401–18.

Delaissé, L. M. J. "Towards a History of the Medieval Book." *Codicologica* 1 (1976): 75–83.

Deleuze, Gilles, and Félix Guattari. *A Thousand Plateaus: Capitalism and Schizophrenia*. Translated by Brian Massumi. Minneapolis: University of Minnesota Press, 1987.

Desmond, Marilynn, and Pamela Sheingorn. *Myth, Montage, and Visuality in Late Medieval Manuscript Culture: Christine de Pizan's* Epistre Othea. Ann Arbor: University of Michigan Press, 2003.

Di Bacco, Giuliano, Yolanda Plumley, and Stefano Jossa, eds. *Citation, Intertextuality and Memory in the Middle Ages and Renaissance,* Vol. 1, *Text, Music and Image from Machaut to Ariosto*. Exeter: University of Exeter Press, 2011.

Di Bacco, Giuliano, and Yolanda Plumley, eds. *Citation, Intertextuality and Memory in the Middle Ages and Renaissance,* Vol. 2, *Cross-Disciplinary Perspectives on Medieval Culture*. Liverpool: University of Liverpool Press, 2013.

Dickens, A. G. "The Tudor-Percy Emblem in Royal 18 D II." *Archaeological Journal* 112 (1955): 95–99.

Didi-Huberman, Georges. "Before the Image, Before Time: The Sovereignty of Anachronism." Translated by Peter Mason. In *Compelling Visuality: The Work of Art in and out of History*, edited by Claire Farago and Robert Zwijnenberg, 31–44. Minneapolis: University of Minnesota Press, 2003.

———. *Confronting Images: Questioning the Ends of a Certain History of Art*. Translated by John Goodman. University Park: Pennsylvania State University Press, 2005.

———. "History and the Image: Has the 'Epistemological Transformation' Taken Place?" In *The Art Historian: National Traditions and Institutional Practices*, edited by Michael Zimmermann, 128–43. Williamstown, MA: Clark Art Institute, 2003.

———. "The Portrait, the Individual and the Singular. Remarks on the Legacy of Aby Warburg." In *The Image of the Individual: Portraits in the Renaissance*, edited by Nicholas Mann and Luke Syson, translated by C. Plazzotta, 165–88. London: British Museum Press, 1998.

Dinshaw, Carolyn. *How Soon Is Now? Medieval Texts, Amateur Readers, and the Queerness of Time*. Durham, NC: Duke University Press, 2012.

Donaldson, E. Talbot. "Chaucer the Pilgrim." *PMLA* 69 (1954): 928–36.

Doyle, A. I. "Penwork Flourishing of Initials in England from c. 1380." In *Tributes to Kathleen L. Scott: English Medieval Manuscripts: Readers, Makers and Illuminators,* edited by Marlene Villalobos Hennessy, 65–72. London: Harvey Miller, 2009.

———. "The Work of a Late Fifteenth-Century English Scribe, William Ebesham." *Bulletin of the John Rylands Library* 39 (1957): 289–325.

Doyle, A. I. and M. B. Parkes. "The Production of Copies of the *Canterbury Tales* and the *Confessio Amantis* in the Early Fifteenth Century." In *Medieval Scribes, Manuscripts, and Libraries: Essays Presented to N. R. Ker*, edited by M. B. Parkes and A. G. Watson, 163–203. London: Scolar, 1978.

Doyle, Kathleen. "The Old Royal Library: 'A Great Many Noble Manuscripts Yet Remaining?'" In *Royal Manuscripts: The Genius of Illumination*, edited by Kathleen Doyle, John Lowden, and Scot McKendrick, 67–93. London: British Library, 2011.

Doyle, Kathleen, John Lowden, and Scot McKendrick, eds. *Royal Manuscripts: The Genius of Illumination*. London: British Library, 2011.

Drimmer, Sonja. "Beyond Private Matter: A Prayer Roll for Queen Margaret of Anjou." *Gesta* 53 (2014): 95–120.

———. "The Disorder of Operations: Illuminators, Scribes, and John Gower's *Confessio Amantis*." *LIAS* 44 (2017): 5–28.

———. "Failure Before Print (the Case of Stephen Scrope)" *Viator* 46 (2015): 343–72.

———. "The Manuscript as an Ambigraphic Medium: Hoccleve's Scribes, Illuminators, and Their Problems." *Exemplaria* 29 (2017): 175–94.

———. "The Painters of Late Medieval London and Westminster." *Burlington Magazine* 159 (2017): 445–59.

———. "Picturing the King or Picturing the Saint: Two Miniature Programmes for Lydgate's *Lives of Saints Edmund and Fremund*." In *Manuscripts and Printed Books in Europe, 1350–1550: Packaging, Presentation and Consumption*, edited by Emma Cayley and Sue Powell, 48–67. Liverpool: Liverpool University Press, 2013.

———. "Unnoticed and Unusual: An Illustration in a Manuscript of John Lydgate's *Fall of Princes*." *Journal of the Early Book Society* 20 (2017): 209–18.

———. "The Visual Language of Vernacular Manuscript Illumination: John Gower's *Confessio Amantis* (Pierpont Morgan MS M.126)." PhD dissertation, Columbia University, 2011.

———. "Visualizing Intertextuality: Conflating Forms of Creativity in Late Medieval 'Author Portraits.'" In *Citation, Intertextuality and Memory in the Middle Ages and Renaissance vol. 2: Cross-Disciplinary Perspectives on Medieval Culture*, edited by Yolanda Plumley and Giuliano Di Bacco, 82–101. Liverpool: University of Liverpool Press, 2013.

Driver, Martha W. *The Image in Print: Book Illustration in Late Medieval England and Its Sources.* London: British Library, 2004.

———. "Mapping Chaucer: John Speed and the Later Portraits." *Chaucer Review* 36 (2002): 228–49.

———. "'Me Fault Faire': French Makers of Manuscripts for English Patrons." In *Language and Culture in Medieval Britain: The French of England c. 1100–c. 1500*, edited by Jocelyn Wogan-Browne, Carolyn Collette, Maryanne Kowaleski, Linne Mooney, Ad Putter, and David Trotter, 420–43. Woodbridge, UK: York Medieval Press, 2009.

———. "Medievalizing the Classical Past in Pierpont Morgan MS M 876." In *Middle English Poetry: Texts and Traditions—Essays in Honour of Derek Pearsall*, edited by Alastair J. Minnis, 211–39. Woodbridge, UK: York Medieval Press, 2001.

———. "Printing the *Confessio Amantis*: Caxton's Edition in Context." In *Re-Visioning Gower*, edited by Robert F. Yeager, 269–304. Asheville, NC: Pegasus, 1998.

———. "Women Readers and Pierpont Morgan MS M.126." In *John Gower: Manuscripts, Readers and Contexts*, edited by Malte Urban and Georgiana Donavin, 71–107. Turnhout, Belgium: Brepols, 2009.

Driver, Martha, and Michael Orr. "Decorating the Page." In *The Production of Books in England, 1350–1500*, edited by Alexandra Gillespie and Daniel Wakelin, 104–28. Cambridge: Cambridge University Press, 2011.

Duffy, Eamon. *Stripping of the Altars: Traditional Religion in England, c. 1400–c. 1580*. 2nd ed. New Haven, CT: Yale University Press, 2005.

Dunn, Thomas. "The Manuscript Source of Caxton's 2nd Edition of the *Canterbury Tales*." PhD dissertation, University of Chicago, 1939.

Eames, Penelope. "Documentary Evidence Concerning the Character and Use of Domestic Furnishings in England in the Fourteenth and Fifteenth Centuries." *Furniture History* 7 (1971): 41–60.

Earp, Lawrence. "Machaut's Role in the Production of His Works." *Journal of the American Musicological Society* 42 (1989): 461–503.

Eberle, Patricia. "Miniatures as Evidence of Reading in a Manuscript of the *Confessio Amantis*." In *John Gower: Recent Readings*, edited by Robert F. Yeager, 311–64. Kalamazoo, MI: Medieval Institute Publications, 1989.

Echard, Siân. "Designs for Reading: Some Manuscripts of Gower's 'Confessio Amantis.'" *Trivium* 31 (1999): 59–72.

———. "Dialogues and Monologues: Manuscript Representations of the Conversation of the *Confessio Amantis*." In *Middle English Poetry: Texts and Traditions—Essays in Honour of Derek Pearsall*, edited by Alastair J. Minnis, 57–75. Woodbridge, UK: York Medieval Press, 2001.

———. "Glossing Gower: in English, in Latin, and in Absentia: The Case of Bodleian Ashmole 35." In *Re-visioning Gower*, edited by R. F. Yeager, 237–56. Asheville, NC: Pegasus Press, 1998.

———. "Last Words: Latin at the End of the *Confessio Amantis*." In *Interstices: Studies in Middle English and Anglo-Latin Texts in Honour of A. G. Rigg*, edited by Richard Firth Green and Linne R. Mooney, 99–121. Toronto: University of Toronto Press, 2004.

———. "Pre-texts: Tables of Contents and the Reading of John Gower's *Confessio Amantis*." *Medium Aevum* 66 (1997):270–87.

———. "With Carmen's Help: Latin Authorities in the 'Confessio Amantis.'" *Studies in Philology* 94 (1998): 1–40.

Economou, George D. "The Character Genius in Alain de Lille, Jean de Meun, and John Gower." *Chaucer Review* 4 (1970): 203–10.

Edwards, A. S. G. "The Author as Scribe: Cavendish's Metrical Visions and MS. Egerton 2402." *Library: Transactions of the Bibliographical Society* (5th series) 29 (1974): 446–49.

———. "Beinecke MS 661 and Early Fifteenth-Century Manuscript Production." *Yale University Library Gazette* 66 (1991): 181–96.

———. "Books Owned by Medieval Members of the Percy Family." In *Tributes to Kathleen L. Scott—English Medieval Manuscripts: Readers, Makers and Illuminators*, edited by Marlene Villalobos Hennessy, 73–82. London: Harvey Miller, 2009.

———. "Hoccleve's *Regiment of Princes*: A Further Manuscript." *Edinburgh Bibliographical Society Transactions* 5 (1978): 32.

———. "Lydgate Manuscripts: Some Directions for Future Research." In *Manuscripts and Readers in Fifteenth-Century England: The Literary Implications of Manuscript Study, Essays from the 1981 Conference at the University of York*, edited by Derek Pearsall, 15–26. Cambridge: D. S. Brewer, 1983.

———. "The McGill Fragment of Lydgate's *Fall of Princes*." *Scriptorium* 28 (1974): 75–77.

———. "Middle English Inscriptional Verse Texts." In *Texts and Their Contexts: Papers from the Early Book Society*, edited by Julia Boffey and John Scattergood, 26–43. Dublin: Four Courts, 1997.

———. Review of *Scribes and the City: London Guildhall Clerks and the Dissemination of Middle English Literature 1375–1425* by Linne R. Mooney and Estelle Stubbs. *Library: Transactions of the Bibliographical Society* 15 (2014): 79–81.

Edwards, A. S. G. and Derek Pearsall. "The Manuscripts of the Major English Poetic Texts." In *Book Production and Publishing in Britain 1375–1475*, edited by Jeremy Griffiths and Derek Pearsall, 257–78. Cambridge: Cambridge University Press, 1989.

Eliot, T. S. *The Three Voices of Poetry*. London: Cambridge University Press, 1953.

Ellis, Stephen G. "Percy, Henry, Fourth Earl of Northumberland (c. 1449–1489)." In *Oxford Dictionary of National Biography*. Oxford: Oxford University Press, 2004.

Emmerson, Richard K. "*Figura* and the Medieval Typological Imagination." In *Typology and English Medieval Literature*, edited by Hugh T. Keenan, 7–42. New York: AMS, 1990.

———. "Middle English Literature and Illustrated Manuscripts: New Approaches to the Disciplinary and the Interdisciplinary." *Journal of English and Germanic Philology* 105 (2006): 118–36.

———. "Reading Gower in a Manuscript Culture: Latin and English in Illustrated Manuscripts of the *Confessio Amantis*." *Studies in the Age of Chaucer* 21 (1999): 143–86.

———. Review of *Telling Images: Chaucer and the Imagery of Narrative* by V. A. Kolve. *Studies in the Age of Chaucer* 32 (2010): 441–45.

———. "Text and Image in the Ellesmere Portraits of the Tale-Tellers." In *The Ellesmere Chaucer: Essays in Interpretation*, edited by Martin Stevens and Daniel Woodward, 143–70. San Marino, CA: Huntington Library, 1995.

———. "Translating Images: Image and Poetic Reception in French, English, and Latin Versions of Guillaume de Deguileville's *Trois Pèlerinages*." In *Poetry, Place and Gender: Studies in Medieval Culture in Honor of Helen Damico*, edited by Catherine E. Karkov, 275–301. Kalamazoo, MI: Medieval Institute Publications, 2009.

———. "Visual Translation in Fifteenth-Century English Manuscripts." In *Medieval Poetics and Social Practice: Responding to the Work of Penn R. Szittya*, edited by Seeta Chaganti, 11–32. New York: Fordham University Press, 2012.

———. "Visualizing the Vernacular: Middle English in Early Fourteenth-Century Bilingual and Trilingual Manuscript Illustrations." In *Studies in Manuscript Illumination: A Tribute to Lucy Freeman Sandler*, edited by Carol Krinsky and Kathryn A. Smith, 187–204. London: Harvey Miller, 2008.

Erler, Mary. "Hoccleve's Portrait? In British Library Manuscript Arundel 38." *Ricardian* 23 (2003): 221–28.

Ettlinger, Ellen. "Notes on a Woodcut Depicting King Henry VI Being Invoked as a Saint." *Folklore* 84 (1973): 115–19.

Evans, Ruth. "An Afterword on the Prologue." In *The Idea of the Vernacular: An Anthology of Middle English Literary Theory 1280–1520*, edited by Jocelyn Wogan-Browne, Nicholas Watson, Andrew Taylor, and Ruth Evans, 371–78. University Park: Pennsylvania State University Press, 1999.

Farquhar, James Douglas. "Identity in an Anonymous Age: Bruges Manuscript Illuminators and Their Signs." *Viator* 11 (1980): 371–84.

Federico, Sylvia. *New Troy: Fantasies of Empire in the Late Middle Ages*. Minneapolis: University of Minnesota Press, 2003.

Fehrmann, Antje. "Politics and Posterity: English Royal Chantry Provision." *Journal of the British Archaeological Association* 164 (2011): 74–99.

Feldman, Marian H. *Communities of Style: Portable Luxury Arts, Identity, and Collective Memory*. Chicago: University of Chicago Press, 2014.

Ferster, Judith. *Fictions of Advice: The Literature and Politics of Counsel in Late Medieval England*. Philadelphia: University of Pennsylvania Press, 1996.

Fisher, John. *John Gower, Moral Philosopher and Friend of Chaucer*. New York: New York University Press, 1964.

———. "A Language Policy for Lancastrian England." *PMLA* 107 (1992): 1168–80.

———. "*Piers Plowman* and the Chancery Tradition." In *Medieval English Studies Presented to George Kane*, edited by E. D. Kennedy, R. Waldron, and J. S. Wittig, 267–78. Cambridge: D. S. Brewer, 1988.

Fisher, Matthew. *Scribal Authorship and the Writing of History in Medieval England*. Columbus: Ohio State University Press, 2012.

Fleming, John V. "Medieval Manuscripts in the Taylor Library." *Princeton University Library Chronicle* 38 (1977): 107–19.

Fletcher, Bradford Y. "The Textual Tradition of the *Assembly of Gods*." *Publications of the Bibliographical Society of America* 71 (1977): 191–94.

Fletcher, D. "The Lancastrian Collar of Esses: Its Origins and Transformations down the Centuries." In *The Age of Richard II*, edited by James L. Gillespie, 191–204. New York: St. Martin's, 1997.

Flett, Alison R. "The Significance of Text Scrolls." In *Medieval Texts and Images: Studies of Manuscripts from the Middle Ages*, edited by Bernard Muir and Margaret M. Manion, 43–56. Melbourne: Harwood Academic, 1991.

Floyd, Jennifer. "St. George and the 'Steyned Halle': Lydgate's Verse for the London Armourers." In *Lydgate Matters: Poetry and Material Culture in the Fifteenth Century*, edited by Lisa H. Cooper and Andrea Denny-Brown, 139–64. New York: Palgrave, 2008.

———. "Writing on the Wall: John Lydgate's Architectural Verse." PhD dissertation, Stanford University, 2008.

Flügel, Ewald. "Kleinere Mitteilungen aus Handschriften." *Anglia* 14 (1892): 463–501.

Foucault, Michel. *The History of Sexuality*. Translated by Robert Hurley. 3 vols. New York: Pantheon, 1978–86.

———. "What Is an Author?" In *Michel Foucault: Language, Counter-Memory, Practice: Selected Essays and Interviews*, edited by Donald F. Bouchard, translated by Donald F. Bouchard and Sherry Simon, 113–38. Ithaca, NY: Cornell University Press, 1977.

Fredell, Joel. "The Gower Manuscripts: Some Inconvenient Truths." *Viator* 41 (2010): 231–50.

———. "Reading the Dream Miniature in the *Confessio Amantis*." *Medievalia et Humanistica* 22 (1995): 61–93.

Freed, John B. "The Creation of the *Codex Falkensteinensis* (1166): Self-Representation and Reality." In *Representations of Power in Medieval Germany 800–1500*, edited by Björn Weiler and Simon MacLean, 189–210. Turnhout, Belgium: Brepols, 2006.

Freedberg, David. *The Power of Images: Studies in the History and Theory of Response*. Chicago: University of Chicago Press, 1989.

———. "Why Connoisseurship Matters." In *Munuscula Amicorum: Contributions on Rubens and His Colleagues in Honour of Hans Vlieghe*, Vol 1, edited by Katlijne van der Stighelen, 29–43. Turnhout, Belgium: Brepols, 2006.

Freud, Sigmund. *Beyond the Pleasure Principle*. Translated and edited by James Strachey. New York: Norton, 1961.

Friend, Albert Mathias. "The Portraits of Evangelists in Greek and Latin Manuscripts." *Art Studies* 5 (1927): 114–150; 7 (1929): 3–29.

Fugelso, Karl. "Dante as Auctor in Musée Condé MS 597." *Gesta* 49 (2010): 1–16.

Galloway, Andrew. "Fame's Penitent: Deconstructive Chaucer Among the Lancastrians." In *Chaucer and Fame: Reputation and Reception*, edited by Isabel Davis and Catherine Nall, 103–26. Cambridge, UK: D. S. Brewer, 2015.

Garbáty, Thomas J. "A Description of the Confession Miniatures for Gower's *Confessio Amantis* with Special Reference to the Illustrator's Role as Reader and Critic." *Mediaevalia* 19 (1996): 319–43.

Gardner, Arthur. *English Medieval Sculpture*. Cambridge: Cambridge University Press, 1951.

Gayk, Shannon Noelle. *Image, Text, and Religious Reform in Fifteenth-Century England*. Cambridge: Cambridge University Press, 2010.

Gaylord, Alan T. "Portrait of a Poet." In *The Ellesmere Chaucer: Essays in Interpretation*, edited by Martin Stevens and Daniel Woodward, 121–42. San Marino, CA: Huntington Library, 1995.

Geary, Patrick J. *Phantoms of Remembrance: Memory and Oblivion at the End of the First Millennium*. Princeton: Princeton University Press, 1994.

Gelfand, Laura D., and Walter S. Gibson. "Surrogate Selves: The Rolin Madonna and the Late-Medieval Devotional Portrait." *Simiolus* 29 (2002): 119–38.

Genette, Gérard. *Palimpsests: Literature in the Second Degree*. Translated by Channa Newman and Claude Doubinsky. Lincoln: University of Nebraska Press, 1997.

Gillespie, Alexandra. "Books." In *Oxford Twenty-First-Century Approaches to Literature: Middle English*, edited by Paul Strohm, 86–103. Oxford: Oxford University Press, 2007.

———. "Framing Lydgate's *Fall of Princes*: The Evidence of Book History." *Mediaevalia* 20 (2001): 153–78.

———. *Print Culture and the Medieval Author: Chaucer, Lydgate, and Their Books, 1473–1557*. Oxford: Oxford University Press, 2006.

———. "Reading Chaucer's Words to Adam." *Chaucer Review* 42 (2008): 269–83.

———. "'These Proverbes Yet Do Last': Lydgate, the Fifth Earl of Northumberland, and Tudor Miscellanies from Print to Manuscript." *Yearbook of English Studies* 33 (2003): 215–32.

Gillespie, Alexandra, and Daniel Wakelin, "Introduction." In *The Production of Books in England, 1350–1500*, edited by Alexandra Gillespie and Daniel Wakelin, 1–11. Cambridge: Cambridge University Press, 2011.

———, eds. *The Production of Books in England, 1350–1500*. Cambridge: Cambridge University Press, 2011.

Gillespie, Vincent. "Introduction." In *A Companion to the Early Printed Book in Britain, 1476–1558*, edited by Vincent Gillespie and Susan Powell, 1–9. Cambridge: D. S. Brewer, 2014.

Gougaud, Louis. *Devotional and Ascetic Practices in the Middle Ages*. London: Burns Oates & Washbourne, 1927.

Gould, Karen. "Terms for Book Production in a Fifteenth-Century Latin-English Nominale (Harvard Law School Library MS. 43)." *Papers of the Bibliographical Society of America* 79 (1985): 75–100.

Grady, Frank. "Gower's Boat, Richard's Barge, and the True Story of the *Confessio Amantis* : Text and Gloss." *Texas Studies in Literature and Language* 44 (2001): 1–15.

Gransden, Antonia. *Historical Writing in England II: c. 1307 to the Early Sixteenth Century*. Ithaca, NY: Cornell University Press, 1974.

Green, Richard Firth. "The Early History of the Scriveners' Company Common Paper and Its So-Called 'Oaths.'" In *Middle English Texts in Transition: A Festschrift Dedicated to Toshiyuki Takamiya on His 70th Birthday*, edited by Simon Horobin and Linne R. Mooney, 1–20. Woodbridge, UK: York Medieval Press, 2014.

———. *Poets and Princepleasers: Literature and the English Court in the Late Middle Ages*. Toronto: University of Toronto Press, 1980.

Greene, Richard Leighton. *Early English Carols*. Oxford: Clarendon, 1977.

Greetham, D. C. "Self-Referential Artifacts: Hoccleve's Persona as a Literary Device." *Modern Philology* 86 (1989): 242–51.

Griffiths, Jane. *Diverting Authorities: Experimental Glossing Practices in Manuscript and Print*. Oxford: Oxford University Press, 2014.

———. *John Skelton and Poetic Authority: Defining the Liberty to Speak*. Oxford: Clarendon, 2006.

Griffiths, Jeremy. "Book Production Terms in Nicholas Munshull's Nominale." In *Art into Life: Collected Papers from the Kresge Art Museum Medieval Symposia*, edited by Carol G. Fisher and Kathleen L. Scott, 49–71. East Lansing: Michigan State University Press, 1995.

———. "*Confessio Amantis*: The Poem and Its Pictures." In *Gower's* Confessio Amantis: *Responses and Reassessments*, edited by Alastair J. Minnis, 163–78. Cambridge: D. S. Brewer, 1983.

———. "Thomas Hyngham, Monk of Bury and the Macro Plays Manuscript." *English Manuscript Studies 1100–1700* 5 (1995): 214–19.

Griffiths, Jeremy, and Derek Pearsall, eds. *Book Production and Publishing in Britain 1375–1475.* Cambridge: Cambridge University Press, 1989.

Griffiths, Ralph A. "Herbert, William, First Earl of Pembroke (c. 1423–1469)." In *Oxford Dictionary of National Biography*. Oxford: Oxford University Press, 2004.

———. *The Reign of Henry VI: The Exercise of Royal Authority, 1422–1461.* Berkeley: University of California Press, 1981.

Grummitt, David. *A Short History of the Wars of the Roses.* London: I. B. Tauris, 2013.

Gumbert, J. Peter. "Codicological Units: Towards a Terminology for the Stratigraphy of the Non-Homogeneous Codex." *Segno e testo* 2 (2004): 17–42.

Hamburger, Jeffrey F. "The Hand of God and the Hand of the Scribe: Craft and Collaboration at Arnstein." In *Die Bibliothek des Mittelalters als dynamischer Prozess*, edited by Michael Embach, Claudine Moulin, and Andrea Rapp, 53–78. Wiesbaden, Germany: Reichert, 2012.

———. "The Medieval Work of Art: Wherein the 'Work'? Wherein the 'Art'?" In *The Mind's Eye: Art and Theological Argument in the Middle Ages*, edited by Jeffrey Hamburger and Anne-Marie Bouché, 374–412. Princeton: Princeton University Press, 2005.

———. *Nuns as Artists: The Visual Culture of a Medieval Convent.* Berkeley: University of California Press, 1997.

———. "Openings." In *Imagination, Books and Community in Medieval Europe: A Conference at the State Library of Victoria (Melbourne, Australia), 29–31 May, 2008*, edited by Constant Mews, 50–133. Melbourne, Australia: Macmillan Art, 2009.

———. "Rewriting History: The Visual and the Vernacular in Late Medieval History Bibles." In *Re-textualisierung in der mittelalterlichen Literatur: Sonderheft der Zeitschrift für deutsche Philologie*, edited by Ursula Peters and Joachim Bumke, 259–307. Berlin: Schmidt, 2005.

———. *The Visual and the Visionary: Art and Female Spirituality in Late Medieval Germany.* New York: Zone Books, 1998.

Hanna, Ralph. "Auchinleck 'Scribe 6' and Some Corollary Issues." In *The Auchinleck Manuscript: New Perspectives*, edited by Susanna Fein, 209–21. Woodbridge, UK: Boydell and Brewer, 2016.

———. *Introducing English Medieval Book History: Manuscripts, Their Producers and Their Readers.* Liverpool: Liverpool University Press, 2013.

———. Review of *Scribes and the City: London Guildhall Clerks and the Dissemination of Middle English Literature, 1375–1425* by Linne R. Mooney and Estelle Stubbs. *Times Literary Supplement* 5750 (2013): 29.

———. "The Scribe of Huntington HM 114." *Studies in Bibliography* 42 (1989): 120–33.

Hardman, Phillipa. "Presenting the Text: Pictorial Tradition in Fifteenth-Century Manuscripts of the *Canterbury Tales*." In *Chaucer Illustrated: Five Hundred Years of the Canterbury Tales in Pictures*, edited by William K. Finley and Joseph Rosenblum, 37–72. New Castle, DE: Oak Knoll, 2003.

———. "Windows into the Text: Unfilled Spaces in Some Fifteenth-Century English Manuscripts." In *Texts and Their Contexts: Papers from the Early Book Society*, edited by Julia Boffey and John Scattergood, 44–70. Dublin: Four Courts, 1997.

Harris, Kate. "Ownership and Readership: Studies in the Provenance of the Manuscripts of Gower's *Confessio Amantis*." PhD dissertation, University of York, 1993.

———. "The Patron of British Library MS Arundel 38." *Notes and Queries* 229 (1984): 462–63.

———. "Patrons, Buyers and Owners: The Evidence for Ownership and the Role of Book Owners in Book Production and the Book Trade." In *Book Production and Publishing in Britain 1375–1475*, edited by Jeremy Griffiths and Derek Pearsall, 163–200. Cambridge: Cambridge University Press, 1989.

Haynes, Christine. "Reassessing 'Genius' in Studies of Authorship: The State of the Discipline." *Book History* 8 (2005): 287–320.

Hedeman, Anne D. "Making Memories for a Mad King: Illustrating the *Dialogues* of Pierre Salmon." *Gesta* 48 (2009): 169–184.

———. "Making the Past Present in Laurent de Premierfait's Translation of *De senectute*." In *Excavating the Medieval Image: Manuscripts, Artists, Audiences. Essays in Honor of Sandra Hindman.*, edited by David S. Areford and Nina A. Rowe, 59–80. Aldershot, UK: Ashgate, 2004.

———. "Making the Past Present: Visual Translation in Jean Lebègue's 'Twin' Manuscripts of Sallust." In *Patrons, Authors and Workshops: Books and Book Production in Paris Around 1400*, edited by Godfried Croenen and Peter Ainsworth, 173–96. Louvain: Peeters, 2006.

———. *Of Counselors and Kings: The Three Versions of Pierre Salmon's Dialogues.* Urbana: University of Illinois Press, 2001.

———. "Presenting the Past: Visual Translation in Thirteenth- to Fifteenth-Century France." In *Imagining the Past in France: History in Manuscript Painting, 1250–1500*, edited by Elizabeth Morrison and Anne D. Hedeman, 69–85. Los Angeles: J. Paul Getty Museum, 2010.

———. "Roger van der Weyden's Escorial *Crucifixion* and Carthusian Devotional Practices." In *The Sacred Image: East and West*, edited by Robert Ousterhout and Leslie Brubaker, 191–203. Urbana: University of Illinois Press, 1995.

———. *The Royal Image: Illustrations of the Grandes Chroniques de France, 1274–1422.* Berkeley: University of California Press, 1991.

———. *Translating the Past: Laurent de Premierfait and Boccaccio's* De Casibus. Los Angeles: J. Paul Getty Museum, 2008.

Hellinga, Lotte. "Printing." In *The Cambridge History of the Book in Britain*, Vol. 3, edited by Lotte Hellinga and J. B. Trapp, 65–108. Cambridge: Cambridge University Press, 1999.

Hellinga, Lotte, and J. B. Trapp, eds. *The Cambridge History of the Book in Britain,* Vol. 3, *1400–1557.* Cambridge: Cambridge University Press, 1999.

Helmbold, Anita. "Chaucer Appropriated: The Troilus Frontispiece as Lancastrian Propaganda." *Studies in the Age of Chaucer* 30 (2008): 205–34.

Henderson, George. "Cassiodorus and Eadfrith Once Again." In *The Age of Migrating Ideas: Early Medieval Art in Northern Britain and Ireland*, edited by R. Michael Spearman and John Higgit, 82–91. Edinburgh: National Museums of Scotland, 1991.

Hicks, M. A. "The 1468 Statute of Livery." *Historical Research* 64 (1991): 15–28.

Higl, Andrew. *Playing the* Canterbury Tales: *The Continuations and Additions.* Burlington, VT: Ashgate, 2012.

Hilmo, Maidie. "The Clerk's 'Unscholarly Bow': Seeing and Reading Chaucer's Clerk from the Ellesmere MS to Caxton." *Journal of the Early Book Society* 10 (2007): 71–105.

———. "Illuminating Chaucer's *Canterbury Tales*: Portraits of the Author and Selected Pilgrim Authors." In *Opening Up Middle English Manuscripts: Literary and Visual Approaches*, 256–59. Ithaca, NY: Cornell University Press, 2012.

———. *Medieval Images, Icons, and Illustrated English Literary Texts: From Ruthwell Cross to the Ellesmere Chaucer.* Burlington, VT: Ashgate, 2004.

Hindman, Sandra. *Christine de Pizan's "Epistre Othéa": Painting and Politics at the Court of Charles VI.* Toronto: Pontifical Institute of Mediaeval Studies, 1986.

———. "The Role of Author and Artist in the Procedure of Illustrating Late Medieval Texts." *Acta* 10 (1986): 27–62.

Hines, John, Natalie Cohen, and Simon Roffey. "Iohannes Gower, Armiger, Poeta: Records and Memorials of His Life and Death." In *A Companion to Gower*, edited by Siân Echard, 36–41. Cambridge: D. S. Brewer, 2004.

Holly, Michael Ann. *Panofsky and the Foundations of Art History.* Ithaca, NY: Cornell University Press, 1984.

———. *Past Looking: Historical Imagination and the Rhetoric of the Image.* Ithaca, NY: Cornell University Press, 1996.

Horobin, Simon. "Adam Pinkhurst and the Copying of British Library MS Additional 35287 of the B Version of Piers Plowman." *Yearbook of Langland Studies* 23 (2009): 61–83.

———. "Adam Pinkhurst, Geoffrey Chaucer and the Hengwrt Manuscript of the *Canterbury Tales*." *The Chaucer Review* 44 (2010): 351–67.

———. "Compiling the *Canterbury Tales* in Fifteenth-Century Manuscripts." *Chaucer Review* 47 (2013): 372–89.

———. "The Edmund-Fremund Scribe Copying Chaucer." *Journal of the Early Book Society* 12 (2009): 195–203.

———. "The 'Hooked G' Scribe and His Work on Three Manuscripts of the *Canterbury Tales*." *Neuphilologische Mitteilungen* 99 (1998): 411–17.

———. "The Professionalization of Writing." In *The Oxford Handbook of Medieval Literature in English*, edited by Elaine Treharne and Greg Walker, 57–67. Oxford: Oxford University Press, 2010.

———. "Thomas Hoccleve: Chaucer's First Editor?" *Chaucer Review* 50 (2015): 228–50.

Horobin, Simon, and Daniel W. Mosser. "Scribe D's SW Midlands Roots: A Reconsideration." *Neuphilologische Mitteilungen* 106 (2005): 289–305.

Houston, Keith. *Shady Characters: The Secret Life of Punctuation, Symbols, and Other Typographical Marks*. New York: Norton, 2013.

Hughes, Jonathan. *Arthurian Myths and Alchemy: The Kingship of Edward IV*. Stroud: Sutton, 2002.

Hui, Andrew. "The Many Returns of Philology: A State of the Field Report." *Journal of the History of Ideas* 78 (2017): 137–56.

Hult, David F. *Self-Fulfilling Prophecies: Readership and Authority in the First* Roman de La Rose. Cambridge: Cambridge University Press, 1986.

Huot, Sylvia. "The Writer's Mirror: Watriquet de Couvin and the Development of the Author-Centered Book." In *Across Boundaries: The Book in Culture and Commerce*, edited by Bill Bell, Philip Benet, and Jonquil Bevan, 29–46. New Castle, DE: Oak Knoll, 2000.

Ingledew, Francis. "The Book of Troy and the Genealogical Construction of History: The Case of Geoffrey of Monmouth's *Historia regum Britanniae*." *Speculum* 69 (1994): 665–704.

Inglis, Erik. "A Book in the Hand: Some Late Medieval Accounts of Manuscript Presentations." *Journal of the Early Book Society* 5 (2002): 57–97.

———. "History in French Manuscripts." *Burlington Magazine* 153 (2011): 210–11.

———. "Image and Ilustration in Jean Fouquet's *Grandes Chroniques de France*." *French Historical Studies* 26 (2003): 185–224.

———. *Jean Fouquet and the Invention of France: Art and Nation after the Hundred Years War*. New Haven: Yale University Press, 2011.

Irvin, Matthew W. *The Poetic Voices of John Gower: Politics and Personae in the* Confessio Amantis. Woodbridge, UK: D. S. Brewer, 2014.

Irwin, William. "What Is an Allusion?" *Journal of Aesthetics and Art Criticism* 59 (2001): 287–97.

Jager, Eric. *The Book of the Heart*. Chicago: University of Chicago Press, 2000.

James, M. R., and Armitage Robinson. *The Manuscripts of Westminster Abbey*. Cambridge: Cambridge University Press, 1909.

James-Maddocks, Holly. "The Illuminators of the Hooked-G Scribe(s) and the Production of Middle English Literature, c. 1460–c. 1490." *Chaucer Review* 51 (2016): 151–86.

James-Maddocks, Holly, and Deborah E. Thorpe. "A Petition Written by Ricardus Franciscus." *Journal of the Early Book Society* 15 (2012): 245–75.

Jameson, Fredric. *Ideologies of Theory*. London: Verso, 2008.

Jefferson, Lisa. *The Medieval Account Books of the Mercers of London, an Edition and Translation*. 2 vols. Surrey, UK: Ashgate, 2009.

Jenkinson, Hilary. *The Later Court Hands in England from the Fifteenth to the Seventeenth Century*. New York: Ungar, 1969.

Jones, Terry. "Did John Gower Rededicate His 'Confessio Amantis' Before Henry IV's Usurpation?" In *Middle English Texts in Transition: A Festschrift Dedicated to Toshiyuki Takamiya on His 70th Birthday*, edited by Toshiyuki Takamiya, Simon Horobin, and Linne R. Mooney, 40–74. Woodbridge, UK: York Medieval Press, 2014.

Kamerick, Kathleen. *Popular Piety and Art in the Late Middle Ages: Image Worship and Idolatry in England 1350–1500*. New York: Palgrave, 2002.

Kelliher, Hilton. "The Historiated Initial in the Devonshire Chaucer." *Notes and Queries* 24 (1977): 197.

Kennedy, Kathleen E. *The Courtly and Commercial Art of the Wycliffite Bible*. Turnhout, Belgium: Brepols, 2014.

Ker, N. R, ed. *Eton College, Quincentenary Exhibition*. Eton: Aldon and Blackwell, 1947.

Kerby-Fulton, Kathryn. "Langlandian Reading Circles and the Civil Service in London and Dublin, 1380–1427." *New Medieval Literatures* 1 (1997): 59–83.

———. Review of *Scribes and the City: London Guildhall Clerks and the Dissemination of Middle English Literature 1375–1425* by Linne R. Mooney and Estelle Stubbs. *Medium Aevum* 84 (2015): 178–81.

Kerby-Fulton, Kathryn, and Denise Louise Despres. *Iconography and the Professional Reader: The Politics of Book Production in the Douce Piers Plowman*. Minneapolis: University of Minnesota Press, 1999.

Kerby-Fulton, Kathryn, and Steven Justice. "Scribe D and the Marketing of Ricardian Literature." In *The Medieval Professional Reader at Work: Evidence from Manuscripts of Chaucer, Langland, Kempe, and Gower*, edited by Maidie Hilmo and Kathryn Kerby-Fulton, 217–37. Victoria, BC: University of Victoria, 2001.

Kerby-Fulton, Kathryn, Linda Olson, and Maidie Hilmo. *Opening Up Middle English Manuscripts: Literary and Visual Approaches*. Ithaca, NY: Cornell University Press, 2012.

Kinch, Ashby. *Imago Mortis: Mediating Images of Death in Late Medieval Culture*. Leiden, Netherlands: Brill, 2013.

King, John N. *Foxe's* Book of Martyrs *and Early Modern Print Culture*. Cambridge: Cambridge University Press, 2011.

King'oo, Clare Costley. *Miserere Mei: The Penitential Psalms in Late Medieval and Early Modern England*. Notre Dame, IN: Notre Dame University Press, 2012.

Kipling, Gordon. *Enter the King: Theatre, Liturgy, and Ritual in the Medieval Civic Triumph*. Oxford: Clarendon, 1998.

———. *The Triumph of Honour: Burgundian Origins of the Elizabethan Renaissance*. The Hague: Leiden University Press, 1977.

Kleineke, Wilhelm. *Englische Fürstenspiegel vom Policraticus Johanns von Salisbury bis zum Basilikon doron König Jakobs I*. Halle: Niemeyer, 1937.

Kline, Daniel T. "Father Chaucer and the 'Siege of Thebes': Literary Paternity, Aggressive Deference, and the Prologue to Lydgate's Oedipal Canterbury Tale." *Chaucer Review* 34 (1999): 217–35.

Knapp, Ethan. *The Bureaucratic Muse: Thomas Hoccleve and the Literature of Late Medieval England*. University Park: Pennsylvania State University Press, 2001.

———. "Eulogies and Usurpations: Hoccleve and Chaucer Revisited." *Studies in the Age of Chaucer* 21 (1999): 247–73.

Koerner, Joseph Leo. "Confessional Portraits: Representation as Redundancy." In *Hans Holbein: Paintings, Prints, and Reception*, edited by Mark Roskill and John Oliver Hand, 125–39. New Haven, CT: Yale University Press; Washington, DC: National Gallery of Art, 2001.

———. *The Moment of Self-Portraiture in German Renaissance Art*. Chicago: University of Chicago Press, 1993.

Kolve, V. A. *Chaucer and the Imagery of Narrative: The First Five Canterbury Tales*. Stanford, CA: Stanford University Press, 1984.

———. *Telling Images: Chaucer and the Imagery of Narrative*. Stanford, CA: Stanford University Press, 2009.

Koziol, Geoffrey. *Begging Pardon and Favor: Ritual and Political Order in Early Medieval France.* Ithaca, NY: Cornell University Press, 1992.

Kren, Thomas, and Scot McKendrick, eds. *Illuminating the Renaissance: The Triumph of Flemish Manuscript Painting in Europe.* Los Angeles: J. Paul Getty Museum, 2003.

Kristeva, Julia. *Desire in Language: A Semiotic Approach to Literature and Art.* Translated by Thomas Gora, Alice Jardine, and Leon S. Roudiez. Edited by Leon S. Roudiez. New York: Columbia University Press, 1980.

Krochalis, Jeanne E. "Hoccleve's Chaucer Portrait." *Chaucer Review* 21 (1986): 234–45.

Krynen, Jacques. *Idéal du prince et pouvoir royal en France à la fin du Moyen Age, 1380–1440: Étude de la littérature politique du temps.* Paris: Picard, 1981.

Kumler, Aden. "The Patron-Function." In *Patronage: Power and Agency in Medieval Art,* edited by Colum Hourihane, 297–313. The Index of Christian Art Occasional Papers 15. University Park: Penn State University Press and Index of Christian Art, 2013.

———. "Translating ma dame de Saint-Pol: The Privilege and Predicament of the Devotee in Paris, BnF, MS naf 4338." in *Translating the Middle Ages,* edited by Karen Fresco and Charles Wright, 35–53. Burlington, VT: Ashgate: 2012.

———. *Translating Truth: Ambitious Images and Religious Knowledge in Late Medieval France and England.* New Haven, CT: Yale University Press, 2011.

Kuskin, William. "The Archival Imagination: Reading John Lydgate Toward a Theory of Literary Reproduction." *English Language Notes* 45 (2007): 79–92.

———. *Symbolic Caxton: Literary Culture and Print Capitalism.* Notre Dame, IN: Notre Dame University Press, 2008.

Kwakkel, Erik. "Commercial Organization and Economic Innovation." In *The Production of Books in England, 1350–1500,* edited by Alexandra Gillespie and Daniel Wakelin, 173–91. Cambridge: Cambridge University Press, 2011.

Lacey, Helen. *The Royal Pardon: Access to Mercy in Fourteenth-Century England.* Woodbridge, UK: York Medieval Press, 2009.

Latham, R. E., D. R. Howlett, and R. K. Ashdowne, eds. *Dictionary of Medieval Latin from British Sources.* Oxford: British Academy, 1975–2013.

Lavezzo, Kathy, ed. *Imagining a Medieval English Nation.* Minneapolis: University of Minnesota Press, 2004.

Lawton, David. "Dullness and the Fifteenth Century." *ELH* 54 (1987): 761–99.

Lawton, Lesley. "The Illustration of Late Medieval Secular Texts with Special Reference to Lydgate's 'Troy Book.'" In *Manuscripts and Readers in Fifteenth-Century England: The Literary Implications of Manuscript Study,* edited by Derek Pearsall, 41–69. Cambridge: D. S. Brewer, 1983.

———. "'To Studie in Bookis of Antiquitie': The Illustrated Manuscripts of John Lydgate's *Fall of Princes* as Witnesses of Cultural Practice." *Anglophonia* 29 (2011): 61–77.

Laynesmith, J. L. *The Last Medieval Queens: English Queenship 1445–1503.* Oxford: Oxford University Press, 2004.

Lee, Jenny Veronica. "Confessio Auctoris: Confessional Poetics and Authority in the Literature of Late Medieval England, 1350–1450." PhD dissertation, Northwestern University, 2012.

Leff, Amanda M. "Lydgate Rewrites Chaucer: The General Prologue Revisited." *Chaucer Review* 46 (2012): 472–79.

Leo, Domenic. "Authorial Presence in the Illuminated Manuscripts of Guillaume de Machaut." PhD dissertation, New York University, Institute of Fine Arts, 2005.

Lerer, Seth. *Chaucer and His Readers: Imagining the Author in Late Medieval England.* Princeton: Princeton University Press, 1993.

Levin, William. "Two Gestures of Virtue in Italian Late Medieval and Renaissance Art." *Southeastern College Art Conference Review* 13 (1999): 325–46.

Lindeboom, Wim. "Rethinking the Recensions of the *Confessio Amantis.*" *Viator* 40 (2009): 319–48.

Lindenbaum, Sheila. "London Texts and Literate Practice." In *The Cambridge History of Medieval English Literature*, edited by David Wallace, 284–309. Cambridge: Cambridge University Press, 1999.

Lindley, P. "Retrospective Effigies, the Past and Lies." In *Medieval Art, Architecture and Archaeology at Hereford*, edited by David Whitehead, 111–21. London: British Archaeological Association, 1995.

Little, Katherine C. *Confession and Resistance: Defining the Self in Late Medieval England*. Notre Dame, IN: University of Notre Dame Press, 2006.

Louis, Cameron. "A Yorkist Genealogical Chronicle in Middle English Verse." *Anglia* 1991 (1991): 1–20.

Lowden, John. "The Royal/Imperial Book and the Image or Self-Image of the Medieval Ruler." In *Kings and Kingship in Medieval Europe*, edited by Anne I. Dugan, 213–40. London: King's College Centre for Late Antique and Medieval Studies, 1993.

Lucas, P. J. "An Author as Copyist of His Own Work: John Capgrave OSA (1393–1464)." In *New Science Out of Old Books: Studies in Manuscripts and Early Printed Books in Honour of A. I. Doyle*, edited by Richard Beadle and A. J. Piper, 227–48. Aldershot, UK: Scolar, 1995.

Luxford, Julian M. Review of *Tradition and Innovation in Later Medieval English Manuscripts* by Kathleen L. Scott. *Speculum* 86 (2011): 803–4.

Lynch, Kathryn L. *The High Medieval Dream Vision: Poetry, Philosophy, and Literary Form*. Stanford: Stanford University Press, 1988.

Machan, Tim William. *Textual Criticism and Middle English Texts*. Charlottesville: University Press of Virginia, 1994.

Mackman, J., and M. Stevens, eds. *Court of Common Pleas: The National Archives, CP40: 1399–1500*. London: British History Online, 2010. http://www.british-history.ac.uk/no-series/common-pleas/1399–1500.

Mahoney, Dhira B. "Courtly Presentation and Authorial Self-Fashioning: Frontispiece Miniatures in Late Medieval French and English Manuscripts." *Mediaevalia* 21 (1996): 97–160.

Mâle, Emile. *Religious Art in France—The Thirteenth Century*. Princeton: Princeton University Press, 1984.

Mann, Jill. *Chaucer and Medieval Estates Satire*. Cambridge: Cambridge University Press, 1973.

Marks, Richard. *Image and Devotion in Late Medieval England*. Stroud, UK: Sutton, 2004.

———. "Images of Henry VI." In *The Lancastrian Court. Proceedings of the 2001 Harlaxton Symposium*, edited by Jenny Stratford, 111–24. Donington, UK: Shaun Tyas, 2003.

———. *Stained Glass in England During the Middle Ages*. Toronto: University of Toronto Press, 1993.

———. "Two Illuminated Guild Registers from Bedfordshire." In *Illuminating the Book: Makers and Interpreters, Essays in Honour of Janet Backhouse*, edited by Michelle P. Brown and Scot McKendrick, 121–41. Toronto: University of Toronto Press, 1998.

Marks, Richard and Paul Williamson, eds. *Gothic: Art for England, 1400–1547*. London: Victoria and Albert Museum, 2003.

Marrow, James H. "The Pembroke Psalter-Hours." In *Als Ich Can: Liber Amicorum in Memory of Professor Dr. Maurits Smeyers*, edited by Bert Cardon, Jan Van der Stock, and Dominique Vanwijnsberghe, 861–902. Leuven, Belgium: Peeters, 2002.

McGerr, Rosemarie. *A Lancastrian Mirror for Princes: The Yale Law School New Statutes of England*. Bloomington and Indianapolis: University of Indiana Press, 2011.

———. "Medieval Concepts of Literary Closure: Theory and Practice." *Exemplaria* 1 (1989): 149–79.

McGrady, Deborah L. "Constructing Authorship in the Late Middle Ages: A Study of the Books of Guillaume de Machaut, Christine de Pizan and Jean Lemaire de Belges." PhD dissertation, University of California, Santa Barbara, 1997.

———. "The Rise of Metafiction in the Late Middle Ages." In *The Cambridge History of French Literature*, edited by William E. Burgwinkle, Nicholas Hammond, and Emma Wilson, 172–79. Cambridge: Cambridge University Press, 2011.

McGregor, James H. "The Iconography of Chaucer in Hoccleve's *De Regimine Principum* and in the Troilus Frontispiece." *Chaucer Review* 11 (1977): 338–50.

McKendrick, Scot. "Edward IV: An English Royal Collector of Netherlandish Tapestry." *Burlington Magazine* 129 (1987): 521–24.

———. "*La Grande Histoire César* and the Manuscripts of Edward IV." *English Manuscript Studies 1100–1700* 2 (1990): 109–38.

———. "*The Romuléon* and the Manuscripts of Edward IV." In *England in the Fifteenth Century: Proceedings from the 1992 Harlaxton Symposium*, edited by Nicholas Rogers, 149–69. Stamford, UK: Paul Watkins, 1994.

McKenzie, D. F. "Printers of the Mind: Some Notes on Bibliographical Theories and Printing-House Practices." *Studies in Bibliography* 22 (1969): 1–75.

McKinley, Kathryn. "Lessons for a King from John Gower's 'Confessio Amantis.'" In *Metamorphoses: The Changing Face of Ovid in Medieval and Early Modern Europe*, edited by Allison Keith and Stephen Rupp, 107–28. Toronto: Centre for Reformation and Renaissance Studies, 2007.

McSparran, Frances, gen. ed. *Middle English Dictionary*. Ann Arbor: University of Michigan, 2001. http://quod.lib.umich.edu/m/med/.

Mead, Vance. "Printers, Stationers, and Bookbinders in the Plea Rolls in the Court of Common Pleas, 1460–1540." *Journal of the Printing Historical Society* 24 (2016): 11–33.

Meale, Carol M. "The Patronage of Poetry." In *A Companion to Fifteenth-Century English Poetry*, edited by Julia Boffey and A. S. G. Edwards, 7–20. Cambridge: D. S. Brewer, 2013.

———. "Patrons, Buyers and Owners: Book Production and Social Status." In *Book Production and Publishing in Britain 1375–1475*, edited by Jeremy Griffiths and Derek Pearsall, 201–38. Cambridge: Cambridge University Press, 1989.

Meecham-Jones, Simon. "Prologue—The Poet as Subject: Literary Self-Consciousness in Gower's *Confessio Amantis*," In *Betraying Our Selves: Forms of Self-Representation in Early Modern English Texts*, edited by Hank Dragstra, Sheila Ottway, and Helen Wilcox, 14–30. New York: St. Martin's, 2000.

Meier, Christel. "Ecce auctor: Beiträge zur Ikonographie literarischer Urheberschaft im Mittelalter." *Frühmittelalterliche Studien* 34 (2000): 338–92.

Meyer-Lee, Robert J. *Poets and Power from Chaucer to Wyatt*. Cambridge: Cambridge University Press, 2007.

Meyvaert, Paul. "Bede, Cassiodorus, and the Codex Amiatinus." *Speculum* 71 (1996): 827–83.

Michael, Michael A. "English Illuminators c. 1190–1450: A Survey from Documentary Sources." *English Manuscript Studies, 1100–1700* 4 (1993): 62–113.

———. "The Iconography of Kingship in the Walter of Milemete Treatise." *Journal of the Warburg and Courtauld Institutes* 57 (1994): 35–47.

———. "Oxford, Cambridge and London: Towards a Theory for 'Grouping' Gothic Manuscripts." *Burlington Magazine* 130 (1988): 107–15.

———. "Urban Production of Manuscript Books and the Role of the University Towns." In *The Cambridge History of the Book in Britain,* Vol 2, edited by Nigel Morgan and Rodney M. Thompson, 168–94. Cambridge: Cambridge University Press, 2008.

Miles, Laura Saetveit. "The Annunciation as Model of Meditation: Stillness, Speech and Transformation in Middle English Drama and Lyric." *Marginalia* 2 (2004). http://mcrg.soc.srcf.net/journal/05cambridge/miles.php.

Minnis, Alastair J. "The Author's Two Bodies? Authority and Fallibility in Late-Medieval Textual Theory." In *Of the Making of Books: Medieval Manuscripts, Their Scribes and Readers, Essays*

Presented to M. B. Parkes, edited by P. R. Robinson, and Rivkah Zim, 259–79. Aldershot, UK: Scolar, 1997.

Minnis, Alastair J. "De Vulgari Auctoritate: Chaucer, Gower and the Men of Great Authority." In *Chaucer and Gower: Difference, Mutuality, Exchange*, edited by Robert F. Yeager, 36–74. Victoria, BC: University of Victoria, 1991.

———. *The Medieval Theory of Authorship: Scholastic Literary Attitudes in the Later Middle Ages*. 2nd ed. Philadelphia: University of Pennsylvania Press, 1988.

Mooney, Linne R. "Chaucer's Scribe." *Speculum* 81 (2006): 97–138.

———. "A Holograph Copy of Thomas Hoccleve's *Regiment of Princes*." *Studies in the Age of Chaucer* 33 (2011): 263–96.

———. "Locating Scribal Activity in Late Medieval London." In *Design and Distribution of Late Medieval Manuscripts in England*, edited by Margaret Connolly and Linne R. Mooney, 183–204. York, UK: York Medieval Press, 2008.

———. "Lydgate's *Kings of England* and Another Verse Chronicle of the Kings." *Viator* 20 (1989): 255–90.

———. "Vernacular Literary Manuscripts and Their Scribes." In *The Production of Books in England, 1350–1500*, edited by Alexandra Gillespie and Daniel Wakelin, 192–211. Cambridge: Cambridge University Press, 2011.

Mooney, Linne R., and Daniel W. Mosser. "Hooked-G Scribes and Takamiya Manuscripts." In *The Medieval Book and a Modern Collector: Essays in Honour of Toshiyuki Takamiya*, edited by Takami Matsuda, Richard A. Linenthal, and John Scahill, 179–96. Cambridge: D. S. Brewer, 2004.

Mooney, Linne R., and Estelle Stubbs. *Scribes and the City: London Guildhall Clerks and the Dissemination of Middle English Literature, 1375–1425*. York, UK: York Medieval Press with Boydell Press, 2013.

Morelli, Giovanni. *Italian Painters: Critical Studies of Their Works*. 2 vols. Translated by Constance Jocelyn Ffoulkes. London: John Murray, 1893–1900.

Morgan, Nigel. *Early Gothic Manuscripts*. 2 vols. A Survey of Manuscripts Illuminated in the British Isles, 4. London: Harvey Miller, 1982.

———. "Patrons and Devotional Images in English Art of the International Gothic c. 1350–1450." In *Reading Texts and Images: Essays on Medieval and Renaissance Art and Patronage in Honour of Margaret M. Manion*, edited by Bernard Muir, 98–122. Exeter: University of Exeter Press, 2002.

———. "An SS Collar in the Devotional Context of the Shield of the Five Wounds." In *The Lancastrian Court: Proceedings of the 2001 Harlaxton Symposium*, edited by Jenny Stratford, 147–62. Donington, UK: Shaun Tyas, 2003.

———. "What Are They Saying? Patrons and Their Text Scrolls in Fifteenth-Century English Art." In *Patronage: Power, and Agency in Medieval Art*, edited by Colum Hourihane, 175–93. The Index of Christian Art Occasional Papers 15. Princeton, NJ: Penn State University Press and Index of Christian Art, 2013.

Morgan, Phillip. "'Those Were the Days': A Yorkist Pedigree Roll." In *Estrangement, Enterprise, and Education in Fifteenth-Century England*, edited by Sharon Michalove and A. Compton Reeves, 107–16. Stroud, UK: Sutton, 1998.

Mortimer, Nigel. *John Lydgate's Fall of Princes: Narrative Tragedy in Its Literary and Political Contexts*. Oxford: Oxford University Press, 2005.

Mosser, Daniel W., and Linne R. Mooney. "The Case of the Hooked-G Scribe(s) and the Production of Middle English Literature, c. 1460–c. 1490." *Chaucer Review* 51 (2016): 131–50.

Moxey, Keith. "Impossible Distance: Past and Present in the Study of Dürer and Grünewald." *Art Bulletin* 86 (2004): 750–63.

———. "Mimesis and Iconoclasm." *Art History* 32 (2009): 52–77.

———. *Visual Time: The Image in History.* Durham, NC: Duke University Press, 2013.

Müller, Monika E., ed. *The Use of Models in Medieval Book Painting.* Newcastle upon Tyne, UK: Cambridge Scholars, 2014.

Murray, Stephen. *Plotting Gothic.* Chicago: University of Chicago Press, 2014.

Musson, Anthony. "Ruling 'Virtually'? Royal Images in Medieval English Law Books." In *Every Inch a King: Comparative Studies on Kings and Kingship in the Ancient and Medieval Worlds*, edited by Charles Melville and Lynette Mitchell, 151–72. Leiden, Netherlands: Brill, 2012.

Myers, A. R. "The Household Accounts of Queen Margaret of Anjou, 1452–3." *Bulletin of the John Rylands Library* 40 (1957–58): 79–113.

Nagel, Alexander, and Christopher S. Wood. *Anachronic Renaissance.* New York: Zone, 2010.

———. "Interventions: Toward a New Model of Renaissance Anachronism." *Art Bulletin* 87 (2005): 403–15.

Nash, Susie. "Claus Sluter's 'Well of Moses' for the Chartreuse de Champmol Reconsidered: Part III." *Burlington Magazine* 150 (2008): 724–41.

Naylor, P. "Scribes and Secretaries of the Percy Earls of Northumberland, with Special Reference to William Peeris and Royal MS 18 D. II." *English Manuscript Studies: 1100–1700* 15 (2009): 166–84.

Neer, Richard. "Connoisseurship and the Stakes of Style." *Critical Inquiry* 32 (2005): 1–26.

———. *The Emergence of the Classical Style in Greek Sculpture.* Chicago: University of Chicago Press, 2010.

Newman, Barbara. *God and the Goddesses: Vision, Poetry, and Belief in the Middle Ages.* Philadelphia: University of Pennsylvania Press, 2003.

Nichols, Ann Eljenholm. "The Etiquette of Pre-Reformation Confession in East Anglia." *Sixteenth Century Journal* 17 (1986): 145–63.

———. *Seeable Signs: The Iconography of the Seven Sacraments, 1350–1544.* Woodbridge, UK: Boydell, 1994.

Nichols, Stephen G. "Introduction: Philology in a Manuscript Culture." *Speculum* 65 (1990): 1–10.

Nichols, Stephen G., and Siegfried Wenzel, eds. *The Whole Book Cultural Perspectives on the Medieval Miscellany.* Ann Arbor: University of Michigan Press, 1996.

Nicholson, Peter. "Gower's Manuscript of the *Confessio Amantis.*" In *The Medieval Python: The Purposive and Provocative Work of Terry Jones*, edited by R. F. Yeager and Toshiyuki Takamiya, 75–86. New York: Palgrave, 2012.

———. "Gower's Revisions in the *Confessio Amantis.*" *Chaucer Review* 19 (1984): 123–43.

———. "Poet and Scribe in the Manuscripts of Gower's *Confessio Amantis.*" In *Manuscripts and Texts: Editorial Problems in Later Middle English Literature*, edited by Derek Pearsall, 130–42. Cambridge: D. S. Brewer, 1987.

Nitzsche, Jane Chance. *The Genius Figure in Antiquity and the Middle Ages.* New York: Columbia University Press, 1975.

Nolan, Maura. "Historicism After Historicism." In *The Post-Historical Middle Ages*, edited by Sylvia Federico and Elizabeth Scala, 63–85. New York: Palgrave, 2009.

———. *John Lydgate and the Making of Public Culture.* Cambridge: Cambridge University Press, 2005.

O'Callaghan, Tamara F. "The Fifteen Stars, Stones and Herbs: Book VII of the *Confessio Amantis* and Its Afterlife." In *Gower, Trilingual Poet: Language, Translation, and Tradition*, edited by Elisabeth Dutton, John Hines, and R. F. Yeager, 139–56. Cambridge: D. S. Brewer, 2010.

Oexle, Otto Gerhard. "Memoria und Memorialbild." In *Memoria: Der geschichtliche Zeugniswert des liturgischen Gedenkens im Mittelalter*, edited by Karl Schmid and Joachim Wollasch, 384–440. Munich: Wilhelm Fink, 1984.

Olson, Mary C. "Marginal Portraits and the Fiction of Orality: The Ellesmere Manuscript." In *Chaucer Illustrated: Five Hundred Years of the Canterbury Tales in Pictures*, edited by William K. Finley and Joseph Rosenblum, 1–35. New Castle, DE: Oak Knoll, 2003.

Olsson, Kurt. *John Gower and the Structures of Conversion: A Reading of the* Confessio Amantis. Cambridge: D. S. Brewer, 1992.

Ormrod, W. Mark. "Murmur, Clamour and Noise: Voicing Complaint and Remedy in Petitions to the English Crown, c. 1300–c. 1460." In *Medieval Petitions: Grace and Grievance*, edited by W. Mark Ormrod, Gwilym Dodd, and Anthony Musson, 135–55. Woodbridge, UK: York Medieval Press, 2009.

Os, Henk van. "The Black Death and Sienese Painting: A Problem of Interpretation." *Art History* 4 (1981): 237–49.

Owen, Charles A. *The Manuscripts of* The Canterbury Tales. Cambridge: D. S. Brewer, 1991.

Panofsky, Erwin. "Das Problem des Stils in der bildenden Kunst." *Zeitschrift für Aesthetik und allgemeine Kunstwissenschaft* 10 (1915): 460–67.

———. *Renaissance and Renascences in Western Art*. Stockholm: Almqvist & Wiksell, 1965.

Parkes, M. B. "The Influence of the Concepts of *Ordinatio* and *Compilatio* on the Development of the Book." In *Scribes, Scripts and Readers: Studies in the Communication, Presentation and Dissemination of Medieval Texts*, 35–70. London: Hambledon, 1991.

———. "Patterns of Scribal Activity and Revisions of the Text in Early Copies of Works by John Gower." In *New Science out of Old Books: Studies in Manuscripts and Early Printed Books in Honour of A. I. Doyle*, edited by Richard. Beadle and A. J. Piper, 81–121. Aldershot, UK: Ashgate, 1995.

———. "Richard Frampton, a Commercial Scribe c. 1390–1420." In *Pages from the Past: Medieval Writing Skills and Manuscript Books*, edited by P. R. Robinson and Rivkah Zim, 113–24. Farnham, UK: Ashgate, 2012.

———. *Their Hands Before Our Eyes: A Closer Look at Scribes*. Aldershot, UK: Ashgate, 2008.

Partridge, Stephen. "'The Makere of This Boke': Chaucer's Retraction and the Author as Scribe and Compiler." In *Author, Reader, Book: Medieval Authorship in Theory and Practice*, edited by Erik Kwakkel and Stephen Partridge, 106–53. Toronto: University of Toronto Press, 2012.

Patch, Howard R. *The Goddess Fortuna in Medieval Literature*. Cambridge, MA: Harvard University Press, 1927.

Patterson, Annabel. "'The Human Face Divine': Identity and the Portrait from Locke to Chaucer." In *Crossing Boundaries: Issues of Cultural and Individual Identities in the Middle Ages and the Renaissance*, edited by Sally McKee, 155–86. Turnhout, Belgium: Brepols, 1999.

Patterson, Lee. *Chaucer and the Subject of History*. London: Routledge, 1991.

———. "Making Identities in Fifteenth-Century England: Henry V and John Lydgate." In *New Historical Literary Study: Essays on Reproducing Texts, Representing History*, edited by Jeffrey N. Cox and Larry J. Reynolds, 69–107. Princeton: Princeton University Press, 1993.

———. *Negotiating the Past: The Historical Understanding of Medieval Literature*. Madison: University of Wisconsin Press, 1987.

———. "'What Is Me?': Self and Society in the Poetry of Thomas Hoccleve." *Studies in the Age of Chaucer* 23 (2001): 437–70.

Pearsall, Derek. "The Apotheosis of John Lydgate." *Journal of Medieval and Early Modern Studies* 35 (2005): 25–38.

———. "Beyond Fidelity: The Illustration of Late Medieval Literary Texts." In *Tributes to Kathleen L. Scott: English Medieval Manuscripts: Readers, Makers and Illuminators*, edited by Marlene Villalobos Hennessy, 197–220. London: Harvey Miller, 2009.

———. "The English Chaucerians." In *Chaucer and Chaucerians: Critical Studies in Middle English Literature*, edited by D. S. Brewer, 201–39. London: Thomas Nelson, 1966.

———. "Gower's Latin in the *Confessio Amantis*." In *Latin and Vernacular: Studies in Late-Medieval Texts and Manuscripts*, edited by Alastair J. Minnis, 13–25. Cambridge: D. S. Brewer, 1989.

———. "Hoccleve's *Regement of Princes*: The Poetics of Royal Self-Representation." *Speculum* 69 (1994): 386–410.

———. "The Idea of Englishness in the Fifteenth Century." In *Nation, Court and Culture: New Essays on Fifteenth-Century English Poetry*, edited by Helen Cooney, 15–27. Dublin: Four Courts, 2001.

———. *John Lydgate*. London: Routledge & K. Paul, 1970.

———. *John Lydgate (1371–1449): A Bio-Bibliography*. Victoria, BC: University of Victoria Press, 1997.

———. *The Life of Geoffrey Chaucer: A Critical Biography*. Oxford: Blackwell, 1992.

———. "Lydgate as Innovator." *Modern Language Quarterly* 53 (1992): 5–22.

———. "The Manuscripts and Illustrations of Gower's Works." In *A Companion to Gower*, edited by Siân Echard, 73–97. Cambridge: D. S. Brewer, 2004.

———. "The Organisation of the Latin Apparatus in Gower's *Confessio Amantis*: The Scribes and Their Problems." In *The Medieval Book and a Modern Collector: Essays in Honour of Toshiyuki Takamiya*, edited by Takami Matsuda, Richard A. Linenthal, and John Scahill, 99–112. Cambridge: D. S. Brewer, 2004.

Peck, Russell A. *Kingship and Common Profit in Gower's* Confessio Amantis. Carbondale: Southern Illinois University Press, 1978.

———. "The Phenomenology of Make Believe in Gower's 'Confessio Amantis.'" *Studies in Philology* 91 (1994): 250–69.

———. "The Politics and Psychology of Governance in Gower: Ideas of Kingship and Real Kings." In *A Companion to Gower*, edited by Siân Echard, 215–38. Cambridge: D. S. Brewer, 2004.

Perkins, Nicholas. *Hoccleve's* Regiment of Princes: *Counsel and Constraint*. Cambridge: D. S. Brewer, 2001.

Perkinson, Stephen. "From an 'Art De Memoire' to the Art of Portraiture: Printed Effigy Books of the Sixteenth Century." *Sixteenth Century Journal* 33 (2002): 687–723.

———. "Likeness." *Studies in Iconography (Special Issue: Medieval Art History Today: Critical Terms*, edited by Nina Rowe) 33 (2012): 15–28.

———. *The Likeness of the King: A Prehistory of Portraiture in Late Medieval France*. Chicago: University of Chicago Press, 2009.

———. "Rethinking the Origins of Portraiture." *Gesta* 46 (2007): 135–57.

Peters, Ursula. *Das Ich im Bild: Die Figur des Autors in volkssprachigen Bilderhandschriften des 13. bis 16. Jahrhunderts*. Cologne: Böhlau, 2008.

Peverley, Sarah L. "Political Consciousness and the Literary Mind in Late Medieval England: Men 'Brought up of Nought' in Vale, Hardyng, Mankind, and Malory." *Studies in Philology* 105 (2008): 1–29.

Pinner, Rebecca. "Medieval Images of St. Edmund in Norfolk Churches." In *St. Edmund, King and Martyr: Changing Images of a Medieval Saint*, edited by Anthony Bale, 111–32. Woodbridge, UK: York Medieval Press, 2009.

Piponnier, Françoise. *Costume et vie sociale: La cour d'Anjou XIVe–XVe siècles*. Paris: Mouton, 1970.

Pittaway, Sarah Louise. "The Political Appropriation of John Lydgate's *Fall of Princes*: A Manuscript Study of British Library MS Harley 1766." PhD dissertation, University of Birmingham, 2011.

Pollard, Graham. "The Company of Stationers Before 1557." *Library* 1937 (18): 1–38.

Porter, Elizabeth. "Gower's Ethical Microcosm and Political Macrocosm." In *Gower's* Confessio Amantis: *Responses and Reassessments*, edited by Alastair J. Minnis, 135–62. Cambridge: D. S. Brewer, 1983.

Prendergast, Thomas A. "Canon Formation." In *A Handbook of Middle English Studies*, edited by Marion Turner, 239–51. London: Wiley-Blackwell, 2013.

Prendergast, Thomas A. *Chaucer's Dead Body: From Corpse to Corpus.* New York: Routledge, 2004.

Prior, Edward S., and Arthur Gardner. *An Account of Medieval Figure-Sculpture in England, with 855 Photographs.* Cambridge: Cambridge University Press, 1912.

Prochno, Joachim. *Das Schreiber- und Dedikationsbild in der deutschen Buchmalerei.* Leipzig: B. G. Teubner, 1929.

Quilligan, Maureen. *The Allegory of Female Authority: Christine de Pizan's* "Cité des dames." Ithaca, NY: Cornell University Press, 1991.

Radulescu, Raluca L. "The Political Mentality of the English Gentry at the End of the Fifteenth Century." *New Europe College Yearbook* 8 (2000/2001): 355–89.

———. *The Gentry Context for Malory's* Morte Darthur. Woodbridge, UK: D. S. Brewer, 2003.

Rajsic, Jaclyn. "The English Prose *Brut* Chronicle on a Roll: Cambridge, Corpus Christi College MS 546 and Its History." In *The Prose Brut and Other Late Medieval Chronicles: Books Have Their Histories, Essays in Honour of Lister Matheson,* edited by Jaclyn Rajsic, Erik Kooper, and Dominique Hoche, 105–24. York: Boydell and Brewer, 2016.

Ramsay, Nigel. "Forgery and the Rise of the London Scriveners' Company." In *Fakes and Frauds: Varieties of Deception in Print and Manuscript,* edited by Robin Myers and Michael Harris, 99–108. Winchester: St. Paul's Bibliographies, 1989.

———. "Scriveners as Notaries and Legal Intermediaries in Later Medieval England." In *Enterprise and Individuals in Fifteenth-Century England,* edited by Jennifer Kermode, 118–31. Stroud, UK: Sutton, 1991.

Reichardt, Paul F. "'Several Illuminations, Coarsely Executed': The Illustrations of the *Pearl* Manuscript." *Studies in Iconography* 18 (1997): 119–42.

Reidemeister, Johann. *Superbia und Narziss: Personifikation und Allegorie in miniaturen mittelalterlicher Handschriften.* Turnhout, Belgium: Brepols, 2006.

Renck, Anneliese Pollock. "Reading Medieval Manuscripts Then, Now, and Somewhere in Between: Verbal and Visual Mise en Abyme in Huntington Library MS HM 60 and Bibliothèque nationale de France MS fr. 875." *Manuscripta* 60 (2016): 30–72.

Reynolds, Catherine. "Illustrated Boccaccio Manuscripts in the British Library (London)." *Studi sul Boccaccio* 17 (1988): 113–81.

Rice, Yael. "Between the Brush and the Pen: On the Intertwined Histories of Mughal Painting and Calligraphy." In *Envisioning Islamic Art and Architecture: Essays in Honor of Renata Holod,* edited by David J. Roxburgh, 148–74. Leiden, Netherlands: Brill, 2014.

Richmond, Colin. "The Visual Culture of Fifteenth-Century England." In *The Wars of the Roses,* edited by A. J. Pollard, 186–250. New York: St. Martin's, 1995.

Rickert, Margaret. "Herman the Illuminator." *Burlington Magazine* 66 (1935): 38–40.

———. *Painting in Britain: The Middle Ages.* 2nd ed. London: Penguin, 1965.

———. *The Reconstructed Carmelite Missal: An English Manuscript of the Late XIV Century in the British Museum (Additional 29704-5, 44892).* Chicago: University of Chicago Press, 1952.

Ringler, William A. *Bibliography and Index of English Verse Printed 1476–1558.* New York: Mansell, 1988.

Roberts, Jane. *Guide to Scripts Used in English Writings up to 1500.* 2nd ed. Liverpool: Liverpool University Press, 2015.

———. "On Giving Scribe B a Name and a Clutch of London Manuscripts from c. 1400." *Medium Aevum* 80 (2011): 257–70.

Rogers, Nicholas. "The Location and Iconography of Confession in Late Medieval Europe." In *Ritual and Space in the Middle Ages: Proceedings of the 2009 Harlaxton Symposium,* edited by Francis Andrews, 298–307. Donington, UK: Shaun Tyas, 2011.

Ross, Charles Derek. *Edward IV.* London: Methuen, 1974.

Rosser, Gervase. *The Art of Solidarity in the Middle Ages: Guilds in England 1250–1550.* Oxford: Oxford University Press, 2015.

Rouse, Mary, and Richard Rouse. *Manuscripts and Their Makers: Commercial Book Producers in Medieval Paris, 1200–1500*. 2 vols. London: Harvey Miller, 2000.

Rubin, Miri. *Mother of God: A History of the Virgin Mary*. New Haven, CT: Yale University Press, 2009.

Ruddick, Andrea. *English Identity and Political Culture in the Fourteenth Century*. Cambridge: Cambridge University Press, 2013.

Rudy, Kathryn M. *Postcards on Parchment: The Social Lives of Medieval Books*. New Haven, CT: Yale University Press, 2015.

Rust, Martha Dana. *Imaginary Worlds in Medieval Books: Exploring the Manuscript Matrix*. New York: Palgrave, 2007.

Runacres, Charles. "Art and Ethics in the Exempla of *Confessio Amantis*." In *Gower's* Confessio Amantis: *Responses and Reassessments*, edited by Alastair J. Minnis, 106–34. Cambridge: D. S. Brewer, 1983.

Saenger, Paul. "Silent Reading: Its Impact on Late Medieval Script and Society." *Viator* 13 (1982): 367–414.

Safran, Linda. "Deconstructing 'Donors' in Medieval Southern Italy." In *Female Founders in Byzantium and Beyond*, edited by Lioba Theis, Margaret Mullett, and Michael Grünbart, with Galina Fingarova and Matthew Savage, 135–51. Vienna: Böhlau, 2013.

Salter, Elizabeth, and Derek Pearsall. "Pictorial Illustration of Late Medieval Poetic Texts: The Role of the Frontispiece or Prefatory Picture." In *Medieval Iconography and Narrative, A Symposium*, edited by F. G. Anderson, E. Nyholm, M. Powell, and F. T. Stubkjaer, 100–23. Odense, Denmark: Odense University Press, 1980.

Sánchez, Reuben. *Persona and Decorum in Milton's Prose*. Madison, NJ: Fairleigh Dickinson University Press, 1997.

Sand, Alexa. *Vision, Devotion, and Self-Representation in Late Medieval Art*. Cambridge: Cambridge University Press, 2014.

Sandler, Lucy Freeman. *Gothic Manuscripts 1285–1385*. 2 vols. A Survey of Manuscripts Illuminated in the British Isles 5. London: Harvey Miller, 1986.

———. "Illuminated in the British Isles: French Influence and/or the Englishness of English Art, 1285–1345." *Gesta* 45 (2006): 177–88.

———. *Illuminators and Patrons in Fourteenth-Century England: The Psalter and Hours of Humphrey de Bohun and the Manuscripts of the Bohun Family*. London: British Library and University of Toronto, 2014.

———. "Notes for the Illuminator: The Case of the *Omne Bonum*." *Art Bulletin* 71 (1989): 551–64.

———. Omne Bonum: *A Fourteenth-Century Encyclopedia of Universal Knowledge*. 2 vols. London: Harvey Miller, 1996.

———. "One Hundred and Fifty Years of the Study of the Illuminated Book in England: The Bohun Manuscripts from the Nineteenth Century to the Present." In *Gothic Art and Thought in the Later Medieval Period: Essays in Honor of Willibald Sauerländer*, edited by Colum Hourihane, 243–63. University Park: Penn State University Press, 2011.

———. "Political Imagery in the Bohun Manuscripts." *English Manuscript Studies 1100–1700* 10 (2002): 114–53.

———. *The Psalter of Robert de Lisle in the British Library*. London: Harvey Miller and Oxford University Press, 1983.

———. "The Wilton Diptych and Images of Devotion in Illuminated Manuscripts." In *The Regal Image of Richard II and the Wilton Diptych*, edited by Dillian Gordon, Lisa Monnas, and Caroline Elam, 137–54. Turnhout, Belgium: Brepols, 1997.

———. "'Written with the Finger of God': Fourteenth-Century Images of Scribal Practice in the Lichtenthal Psalter." In *Teaching Writing, Learning to Write: Proceedings of the XVIth Collo-*

quium of the Comité International de Paléographie Latine, edited by Pamela R. Robinson, 275–91. London: Centre for Late Antique and Medieval Studies, King's College London, 2010.

Scallen, Catherine B. *Rembrandt, Reputation, and the Practice of Connoisseurship*. Amsterdam: Amsterdam University Press, 2004.

Scanlon, Larry. *Narrative, Authority, and Power: The Medieval Exemplum and the Chaucerian Tradition*. Cambridge: Cambridge University Press, 1994.

Scanlon, Larry, and James Simpson, "Introduction." In *John Lydgate: Poetry, Culture, and Lancastrian England*, edited by Larry Scanlon and James Simpson, 1–11. Notre Dame, IN: University of Notre Dame Press, 2006.

Scase, Wendy. "Writing and the 'Poetics of Spectacle': Political Epiphanies in 'The Arrivall of Edward IV' and Some Contemporary Lancastrian and Yorkist Texts." In *Images, Idolatry and Iconoclasm: Textuality and the Visual Image*, edited by Jeremy Dimmick, James Simpson, and Nicolette Zeeman, 172–84. Oxford: Oxford University Press, 2002.

Scattergood, V. J. *Politics and Poetry in the Fifteenth Century*. London: Blandford, 1971.

Scheller, Robert Walter. *Exemplum: Model Book Drawings and the Practice of Artistic Transmission in the Middle Ages (ca. 900–ca. 1450)*. Amsterdam: Amsterdam University Press, 1995.

Schleif, Corine. "Hands That Appoint, Anoint and Ally: Late Medieval Donor Strategies for Appropriating Approbation Through Painting." *Art History* 16 (1993): 1–32.

Schueler, Donald. "The Age of the Lover in Gower's *Confessio Amantis*." *Medium Aevum* 36 (1967): 152–58.

Scott, Kathleen L. "*Caveat Lector*: Ownership and Standardization in the Illustration of Fifteenth-Century English Manuscripts." *English Manuscript Studies 1100–1700* 1 (1989): 19–63.

——. "Dated and Datable Borders in English Books, c. 1395–c. 1504: Preliminary Thoughts on a Project Sponsored by the Bibliographical Society of London." *Papers of the Bibliographical Society of America* 91 (1997): 635–44.

——. *Dated and Datable English Manuscript Borders, c. 1395–1499*. London: Bibliographical Society and the British Library, 2002.

——. "The Decorated Letters of Two Cotton Manuscripts." In *Tributes to Jonathan J. G. Alexander: The Making and Meaning of Illuminated Medieval and Renaissance Manuscripts, Art and Architecture*, edited by Susan L'Engle and Gerald B. Guest, 99–110. London: Harvey Miller, 2006.

——. "Design, Decoration and Illustration." In *Book Production and Publishing in Britain 1375–1475*, edited by Jeremy Griffiths and Derek Pearsall, 31–64. Cambridge: Cambridge University Press, 1989.

——. "An Hours and Psalter by Two Ellesmere Illuminators." In *The Ellesmere Chaucer: Essays in Interpretation*, edited by Martin Stevens and Daniel Woodward, 87–119. San Marino, CA: Huntington Library, 1995.

——. "Instructions to a Limner in Beinecke MS 223." *Yale University Library Gazette* 72 (1997): 13–16.

——. *Later Gothic Manuscripts, 1390–1490*. 2 vols. A Survey of Manuscripts Illuminated in the British Isles 6. London: Harvey Miller, 1996.

——. "Limning and Book-Producing Terms and Signs in Situ in Late-Medieval English Manuscripts: A First Listing." In *New Science out of Old Books: Studies in Manuscripts and Early Printed Books in Honour of A. I. Doyle*, edited by Richard Beadle and A. J. Piper, 142–88. Aldershot, UK: Scolar, 1995.

——. "Lydgate's *Lives of Saints Edmund and Fremund*: A Newly-Located Manuscript in Arundel Castle." *Viator* 13 (1982): 335–66.

——. "A Mid-Fifteenth-Century Illuminating Shop and Its Customers." *Journal of the Warburg and Courtauld Institutes* 31 (1968): 170–96.

———. "Representations of Scribal Activity in English Manuscripts c. 1400–c. 1490: A Mirror of the Craft?" In *Pen in Hand: Medieval Scribal Portraits, Colophons and Tools*, edited by Michael Gullick, 115–49. Walkern, UK: Red Gull, 2006.

———. *Tradition and Innovation in Later Medieval English Manuscripts*. London: British Library, 2007.

Sears, Elizabeth. "Portraits in Counterpoint : Jerome and Jeremiah in an Augsburg Manuscript." In *Reading Medieval Images*, edited by Elizabeth Sears and Thelma K. Thomas, 61–74. Ann Arbor: University of Michigan Press, 2002.

Seymour, M. C., "Manuscripts of Hoccleve's *Regiment of Princes*." *Edinburgh Bibliographical Transactions* 4 (1974): 253–97.

———. "Manuscript Portraits of Chaucer and Hoccleve." *Burlington Magazine* 124 (1982): 618–23.

Shahar, Shulamith. *Growing Old in the Middle Ages: Winter Clothes Us in Shadow and Pain*. Translated by Yael Lotan. New York: Routledge, 1997.

Sherman, Claire Richter. *Imaging Aristotle: Verbal and Visual Representation in Fourteenth-Century France*. Berkeley: University of California Press, 1995.

———. *The Portraits of Charles V of France (1338–1380)*. University Park: Penn State University Press and College Art Association, 1969.

Sherman, William H. *Used Books: Marking Readers in Renaissance England*. Philadelphia: University of Pennsylvania Press, 2007.

Siddons, Michael Powell. *Heraldic Badges in England and Wales*. 4 vols. Woodbridge, UK: Boydell and Brewer for the Society of Antiquaries of London, 2009.

Simpson, James. "Bulldozing the Middle Ages: The Case of John Lydgate." *New Medieval Literatures* 4 (2001): 213–42.

———. "Madness and Texts: Hoccleve's Series." In *Chaucer and Fifteenth Century Poetry*, edited by Janet Cowen and Julia Boffey, 15–29. London: King's College, London, 1991.

———. "Nobody's Man: Thomas Hoccleve's *Regement of Princes*." In *London and Europe in the Later Middle Ages*, edited by Julia Boffey and Pamela King, 149–80. London: Centre for Medieval and Renaissance Studies, Queen Mary and Westfield College, 1995.

———. *Sciences and the Self in Medieval Poetry: Alan of Lille's* Anticlaudianus *and John Gower's* Confessio Amantis. Cambridge: Cambridge University Press, 1995.

Sklute, Larry. *Virtue of Necessity: Inconclusiveness and Narrative Form in Chaucer's Poetry*. Columbus: Ohio State University Press, 1984.

Slights, William W. E. *Managing Readers: Printed Marginalia in English Renaissance Books*. Ann Arbor: University of Michigan Press, 2001.

Smith, Kathryn A. "Accident, Play, and Invention: Three Infancy Miracles in the Holkham Bible Picture Book." In *Tributes to Jonathan J. G. Alexander: The Making and Meaning of Illuminated Medieval and Renaissance Manuscripts, Art and Architecture*, edited by Susan L'Engle and Gerald B. Guest, 357–69. London: Harvey Miller, 2006.

———. *Art, Identity, and Devotion in Fourteenth-Century England: Three Women and Their Books of Hours*. London: British Library and University of Toronto, 2003.

———. "History, Typology and Homily: The Jospeh Cycle in the *Queen Mary Psalter*." *Gesta* 32 (1993): 147–59.

———. "The Monk Who Crucified Himself." In *Thresholds of Medieval Visual Culture: Liminal Spaces*, edited by Elina Gertsman and Jill Stevenson, 43–72. Woodbridge, UK: Boydell and Brewer, 2012.

———. "The Neville of Hornby Hours and the Design of Literate Devotion." *Art Bulletin* 81 (1999): 72–92.

———. *The Taymouth Hours: Stories and Construction of the Self in Late Medieval England*. London: British Library and the University of Toronto, 2012.

Smyth, Karen Elaine. "Changing Times in the Cultural Discourse of Late Medieval England." *Viator* 35 (2004): 435–53.

———. *Imaginings of Time in Lydgate and Hoccleve's Verse*. Burlington, VT: Ashgate, 2011.

Sobecki, Sebastian. "*Ecce Patet Tensus*: The Trentham Manuscript, in Praise of Peace, and John Gower's Autograph Hand." *Speculum* 90 (2015): 925–59.

———. "Lydgate's Kneeling Retraction: The Testament as a Literary Palinode." *Chaucer Review* 49 (2015): 265–93.

———. "A Southwark Tale: Gower, the 1381 Poll Tax, and Chaucer's *The Canterbury Tales*." *Speculum* 92 (2017): 630–60.

Somerset, Fiona. "'Hard Is with Seyntis for to Make Affray': Lydgate the 'Poet-Propagandist' as Hagiographer." In *John Lydgate: Poetry, Culture, and Lancastrian England*, edited by Larry Scanlon and James Simpson, 258–78. Notre Dame, IN: University of Notre Dame Press, 2006.

Somerville, R. "The Cowcher Books of the Duchy of Lancaster." *English Historical Review* 51 (1936): 598–615.

Spearing, A. C. *Medieval Autographies: The "I" of the Text*. Notre Dame, IN: University of Notre Dame Press, 2012.

———. *Textual Subjectivity: The Encoding of Subjectivity in Medieval Narratives and Lyrics*. New York: Oxford University Press, 2005.

Spiegel, Gabrielle M. *The Past as Text: The Theory and Practice of Medieval Historiography*. Baltimore, MD: Johns Hopkins University Press, 1997.

———. "Revising the Past/Revisiting the Present: How Change Happens in Historiography." *History and Theory* 46 (2007): 1–19.

Spitzer, Leo. "Note on the Poetic and Empirical 'I' in Mediaeval Authors." *Traditio* 4 (1946): 414–22.

Sponsler, Claire. "Lydgate and London's Public Culture." In *Lydgate Matters: Poetry and Material Culture in the Fifteenth Century*, edited by Lisa H. Cooper and Andrea Denny-Brown, 13–33. New York: Palgrave, 2008.

———. *The Queen's Dumbshows: John Lydgate and the Making of Early Theater*. Philadelphia: University of Pennsylvania Press, 2014.

Spriggs, Gereth M. "Unnoticed Bodleian Library Manuscripts, Illuminated by Herman Scheere and His School." *Bodleian Library Record* 7 (1964): 193–203.

Stanbury, Sarah. *The Visual Object of Desire in Late Medieval England*. Philadelphia: University of Pennsylvania Press, 2007.

Stanton, Anne Rudloff. "Margaret Rickert (1888–1973): Art Historian." In *Women Medievalists and the Academy*, edited by Jane Chance, 285–94. Madison: University of Wisconsin Press, 2005.

———. *The Queen Mary Psalter: A Study of Affect and Audience*. Philadelphia: American Philosophical Society, 2001.

Steinberg, Leo. *The Sexuality of Christ in Renaissance Art and in Modern Oblivion*. 2nd ed. Chicago: University of Chicago Press, 1996.

Steiner, Emily. *Documentary Culture and the Making of Medieval English Literature*. Cambridge: Cambridge University Press, 2003.

Stevens, Martin. "The Ellesmere Miniatures as Illustrations of Chaucer's *Canterbury Tales*." *Studies in Iconography* 7–8 (1981–82): 113–34.

Straker, Scott-Morgan. "Deference and Difference: Lydgate, Chaucer, and the 'Siege of Thebes.'" *Review of English Studies* 52 (2001): 1–21.

Stratford, Jenny. "The Early Royal Collections and the Royal Library to 1461." In *The Cambridge History of the Book in Britain*, Vol. 3, edited by Lotte Hellinga and J. B. Trapp, 255–66. Cambridge: Cambridge University Press, 1999.

Strohm, Paul. "Chaucer's Fifteenth-Century Audience and the Narrowing of the 'Chaucer Tradition.'" *Studies in the Age of Chaucer* 4 (1982): 3–32.

——. *England's Empty Throne: Usurpation and the Language of Legitimation, 1399–1422*. New Haven, CT: Yale University Press, 1998.

——. "Hoccleve, Lydgate and the Lancastrian Court." In *The Cambridge History of Medieval English Literature*, edited by David Wallace, 640–61. Cambridge: Cambridge University Press, 1999.

——. "John Lydgate, Jacque of Holland, and the Poetics of Complicity." In *Medieval Literature and Historical Inquiry: Essays in Honor of Derek Pearsall*, edited by David Aers, 115–32. Woodbridge, UK: Boydell & Brewer, 2000.

——. "A Note on Gower's Persona." In *Acts of Interpretation: The Text and Its Contexts 700–1600, Essays on Medieval and Renaissance Literature in Honor of E. Talbot Donaldson*, edited by Mary Carruthers and Elizabeth D. Kirk, 293–98. Norman, OK: Pilgrim, 1982.

——. *Politique: Languages of Statecraft Between Chaucer and Shakespeare*. Notre Dame, IN: University of Notre Dame Press, 2005.

——. *Theory and the Premodern Text*. Minneapolis: University of Minnesota Press, 2000.

Stubbs, Estelle. "'Here's One I Prepared Earlier': The Work of Scribe D on Oxford, Corpus Christi College MS 198." *Review of English Studies* 58 (2007): 133–53.

——. "Richard Frampton and Two Manuscripts in the Parker Library." *Digital Philology* 4 (2015): 225–62.

Summit, Jennifer. *Lost Property: The Woman Writer and English Literary History, 1380–1589*. Chicago: University of Chicago Press, 2000.

——. *Memory's Library: Medieval Books in Early Modern England*. Chicago: University of Chicago Press, 2008.

——. "'Stable in Study': Lydgate's *Fall of Princes* and Duke Humphrey's Library." In *John Lydgate: Poetry, Culture, and Lancastrian England*, edited by Larry Scanlon and James Simpson, 207–31. Notre Dame, IN: University of Notre Dame Press, 2006.

Sutton, Anne F. "An Unfinished Celebration of the Yorkist Accession by a Clerk of the Merchant Staplers of Calais." In *The Fifteenth Century VIII—Rule, Redemption, and Representations in Late Medieval England and France*, edited by Linda Clark, 135–61. Woodbridge, UK: Boydell, 2008.

Sutton, Anne F., and Livia Visser-Fuchs. "The Cult of Angels in Late Fifteenth-Century England: An Hours of the Guardian Angel Presented to Queen Elizabeth Woodville." In *Women and the Book: Assessing the Visual Evidence*, edited by Jane H. M. Taylor and Lesley Smith, 230–65. London: British Library and University of Toronto Press, 1996.

——. *Richard III's Books: Ideal and Reality in the Life and Library of a Medieval Prince*. Stroud, UK: Sutton, 1997.

Takamiya, Toshiyuki. "A Handlist of Western Medieval Manuscripts in the Takamiya Collection." In *The Medieval Book: Glosses from Friends and Colleagues of Christopher de Hamel*, edited by James Marrow, William Noel, and Richard A. Linenthal, 421–40. Houten, Netherlands: Hes and De Graaf, 2010.

Tanselle, G. Thomas. *Bibliographical Analysis: A Historical Introduction*. Cambridge: Cambridge University Press, 2009.

Taylor, Andrew. "Vernacular Authorship and the Control of Manuscript Production." In *The Medieval Manuscript Book : Cultural Approaches*, edited by Michael Johnston and Michael Van Dussen, 199–214. Cambridge: Cambridge University Press, 2015.

Taylor, Chloë. *The Culture of Confession from Augustine to Foucault: A Genealogy of the "Confessing Animal."* New York: Routledge, 2009.

Tentler, Thomas N. *Sin and Confession on the Eve of the Reformation*. Princeton: Princeton University Press, 1977.

Thaisen, Jacob. "The Trinity Gower D Scribe's Two *Canterbury Tales* Manuscripts Revisited." In *Design and Distribution of Late Medieval Manuscripts in England*, edited by Margaret Connolly and Linne R. Mooney, 41–60. York, UK: York Medieval Press, 2008.

Thompson, John J. "Thomas Hoccleve and Manuscript Culture." In *Nation, Court and Culture: New Essays on Fifteenth-Century English Poetry*, edited by Helen Cooney, 81–94. Dublin: Four Courts, 2001.

Thorpe, Deborah E. "British Library MS Arundel 249: Another Manuscript in the Hand of Ricardus Franciscus." *Notes and Queries* 61 (2014): 189–96.

Tilghman, Benjamin C. "Pattern, Process, and the Creation of Meaning in *The Lindisfarne Gospels*." *West 86th* 24 (2017): 3–28.

Tinkle, Theresa Lynn. *Medieval Venuses and Cupids: Sexuality, Hermeneutics, and English Poetry*. Stanford, CA: Stanford University Press, 1996.

Todoroki, Yoshiaki. "A List of Miniatures of Goddess Fortune in Medieval Manuscripts." *Cultural and Social Sciences* 41 (1990): 71–114.

Town, Edward. "A Biographical Dictionary of London Painters, 1547–1625." *Walpole Society* 76 (2014): 1–235.

Trigg, Stephanie. *Congenial Souls: Reading Chaucer from Medieval to Postmodern*. Minneapolis: University of Minnesota Press, 2002.

Turville-Petre, Thorlac. *England the Nation: Language, Literature, and National Identity, 1290–1340*. Oxford: Clarendon, 1996.

Urban, Malte. *Fragments: Past and Present in Chaucer and Gower*. Bern: Peter Lang, 2009.

Velden, Hugo van der. *The Donor's Image: Gerard Loyet and the Votive Portraits of Charles the Bold*. Turnhout, Belgium: Brepols, 2000.

Vines, Amy N. "The Rehabilitation of Patronage in Hoccleve's Series." *Digital Philology* 2 (2013): 201–21.

Wakelin, Daniel. *Scribal Correction and Literary Craft: English Manuscripts 1375–1510*. Cambridge: Cambridge University Press, 2014.

Wallace, David. *Chaucerian Polity: Absolutist Lineages and Associational Forms in England and Italy*. Stanford, CA: Stanford University Press, 1997.

Ward, Matthew. "The Livery Collar: Politics and Identity in Fifteenth-Century England." PhD dissertation, University of Nottingham, 2014.

———. "The Livery Collar: Politics and Identity During the Fifteenth Century." In *The Fifteenth Century XIII—Exploring the Evidence: Commemoration, Administration, and The Economy*, edited by Linda Clark, 41–61. Woodbridge, UK: Boydell & Brewer, 2014.

Warner, George F., and Julius P. Gilson. *Catalogue of Western Manuscripts in the Old Royal and King's Collections*. 4 vols. London: British Museum, 1921.

Warner, Kathryn. "The Provenance and Early Ownership of John Ryland MS English 1." *Bulletin of the John Rylands Library* 81 (1999): 127–40.

Warner, Lawrence. "Scribes, Misattributed: Hoccleve and Pinkhurst." *Studies in the Age of Chaucer* 37 (2015): 55–100.

Watt, David. *The Making of Thomas Hoccleve's Series*. Liverpool: Liverpool University Press, 2013.

Watt, Diane. *Amoral Gower: Language, Sex, and Politics*. Minneapolis: University of Minnesota Press, 2003.

Weinryb, Ittai. "Introduction: Ex-Voto as Material Culture." In *Ex Voto: Votive Giving Across Cultures*, edited by Ittai Weinryb, 1–22. Chicago: University of Chicago Press, 2015.

Wenzel, Horst. "Autorenbilder: Zur Ausdifferenzierung von Autorenfunktionen in mittelalterlichen Miniaturen." In *Autor und Autorschaft im Mittelalter*, edited by Elizabeth Anderson, Jens Haustein, Anne Simon, and Peter Strohschneider, 1–28. Tübingen, Germany: Niemeyer, 1998.

Werner, Thomas. "Das Rad der Fortuna: Variationen über ein altes Thema." In *Thiasos Ton Mouson: Studien zu Antike und Christentum—Festschrift für Josef Fink zum 70. Geburtstag*, edited by Dieter Ahrens, 233–44. Cologne: Böhlau, 1984.

Wetherbee, Winthrop. "Classical and Boethian Tradition in the *Confessio Amantis*." In *A Companion to Gower*, edited by Siân Echard, 181–96. Cambridge: D. S. Brewer, 2004.

———. "Genius and Interpretation in the 'Confessio Amantis.'" In *Magister Regis: Studies in Honor of Robert Earl Kaske*, edited by Arthur Groos, with Emerson Brown, Giuseppe Mazzotta, Thomas D. Hill, and Joseph S. Wittig, 241–60. New York: Fordham University Press, 1986.

———. "Latin Structure and Vernacular Space: Gower, Chaucer, and the Boethian Tradition." In *Chaucer and Gower: Difference, Mutuality, Exchange*, edited by R. F. Yeager, 7–35. Victoria, BC: University of Victoria, 1991.

W. H. B. "Will of John Gower the Poet, Anno 1408." *Gentleman's Magazine* 3 (1835): 49–51.

Williams, Sarah Jane. "An Author's Role in Fourteenth-Century Book Production: Guillaume de Machaut's 'Livre ou je mets toutes mes choses.'" *Romania* 90 (1969): 433–54.

Williamson, Beth. *The Madonna of Humility: Development, Dissemination and Reception, c. 1340–1400*. Woodbridge, UK: Boydell and Brewer, 2009.

Wirth, Karl-August, ed. *Pictor in Carmine. Ein Handbuch der Typologie aus der Zeit um 1200, nach MS 300 des Corpus Christi College in Cambridge*. Berlin: Gebr. Mann, 2006.

Wittgenstein, Ludwig. *Philosophical Investigations*, translated by Gertrude E. M. Anscombe, Peter M. S. Hacker, and Joachim Schulte. Chichester, UK: Wiley-Blackwell, 2009.

Wogan-Browne, Jocelyn, Nicholas Watson, Andrew Taylor, and Ruth Evans, eds. *The Idea of the Vernacular: An Anthology of Middle English Literary Theory, 1280–1520*. Exeter, UK: University of Exeter Press, 1999.

Wölfflin, Heinrich. *Principles of Art History: The Problem of the Development of Style in Later Art*, translated by Mary Hottinger. New York: Dover, 1950.

Wollheim, Richard. *On Art and the Mind*. Cambridge, MA: Harvard University Press, 1974.

———. "Pictorial Style : Two Views." In *The Concept of Style*, edited by Berel Lang, 183–202. Philadelphia: University of Pennsylvania Press, 1979.

Wood, Christopher S. *Forgery, Replica, Fiction: Temporalities of German Renaissance Art*. Chicago: University of Chicago Press, 2008.

———. "The Votive Scenario." *RES: Anthropology and Aesthetics* 59/60 (2011): 206–27.

Wright, Sylvia. "The Author Portraits in the Bedford Psalter-Hours: Gower, Chaucer, and Hoccleve." *British Library Journal* 18 (1992): 190–201.

———. "Bruges Artists in London: The Patronage of the House of Lancaster." In *Flanders in a European Perspective: Manuscript Illumination Around 1400 in Flanders and Abroad*, edited by Maurits Smeyers and Bert Cardon, 93–109. Leuven: Peeters, 1995.

Yeager, Robert F. *John Gower's Poetic: The Search for a New Arion*. Woodbridge, UK: D. S. Brewer, 1990.

———. "'Scripture Veteris Capiunt Exempla Futuri': John Gower's Transformation of a Fable of Avianus." In *Retelling Tales: Essays in Honor of Russell Peck*, edited by Thomas Hahn and Alan Lupack, 341–54. Cambridge: D. S. Brewer, 1997.

Zink, Michel. *La subjectivité littéraire: Autour de siècle de Saint Louis*. Paris: Presses Universitaires de France, 1983

Ziolkowski, Jan M. "Do Actions Speak Louder Than Words? The Scope and Role of *Pronuntiatio* in the Latin Rhetorical Tradition with Special Reference to the Cistercians." In *Rhetoric Beyond Words: Delight And Persuasion in the Arts of the Middle Ages*, edited by Mary Carruthers, 124–50. New York: Cambridge University Press, 2010.

Zumthor, Paul. *Essai de poétique médiévale*. Paris: Éditions du Seuil, 1972.

INDEX

heraldry, **82**, 83, 138, 142, 148, 160–62, 165, 184, 248 n.84, 272 n.58; arms of England, 197, 207, 212, **213**, 223, 240 n.7, plate 25; heraldic badge of the Lion of March, **200**, 200–201, plate 23; heraldic badge of the sun in splendor, **200**, 200–201, plate 23; heraldic device, 198, 201, 204; heraldic emblem, 179–81, **182**, 183–84, **185**, 186; heraldic insignia, 165, 181–83, 203–4, plate 22

Herbert, Maud, 180

Herbert household, 12, 134, 162–65, 169, 178, 181, 228

Hilmo, Maidie, 66

Hindman, Sandra, 11

historicity, 74, 77, 78, 112

history, 157–59, 165–66, 190–93, 207–10, 213, 218–21; historical present, 218–19; and historicism, 155; visual historiography, 22. *See also* temporality

Hoccleve, Thomas: and autobiography, 70; and Chaucer, 69–80; *Lerne for to Die*, 106, plate 13; *Regiment of Princes*, 69–79, 83, 137, 139, 144–45; as scribe, 38, 39, 73

Holly, Michael Ann, 151, 153

hooked-G scribe(s), 141

Horobin, Simon, 38

Hult, David, 58

humilitatio (gesture), 100–109

humility, 16, 100–109, 119, 162, 216–18

Hundred Years' War, 3, 152

Huot, Sylvia, 58

illuminator. *See* producers of books and documents

incipit, 143, 145, 148

incompletion, 26, 153, 163, 166, 178–79, 183

index, 197

individuality, 59–60, 201–2, 207

Ingledew, Francis, 199

Inglis, Erik, 11

instructional literature. *See* Mirror for Princes

instructions (in book production), 26, 91, 99, 102, 255 n.92

intercession, 75, 130

interiority, 106, 111–12

intertextuality, 3, 5, 9–10, 13, 93

intervisuality, 13, 232 n.18

invention, 3, 5, 8, 10, 13–15

inventory, 13, 201, 248 n.84

Irvin, Matthew, 96

Irwin, William, 4, 13

Jean de Meun, 244 n.12, 252 n.42

Jerome (Saint), 113

Joshua (biblical figure), 219, 220, 223

Kennedy, Kathleen E., 49

Kew: National Archives C 81/1505, 242 n.109, plate 3; National Archives CP 40/647, 35, 239 n.60; National Archives CP 40/660, 242 n.118; National Archives CP 40/802, 238 n.46; National Archives CP 40/810, 162, 265 n.57; National Archives CP 40/819, 41, **43**, 44; National Archives CP 40/823, 238 n.46; National Archives CP 40/861, 260 n.71; National Archives E 361/6, 48, 252 n.117; National Archives KB 27/714, 242 n.118

Kinch, Ashby, 106

Kipling Gordon, 134

Kirkby, 44, 47, 241 n.105

kneeling, 15–16, 95, 101–2, 104, 109–10, 116–25, 127, 129, 132–38, 140, 142–43, 160–62, 193. *See also* deference; submission; supplication; humility

Kristeva, Julia, 13

Krochalis, Jeanne, 58, 74

Kumler, Aden, 11

Kuskin, William, 151, 153

Lancastrian, 75, 114, 128, 155, 161, 198, 201

Latini, Brunetto, 244 n.12

laureate, 16, 112, 114, 116, 131–32, 140, 183, 259 n.59

Lawton, David, 132, 155

Lawton, Lesley, 161, 168

Leland, John, 186

Lerer, Seth, 138

Liber Niger. See *Black Book of Edward IV*

library, 186, 190, 207, 209, 221

likeness, 58, 76–79, 83

limner. *See* producers of books and documents

Lincoln, Stone Bow, 104

lineage, royal or noble, 18, 184, 189, 201, 204; literary, 73–74, 228, 264 n.30

Liverpool: Cathedral of Christ MS 6, 134, **136**

livery, 95, 197–201, **200**, 203–4, 206–7. *See also* heraldry

Livery Companies of London: Armourers, 44, **45**, 155; Brewers, 242 n.114; Carpenters, 34;

Company of Drapers WA/1, 47–48, 242 n.116; Worshipful Company of Haberdashers Grant of Arms of 1446, 29, **30**, 237 n.40; Worshipful Company of Ironmongers Grant of Arms of 1455, **46**, 46–47, 242 n.114, plate 4; Worshipful Company of Tallow Chandlers Grant of Arms of 1456, 242 n.114

Los Angeles: J. Paul Getty Museum MS 5, 84 ML.723, 268 n.5

Louis de Bruges, Lord of Gruuthuse, 44–45,

love, 86–90, 111, 192–93

Lowden, John, 198

loyalty, 161, 164, 186,

Luton: Museum of Luton, Luton Guild Register, 239 n.55

Lydgate, John: and Chaucer, 140–41, 145–46; *Danse Macabre*, 155; depictions of, **117–24, 126–27**, plates 15–18; *Fall of Princes*, 1–2, 116, 121, 126, 128–32, 134, 138–39, 152, 226, 228, plates 1, 16; fortunes of, 154–56; as laureate, 16, 114, 131–32, 140, 183; *Lives of Saints Edmund and Fremund*, 105, 116, 122–24, 131–32, 257 n.10, 257 n.21, 257 n.22, 260 n. 65, plates 17, 19; and manuscript production, 125; mistaken for another author or character, 132, 137, 144–46; patronage of, 114, 116, 119–20, 128, 140, 141, 146; as pilgrim, 140–45, **146**, 147–48, plate 18; as poet propagandist, 114, 256 n.2; *Proverbs*, 186; *Secrets of the Philosophers*, 116, 121–23, 257 n.10; *Siege of Thebes*, 41, 43, 140–48, 165–67, 171, 183–84; "Verses on the Kings of England," 187, 263 n.19. See also *Troy Book*

Lytlington Missal. *See* London, Westminster Abbey MS 37

Machaut, Guillaume de, 244 n.12, 252 n.42

magnificence, 206–8

Mahoney, Dhira B., 125

maker (as producer of book), 14, 25, 60, 90, 145, 166, 235 n.66

Malory, Sir Thomas: *Morte d'Arthur*, 162

Man, Paul de, 88

Manchester: Rylands Library MS English 1, 172, **174**, 176, 256 n.10, 260 n.77, 265 n.67, 266 n.81, plate 15; Rylands Library MS English 2, 132, **134**, 259 n.60, 259 n.61; Rylands Library MS English 63, 225, 245 n.24, 246 n.38, 274 n.8

Mandeville, John, 146–47, 244 n.11

manicule, 80–83

Mankind, 202–3

Marchaunt, John, 38. *See also* Scribe D

Margaret of Anjou, 237 n.40, 271 n.74

marginalia, 81, 132, 134, 143–44, 255 n.92. *See also* gloss

master (of artistic school), 27, 32–34, 36–37, 39–40, 44, 49–50

McGrady, Deborah L., 58

McKenzie, D. F., 23

Meale, Carol M., 186

medievalization. *See* translation, visual

Memling, Hans, 200–201

memorial, 70, 76–77. *See also* commemoration

memory, 77–80, 192–93

mercy, 71–76, 162

metafiction, 60, 78, 112

Meyer-Lee, Robert J., 116

Miles, Laura Saetveit, 103

mirror: as metaphor for introspection, 106–7, 197

Mirror for Princes, 70, 146, 159–60, 172, 192–97. *See also* Hoccleve, Thomas, *Regiment of Princes*

misbinding, 186–86

miscellany, 153–54, 186

missal, 21–22, 36

mistery, 24

model book, 10, 37

Montreal: McGill University MS 143, 120, **121**, 257 n.10, 257 n.21, 257 n.22, 259 n.52

monument 27, 74–75, 78

Mooney, Linne R., 38, 41

moral instruction, 86, 159, 191–93

Morecroft, Roger, 272 n.74

Morelli, Giovanni, 39–40

Morgan *Confessio*. *See* New York, Morgan Library and Museum MS M.126

Mortimer, Nigel, 155

Moses (biblical figure), 219–20, **221**, 223

Mosser, Daniel, 41

motto, 63, 160–61, 184–85, 187, 189

mouvance, 10

Moxey, Keith, 187

multivocality, 15, 84, 87–93, 113, 228

Murray, Stephen, 166

muse, 87, 114, 119, 157

Nebuchadnezzar (biblical figure), 84–86, 88, 99, 111, 206

Neer, Richard, 39, 40

New Haven: Beinecke Library Takamiya MS 24, 64, 66–68, 245 n.24, plate 5; Beinecke Library Takamiya MS 54, 261 n.87

New York: Columbia University Rare Book and
Manuscript Library Plimpton MS 265, 240
n.77; Morgan Library and Museum MS M.125,
249 n.5; Morgan Library and Museum MS
M.126, 109–11, 189–95, **194**, **195**, **196**, 196–201,
203–4, 206–18, **211**, **213**, **214**, **215**, **216**, 221–23,
249 n. 5, plates 23–25; Morgan Library and
Museum MS M.231, 255 n.91; Morgan Library
and Museum MS M.690, 249 n.5; Morgan
Library and Museum MS M.876, 172, **175**, 266
n.81

Nichols, Stephen, 156

Noah (biblical figure), 206

Nolan, Maura, 151, 155

Northumberland, Henry Percy, fourth earl of,
179–82

Nottingham: University Library Middleton MS
Mi LM 8, 249 n.5

Nova Statuta, 162–63

oath, 42, 199–200, 223

Office of the Dead, 106, **107**

ontology (textual), 53, 56, 60, 140

orb (royal), 160–62

Ordinance of 1478, 201–3

orthodoxy, 75–76, 106, 134, 145

Oslo: Schøyen Collection 615, 261 n.87

Ovid: *Heroides*, 203

Oxford: Bodleian Library MS Arch Selden B 10,
186, 267 n.104; Bodleian Library MS Arch
Selden B 11, 91, 251 n.38; Bodleian Library MS
Arch Selden B 24, 186, 267 n.106; Bodleian
Library MS Ashmole 34, 248 n.99; Bodleian
Library MS Ashmole 35, 90, 251 n.33; Bodleian
Library MS Ashmole 46, 131, 257 n.10, 257
n.21, 259 n.49, 259 n.56, plate 17; Bodleian
Library MS Bodley 263, 130, 259, n.53; Bodle-
ian Library MS Bodley 277, 133, 135; Bodleian
Library MS Bodley 294, 91, **94**–95, 240 n.77,
249 n.5, 251 n.36, 252 n.47, 253 n.72; Bodle-
ian Library MS Bodley 596, **104**; Bodleian
Library MS Bodley 623, 268 n.6; Bodleian
Library MS Bodley 686, 62–64, 65, 145, **146**,
245 n.24, 245 n.29, 262 n.103, 262 n.105, 262
n.106; Bodleian Library MS Bodley 693, 91,
plate 9, 249 n.5, 252 n.47254 n.72; Bodleian
Library MS Bodley 902, 95, **96**, 102, 240 n.77,
249 n.5, 252 n.51, 254 n.72; Bodleian Library
MS Digby 230, 262 n.82, 266 n.71; Bodleian
Library MS Digby 232, **117**, 165, 256 n.10, 257

n.19, 265 n.64, 2662 n.75, 266 n.78; Bodleian
Library MS Digby 233, 136, 258 n.41, 260 n.72;
Bodleian Library MS Douce 104, 241 n.105,
253 n.69; Bodleian Library MS Douce 158, 258
n.99; Bodleian Library MS Duke Humfrey b
1, 129, 258 n.41; Bodleian Library MS Fairfax
3, 95, **98**, plate 11, 249 n.5, 250 n.9, 252 n.51;
Bodleian Library MS Laud Misc. 609, 91, **92**,
249 n.5, 252 n.47, 254 n.72, 257 n.21; Bodleian
Library MS Laud Misc. 673, 257 n.21; Bodleian
Library MS Rawlinson C 48, 41, **43**; Bodleian
Library MS Rawlinson C 446, 119, **120**, 165,
257 n.10, 257 n.19, 265 n.65, 266 n.75, 266 n.78;
Bodleian Library MS Rawlinson Poet. 223,
41, **42**, 67–68, 241 n.102, 245 n.24, 246 n.40,
plates 6, 7; Bodleian Library MS Selden Supra
53, 106, plate 13; Bodleian Library MS Wood
Empt. 1, 260 n.71; Christ Church College
MS 148, 234 n.53, 240 n.77, 249 n.5; Corpus
Christi College MS 67, 91, 240 n.77, 249 n.5,
252 n.47, 254 n.72, 266 n.70; Jesus College MS
124, 237 n.40; Magdalene College MS 213, 91;
New College MS 266, 210, **212**, **217**, 249 n.5;
St. John's College MS 18, 237 n.40; St. John's
College MS 266, 262 n.82, plate 27; University
College MS 85, 159, 264 n.43;

paleography, 39–44

Panofsky, Erwin, 241 n.99, 268 n.11, 199, 271 n.54

paratext, 58, 132

pardon, 133, 161–64, 210,

parhelion, 271 n.63

Paris, 49, 236 n.24, 236 n.25, 237 n.34, 238 n.45

Paris: Bibliothèque mazarine MS 507, 106, **107**

Paris (of Troy), 206

parish churches of London and Westminster, 23,
34; St. Dunstan in the East, 36; St. Egidius beyond Cripplegate, 32; St. Margaret's Westminster, 35; St. Martin Orgar, 239 n.66; St. Mary
at Hill, 36, 239 n.66; St. Nicholas Shambles,
33, 35, 36

Paris, Matthew, 129

Parkes, M. B., 34, 38, 165

Paternoster Row, 25–26, 33

patronage, 11–12, 16–18, 26, 48, 73, 75–76, 114–16,
119–21, 127, 138–41, 146, 154, 156, 160–61, 164,
170, 189–90, 197, 200, 206–7

Patterson, Lee, 155, 226

Pearsall, Derek, 10, 58, 66, 74, 116, 154, 197, 218

Peck, Russell, 194

Scribe B, 240 n.83, 246 n.53. *See also* Pinkhurst, Adam

Scribe D, 38. *See also* Marchaunt, John

script, 41–42, 44, 156, 184

scriptorium, 25, 38

scrivener. *See* producers of books and documents

scroll (containing speech or motto), 16, 17, 22, 26, **28**, **29**, **32**, 63, **65**, 84, **85**, 112, 113, 129–30, 134, **136**

Secretum secretorum, 144, 159. *See also* Mirror for Princes

self-fashioning (authorial), 93, 120, 125

Sherborne Missal. *See* London, British Library Additional MS 74236

Sherman, Claire Richter, 11

shrift. *See* confession

Siferwas, John, 27, 35

Simpson, James, 159

Sin, 86, 101–2, 106; pride, 90, 215–18; sloth 250 n.5; vanity, 106; wrath, 250 n.5

Skelton, John: "On the Death of the Earl of Northumberland," 184; "Phyllyp Sparrow," 255 n.90

Smith, Kathryn A., 11, 48, 101, 187, 200

Smyth, Karen E., 159

Sobecki, Sebastian, 123, 125

Solomon (biblical figure), **32**, 208

Southwark Cathedral, 99

spectacle, 189

Speculum sacerdotale, 75

Speed, John, 81–83

Speght, Thomas, 81–82, 228

sphragides, 81

spolia, 187

Sponsler, Claire, 155

sponsorship. *See* patronage

standardization, 87, 249 n.5

stationer. *See* producers of books and documents

stile, 89

strapwork, **28**, **29**, 41, **42–43**, 46

stratigraphy. *See* archaeology of the book

Strayler, Alanus, 76, plate 8

Strohm, Paul, 78, 155, 208

Stubbs, Estelle, 38, 44

style, 26, 29–34, 48–49; communal or group, 41; individual, 36, 41; literary, 89, 116, 129; and periodization, 159, 187; script as 44

Summit, Jennifer, 128

symbolic bibliography, 153

submission, 102–3, 140, 165, 186

Suffolk, William de la Pole, duke of, 142, 147–48

supplication, 121–22, 133, 161–63

table of contents, 91, 131–32

tapestry, 189, 206–8

temporality, 17, 81, 151–54, 156–59, 164–67, 187–88, 190–93, 199, 204–7, 210, 218–23. *See also* history

Tentler, Thomas, 101

time. *See* temporality; history

tomb, 75–78, 81–83, 99

Traditionsbuch, 76

translation: linguistic, 3, 9–10, 93, 128, 132, 158, 160, 227; visual, 12, 191, 218–19, 234 n.54

treason, 161, 196

Troy Book, 17, 116–20, 128, 133, 151–88; Agamemnon, **171**, **177**, **178**; Hector, **169**, **170**, **176**; manuscripts of, 116–20, 153, 156, 160–83; Patroclus, **169**, **176**; Peleus, **167**, 172; Priam, **168**, 172; Prologue, 157–59; Thessalians, **167**, 172; Troilus, 176; Trojan horse, **180**, 183

Tudor Rose, 184, **185**

typology, 209–13, 218–23

unmarked present, 218–19

variance, 10

Venus, 86, 89–91, 93, 96, 102, 232 n.17

vernacular (English), 3–4, 9–10, 14, 15, 23, 24, 37, 57–59, 77, 93, 128, 132, 140, 152, 218

vices, 101, 193, 274 n.10

Virgin Mary, 4, 75–76, 102–4, **104**, 106, 108, 112, **127**, 129

virtues, 193

Wakefield, Battle of, 219, plate 26

Wallace, David, 229

Warburg, Aby, 201

wardens' accounts (of London), 21, 22, 33, 34, 35–36

Warner, Lawrence, 39

Wars of the Roses, 3, 7, 152, 198, 202

Westminster, 23, 35, 41, 162; Abbey, 53, 104, 203

Wheel of Fortune. *See* Fortune

White, William, 35

Wittgenstein, Ludwig, 40

Wood, Christopher S., 130, 133, 159

woodcut, **67**, 133–34, **135**, 226, 227–29, plate 27

Woodville, Elizabeth, 34, 134, **136**, 189, 203

word-and-image, 14, 59

Worde, Wynkyn de, 67, 184

workshop, 26, 36

writing, agricultural metaphors of, 1–3; as a conduit, 5–8; as craft 8–9; from reference material, 1–3, 5, 9; representation of, **1–2**, 5–8, **6**, **7**, 9–10, 58–59, 94, 228, plates 1, 10

Yeoman of the Crown, 197, 199, 203, plates 23, 24

Yorkist, 161, 189, 191, 197, 198, 200, 202, 206, 209

ACKNOWLEDGMENTS

If the price of a book reflected the debts of gratitude owed by its author to the friends and colleagues who helped make it, then this one would be obscenely expensive.

Whether because of their friendship, advice, feedback, mentorship, or any combination of the four, the following people have all helped me along the way: Jenny Adams, Alixe Bovey, Nancy Bradbury, Elizabeth J. Bryan, Brigitte Buettner, Kathleen Doyle, Consuelo Dutschke, Shirin Fozi, Anna Ratner Hetherington, Michael Johnston, Jacqueline Jung, Aden Kumler, Evelyn Lincoln, Sheila Lindenbaum, Jessica Maier, Richard Marks, Janet Marquardt, Scot McKendrick, Robert Meyer-Lee, Laura Saetveit Miles, Asa Mittman, Stephen Murray, Ingrid Nelson, Elizabeth Perkins, Stephen Perkinson, Sarah Peverley, Olivia Powell, Nigel Ramsay, Yael Rice, Kathryn Rudy, Lucy Freeman Sandler, Misty Schieberle, Barbara Shailor, James Simpson, Kathryn A. Smith, Sebastian Sobecki, Zachary Stewart, Paul Strohm, Amy Vines, and Barbara Zimbalist. My colleagues in the Department of the History of Art and Architecture at the University of Massachusetts, Amherst, and fellow art historians of the Five Colleges have given me a stimulating and supportive environment in which to work. Richard K. Emmerson and Alexandra Gillespie read the entire manuscript and offered detailed and dedicated feedback that vastly improved the resulting book. Annie Sollinger has been terrifically helpful with images, and Cassandra Duncanson and Casey Simring were wonderful research assistants. To all of these people, I extend my warmest thanks.

It has been a pleasure to work with the University of Pennsylvania Press and especially to benefit from the insights and guidance of Jerry Singerman. Hannah Blake, Noreen O'Connor-Abel, and Patricia Wieland have all likewise assisted in bringing this book to print, and I am fortunate to have had the opportunity to collaborate with them.

I am also grateful to the following organizations and institutions for providing financial support for my research and writing: the Bibliographical Society of America (Short-Term Fellowship); the British Academy (Neil R. Ker Memorial Fund); the Huntington Library (Riley Fellowship); the Massachusetts Society of Professors (research support funds); the National Endowment for the Humanities (summer stipend); and the University of Massachusetts, Amherst (research intensive semester and junior faculty start-up funds). I am also indebted to the institutions that supported my early work, including Columbia University (faculty fellowships for doctoral study and the C. V. Starr Fellowship for Dissertation Research); the Medieval Academy of America in Association with the Richard III Society (Schallek Award); CASVA at the National Gallery of Art (Robert H. and Clarice Smith Fellowship); the Whiting Foundation (dissertation completion fellowship); and the Paul Mellon Centre for the Study of British Art (research support grant). I also benefited enormously from a curatorial internship for the exhibition *Royal Manuscripts: The Genius of Illumination*, funded by the American Trust for the British Library.

In addition, a three-year Andrew W. Mellon Fellowship of Scholars in Critical Bibliography at the Rare Book School, University of Virginia allowed me to learn and refine skills that were essential to the writing of this book. It also gave me a fellowship, in the true sense of the word, a group of friends who with their kindness and intelligence have shown me how to be a better scholar.

It has been a privilege to visit so many archives and libraries in the United States and the United Kingdom, where I was met with knowledgeable and helpful librarians, curators, and archivists at every turn. I thank them all for sharing so generously with me their wisdom and their manuscripts.

Also Casey.